EVERY MOVE SHE MAKES

They'd parked her Beamer under a streetlight. It shone down on an envelope tucked between the windshield wiper and the glass.

"It can't be a parking ticket," she said as they approached.

"Don't touch it."

They stared down at the envelope. In big, bold computer-generated letters, *TAYLOR MAXWELL* was written across the front.

Taylor pulled it out, and Shane grabbed her hand. "It's probably just a condolence note."

"True, but let me open it."

He walked about ten feet away, turned his back to her, and she heard him rip open the envelope.

Silence.

He turned around and strode back to her, a grim expression on his face.

"I was right." He handed her the single sheet of paper. "You're in danger."

Taylor scanned the words:

EVERY WAKING MOMENT YOUR KILLER IS WATCHING YOU.
PREPARE TO DIE, TAYLOR.

Books by Meryl Sawyer

UNFORGETTABLE

THE HIDEAWAY

TEMPTING FATE

HALF-MOON BAY

THUNDER ISLAND

TRUST NO ONE

CLOSER THAN SHE THINKS

EVERY WAKING MOMENT

Published by Zebra Books

EVERY WAKING MOMENT

Meryl Sawyer

ZEBRA BOOKS
KENSINGTON PUBLISHING CORP.
http://www.kensingtonbooks.com

*This book is dedicated to Dottie Dozal for all
she's done to help so many others.
And always with a smile!*

The best way to love anything is as if it might be lost.

—G. K. Chesterton

Prologue
Final Destination

A gem of inspiration could appear anywhere. Out of the blue or from the Psalms. Today it had come over the radio.

"From the moment of conception, the journey begins. The final destination never alters. It is always death."

Perfect.

"Why hadn't you thought of putting death in such simple terms?" he asked his reflection in the bathroom mirror.

It was so true. Man was conceived and ultimately died. Some died sooner, and more violently, than others.

But eventually, everyone died.

Death fascinated people—especially brutal deaths. No doubt about it. Just tune into the evening news. Plane crashes. Car accidents. Drive-by shootings.

Brutal murder.

Well, he had to admit, murder could be interesting.

It beat death by natural causes, which was a major snoozer. Unless you were someone important, it was a nonevent for television. Your demise was confined to a few lines in the obituaries.

Not all murders were worthy of attention, he noted not for the first time. Most killings were pathetic, botched jobs.

Crimes of passion, not crimes of expertise.

The police had absolutely no trouble catching those idiots. But a cunning killer was a different story. Murder could be handled with finesse, and not be an impulsive, stupid act that left a trail of clues a blind squirrel could follow.

No. If he remained clever—and patient—murder could be elevated to an art.

"Wait!" he said, studying his reflection for a flaw and finding none. "Art is the wrong word. A game. Now, that's a better description."

Not just an ordinary game, but an intellectual challenge requiring strategy, like chess. He had to plan his moves, one. . . two . . . three and even four steps ahead of his unsuspecting opponent.

Revenge took time and a well-crafted scheme.

"Have no doubt. I can plan the perfect crime," he said, flicking out the light and leaving the bathroom.

It required the proper subtlety to carefully plot murder. He refused to rush it and have his name added to the list of bunglers who killed and were so easily caught.

When it all came together, the way it was now— nothing, but nothing was sweeter. Or more fun than orchestrating the final moments of the adventure called life.

A dead gasp of a laugh ricocheted through the room, music to his ears.

"Death *is* the final destination."

Chapter 1

It was nearly ten o'clock, but South Beach was just beginning to wake up, Taylor Maxwell noticed as she strolled along Ocean Drive toward Brew Ha-Ha. SoBe thrived on the club life, which meant dancing until dawn to frenetic music. Not that she was part of the club scene. Taylor lived in SoBe to enjoy the diverse culture.

Or so she told her family and friends.

Taylor secretly admitted she'd stayed in the apartment she'd shared with Paul Ashton to feel closer to him. He'd adored South Beach, and before he had disappeared, Taylor had spent her free time here with him. SoBe wasn't far from Coral Gables, where she'd grown up, but it was another world entirely.

A teenage boy sauntered toward her, his bopping walk swaying to a beat only he could hear. Attitude blazed from his dark eyes, half hidden by a Dolphins ball cap.

"Yo, mama. Lookin' good."

Taylor knew better than to respond. If she did, he'd follow her down the street, refusing to take no for an answer. She'd dressed conservatively—for SoBe—white shorts, strappy high-heeled red sandals, and a sky blue blouse tied at the midriff, baring only a few inches of skin. No exposed navel pierced with rings or studs for her.

The kid strutted into a newsstand specializing in magazines featuring nude women. She walked along the nearly deserted sidewalk, gazing beyond the stately royal palms at the beach. Sparkling blue waves swelled, crested, then tumbled onto the sand, leaving a trail of froth as they lazily retreated.

In the distance, a pale mist hung over the ocean, blurring the horizon where the blue sea met the even bluer sky. A cat's paw of wind ruffled the umbrellas and towels early beachgoers had set up to stake out their places on the white sand.

It was February and pleasantly warm, the weather that made Florida a mecca for snowbirds. Taylor had lived here for almost thirty-two years, her entire life, but she never took the climate or the scenery for granted.

One of the bitterest lessons she'd learned was *nothing* could be taken for granted.

The ability to—survive and thrive—despite being so heartsick over Paul, was one of her strongest points. Through sheer determination, she'd concentrated on her job and had become very successful.

Nights were the hardest time

Hours of hope would crash into mind-numbing fear that she would never see Paul again. The only escape was to work until it was almost dawn on her computer trivia game.

Driving herself hard and forcing herself to tamp down her grief, her fear kept her mind off Paul.

Most of the time.

But on sunny mornings like this, she couldn't help thinking he should be at her side, enjoying the beautiful day.

Taylor strolled into Brew Ha-Ha, and the fragrant scent of coffee greeted her. Salsa music pulsed from speakers that hung from the rafters. The coffeehouse was little more than a bamboo shack with palm fronds for a roof, but its Cuban-style coffee drinks made it a popular hangout.

She looked around for her friend, but Lisa hadn't arrived yet. A glance at her Ebell confirmed that she was a few minutes early. She decided to order and relax with coffee while she waited.

"*Café cubano,*" she told the girl behind the counter. "A double."

It would be like mainlining high-octane caffeine—a legal high. Taylor could almost feel the adrenaline rush just watching the girl pour the thick, sugar-laced Cuban coffee into a pink cup not much bigger than a shot glass. The scent of the *pan cubano* slathered with butter and toasting on the grill reminded Taylor she'd neglected to have dinner last night.

"I'll have a slice of *pan cubano tostado,* too."

She paid for the coffee and toasted Cuban bread, then found a small table under the shade of the ancient banyan tree that arched over the area like an umbrella. She added a touch of cream to the coffee even though this was a no-no to most who drank the Cuban coffee for its pure, intense flavor. As she was stirring the mixture and munching on the crusty

Cuban bread, Taylor spotted Lisa coming up the street with her usual jaunty stride.

Even though they were the same age and height, Lisa Abbott was like the flip side of a coin. While Taylor was fair with blond hair and blue eyes, Lisa had raven-black hair and melt-your-heart chocolate brown eyes. The hot-pink bustier and matching shorts she was wearing captured the attention of every male in the vicinity.

Taylor sprang to her feet, waving. "Lisa! Over here!"

Lisa rushed up and flung herself into Taylor's open arms. "Oh, God, I've missed you!"

Tears welled up in Taylor's eyes as she bear-hugged her closest friend. Nine months had passed since they had seen each other, but to Taylor, it seemed like years. With her brother, Trent, immersed in a new relationship, and with Paul gone for two years, Taylor had missed Lisa more than she ever could have imagined.

"Sit, sit," Taylor said. "Tell me everything."

Lisa rolled her dark eyes. "Do I have time to get coffee first?"

"Sure, but hurry. I want to hear all about your trip."

She sat down, taking a careful sip of her very hot coffee, and watched Lisa put in her order. Brew Ha-Ha was beginning to fill, and Taylor recognized several of the regulars. Most mornings she stopped in here for coffee to-go before climbing into her small Beamer to head to the Coral Gables offices of To The Maxx where she worked in the family business with her uncle and brother.

Lisa returned with a cup of flavored coffee and a double thick slice of *pan cubano tostado*. The scent of vanilla wafted across the table as her friend gently blew on the coffee to cool it.

"What's new?" Lisa asked.

"You don't want to know."

Taylor realized Lisa didn't inquire about Trent because she wanted Taylor to volunteer the news about her younger brother. Trent and Lisa had been happily married for six years—or so everyone assumed—until Trent asked for a divorce.

Lisa had been devastated. As soon as the papers had been signed, she'd gone on an around the world trip to find herself. Since she'd left, no one had spoken to her, but she'd e-mailed Taylor and her parents to say she was okay.

Still, Taylor had been worried. After the way Paul had vanished while abroad, she'd wondered if someone had stolen Lisa's laptop and she'd met a similar fate. Taylor had answered the telephone last night and discovered Lisa had returned.

"Tell me about your trip. Which country did you like best?" Taylor asked, calculatedly avoiding the subjects it would be painful to discuss—Trent's new love, Paul Ashton, her mother.

"I've been dying for this bread." Lisa took a bite of the *pan cubano*. "India is my favorite country—hands down."

Interesting, Taylor thought. She wouldn't have pictured Lisa in India.

"I spent six months there studying the *Kama Sutra*."

"Really?"

Taylor sipped her coffee to hide her shock, thankful she was wearing shades. It was difficult to imagine one of Miami's up-and-coming financial advisors spending months studying the art of making love.

Lisa flipped her long hair back over one shoulder with her hand, a gesture Taylor had noticed the day they first met at Yale. "I'm changing careers. I'm opening a shop here in South Beach as soon as I can find space."

Changing careers? This was not like the steady, goal-oriented Lisa who had married her brother.

Tragedy changes you, Taylor decided.

She'd like to make a career change as well. She wanted to start her own company and develop computer games. She was a trivia buff and had a game already half finished, but now, with her mother so ill, was not the time to leave the family's cosmetics business.

"What kind of shop do you plan to open?"

Lisa smiled at Taylor over the rim of her cup. "I'm not sure what I'm going to call it yet, but it'll be a boutique that sells everything from sexy lingerie to love potions. There'll be classes for women in the evening to teach them the arts of the *Kama Sutra*."

It was such an outrageous career change that Taylor might have laughed, if she hadn't known Lisa for fourteen years. What was Lisa thinking? This was a ridiculous idea—even in SoBe.

Then the light dawned. Trent. Lisa hadn't seen the divorce coming, hadn't suspected a thing.

Lisa blamed herself.

Taylor recognized the pain in Lisa's eyes because it mirrored her own loss. At times she wanted to break something, hit something. Scream.

The only solution was to maintain inner strength and deal with grim reality any way you could. For Lisa it might just be a *Kama Sutra* shop.

Only the strong survive, Taylor reminded herself.

"You think I've lost it, don't you?" Lisa asked, her voice pitched low.

Taylor couldn't lie, not to Lisa. She'd pick up on it in a heartbeat.

"No. I don't think you're crazy. I think you're blaming yourself for something that was beyond your control."

Lisa downed the last of her coffee, got up from

the table, and went back for a refill. By the time she returned, Taylor had marshaled her thoughts.

"If you want to help people, why don't you go back to school and become a therapist?" Taylor suggested. "Better yet, become a personal coach. That's what many therapists are calling themselves. Men don't like to admit they need a therapist, but a coach—"

"You don't understand. That's the Western way. I'm into Eastern methods. It's a sensual, hands-on technique."

Taylor didn't know what to say. This was her best friend, but after her trip Lisa seemed like a stranger. Her mind wandered and she couldn't help wondering what Paul would be like if he should suddenly reappear after an absence of two long years.

Time had changed her, too. She'd never been afraid to make business decisions, but she was much more confident now. Some of her innovations had received attention from the major cosmetics firms. Now they were fielding offers for their small company.

"Your turn," Lisa said. "What's been happening?"

Taylor took another sip of coffee, stalling, trying to decide if she should mention Trent's new love or not. She caught sight of a tall, dark-haired man and a dog in the line that had formed at the counter. She pushed her shades to the top of her head, leaned closer to Lisa, keeping her voice low.

"There's the mole."

Lisa's dark eyes widened. "Mole?"

"The creep who moved into my building. He lives right across the courtyard. This is the first time I've seen him out in the light of day. He slinks off to work at nine or so and comes back at dawn like a mole."

Lisa wrinkled her nose. "The guy in the wife beater?"

Taylor shook her head, realizing Lisa meant the

man in the tank top cut extra wide at the arms to reveal bulging pecs and biceps. "No, the guy with the dog."

"The hunk with the Labrador retriever?" Lisa flipped her hair over her shoulder. "A mole? Nah. He probably works in one of the nightclubs."

"I doubt it. He takes his dog to work with him."

Lisa studied her for a moment. "Okay, what gives? Why don't you like him?"

"I've never met the man. There's something strange about him, that's all."

"Like what?"

"I'm not sure exactly. Twice now I've caught him looking at my apartment in an odd way."

"He wouldn't be the first guy to be curious about a knockout blonde, especially if she's right across the courtyard."

"He's never seen me. Both times, I was upstairs in my office, hidden by that humungous fern. I looked down and he was staring at the first floor of my apartment."

"Maybe he's new to the area. You know how people are about South Beach architecture. He was probably studying the cool etched-glass mermaid panels beside your front door or the rounded art deco corners of the building."

Taylor glanced at the man, who was now placing his order. "True, but it . . ."

"Gave you the creeps? Well, I think the guy could benefit from some *Kama Sutra* enlightenment. Introduce me."

"I told you. We haven't met." She stole another peek at the guy. He was ordering, his back to them, but the dog was watching her. "His dog is positively scary. See the way he's glaring at me?"

Lisa looked, but the Labrador had turned away.

"You love dogs, especially Labs and retrievers. If it weren't for Paul, you'd have a golden retriever, right?"

Taylor nodded; Paul had been allergic to dogs. It had kept her from adopting one from Retriever Rescue. She adored dogs, always had, so much so her family and friends teased her about it. This was the longest she'd been without a pet. Only the hope of Paul's return kept her from getting one.

"This dog is different," she told Lisa. "He never barks. He just stares."

"I don't get it. If you've never met the man, how do you know so much about his dog?"

"I was in the laundry room one night. I could feel someone watching me. I turned around, and that dog was in the doorway. It was staring at me, one leg up, pointing like he'd spotted fresh kill."

A shadow of alarm touched Lisa's dark eyes. "Did he growl or bare his teeth?"

"No. He just kept his eyes trained on me, and his nostrils were flaring. Then someone whistled, and the dog ran off."

"That is a little weird. Did you report it to the building manager?"

"No. You know old Mrs. Bryant. She's nosy as all get-out, and she upsets so-o-o easily. I didn't want to make trouble for the dog. What if he's harmless?"

"If he does anything, even growls at you, take action. Remember that woman in San Francisco." Lisa brought the last of her *pan cubano* up to her mouth. "Oh, my God. The stud with the dog is coming this way. Be still, my heart!"

Taylor turned her head toward the busy street but kept her neighbor in sight. He *was* coming over to them.

He stopped directly in front of their small table and

spoke to Taylor. "Hi, there. I'm Shane Donovan, your new neighbor."

"Wow! You live in Taylor's building," Lisa said, managing to sound as if this were news to her. "Sit down."

"I'm Taylor Maxwell," she replied, kicking Lisa under the table. Why would she ask him to join them?

"I know." Shane swung a chair around backward and sat down, straddling it. He placed his coffee mug on the table. He pulled off aviator style shades and shoved them into the pocket of his black T-shirt. His dark blue eyes seemed unusually intense under brows a shade lighter than his black hair.

She supposed most women would be attracted to Shane Donovan, if you went for tall jocks with linebacker shoulders. Personally, Taylor preferred lean runner types with sandy hair and green eyes.

Men like Paul Ashford.

"How do you know who I am?" she asked.

He smiled, his mouth canting slightly to one side and giving him a mischievous, boyish expression. "I'd seen you around, and Mrs. Bryant told me who you were."

Mrs. Bryant. It figured. The old biddy probably was trying her hand at matchmaking. She knew Taylor didn't date and had commented on it several times.

When had Shane Donovan seen her? Taylor wondered. She was certain he hadn't, but obviously she was mistaken. He must have been peeking through the curtains when she wasn't looking.

Creepy.

"Where are you from?" Lisa asked Shane.

"Germany originally, but I've been around a lot."

The way he said "a lot" implied something, Taylor decided. Danger or a situation he'd rather not discuss.

His expression kept his secret—whatever it was—but the intensity in his gaze as he looked at Taylor revealed deep, powerful emotions.

She wasn't easily frightened, and she wasn't afraid now, but she had to admit this man made her uneasy. It was a subliminal message that Lisa wasn't picking up. Just from Lisa's smile, Taylor could see how taken her friend was with this stranger.

"I just returned from nine months abroad," Lisa told Shane.

"Lucky you."

He had an attitude, she decided. A grown-up, more sophisticated version of the teenager she'd passed on the street earlier. He was the kind of man who went after what he wanted, and he probably got it.

His dog had sat down next to Shane, but its eyes were locked on Taylor. This close, the dog appeared less threatening. His eyes were soulful as if he were sad or profoundly troubled about something.

Shane stroked the dog's back while continuing to listen to Lisa, who was asking if Shane had ever been in India. He hadn't.

"What's your dog's name?" Taylor asked.

"Auggie. That's short for Augustus." He jostled the dog's ears. "Right, boy?"

The dog's tail flitted, but it wasn't what Taylor would have called a real wag. "Your dog seems . . . different. He sniffs a lot, but I've never heard him bark."

Shane studied her for a moment in a way that unsettled her more than it should have. "Auggie's a Braveheart military dog. I'm detraining him, getting him used to civilian life."

"Really? Was he an attack dog?"

Shane chuckled. "No way. Auggie has an A-rated sense of smell. He's trained to detect explosives."

Taylor gazed down at the dog, intrigued. "Why isn't he still in the military?"

"Bad hips. He flunked the last field test. He had to be able to jump over a four-foot wall, but he couldn't make it." There was something almost wistful in Shane's voice, as if he'd personally failed the test.

"Were you his handler?" Lisa asked.

Shane shook his head, then drank a little of what appeared to be *café con leche*—Cuban espresso with steamed milk.

"No. I had connections and was able to bring Auggie here. Ex-military dogs need a lot of retraining. They've never been taught to play or enjoy people the way other dogs have. All they've done is work."

Interesting, Taylor thought. That would account for the dog's watchfulness. As if sensing her thoughts, Auggie inched a bit closer, and Taylor stroked the gloss-black fur on his head. The dog's tail thumped once.

Something inside Taylor ignited, a small spark of happiness. For a second she didn't recognize the feeling. It had been so long since she'd experienced a flicker of joy.

Her life had been reduced to hard work, business deals. And loneliness. And worries about her mother's failing health.

She reached down and rubbed the dog's chest, a touch she knew all dogs liked. Auggie leaned forward to get closer to her hand and flicked his tongue across the back of her fingers.

Maybe it was time to give up on Paul and rescue a dog. The minute the traitorous thought hit her brain, she yanked back her hand. Paul was still alive. If he'd been killed, she'd know it, feel it.

Wouldn't she?

"What business are you in?" Lisa asked.

"Security. Computer security."

No way, Taylor thought. There was an air of ruth-lessness about this man that didn't jibe with the computer types she knew.

"Oh, gosh! Look at the time," Taylor cried, standing up. "We're late." She grabbed Lisa by the arm. "Nice to meet you," she said to Shane.

"Well, that was *so* not like you," Lisa said once they were outside Brew Ha-Ha. "You're never rude."

"That man is not a computer expert."

Lisa stopped, put her hands on her hips, and studied Taylor for a moment. "How can you tell? Did you turn into a mind reader while I was away?"

"No, of course not. I—I just feel something's wrong with him."

"Yeah, right. What's wrong with Shane Donovan is that he's interested in you."

Lisa put her arm around Taylor and gave her a heartfelt hug. "You're young and pretty . . . and alive. You have to face reality."

"Reality?" Taylor repeated, the word a hollow echo in her head.

"It's been two years since Paul disappeared." Lisa gazed directly into Taylor's eyes, hesitated a moment before saying, "He must be dead. It's all right to be attracted to another man."

Taylor squinted against the bright sunlight through a sheen of tears that appeared without warning. Trust Lisa, her dearest friend, to say what her mother and brother must have wanted to tell her for months.

Like a crack in the universe, hope drained from the pool of inner strength that had supported her all this time. A silent scream tore through her, as much a cry for what had been lost as a cry for help.

A dark and terrifying moment of truth nearly knocked Taylor to her knees. Every waking moment, she'd kept this thought at bay, but Lisa had forced her to face the truth.

She was never going to see Paul Ashton again.

Chapter 2

"Can you believe it?" Shane muttered to Auggie. "Taylor's crazy about me—already."

Had me fooled, Auggie's dark eyes seemed to say.

"What is there about me? Women either hate me on sight or want to jump my bones."

He shrugged. "Go figure."

Auggie put his sleek head on Shane's bare knee. Shane patted him, thinking about Taylor Maxwell. A knockout. Sexy as hell.

But she didn't like him one damn bit.

"I'm counting on you, boy," he told Auggie. "You'll have to be the one to break the ice."

Shane caught the strange look the men at the next table were giving him. Aw, hell. Hadn't they seen a man carry on a conversation with his dog before?

The real kicker was, now that he was back among the living, he still didn't have anyone to talk to except his dog. There must be some cosmic purpose to all this, he decided.

Either that or he was his own crown of thorns.

He tossed back the rest of his *café con leche*—not bad—but nothing like the brew in Colombia. He watched Taylor and her friend disappear around the corner, wondering what move to make next. He refused to allow her to write him off like he was a major scumbag.

He hadn't thought about her all this time for nothing. He was damn well going to get to know her. To find out if the image in his head was real.

The cell phone in the pocket of his khaki shorts rang. It had to be Vince. No one else had this number.

"What's up?" Shane asked when he'd flipped open the phone, walking out of Brew Ha-Ha. He didn't trust cell phones. Everyone else talked on them in the cafés lining the sidewalks of South Beach, but anyone with the right equipment could eavesdrop on your conversation.

"I'm taking you off the Starline case," his boss told him.

"Why? I'm almost finished. I should wrap it tonight."

"Something's come up. I need you with me."

Shane listened, then let out a low whistle. "Son of a bitch!"

Taylor allowed Lisa to drag her into Ruby's Diner for feta cheese and spinach omelets. Lisa claimed she was starving, but Taylor suspected her friend had noticed how much weight Taylor had lost.

Lisa ordered an omelet for each of them and fresh squeezed orange juice without consulting the menu. Taylor couldn't help remembering all the times she and Paul had joined Lisa and Trent for breakfast here on Saturday morning.

"I didn't mean to upset you," Lisa said, her dark eyes filled with concern. "I just think you need to face reality. The American Embassy in Colombia can't find a trace of Paul.

"You went down there. Nothing. Even the private detective you hired came up empty. At some point, you've got to get on with your life."

Taylor gazed across the diner decorated in retro sixties style complete with red vinyl booths and chrome-banded stools at the counter. Instead of salsa music, the jukebox played "Jailhouse Rock." She toyed with her spoon for a moment, then looked at her friend.

"I know you're right, Lisa, but it's so hard. How can a photographer disappear without a trace?"

"Colombia's famous for drugs and terrorists and God knows what. Anything is possible. Why did he have to go to such a dangerous country? Why not Brazil or Venezuela?"

She'd been over this so many times, Taylor could barely muster yet another response. "You know Paul. He never worried about danger. He wanted to photograph the indigenous tribes along the border with Brazil. He planned to sell the video to the Discovery Channel."

Taylor blamed herself for encouraging Paul to go. He was a commercial photographer, but his career had been going nowhere while hers skyrocketed. She hadn't wanted him to become resentful.

Paul had been moody those last few weeks before he left. She often asked herself if she'd been spending too much time with her family. Had he resented it?

Paul was an only child who wasn't accustomed to family gatherings, and he rarely came with her to the

Coral Gables home where she'd grown up. Taylor could almost feel the lump of lead forming in her chest the way it had the night she'd introduced Paul to her family. Without a flicker of her usual charm, Vanessa Maxwell had questioned Paul relentlessly about his parents.

What did it matter?

His parents were dead, and they hadn't lived in the city. They couldn't have been expected to be part of Miami's society.

Taylor had cut off her mother's questions, but not before the damage had been done. Paul was a sensitive man, a person who took offense more easily than most men she knew.

The waiter delivered their glasses of juice. Lisa let him set them down before saying, "I think drug traffickers believed Paul was up to something and killed him. I thought so when he disappeared, and no one's discovered anything to change my mind."

"You could be right." After a moment of silence, Taylor added, "I have to face the fact that I may never know what happened to Paul."

Lisa put her hand on Taylor's. "Can you get on with your life? I'm moving on with mine. That's what I learned while I was in India."

"Did you? Really?"

For the second time that day, Taylor experienced a surge of happiness. She'd been worried that Lisa had returned as in love as ever with Trent.

"Yes. I'm at peace with myself. What's meant to be—will be. The teachers at the Bidar Latur taught me to accept what is 'written'—your fate. If something is not meant to be, you have to let it go or it will bleed the energy from your spirit."

Taylor nodded, not sure how to respond.

She hesitated a moment. "That's what's happening to you. I can see it."

Taylor didn't believe in a lot of pooky-pooky stuff, but she knew that on one level Lisa was right. Her body seemed to be drained of any inner spirit. She hadn't been like this before Paul disappeared.

While she was searching for him, Trent had left Lisa, and her mother had become ill. Taylor had been forced to cope with a series of blows. She'd done very well, being all things to her family while taking care of the business.

Everyone commented on her strength and praised her. But she knew something was missing.

"You're right. I have to go on with my life . . . and assume Paul is dead."

Lisa nodded. "That's why I flirted with Shane for you. He—"

"Don't do me any favors. Accepting Paul might be dead is one thing. Flirting with another man is a quantum leap."

"I understand, but Shane is interested in you. He talked to me, but he never stopped looking at you."

Taylor questioned Lisa's analysis of the situation. There was something alarmingly intense about Shane Donovan. Something profoundly disturbing.

It wasn't just that he was a big, tall man with an athletic build. His size and strength didn't intimidate her. She held her own in a cutthroat business against men who thought nothing of taking advantage of a woman's weakness.

No, this was different.

She didn't know what about Shane Donovan bothered her. No denying he was an attractive man, but danger lurked in his eyes. Since she didn't intend to have anything to do with him, she'd never find out what was wrong with him.

The waiter arrived with their omelets and placed the large dishes garnished with fresh fruit and home-baked banana nut bread in front of them. For several moments neither of them said anything as they ate.

Taylor remembered other Saturday mornings, when the four of them had sat in the booth across the room—their table—and had breakfast together.

Who would have thought that one day it would be just Taylor and Lisa?

"How's your mother?" Lisa asked.

"Her health's the same. The cancer hasn't spread."

A year after her father had died, Taylor's mother had been diagnosed with myeloma. Although her blood test results were still good, Vanessa Maxwell acted as if each day might be her last. With Trent spending most of his time with his new love, Taylor was left to console her mother.

"I'm glad your mother isn't worse," Lisa said. "I'll drop by and see her."

Taylor waited for her friend to say something more, but she kept eating. Taylor couldn't force down another bite. She pushed her plate aside, thinking of how she was going to deal with her mother.

Last night, she'd called and insisted Taylor had to come over for dinner, saying something important had come up.

"You didn't hear anything about my mother when you were traveling?"

Lisa stopped, her fork in midair. "I was at Bidar Latur outside New Delhi. No phones. No television or radio. No newspapers. What did I miss?"

Taylor waited a moment, not sure how to say this, although it was pretty straightforward. She hadn't discussed the details with anyone but Trent and her mother.

"It seems Trent and I have an older sister."

Lisa almost dropped her fork. "Are you telling me your mother had a child—"

"And gave it up for adoption. Or so she thought."

"What?" Lisa shoved her plate aside. "I don't get it."

Neither did Taylor. She let her eyes drift to their corner booth where a couple was being seated. They seemed so young and so very much in love.

"Explain what happened."

"I guess Mother always had wondered what had happened to the baby she'd given up for adoption."

What mother wouldn't? Taylor assured herself. Still, there was a tiny part of her that was hurt by the way her mother had become obsessed by this other daughter.

"As soon as my father died—over a year before my mother knew she had cancer—she hired a private detective to look for the child."

"Woman," Lisa corrected. "She must be what? Thirty-one? Thirty-two?"

"She's thirty-three."

Lisa's dark eyes narrowed. "Uh-oh! Vanessa must have been barely eighteen when she had the baby."

"Actually, she was still seventeen. Just shy of her next birthday."

"That's awfully young. Who was the father?"

Taylor hesitated. "Mother says it was one of the other boys in the foster home."

Lisa caught the missed beat. "You don't believe her."

A hundred times Taylor had asked herself why she doubted her mother's explanation, but she'd never come up with an answer. "Maybe she's telling the truth, but I think she's holding back something."

"Why?"

"I don't know. It's just a gut instinct." Like her reaction to Shane Donovan, she silently added.

"Trust your intuition. That's what they taught me at Bidar Latur."

Taylor could almost hear Lisa thinking, "What does Trent say?" Unfortunately, her astute brother was so absorbed by his new life that he took their mother at her word.

"Obviously, they haven't located your mother's child."

"No. Trust me, Mother has thrown megabucks at it, but the private investigators can't find any evidence that the baby was ever put up for adoption."

Doyle Maxwell shot his cuffs, pulling the sleeves of the white shirt down so the lapis cufflinks showed beneath the navy sport coat. He checked in the mirror to be sure his gray linen slacks still had a stiletto crease.

Perfect.

He wandered across the mammoth bedroom into his wife's dressing area. Brianna was preening in the makeup mirror. She was wearing a black lace bra and matching thong—and black satin high heels.

It was her come-fuck-me outfit, but he wasn't interested. Something was happening with Vanessa and it made him uneasy.

"Hurry up. We're going to be late."

Brianna turned and her shoulder-length blond hair cascaded downward, brushing the valley between her lush breasts like a kiss. "So? Vanessa will hold court for two hours before anyone sits down to eat. Trust me. Do we have to be there the entire time?"

"Yes. Something's going on."

Brianna cocked one perfectly arched eyebrow. "Is it about her missing baby or does Raoul Cathcart have another brilliant idea?"

"I don't know. Vanessa sounded . . . happy when she invited us for dinner."

"Invited—ha! *Demanded* is more like it."

"True, so true," he admitted.

One of the unexpected bonuses of having a trophy wife was finding one who was sexy and smart. Even though Brianna was the same age as his niece, Taylor, his wife was savvy beyond her years. He could tell her anything and count on her to come up with insightful comments.

Brianna had Vanessa's number the first time the two women had met. She'd insisted Vanessa wore the pants even though Doyle's macho twin brother, Duncan, had been alive then, and most people believed he ran the family.

She'd seen right through Raoul Cathcart the instant the guy had shaken her hand. She had immediately whispered, "Raoul Cathcart will be trouble. Trust me."

Brianna had been a lap dancer in a club off *Calle Ocho* in Little Havana when he'd met her. Brianna's mother had immigrated from Cuba, then married an American just the way Raoul Cathcart's mother had.

They were YUCAs—young, urban, Cuban-Americans—and they understood each other in a way Doyle couldn't quite explain. But he had no doubt Brianna was right.

Raoul was trouble.

"I'm going to drive over in the Maserati," he told his wife. "You come when you're ready."

He turned to leave, but Brianna jumped up and blocked his way, saying, "You're leaving without a kiss good-bye?"

He shrugged. Brianna didn't want a kiss, and they both knew it. She had sex in mind—as usual.

When he'd dumped his wife for a blond bombshell, he'd counted on many things. Demands for jewelry.

An insatiable appetite for designer clothes. A thirst for travel.

He gave Brianna those things, but she didn't lust for them the way he'd expected.

When he'd traded up, leaving a dowdy childless wife who asked for nothing, he hadn't counted on getting a sexpot with brains who wanted to fuck all the time. He was way, way too old for this, but he kept it a secret.

It wasn't the only thing he hid from Brianna.

"Good-bye." He kissed her on the cheek, teasing her, pretending that's all that would happen.

"Bye-bye," she replied with a little wave.

He marched out of the bedroom, taken aback. Brianna always insisted on screwing before they went out for the evening. "To take the edge off," she claimed. When they returned home, she'd expect him to spend hours making love to her again.

She wasn't having an affair, was she?

It was possible, he conceded. He couldn't get it up more than twice a day unless he popped Viagra, but Brianna was insatiable. She could be juggling several men and still want to fuck.

He mulled over the situation, silently cursing. Right now he didn't need another problem. The situation at To The Maxx was volatile with Raoul Cartcart butting in all the time.

Worse, he was in serious financial trouble. The divorce, the meltdown in the stock market, and an expensive young wife had drained his finances. He desperately needed To The Maxx to be sold.

An infusion of cash would solve his financial woes. His sex problems were another story.

He walked into the garage, then flicked on the light switch. Brianna was sprawled buck-naked on the hood of his red Maserati like some centerfold. She must have raced down the back stairs to beat him to the garage.

She used her index finger to motion for him to come closer. "Don't ever think you can just walk out on me like that. You know what I need."

"I don't want to wrinkle my pants."

"Don't worry about it." She rose to her feet and stood so her pussy was inches from his lips.

He was going to have to service her. There was no getting out of it, he thought. She waxed her crotch so there was never a suggestion of dark pubic hair, which would have been a startling contrast to her golden mane.

Her skin was creamy smooth and softer than a baby's ass. She slid her hand down her flat tummy and touched herself with an index finger crowned by a ruby-red nail.

"Your turn," she whispered, in a tone that told him she was already aroused.

Dusk was gathering when Taylor drove toward Alhambra Street, one of the many streets in Coral Gables with Spanish names. A canopy of noble banyan trees deepened the shadows. The neighborhood had the reputation of being one of the most exclusive areas in the city, but to Taylor it was home, a reminder of a time when her life had been simple, happy.

She parked and entered the sprawling Spanish-style mansion with a high wall capped in coral rock, where she had been raised. The home opened onto a swimming pool with a coral rock waterfall. As usual at this time of day, her mother would be near the bubbling fountain, sipping a mint julep. Even though she was older and ill, Vanessa Maxwell was still a striking blonde who turned men's heads.

"Taylor, lookin' way cool," Raoul Cathcart greeted her when she walked into the pool area. "Miami Spice, right?" he said, referring to the popular boutique where she'd purchased the red halter dress.

"Yes. It's a great shop." She managed a smile at the man who'd captured her brother's heart.

She loved Trent in a way only siblings born fourteen months apart can love each other, but she hadn't known Trent. Not at all. When he'd announced he was gay and was divorcing Lisa, no one had been more surprised than Taylor.

Raoul, like most men of Cuban descent, dressed with a flair even when he was wearing shorts and a T-shirt. Add that to his sexual orientation, where clothing was almost an art, and Taylor wasn't in the least surprised he could spot a Miami Spice outfit.

He was dressed in a white-on-white suit that made his skin seem more bronze, a soft blue shirt, and a creamy yellow tie. His honey blond hair stood up in spikes that might have made some men look foolish.

Not Raoul. He rode the crest of every trend as if he'd invented it.

His most unusual feature was his eyes. He'd inherited his father's pale blue eyes, which seemed even paler in his tanned face. He was a striking man, a fact that had not escaped his own attention.

"Where's Trent?" she asked.

"With Her Majesty."

Taylor resisted the urge to slap his handsome face, a square jawline and chiseled cheekbones women adored—for all the good it did them. A grudging little voice inside her acknowledged the truth behind the phrase "Her Majesty."

Taylor's mother had an imperial attitude. Granted, she was loving, supportive—never once criticizing

Trent—but Vanessa Maxwell had an air of entitlement that usually came from wealth.

In her case, it did not. Taylor's mother had been born May Ella Jones. She'd changed her name the second she'd been released from foster care on her eighteenth birthday. She'd moved to Miami and reinvented herself.

She'd married a man who had family money, and who then went on to make even more with his own business. Vanessa Maxwell ran with a society crowd, a fact Paul Ashton had noted immediately.

He was a struggling photographer without much money. Taylor hadn't cared. She was thankful she'd inherited her father's attitude about people. *Money isn't everything.*

Taylor's father had suffered a heart attack and died shortly before Paul vanished in South America. If her father had lived, she would have amended his saying about money.

There are things in life money can buy, then there are those things in life no amount of money can buy.

When you lost someone you loved, no amount of money was ever going to bring them back.

"I see Trent now," she said, spotting her brother talking to a tall, powerfully built man whose back was to her. Until the guy had moved, he'd blocked her view of Trent.

Off to the side stood another man she didn't recognize either. She wanted to ask what was going on, but she refused to give Raoul the satisfaction of realizing he knew more than she did.

"Hey, Taylor. That's a dynamite dress," her uncle said, coming up beside her and giving her a quick peck on the cheek.

"Thanks."

She hugged Doyle Maxwell and secretly pretended

he was her father. It wasn't difficult. Duncan and Doyle Maxwell had been identical twins and looked so much alike that many people hadn't been able to tell them apart.

Pewter hair wisped with silver at the temples offset the same blue eyes Taylor saw in the mirror each morning. She adored her uncle, and in many ways, he'd been more supportive of her than her own father who had lived for the company.

Uncle Doyle shared her love of games and had encouraged her to make up her own games since she was a child. She'd told him about her plans to start her own game company, something she'd never told her father. It would have disappointed him to know she really wasn't crazy about the cosmetics business.

"I wore a dress," she told him. "You know how Mother is. One always dresses for dinner."

Doyle chuckled. "Yep. That's why I put on a jacket."

"I got out one of my white suits because I adore white suits," Raoul chimed in.

"Looks good on you," her uncle said.

Uncle Doyle was being polite, but she didn't have to ask what he really thought of Raoul Cathcart. Her uncle didn't like the man. When Taylor's father had died, Doyle had stepped in to help run To The Maxx.

Things had gone smoothly until Raoul came into Trent's life. Even though Raoul didn't work for the company, he wanted to start a similar business. He had an opinion about everything at To The Maxx and voiced it through Trent.

Raoul moved away to join the cluster of men talking to her mother, and Taylor asked, "What's going on?"

"Who knows?"

Her uncle shrugged one shoulder, a gesture that reminded Taylor so much of her father. His hair had receded just a bit, and the high, noble foreheads coupled with blue eyes were male family traits. One day Trent would look like this.

Vanessa Maxwell turned and saw them. She smiled and headed their way as she tapped on her glass to signal Pablo, the houseboy, for another mint julep. Taylor couldn't help returning her mother's smile.

When was the last time she'd seen her mother look so happy?

"Darling." Her mother kissed the air beside Taylor's cheek, then said hello to Doyle.

"That's some dress." She twirled her finger, motioning for Taylor to turn around.

Taylor did a slow pirouette so her mother could inspect the glowing red halter dress. It was backless and skimmed her thighs and clung to every curve, a typical SoBe club outfit.

Ordinarily, her mother wouldn't approve, but it had been almost two years since she'd bought a new dress. When Paul vanished from her life, there didn't seem to be any point in trying to look good.

Work and finding Paul had been all that mattered. Then her mother became ill, and buying clothes mattered even less.

Tonight she was wearing a new dress and makeup. "Getting a grip" is what Lisa called it.

"Lisa insisted I buy it," Taylor told her mother. "The shoes, too."

She wiggled one foot to show off the red sandals with stiletto heels of clear Lucite. In the center of each heel was a red butterfly with flecks of iridescent green on its wings.

"Lisa's finally come home?" Her mother's eyes were troubled. "How is she?"

"Really happy." Taylor didn't mention the *Kama Sutra* business, knowing it would worry her mother.

"I'm glad. I miss her."

"Ditto," Uncle Doyle added, his eyes narrowing as he watched Raoul.

There was no point dwelling on the past, Taylor decided. "Who are those men?"

"Come with me." Her mother tugged on her arm. "I'll introduce you."

Taylor linked her arm with her uncle's and followed her mother toward the group of men. Over the shoulder of the tall man, Trent caught Taylor's eye. No one else would have noticed the subtle change in his expression, but Taylor did.

A frisson of alarm skittered down her bare back. *Trouble.*

Uh-oh. Now what?

"This is my daughter, Taylor Maxwell," her mother announced. "And my brother-in-law, Doyle Maxwell."

The men turned and Taylor found herself staring at one of them. For a split second she didn't recognize the tall man who was smiling at her. His wide shoulders did wonders for the light-weight navy blazer. His crisp white shirt was open at the throat, revealing a strong neck and a silver chain.

Shane Donovan.

Well, well. Take a jock out of T-shirts and shorts and look what happened. Who would have guessed?

"Vince Walker and Shane Donovan are with TriTech Security," her mother told them.

Shane's smile had a disturbing nuance to it. She looked away, thinking she'd been right. He wasn't the computer type. He was a security guard.

"They've located Renata." Raw emotion charged each word her mother uttered.

"Renata?" Taylor heard herself ask, her mind making another mental adjustment. Shane was a private investigator.

Then her mother's words registered with unexpected force.

Renata.

The missing baby.

Her sister.

Chapter 3

"We didn't actually find Renata Rollins," Vince Walker told them. "Putting the case on *Missing!* brought in a number of leads. They contacted your mother about this woman."

"What happened to her?" asked Taylor.

"Why was there no record of her adoption?" added Trent.

"She wasn't adopted through the state agency," her mother replied. "In the hospital, I handed the baby to my foster mother. She was supposed to give her to the social worker to arrange the adoption. Instead, she took my baby to an attorney who handled private adoptions for wealthy clients."

"She made a bundle and so did the attorney," Trent guessed.

"Assuming this woman is your baby," Raoul said to her mother.

"Is there some question?" Taylor asked, stunned her mysterious neighbor was involved in this.

"Yes," Shane said. "We haven't spoken with the woman, but her father claims he adopted her the same week your mother gave birth. It was a private adoption, but he doesn't recall the name of the attorney, and the papers have been conveniently lost in a fire."

"Wouldn't the state have some record?" she asked.

"Not with a private adoption in Alabama over thirty years ago," Shane replied. "The attorney just needed to have the mother and father's signatures on the consent form."

"Did the father sign the form?" Trent asked their mother.

"I assume so. I never saw him again."

There was something in her mother's voice that didn't sound right to Taylor. Wouldn't it be natural to communicate with the father of your child? She'd asked her mother about it before, but she'd merely said she'd been young and had made a mistake.

"I turned eighteen two weeks after I gave the baby away. The second you're eighteen the state no longer provides foster care. I hitchhiked to Miami, changed my name, and started over." Taylor heard the threat of tears in her mother's voice. "But I never forgot my baby, and I always wondered what happened to her."

Trent shot Taylor a look that said he had misgivings about this situation. "How will we know if she's really your child?"

"I've spoken with Caleb Bassett. He's the adoptive father," Vanessa said. "I'm certain Renata is my daughter. He adopted her in a town that was close by."

"A DNA test will prove it," Shane said.

"It's taking about three months to get a test," Vince informed them.

"I may run out of time." Vanessa's voice was tight.

"Grease the wheels," Raoul said. "A little money should—"

"I'm afraid it doesn't work that way," Shane responded to Raoul, but his eyes were on Taylor. "There are hundreds of men sitting in prison, waiting for a DNA test to clear them. They have top priority except for current criminal investigations."

"What about ads I've seen touting quick paternity checks?" Trent asked.

"Those labs are being shut down almost as fast as they open," Shane said. "A lab is only as good as the equipment and the expert interpreting the results."

"Just the largest, most sophisticated labs can afford the newest equipment," Vince added. "It's the only place to send a sample."

Trent shook his head. "I guess we don't have any choice—"

"Doyle! There you are." Brianna sashayed across the terrace and rushed up to her husband.

Taylor noted the way Vince Walker's mouth gaped open as if he wanted to swallow Brianna whole. She affected most men that way. She was one of the most stunning women Taylor had ever seen.

She had her hair colored a glistening butterscotch blond, but everything else about her was natural, which was unusual in SoBe, where boob jobs were as common as sunglasses.

As usual, Brianna was wearing a form-fitting dress. She didn't seem to own anything except clingy sundresses and could be found wearing one at breakfast. This outfit was fluorescent green, a SoBe club outfit not unlike the one Taylor was wearing.

The difference was, Taylor planned to meet Lisa at Bash later. Brianna would be going home with her older husband. What the two had in common, Taylor couldn't imagine, but Brianna played it to the hilt, acting as if she were ga-ga over Doyle.

"What's going on?" Brianna asked. "Why is everyone so serious?"

"They may have located the baby Mother gave up," Taylor said.

Out of the corner of her eye, she'd kept track of Shane. He'd given Brianna one swift, appraising glance, then refocused his attention on Taylor.

He was up to something; she was sure of it.

"Really?" Brianna's cheery voice slipped a notch. "How?"

Vince gave Brianna the details, including their misgivings about the authenticity of this woman's claim. Taylor glanced to the side and caught Shane staring at her. Instead of looking away, he grinned, forcing her to show him her teeth—as close to a smile as she could manage for a man like him.

"Who are you two?" Brianna asked Vince, but her look included Shane.

"Private investigators who specialize in computer security," Vince replied. "We've been hired to inspect the system at To The Maxx."

"What's wrong with the security firm the company has been using?" Brianna asked.

Good question, Taylor thought.

Leave it to Brianna to hone in on anything unusual. Her beauty kept most people off guard, but Taylor had discovered Brianna was one of the most intelligent women she'd ever known.

Taylor liked her, but she couldn't help feeling disloyal to Aunt Sophie. Taylor had never much cared for her aunt, having learned over the years how self-centered and cold the woman was. But she sympathized with the betrayal her aunt had suffered, the humiliation.

No one had expected strait-laced Doyle Maxwell to divorce his wife, then turn up later that year with a sexpot young enough to be his daughter.

Everyone claimed Brianna was after his money, and Taylor suspected it was true. Even so, Brianna was likable and easy to get along with—much more so than Aunt Sophie had been.

The only problem was Vanessa's snotty friends. They never included Brianna in their plans. Taylor's mother—always sensitive to her friend's opinions—never saw Brianna unless Doyle was with her in a small family gathering that did not include Vanessa's society buddies.

Taylor had spoken to her mother several times about it, but Vanessa brushed off her suggestion that she should develop a relationship with Brianna. Taylor had made it a point to meet Brianna once a week for lunch.

"Many of our orders come in through the Web site. One of the employees, a young man just out of college, picked up a glitch. Our financial records, our sales info—a number of sensitive matters are at risk if some hacker is after us," announced Vanessa.

Since when? Taylor wondered.

She'd been at the office all day yesterday and no one mentioned this. Something in her brain clicked, and she looked at Trent. He was carefully inspecting the polished marble beneath his feet.

He knew all about the change in security companies and hadn't mentioned it. Why not?

Raoul.

Raoul Cathcart was involved, the way he was so often now. Did he have anything to do with "discovering" this Renata person, Taylor wondered, her thoughts skipping from one subject to the other. She forced herself to concentrate on the computer problems.

She ventured a glance at her uncle. Doyle was staring at Vanessa, his eyes narrowed. Taylor knew he was feeling as betrayed as she was. Normally, they would have been told about the problem and been consulted before the company changed security firms.

But this wasn't like old times, when Trent and Taylor ran the company and Uncle Doyle handled the finances while Vanessa swanned through the office once a week, giving creative input.

Since Raoul had moved in with Trent, her brother began to have more and more opinions about how To The Maxx should be run, infringing on areas Taylor and Doyle oversaw. Vanessa was being increasingly dragged into the business even though her health should have kept her at home.

"The formulas are still secure, aren't they?" asked Brianna.

"Of course," Trent assured everyone. "They're all in the safe here. None of them are in any computer."

"Still, there is enough valuable information on company computers to be concerned," Shane said, his tone firm.

Now Taylor was confused. Maybe he actually knew computers. Then what was it about him that made her so edgy?

"We've gotten off course here," Vanessa said. "This afternoon we hired Vince and Shane to work on our computer security."

"It's so important I pulled Shane off another case," Vince added.

"Since I had received the tip from the *Missing!* hot line, I thought Vince and Shane should investigate, since they are now handling our security."

"Does your firm have experience with this sort of case?" Taylor asked. She knew she sounded snappish, but she couldn't help herself. Her world seemed to be veering out of control and she was powerless to do anything about it.

"No," Vince admitted. "We focus on computer security, but that often branches out to other concerns."

"When there's been a computer breach, we review the security camera tapes to see who's been in the building, and we also follow the computer trail," Shane explained. "That often forces us to use surveillance and other types of investigative tools."

"Checking Renata Rollins's claim isn't exactly rocket science." Vince tried for a laugh but it fell flat.

"You haven't been able to verify or disprove," Brianna pointed out. "I guess it isn't so easy."

"All it will take is a DNA test," Shane responded.

"And the time to process it." Vanessa spread her hands wide. "I don't have the time to waste. I want you to interview Renata," she said to Shane. "If there's even an outside chance she's my daughter, I want to meet her. I'd go there myself, but . . ."

No one had to be reminded that Vanessa was too ill to travel. Her blood had to be monitored every few days, and she was on a regime of more medications than Taylor cared to count.

"Go with him, Taylor," her mother added. "I need Trent and Doyle to tackle the computer problem with Vince. Let me know if I'm right. Renata is my daughter."

Doyle allowed Brianna to pull him aside while everyone filed into the enormous dining room often used for Vanessa's charity galas. Tonight it was set for an intimate five-course family dinner.

"You don't trust me." Brianna's full lower lip jutted out and her eyes widened.

"Of course I do," Doyle lied.

When Brianna had volunteered to go to New Orleans to help Taylor and Shane, Doyle had insisted he needed Brianna here to help sort information on his home computer, to cross-check info that might also be on the company computers.

"I need you to help me, that's all."

Her sexy pout remained in place. "We could do it in a few hours, tonight. Then I could go with Taylor."

He didn't know what to say. There was no skirting the truth. Shane was a stud, if ever Doyle had seen one. He didn't have matinee idol looks like Raoul, but he was a man's man with the kind of rough-hewn good looks that appealed to women.

Doyle wasn't giving sixty a hard shove for nothing. If he'd learned anything in all these years, it was not to throw two oversexed people together.

Once, Doyle had been a sex-starved man married to a good Catholic who thought sex, except for procreation, was a mortal sin. Brianna had been a brunette lap dancer in Little Havana.

The rest was history.

"It's not that I don't trust you, Brianna. I just don't want you in the middle of this."

"What if Taylor were going alone?" she challenged. "Would you let me go then?"

"Well . . . I guess," he hedged. "But that isn't the case. Shane—"

"Is walking testosterone, and you don't trust me near him."

She had her hands on her hips now, the way she'd had the night he'd suggested she become a blonde. It had taken a little convincing, but the result had been sensational. Blond Brianna became so much in demand, Doyle had been forced to marry her or lose her.

"Don't worry. Shane has the hots for Taylor. He doesn't even know I exist."

Doyle had to admit his niece was beautiful. A cool blonde while Brianna was a hot blonde. He trusted Taylor. She'd spent her youth in Catholic schools, but his wife was another story. Part Cuban, part white trailer trash, Brianna was too sexy for her own good.

"I trust you," he replied, struggling for something, anything, to strengthen his argument. "I just—"

Brianna sidled up to him, her searing green eyes staring into his. She kissed him lightly on the mouth, but in the instant their lips met, her tongue grazed his, sending a current of arousal to his groin.

"Then it's settled, darling. I'm going with Taylor."

Brianna bolted into the dining room, announcing, "We've worked out our scheduling problems, Taylor. I'm going with you."

Doyle hadn't seen Taylor look so happy since that worthless photographer had vanished. It was almost enough to make him smile. Almost.

"How many times do you have to keep telling me the same shit?"

"Until you get it right."

"Fuck you!"

"Is that any way to talk to me?"

Renata swung around so her back was on the sofa and her long, bare legs were flung over the top. She looked backward at Caleb Bassett—the upside-down image no better than the face-to-face version. He was munching on take-out pepperoni pizza—her favorite—and chugging Abita beer.

"I have to dance at nine," she told him, her stomach rumbling. "I can't eat until two, when I finish."

"One bite." He rose to his feet and hovered above her head. "To tide you over."

Renata twirled around, her feet hitting the wood floor in her French Quarter flat with a dull thud.

"I can't have one bite and you know it."

She snatched the slice of pepperoni pizza from his hand and hurled it against the fireplace. It landed with a wet splat and plopped onto the hearth.

Caleb sauntered back to his chair, his loose-limbed gait not fooling her for one second. He was pissed. Caleb reached into the cardboard box for another slice, took a loud, satisfying bite, then dropped into the chair.

Renata's tummy protested with a bleak roar that she was certain Caleb heard. She was hungry all the time—it seemed. She finally made decent money, but she still couldn't eat.

Not if she wanted to keep her job at Puss 'N Boots, the nightclub where she worked.

If she ate now, her stomach would pooch out, and her body would no longer be perfect. She had to wait until after work, then eat as little as possible, or stick her finger down her throat so her stomach was flat again for tomorrow's show.

Caleb smacked his lips—because it drover her crazy—and polished off the slice of pizza before speaking. "This could be the last week at the Puss."

She hated the way he made the P 'n B—the workers' nickname for the club—sound disgusting. But she didn't call him on it. Time had taught her a few lessons.

This man got off on baiting her.

Don't play into his hands.

"I know the drill." Renata stood up and strutted across the room, practicing her stage walk. "I know how to handle May Ella—"

"No, no! Her name is Vanessa now. Forget she was

ever May Ella Jones. All you need to know is that you're her long-lost daughter.''

Sometimes she hated Caleb with every bone in her body. He often felt the same way about her. But she had to admit they were a good team.

Life sucked the big one.

She jumped to her feet, grabbed her purse, and headed out the door.

"Where are you going?"

"To visit Marie."

"That's crazy and you know it. You should—"

Renata slammed the door behind her, cutting off his final words. She knew Caleb thought she was a nut to be so superstitious, but she couldn't help herself. Visiting the grave of Marie Laveau, the legendary voodoo queen brought good luck.

Her tombstone was covered with triple X's and had candles placed on it by people who believed in the black arts. Renata's luck had changed the day she'd come across Marie's grave in the St. Louis Cemetery in New Orleans.

She had run her hands across the triple X's and lit a candle. Miracle of miracles—a long string of bad luck had changed. She'd been offered a job at Puss 'N Boots and began to make real money.

"Call me superstitious," she mumbled to herself. "My luck is about to change again."

Chapter 4

Blowback.

An interesting concept. It hadn't been on anyone's radar screen until terrorists had struck the World Trade Center and the Pentagon. Then the idiots in the media interviewed the military, who had coined the term.

Blowback meant something you did could backfire and return—with a vengeance—to haunt you.

Unintended negative consequences.

The CIA trained Afghan men during the Soviet occupation of Afghanistan in the days of the Cold War, when limiting the spread of Communism was a priority for this country. Later those same men took their experience and unleashed it on American targets.

Blowback. Big time.

"That's biting the hand that fed you." He chuckled,

then amended his statement. "No, it's cutting off the hand that fed you. That's blowback. It's worse than what you put out in the first place. It intensifies with time, feeds on hate."

He looked out the window at the heat shimmering upward in moist curls from the damp pavement, bringing with it a whiff of the loamy soil in the planters, thinking.

Another interesting aspect of blowback was its unexpectedness. It wasn't the old "you reap what you sow."

Not at all. Things done with the best of intentions—even love—could boomerang after sulking in the shadows for years.

"No good deed goes unpunished."

That was certainly an aspect of blowback in this case. He couldn't help being pleased with himself. The Maxwells were experiencing big-time blowback.

The past was coming back to haunt them. No. Torture them is a better way of putting it.

Death would be the ultimate price for crossing him.

Too bad no one would be smart enough to figure the blowback angle. It was a killer concept.

Accurate.

Deadly.

Utterly fascinating.

"I'm finally enjoying myself."

Shane stood beside Brianna and Taylor, waiting for Caleb Bassett to answer the bell at the Creole town house on the fringe of New Orleans's French Quarter. The paint on the building once had been a warm coral, but it had faded to a dirty, nameless shade. It was cracked and peeling in so many places that the building appeared to be molting. The rancid smell of garbage spilling from an overturned trash can across the narrow street reminded Shane of the places he'd visited in Third World countries.

Shane rang the bell again, conscious of Taylor looking up at him. On the flight from Miami, she'd sat in stony silence and let Brianna do the talking. He didn't press it.

The one thing he had on his side was time.

"Why would he leave if he told us to come over?" Taylor asked.

After they'd checked into the Windsor Court Hotel, Shane had called Caleb Bassett, father of the woman who might be Vanessa's daughter. Renata was unavailable, but Caleb said he would be willing to talk to them.

Where in hell was he?

Unexpectedly, the door swung open. A handsome man with thick black hair burnished with silver at the temples beamed a grin worthy of a televangelist. He was dressed in a maroon something—would it be called a smoking jacket?—and black velvet Hush Puppies.

"Shane Donovan." Shane extended his hand. "This is Brianna Maxwell and Taylor Maxwell."

"Caleb Bassett." He bowed slightly to the women while he shook Shane's hand with a firm grip. "Come on in. I have tea ready."

Tea? What a brilliant idea.

Shane waited for Brianna and Taylor to enter, already dreading interviewing this man. His shit-o-meter had just gone off the chart.

This kind of man would be hard to judge. Shane could already see Bassett had a certain quality some people would find charming. And he knew how to exploit it.

So did most con artists.

They followed Caleb, as he wanted to be called,

down a narrow hallway with wood floors so highly buffed that Shane could almost see his reflection. The living room—Caleb called it the parlor—was a sunny room facing an immaculately maintained rear garden.

The room was decorated in what Shane assumed were period pieces, possibly authentic antiques. The kind of prissy French furniture upholstered in brocade that made a big man like Shane think twice before sitting down.

He planted himself on the end of a chaise across from Caleb and near Taylor who had taken a French chair with flimsy wood legs. Brianna had seated herself next to Caleb and she was saying something about how lovely the home was.

"You were expecting something less . . . refined?" Caleb asked.

"Well, we weren't sure—"

"Security, my dear." Caleb leaned closer to Brianna. "The Quarter is rife with crime. From all appearances, we wouldn't have anything to steal, would we?"

Got that right.

Brianna giggled and Taylor managed a smile. While taking in as much of the rest of the room as he could without making it obvious, Shane kept his gaze on Caleb, who was now offering them tea.

No family photos. Nothing that seemed really personal.

The place reminded Shane of a movie set except for a trace of something in the air. It might have been incense except Shane had spent too much time in Colombia not to recognize kick-ass marijuana.

He listened to Caleb describing the crumpets, scones, and pastries on the coffee table in front of them. A multi-tiered dish held a variety of bite-size sandwiches on bread with the crusts cut off. Shane couldn't help recalling afternoon gatherings in foreign embassies when he'd been with Special Forces. You'd need a mountain of those things to equal half a sandwich.

Real men did not eat cucumber sandwiches.

As he listened, Shane detected more than a hint of the deep South in Caleb's voice. Arkansas. Alabama. Maybe Tennessee.

Linguistics wasn't his expertise, but he'd been in enough dangerous places to know to listen to the difference in intonation that could warn you about a person's background.

In some places like the Middle East and South America, the slightest difference in pronunciation indicated a person was from another tribe—an enemy. Mistaking someone for a member of the wrong group could prove to be deadly.

The world had gone global in many aspects, yet in other ways the world seemed to be hunkering down into nations within nations, split-off states, tribes—and in America—gangs.

"Milk in your tea, Shane?" Caleb was asking.

Shane shook his head and waved off the cube of sugar Caleb was offering with silver tongs. Caleb reached for one of the cucumber sandwiches.

"Just a scone, please."

"I was expecting Vanessa," Caleb said, taking Shane by surprise.

Vanessa? Not Mrs. Maxwell? "She had pressing business. That's why she sent us."

Shane knew Vanessa had spoken with this man on the telephone. Obviously, she hadn't told him about her failing health. Equally as apparent, this was a guy who liked to get real chummy.

He was already using everyone's first name—as if they were his friends. Basset's friends? Now there's a depressing thought.

"We want to verify that your adopted daughter is my mother's—"

"Oh, she is. She is," Caleb cut off Taylor. "We discussed it on the telephone. Your mother agreed that it would be just too much of a coincidence for me to have adopted Renata in such a small town as Titusville just after she'd given birth less than twenty miles away."

"Me?" Taylor asked. "Don't you mean 'us?' Weren't you married when you adopted Renata?"

Damn good point. Taylor had picked up on his word choice.

"Of course." Caleb sounded unfazed. "But Mary Jo has been gone so long now. I've been a single father since Renata was five. There hasn't been an 'us' for almost thirty years."

"You never remarried?" This from Brianna. "A man of your taste and refinement?"

Shane nearly choked on his scone and was forced to wash it down with a swig of tea. Caleb went for it, beaming a white-toothed grin at Brianna. Who could blame him? She was a knockout with a ready smile, unlike Taylor who rarely smiled.

"I was too busy raising Renata and working to bother with romance."

Yeah, yeah. Right.

"What proof do you have that this baby you adopted is Vanessa Maxwell's daughter?" Shane asked.

"Proof?" Caleb asked as if Shane were speaking in tongues. "I explained that a fire had destroyed our home. Everything we owned went up in smoke. I couldn't even save our wedding album or the family photographs."

Well, hell. This just kept getting better and better. Shane had to give him credit, though. The man sounded sincere, but with this much money at stake anyone could deliver an Oscar-worthy performance.

"What year was that?"

It took Caleb a second too long to say, "Nineteen eighty-seven."

"That was in Titusville?"

"No. No. We were living in Brigg's Crossing."

"That's in Alabama, too?"

"No. It's in Arkansas near Little Rock."

Shane nodded, thinking it shouldn't be too hard to verify the fire. Of course, what the family photographs would have shown was a whole other question. He reached into his sport coat's inside pocket for the small pen and notepad.

"Look, we're going to need to verify a few facts before—"

"That's not what Vanessa said."

"My mother is a little impetuous at times," Taylor informed Caleb in the same cool tone she used on Shane so often. "That's why we're here."

"It's a fact finding mission," Brianna added in a voice meant to defuse the tension.

"We need to prove or disprove your claim," Shane said, again wishing they had time to run a DNA test.

"I'm not claiming anything," Caleb said.

"You contacted *Missing!*," Shane reminded him.

"I thought Renata deserved to meet her real mother."

Shane said, "There must be something we could take back to Mrs. Maxwell that would verify your statements."

"Talk to Renata," Caleb said with a wave of his hand toward the garden beyond the window.

"She's here? I thought you said—"

"At this time of day? No. She's out shopping. But she lives in the slave quarters out back."

Beyond the small garden was another house. Even at this distance, Shane could see it had been meticulously restored, unlike the outside of the compound facing the street.

"When do you expect her to return?" Taylor asked.

"She usually comes home between four and five."

Brianna checked her Rolex. "She'll be here any minute. It's almost five now."

Caleb smiled at Brianna, and Shane detected more than a casual hint of interest in the older man's eyes. "Five in the morning. You know, just before sunrise."

"She can't possibly be shopping until then," Taylor said.

"Shopping? Of course not. She'll leave the shops and go directly to the club. Her act starts at eleven and finishes at two." Caleb crossed his legs and gazed at the toes of his Hush Puppies. "You might want to watch her dance at Puss 'N Boots."

The luminous dial on Renata's watch told her it was almost seven o'clock. How long had she been locked in here? She'd dozed off, losing track of time.

That terrible man—what was his name—hadn't left her, had he?

No. That wasn't what this jerk wanted. Since she'd bought her first bra at Walmart when she'd been twelve, Renata had known what men wanted.

Sex.

Once you got with the program life was simple. Most of the time.

Dick-breath Caleb could complicate things, but only if she let him. This man was another story. It wasn't as if she hadn't had kinky sex in the past, but she'd done her level best to stay out of dangerous situations.

Until now.

"Hey! Hey!" She banged on the door and screamed at the top of her lungs.

For all the good it would do. She'd been taken to a shanty supported by rickety wooden stilts deep in the swampy part of the bayou. Nobody was around to hear her except the alligators.

And the mosquitoes. She'd given up swatting them. They buzzed through the cracks between the shack's wooden slats even though someone had tried to plug the gaps with flypaper.

She hadn't lost her *mojo*, had she? A dancer at the club told Renata a *mojo* was a good luck charm that came in the air. You couldn't see it, couldn't feel it, but your *mojo* protected you, bringing good luck.

Where was her *mojo* when she needed it?

The dull thud of boots clacked against the wooden floor. A second later the door opened enough to let in a shaft of light from the lantern, the only light in the one-room shack. A fresh stream of air rife with the mossy, pungent smell of the bayou hit her damp body.

"Ready to do what I say?" asked the gruff voice.

Fuck off and die! Renata silently swallowed those words.

"Yes. I'll do whatever you want."

The door flung back, hitting the wall with a splintering sound like wood shattering. A gush of dank body odor engulfed her.

A meat hook of a hand grabbed her long hair, flung her sideways, then dragged her from the closet. He pulled her across the rough plank floor. A splinter stabbed into her butt with the force of a knife.

"Ow! Ow! Stop!"

She couldn't perform tonight with a red mark on her ass. But he didn't pay any attention to her. The beast kept yanking on her hair until she thought he intended to scalp her.

Suddenly, Puss 'N Boots seemed a distant memory.

He let go of her hair and grabbed her arms, hauling her up to her knees, her face smack against the worn denim covering his crotch. He was fully erect, a bull of a man, suited to whores in Cajun dives along the bayou, not her.

In her own right, Renata was a class act.

Using both hands, he kept her face buried against his cock, her lungs forced to inhale the foulness of his body. His chest was bare and slick with oily sweat dribbling down from a damp mat of curly chest hair.

She opened her mouth wide and bit down on his cock. The denim was worn, but enough protection to elicit a guttural moan of pleasure. She clamped down again and used more force this time.

"Motherfucker!" He jumped away. "You'll pay, bitch!"

"Don't hurt me," she whimpered.

The hulk of a man scooted sideways onto a pallet of straw. Even from a few feet away, she smelled the rank odor of mildew and sex.

"Strip," he ordered, the words coming from between clenched teeth as he gripped his sore dick with both hands.

She heaved herself to her feet, her legs numb and tingling from being imprisoned in the closet for so long. Swaying from the effort, not from any attempt to titillate, she slowly pirouetted, running her hands down her hips. The splinter in her ass throbbed like a tooth in need of a root canal, but she didn't dare stop to pull it out.

"Come on, big guy. Keep that boner up."

She flung her sheer blouse over her head and it swished through the heavy air. A kiss of coolness caressed her uplifted breasts, and she sighed, managing to turn the sound into a moan of delight.

What would satisfy him? she wondered with renewed desperation.

She unzipped her dress a scant inch at a time, revealing a navel that had become her trademark. Diamond studs circled her outtie belly button, surrounding a larger diamond dead in the center.

With a flourish that masked a surge of pain from the splinter in her butt, she managed to fling her gown aside.

"Oh, yeah, babe. Gimme more, else'n I'll cut your pussy to ribbons."

She had no doubt he meant every word. With a few more gyrations, she shed the high heels that had caused blisters on her toes. Could she do this?

She was down to the demi-bra that shoved her boobs skyward and a G-string. She strutted across the coffin of a room, then pivoted and headed back. A dark cloud of mosquitoes hovered overhead like a curse.

From the bleak shadows a foot shot out. She stumbled and fell facedown in his lap. That's when she felt the cold, sharp blade of the knife.

With one precise flick of the blade, he inserted it between her breasts and slit the clasp on her bra. Her boobs tumbled forward, hitting him in the face. Beneath her tummy, a dangerous erection prodded at her.

He sucked one nipple into his mouth while his broad hand shot between her legs, then found the opening. He stroked gently for a moment, his lips suckling with the same cadence, and she prayed her *mojo* had returned.

"Oh, yes," she murmured as if she were enjoying this.

A second later, he flipped her onto her back and

one swipe of his knife cut the G-string. He rammed into her like a bulldozer. Something ripped inside her, forcing out the scream she'd promised she wouldn't let come.

Tiny pinpricks of light exploded in the darkness behind her closed eyelids. Maybe Caleb was right, she decided.

Enough of this shit.

Chapter 5

Taylor hesitated outside the door to Shane's room. She didn't know which was worse, dealing with her mother or with Shane Donovan. Her mother was totally obsessed with Renata Rollins. Vanessa was convinced this woman had to be her lost daughter.

The last thing Taylor wanted was to have her mother's final days ruined by charlatans after her money. Since meeting Caleb Bassett, Taylor was positive the man was an appealing impostor who would cause her mother needless pain.

What did Shane think?

They'd left Caleb and returned to the Windsor Court Hotel without Shane saying anything much except he was going to check the story Caleb had told them. Brianna hadn't been helpful either, claiming Caleb was an unusual person, but he just might be telling the truth.

No getting around it. Caleb Bassett had a way about him. That, combined with his good looks, could very well take in her mother.

Taylor knocked and waited, listening to the thunder grumbling in the distance, promising more rain. She had her hand raised to knock again when the door swung open. Shane had pulled on a pair of khaki slacks and had zipped them up, but the button at the waist was undone and he wasn't wearing a shirt.

He'd just toweled off from the shower. His skin was still moist and his rebellious hair waved in different directions.

"Taylor?" he said as if he didn't recognize her.

"Do you have a minute?"

A beat of silence, then he stepped aside and she walked into the room. He had his laptop set up on the small round table in the corner. Even at this distance, she could see screen saver, the initials *D. I. A.*, and an eagle.

D. I. A.? What did that stand for?

She turned to face him and found him looking at her in a way that was as blatantly sexual as if he were gazing at her from the same pillow. Meeting his fixed stare with an icy glance, she went into her professional mode, not wanting him to think for a second she'd come to his room for any other reason than business.

"My mother called. She wanted to know what we thought. I explained how little information Caleb gave us, but she didn't care. She's convinced Renata Rollins is her daughter."

"That's what she wants to believe." Shane combed his wet hair with his fingers, but it didn't help much. "Is that what you came to see me about? It couldn't wait until dinner?"

His teasing tone implied she had some other motive for visiting him.

"No. I wanted to know if you'd found out anything," she told him in a breathless rush. "The sooner I can persuade my mother we're dealing with impostors, the better off she'll be. I don't want her last months to be ruined by false hopes."

"Don't count on it." Shane crossed the room in a few long strides, hit a key on the computer, and the screen went dark. "So far, what little Caleb Bassett told us appears to be the truth."

"He didn't say anything that would prove—"

"True, but when Peggy Sue Bassett—Renata's real name if she's who Caleb says she is—enrolled in first grade, her next of kin was listed as her father and her grandmother, Alma Bassett."

"The adoptive mother must have died the way he said," Taylor replied, a flicker of compassion for Caleb replacing skepticism.

She crossed the room so she could look into Shane's eyes. This man was hard to read, and something about him kept disturbing her. She didn't know how to talk to him except defensively.

Well, she was going to have to learn. Taylor needed him to thoroughly investigate these people.

"Alma was on welfare and so was Caleb," Shane informed her. "It isn't the profile of a man who could afford an expensive private adoption where you had to pay off a lawyer and the woman who handed over the baby."

"The wife's family may have had money."

"There could be some other explanation." Shane dropped into the chair facing his computer and closed the lid. "Bassett had a daughter, but it doesn't mean she was adopted."

"True. Anything else?"

"The Bassetts moved to Brigg's Crossing when Renata was nine, after the grandmother had died.

Caleb worked as an insurance salesman. The next year the house they were renting burned down, and they lost everything.''

Taylor stifled a groan. "You think he's telling the truth."

"What he's told us so far seems true."

"You don't think that man is charming but a bit off? The way he acted, the way he dressed, that house—"

"He might have been working with glue a little too much."

It took Taylor a second to get it. "Very funny."

"You may not like Caleb Bassett, but what matters to me is verifying whether Renata is the missing baby or not."

"Unless we can prove they're lying, my mother is going to want to meet Renata. Mother is already talking about bringing them both to Miami."

Taylor heard defeat and desperation in her own voice but couldn't help it. She gathered her thoughts for a moment, then asked, "You found out all that online?"

Shane nodded. "You'd be surprised what's out there in cyberspace."

"Like why a seemingly poor man went to an attorney for a private adoption," she replied, then waited while Shane studied her in silence. "Hold it. How old was Caleb when the baby was adopted?"

"You're smarter than you look." Shane's impudent grin canted to one side in a way some women might have found charming or even sexy. It merely annoyed Taylor. "He was twenty-five."

"That's awfully young to adopt a baby."

"Not if you knew—for certain—you couldn't father a child."

"Doesn't it seem unlikely a man that young living

in a backwater town would have consulted a fertility expert?"

"Maybe he had mumps in his teens, and they settled in his testicles. More likely, the mother knew she couldn't have a baby. Women usually push to have children, not men, especially men so young."

"He never had another child, and he never remarried," Taylor observed, thinking of Paul Ashton and knowing how it felt to lose the love of your life. The flicker of sympathy she'd felt moments ago intensified. Maybe she'd been too quick to judge Caleb Bassett.

"He still lives near his daughter even though she's a grown woman," she said. "Strange."

Renata shouldered her way through the back door of Puss 'N Boots with only minutes to spare before her act began. "Buzz, get in here," she yelled at the bouncer who kept the low life creeps from coming backstage.

The three-hundred-pound ex-Marine lumbered over to her. "Hey, babe. What in hell happened? Did a trick go south on you?"

"Sorta', but I got paid plenty."

She grabbed his beefy wrist and pulled him into the makeshift excuse for a dressing room she shared with Cissy LaBuff. Cissy was onstage fan dancing, and as usual, her makeup was strewn across the dressing table. With a sweep of her arm, Renata sent open bottles and jars crashing to the floor.

"Money talks, Buzz. Real loud."

"Yeah? All money ever says to me is bye-bye."

Renata almost laughed as she whipped off the red sundress she was wearing. Underneath she was buck naked. She knew Buzz had the hots for her, but seeing her undressed was nothing new. He was backstage all the time, and the girls pranced around naked while getting ready to perform.

"Whatcha lookin' for?" Buzz asked when she began to rifle through the drawers in the battered Formica dressing table.

"Tweezers. Can't you see that huge splinter in my ass?"

Behind her Buzz cleared his throat. "They're over there." He edged by her and picked up the tweezers from the mess on the floor.

"Great. Thanks." She pointed to her butt. "Pull out the splinter."

Buzz placed one clammy hand on her waist. He grunted as he took his sweet time locating the splinter. He yanked it out with another grunt. She bit the inside of her cheek to keep from crying.

"There's more. It's broken into pieces."

Small wonder, she thought. She'd felt it when she'd driven herself here from the bayou. So, the money was great. It beat flatbacks—regular tricks—to hell.

The john worked on one of the oil rigs in the Gulf and had money to burn when he was on shore. She'd had rough sex with him before. Each incident became more violent.

She swore this was the last time and thought about Caleb's plan as Buzz removed the splinter fragments.

"What were you expecting?" Brianna asked as they walked up to the line of men waiting to get into the club where Renata Rollins worked in the seedy fringe of the French Quarter.

"Dancing at a club called Puss 'N Boots isn't the ballet. I should know. I used to make a living lap dancing in Little Havana, remember?"

"Was it like this?" Taylor asked, conscious of the men leering at them.

She was unexpectedly thankful they had Shane escorting them. Most of the guys waiting to get into the club looked as if they should be in a police lineup.

"It was worse," Brianna replied. "Your uncle was the only gentleman who ever came into the club where I worked."

Taylor grudgingly admired Brianna. She never pretended to be anything she wasn't.

For an instant, Taylor thought of her mother, a woman who kept her background a well-guarded secret and lived to maintain a place in society. She could just imagine what her mother would say if she saw just the outside of this dive and knew Renata worked here.

The sign for Puss 'N Boots featured a comic strip type painting of a nearly nude woman dressed up in a cat outfit with a long tail and a headband with over-sized ears. The nipples of her humungous breasts were covered with fur pasties. She wore shiny black leather boots up to her knees and brandished a whip in one hand.

The thundershower had passed, but water dripped from the roofs and formed oily puddles with cigarette butts floating on them. A pale ghost of a moon momentarily parted the clouds. Moisture formed gauzy haloes around the neon signs for the other joints on the narrow street.

Rain had cleared the air but had done nothing to make this place look better. What could?

"New Orleans gets more rain than Seattle," Taylor said, thinking out loud about a question for her Trivial Moments game.

"No kidding?" Shane said with a hint of humor.

"Bet on it," Brianna told him. "Taylor's hobby is trivia. She knows her facts."

Taylor tried for a nonchalant smile but didn't quite make it. She peered into the alley across the street. Piles of cardboard boxes soggy from the rain. A black cat foraging in a McDonald's bag. Discarded Styrofoam cups.

A world away from the Miami she knew.

"Both of you stick close to me," Shane ordered. "Don't make eye contact with any man. No matter what they say, don't answer."

Shane guided them around the line of men and walked up to the bouncer. "We're guests of Renata Rollins."

Caleb had told them to say this and it would get them inside. The dark man appeared to be Bahamian, and he looked them over while the men nearby whistled and tried to get their attention. Shane slipped the bouncer a folded bill and he stepped aside.

The stench of beer, cigarette smoke, and rank body odor hit Taylor the second she walked into the pitch-dark club lit only by a blue neon sign advertising Abita beer. Off to one side was a long bar with several women in pussycat outfits serving drinks. At the front of the club was a small stage with a brass pole in the center.

"I see a table near the front," Shane said as he guided them through a warren of tables crammed with men.

Several men reached out to grab them, but Shane zapped them with a look that could have backed down a pit bull. Except for the women who worked here, they were the only females in the club.

The three of them huddled around a table the size of a dinner plate in the second row from the stage. A waitress in a threadbare cat costume with limp ears and a tail that dragged behind her collected the cover charge and brought them a pitcher of what she claimed was their famous Hurricane.

The phosphorescent drink so popular on Bourbon Street tasted like lukewarm turpentine in this club.

"I guess they're between acts," Brianna said, stating the obvious.

"Are they lap dancing here?" Taylor asked.

"Nah," Brianna replied. "There's not enough room. Expect a stripper."

A stripper. She'd suspected as much the second she'd heard the club's name, but nothing prepared her for how seedy this place was.

Look on the bright side, she thought. Mother won't be so anxious to bring a stripper home. Especially a stripper with a half-baked story about being her daughter.

Her mother was a snob; no getting around it, Taylor silently conceded. At all times Vanessa Maxwell was conscious of class and background and breeding. Her wealthy friends, the country club, her place in society meant a lot to her.

Now Taylor understood why. Her mother had grown up poor and neglected. Even the love of a wealthy, powerful man hadn't made Vanessa feel secure. Unless Renata Rollins could prove she was Vanessa's daughter, Taylor knew her mother wouldn't want the woman around.

With a drum roll, the stage went dark and a hush charged with anticipation replaced the chatter in the room. Taylor inhaled a calming breath, wondering if this woman would look like her the way Taylor resembled her mother.

She prayed not, but she wasn't positive. Shane's confirming what Caleb had told them had shaken her.

A single spotlight blasted the stage with a circle of blinding light. In its center, leaning against the pole was a tall woman clad in a black leather trench coat and stiletto heels.

Renata Rollins.

Thick hair gleamed blue-black in the intense light. Pouty lips suggested collagen. Those spidery lashes couldn't be real.

Taylor forced herself to admit the woman was beautiful in a hard-looking, overly made-up way. Renata's eyes were as dark as her hair and enhanced by the liberal use of eyeliner.

Taylor examined every feature as the woman strutted across the small stage and untied the belt on her coat to the hoots of the all-male audience.

She didn't see a hint of her mother in this ... person. Thank you, God. Taylor watched, relief morphing into anger. This stripper and the jerk they'd met this afternoon planned to take her mother for a ride.

Over my dead body.

"Typical striptease," Brianna whispered as the woman slowly peeled off the coat, then tossed it aside.

The closest Taylor had been to anything like this was a raunchy show she'd seen in Key West during spring break when she'd been at Yale. The women had danced in skirts and tops that came off with a flick of Velcro, leaving them in black lace bras and matching panties. She stole a glance at Shane to see what he was thinking.

Like every other guy in the place, his eyes were tracking Renata, but his face was expressionless. He was darn good at hiding his thoughts, she decided. This afternoon with Caleb Bassett, she hadn't been able to gauge Shane's reaction to the man.

Renata had shed her skirt and sweater as well as her

boots. She was wearing a red satin slip that Taylor had to admit was sexy. She noticed Shane's eyes narrowed just slightly. So, he wasn't the master of the poker face after all.

"Why is she doing that?" Taylor whispered to Brianna when Renata began to move provocatively against the pole in the center of the stage.

"It's called 'humping the pole.' It drives guys crazy."

Taylor nodded, noticing the men were now banging on the tables or stomping their feet. Many were yelling for her to "Take it off. Take it *all* off."

Shane was silent, but his eyes were still on Renata.

After another shimmy against the pole, Renata sashayed to the front of the stage. Running the tip of her tongue over her cherry-red lips, she gazed out at her enthralled audience. If she noticed two women among the horde of men, Renata gave no sign.

She lifted the hem of her slip up an inch at a time, revealing slender thighs. She stopped just short of showing her panties and waited. And waited.

The men went ballistic, yelling more, stomping louder. Finally, Renata inched the slip upward exposing a swatch of red satin.

"More! More! Go for it!" screamed the apes at the table next to them.

It seemed to take an eternity to pull the slip up enough to reveal a belly button pierced with a circle of rhinestones that glinted like diamonds. A larger stone, too big to be real, winked at the audience from the center of her belly button.

In a split second, she shucked the slip and flung it high into the air above the crowd. Men scrambled to their feet, fighting each other for the garment. A soccer-type fight threatened to break out. A burly bouncer shoved the rowdiest men back into their seats.

Looking mildly amused, Renata stood there in all her glory. A wisp of red satin passed for a G-string and patches of red satin connected by thin straps covered huge breasts. She slowly turned to allow the men to admire every inch of her body.

Taylor fought the urge to run for the exit. What would it be like to have to earn your living by stripping every night? Mortified, Taylor's stomach churned.

How was any woman reduced to this? What had happened to her?

Taylor thought about Caleb's town house. It was in marvelous condition and was furnished with antiques. Why didn't he sell something to save his daughter from humiliating herself like this?

What kind of man was Caleb Bassett? she wondered. He was handsome and had a certain ... charm, but he was odd. He didn't seem fatherly at all.

He couldn't be her father, she decided, anger resurfacing again and getting the better of the analytical train of thought that served her so well in business. That charlatan and this stripper were trying to take advantage of her mother.

"She's good," Brianna whispered. "It's all about timing and she knows it."

Maybe Brianna really did love Doyle, Taylor decided. He'd taken her away from a degrading life like this and put her on a pedestal. Why wouldn't she love him for it?

Renata slowly pivoted and showed her rear end. Her bottom as flawless as a newborn baby's. Red lips were painted on one cheek with what appeared to be lipstick.

Renata looked back over her shoulder, her lips forming a sexy pout. "Renata has an owie. Wanna kiss it and make it better?"

She jumped from the stage and paraded by the

first row. The men took turns kissing her butt. Taylor couldn't force herself to watch.

Some of them smacked so loudly that the rest howled with laughter. She knew, from watching the first few, they were tucking money into the elastic band of her G-string.

She promenaded around the room, collecting more and more bills. Circling back, Renata approached them. Taylor wanted to hide under their table.

To quell her reaction, Taylor concentrated on the woman's face, again checking it for something—any hint—of a family resemblance.

Nothing.

Renata halted right in front of Shane. She smiled and showed him the lips painted on her rear. This close, Taylor could see it had been painted on with nail polish, not lipstick.

"Come on, big boy," Renata purred.

Taylor could see why she'd singled out Shane. He might have looked scruffy in South Beach, but he was GQ material in this crowd. She sucked in her breath and waited for him to kiss ass. The spotlight flooded their table with glaring light, and its heat brought a prickle of moisture to the back of Taylor's neck.

Shane cracked a smile and took out his money clip. He peeled a crisp one-hundred-dollar bill from it. While the other men yelled for Renata to take off her bra, Shane folded the bill into a fan.

He stuck it between her breasts and winked.

Renata grabbed the bill and put it over one ear like a flower. She pranced over to the stage, hopped up, and stood there, smiling. With a flick of her hand, she unhooked the bra.

Little had been left to the imagination before, but seeing those bare breasts thrust upward like some pagan offering sent the men over the top. They hooted and threw money onto the stage. Renata swung the bra in the air the way she had her other clothes and tossed it into the audience.

It landed, the cups down like ear muffs, on Shane's head.

Chapter 6

The sound of the telephone on his nightstand yanked Doyle out of a fitful sleep. His money problems had triggered another nightmare. He'd run out of money and Brianna had left him.

The glow of the digital alarm clock told him it was after two. What in hell was Brianna doing out so late, he thought, reaching for the telephone.

"Doyle, it's me . . . Trent."

He sat bolt upright, thrusting the covers aside. "Your mother! Something's happened."

"No. She's fine." There was a lot of commotion in the background. Doyle could barely hear his nephew. "It's me. I'm in trouble."

Trouble? Trent? Never. Wait. His nephew had changed a lot in the past year.

Goose bumps sprang up beneath Doyle's silk pajama top. "What kind of trouble?"

"I've been arrested. Raoul, too."

Served the interfering Cuban swish right was Doyle's first reaction. Then he reconsidered. No matter how much he despised Raoul, they needed Doyle's help. Maybe he could use this to his advantage.

"Arrested? For what?"

"Possession."

"Aaah." He fought a smile. If he played this right, he could neutralize Raoul or get rid of him entirely. Thinking, he repeated, "Drugs?"

"Crystal meth," Trent replied. "Would you come down to the station with a lawyer? And don't tell Mother."

It was almost dawn before Doyle contacted Alan Friedman. Never having needed a criminal attorney, Doyle had awakened Ridley Pudge, the family attorney for a recommendation. Friedman was the best, and judging by the fee he demanded up front, the man had better be good.

Alan Friedman, a short, wiry man with receding red hair and half-moon glasses, met Doyle in the lobby of the Miami Beach Police Department. The lawyer was waiting in front of the mural of fishes. Doyle wondered how many other parents he'd met in the same spot. Probably too many to count.

"I'm Doyle Maxwell." He stuck out his hand and Friedman gave it a quick shake. He handed over the check for the retainer, and the attorney tucked it into his pocket without looking at it.

"You said your nephew is being held on a drug charge?" the lawyer asked.

The atrium went to the ceiling past four floors marked with turquoise metal railings. His voice seemed to bounce off the walls.

"Which drug?"

"Does it matter?"

"You bet. Which drug and the amount the police found is important."

"Crystal meth."

"He's gay."

It wasn't a question; it was a statement. Doyle nodded.

"It's the drug of choice among gay men. It goes hand in hand with unsafe sex."

Shane leaned one shoulder against the doorjamb of Renata's dressing room. He ignored the hulking bouncer who was eyeing him. Not what he'd call a fun guy. The bouncer had seen more naked butts than a pediatrician, and he didn't want another man on his turf, getting a peek or copping a feel.

Taylor had insisted on talking to the stripper herself, telling Shane and Brianna to come along but keep quiet. Renata sat facing a marquee-style makeup mirror with several of the lights burned out. She was wearing a flimsy robe and hadn't bothered to button it.

Her lush breasts were half exposed, but he figured it wasn't a deliberate attempt to be provocative. The woman was a stripper; being nude was second nature to her.

"So you met Caleb," Renata was saying. "Isn't he a trip?"

Caleb—not Father or Dad or Papa. Interesting, Shane thought.

"He was interesting," Taylor replied.

Renata's whoop of laugher richoted off the walls. "Yeah, ole Caleb is priceless. Bet he pulled that phony English gentleman crap on you, didn't he?"

"We enjoyed having tea with him."

"Sure you did. Musta' been a real party."

Renata gathered her long, dark hair in one hand and secured it to the top of her head with a red clip. She slapped lotion on her face and began removing the stage makeup with wads of Kleenex.

"What's so important that you had to see me?"

Taylor flashed a quick glance at Shane. "It's about your claim that you're Vanessa Maxwell's daughter."

"My claim?" Renata whirled around to face them. Anger flashed in her dark eyes and Shane decided only someone with a death wish would cross this woman. "I never said I was her child."

"*Missing!* received a call," Brianna said, and Taylor shot her a warning look meant to shut her up.

"Ask me if I care."

"My mother spoke with your father, and he—"

"Caleb—being Caleb—insisted I was her daughter, right?"

"Yes, but you don't think you are," Taylor said. "Is that what I'm hearing?"

"You aren't hearing squat. How in hell should I know who my mother is?"

"What did your father tell you about your real mother?" Shane asked even though Taylor was frowning at him.

"I was adopted." Renata turned back to the mirror and continued wiping off the makeup. "He never let me forget it. Claimed I ruined his life. If it hadn't been for me, Caleb would have joined the Navy and seen the world."

Two beats of silence filled the tiny room. In the distance, the drawn-out roll of the drum and loud male hoots signaled another stripper was slowly taking off her clothes.

Finally, Taylor asked, "Do you know *anything* about your real mother?"

Renata stopped wiping off makeup that must have been applied with a trowel and stared hard, her dark eyes meeting Taylor's in the mirror. "She dumped me, then ran off. Caleb and Mary Jo adopted me."

"Why?" Taylor asked. "Couldn't they have children?"

"No. Mary Jo got knocked up when she was fifteen. Some country doctor butchered her during the abortion."

Taylor's gaze shifted in his direction for a fraction of a second, and he knew what she was thinking. This would explain why a young, healthy man like Caleb would adopt a child.

Renata closed an eye and placed a square of cotton soaked in some solution on it. Even with just one eye directed at them, her expression was positively feral. Shane knew Renata Rollins had seen as much of the world as he had.

Maybe more.

When he'd watched her onstage, he'd figured her for another stripper with more silicone than brain cells. The kind of woman who should come with the surgeon general's warning label stamped on her forehead.

Now he could see he was mistaken. Not about the silicone; those boobs were not original equipment. But that didn't mean Renata wasn't smart.

Actually, he'd bet she was more cunning than intelligent, the kind of person who relied on her instincts.

"Things mighta' been okay," Renata continued, "but Mary Jo up and died leaving Caleb to raise me."

"Caleb was mean to you?"

"Caleb? Mean?" Renata dropped the cotton square and peeled off a set of false eyelashes. "Nah, not really.

Gramma Alma was the meanest bitch to walk the earth.''

Again silence filled the room, but outside the strip-tease had reached a crescendo with men yelling and stomping until the floor beneath Shane's feet trembled. The bouncer had edged closer. No doubt he was getting an earful.

"Do you know of any records—anywhere—that could prove who your real parents were?" Taylor asked, her frustration and annoyance evident.

Renata had another square of cotton over the other eye. "Nope."

"Look, my mother is very ill. She gave up a baby a long time ago in a town near where you were adopted. Mother wonders if you might—"

"She can wonder all she wants." Renata peeled off the other strip of false eyelashes and flung it down on the table. "I don't know and I don't give a shit. I have my life. Why should I care about some rich bitch who waits until the grim reaper is calling to look for her child?"

"You're wrong," insisted Taylor. "Mother began searching just after my father died. She wasn't ill then."

"Big fucking deal. She didn't want him to know she wasn't Miss Perfect, so she waited until he was gone. Why should I care if she ever finds her kid?"

"Renata had a point, you know," Taylor told Shane. "Mother didn't want my father—or anybody—to know she isn't perfect. She's always been so concerned with . . . appearances."

They'd returned to Windsor Court and he was sitting with Taylor on a sofa in the deserted lobby. Brianna had gone upstairs to call her husband. At two o'clock in the morning? Obviously, the old geezer kept her on a short leash, Shane decided.

"Yeah, well, meeting Renata should blow your mother away."

Taylor gazed at him with eyes that reflected more hurt than any woman her age should have suffered.

"I don't want my mother to have to deal with Renata. You heard her. She's a hard-as-nails stripper who hates the woman who gave her up for adoption."

Shane could see her point. Renata probably would be unnecessarily cruel to Vanessa Maxwell. Why expose a woman so ill to this?

"If and it's a big IF—Renata was ever adopted. I'll bet it's all an act like the performance she gives when she strips."

"What about your mother's money?" Shane asked before he could stop himself. "That's another reason to hope Renata isn't the missing baby. Your mother would leave her a bundle, wouldn't she?"

"I suppose." The insolence in her blue eyes and the defiant set of her lips sent an erotic charge through him.

"It's not the money I'm worried about. It's my mother's mental state. Knowing you're going to die is one thing. This is another."

Shane believed Taylor. She was tough in some ways, but she wasn't the type who could lie easily and get away with it. Her face, her eyes revealed too much.

Trent and his lover, Raoul, were another story. So was good old Uncle Doyle. Only a man with an IQ in the minus column wouldn't know the money angle worried Doyle Maxwell.

Shane hadn't had a chance to do an in-depth analysis of To The Maxx, but even a preliminary report showed how wealthy Vanessa Maxwell was. Trent and Taylor had small trusts and modest salaries. They both stood to gain by Vanessa's death, especially if To The Maxx was acquired by one of the big cosmetics companies.

From what he'd seen, Vanessa was having a major guilt trip about the baby she'd given up for adoption. If she even *thought* Renata was her child, the stripper would certainly appear in her will.

Who knew? Renata might finagle her way into getting a chunk of money right now, if they actually met.

This could get interesting.

"What am I going to tell Mother?" Taylor asked. "It's too late to call her now, but I'll have to talk to her in the morning."

He picked up on the pleading note in her voice, her eyes. The situation was forcing her to deal with him. He'd thought he was going to have to rely on Auggie to break the ice, but this unexpected twist of fate changed things.

Come to think about it, Lady Luck had been on his side—for once. He'd deliberately sought out Taylor. He hadn't expected to find a vacancy in her building, but there you go.

Luck was with him.

He certainly hadn't anticipated having this case dumped in his lap. Again, he'd gotten lucky.

"What can you tell your mother? The truth. We don't have a clue. This woman might be her daughter or maybe not."

"What do you think? Is Renata the real thing?"

Shane changed positions but resisted the urge to move closer to Taylor. She wasn't treating him like shit any longer, yet he wasn't a fool. It was too soon to make the slightest move. Her riveting eyes narrowed as she waited for an answer.

"Is Renata the missing baby? I wouldn't bet one way or the other."

"Come on. You must have some opinion."

His sixth sense told him Bassett and his daughter were scam artists, but he could be wrong.

"My opinion is that Renata is very clever. Caleb has to have told her how much your mother is worth. Yet she acts as if she doesn't give a damn. She loves her life as a stripper in a two-bit dive. I'm not buying it."

"So you think she's a fraud."

"A fraud? Not exactly. Has she claimed to be the missing baby? No. Caleb says she is. DNA would be proof positive."

"Considering Mother's condition, we may not have time to wait for the results. Are you sure we couldn't slip one of the good labs some money to do a test?"

Taylor's appraising look, instead of putting him down—told him that she honestly valued his opinion. Way to go, Donovan.

"Like I told you in Miami, labs have priority lists. Barry Scheck—one of O. J. Simpson's attorneys—heads up the Innocence Project at Cardozo Law School in New York. They use DNA to prove convicted prisoners are not guilty."

"Really? How can prisoners afford him?"

Shane smiled. "He does it gratis for convicts who can't pay. Celebrities he charges big time."

"I know DNA has cleared several men."

"A lawyer like Scheck knows exactly where everyone is on the lab's waiting list. There'd be hell to pay—if we even tried to get around them."

"You're right," Taylor agreed with a sigh. "Some prisoners have been in jail for years. It wouldn't be fair to make them wait a day longer than necessary if they're innocent."

The dusky sweep of her lashes and slightly parted lips made him want to put his arm around her, but once again he held himself in check. Instead, he kept talking. "Someday every police station will have the ability to run the tests themselves."

"Really?"

"Yes. There are even field kits the size of laptop computers that can be used anywhere. Testing is going on right now."

"How do you know all this?"

He tried for a teasing smile. "If I tell you, I'll have to shoot you. It's classified."

"You worked for the military. That's how you got your dog."

"There you go, clever girl. You figured it out."

"What did you do?"

"A little of this, a little of that."

A suggestion of a smile touched her lips. "Sounds exciting."

"I guess you're the type who's easily excited."

"Oh, stop. Be serious."

Her voice had an almost intimate quality to it that brought him up short. For a moment, Shane was tempted to tell her the truth. But the truth was a double-edged sword.

Chapter 7

Taylor opened the door just a crack, expecting room service to be delivering her morning coffee, and found Brianna outside her hotel room. It was obvious she'd been crying.

"What's the matter?" Taylor pulled Brianna into the room.

"It's Doyle," Brianna said. "He's having an affair."

"What?" Taylor gasped. "I don't believe it. He's crazy about you."

Brianna flopped down onto the unmade bed. "I tried calling him all last night. He wasn't home."

"Maybe he had to go somewhere on business," Taylor suggested, although she couldn't imagine what would take her uncle out of the city.

"He wouldn't go away without leaving me a message." Brianna twisted her pear-shaped wedding ring in a circle, the early morning light catching the facets of a diamond as big as a doorknob.

"Maybe something came up," Taylor said with as much conviction as she could muster.

Brianna kept fidgeting with her ring, spinning it in circles. For a moment, she didn't say anything. Taylor noted the sadness in Brianna's eyes and knew she truly did love Uncle Doyle.

"He needs sex . . . all the time," Brianna said.

Taylor swallowed hard. Uncle Doyle? Sex all the time? Maybe. What did she know?

For some reason Taylor thought of Shane Donovan. Now there was a man who would need sex all the time.

"Brianna, you've only been gone one night," Taylor replied. "My uncle loves you. He wouldn't—"

"You don't know men the way I do."

Brianna stood up, her disheveled blond hair falling across her face, and Taylor noticed this was the first time she'd seen Brianna without makeup. Even in the harsh morning light, Brianna glowed from within, a natural beauty that most women couldn't duplicate with all the cosmetics in the world.

"Brianna, my uncle went through quite an ordeal to marry you. I can't believe he's just gone off and had an affair because you're away one night."

"Not an affair. A one-night stand. Typical of men."

Bitterness underscored every word. Taylor couldn't help imagining what Brianna's life had been like before she'd married Uncle Doyle. She'd worked in a seedy club like Renata.

"What am I going to do?" Brianna asked. "How will I get him back?"

"You haven't lost him. I'm certain there's a reasonable explanation—"

Brianna tossed her mane of blond hair from side

to side and rushed toward the door. "No. I'm all alone again."

"Wait! You'll never be alone. I'm your friend. Don't you understand that? I'm with you no matter what happens."

Brianna looked over her shoulder, tears glistening in her eyes. "You mean it?"

"Of course. We're friends, right?"

Brianna gazed down at the carpet beneath her bare feet. "I guess. I thought you . . . put up with me because of Doyle."

Taylor saw no reason to varnish the truth. "That's how we met, but since then, I've come to appreciate you as a person. No matter what has happened with Uncle Doyle, I'm still your friend."

"Thanks, I had no idea—"

The *brring-brring* of the telephone interrupted Brianna. Taylor dashed across the room to answer it. "Hello."

It was Uncle Doyle. "What's happened to Brianna?"

"Nothing." Taylor waved Brianna toward her. "She's right here. We were talking."

Taylor handed Brianna the telephone, then walked over to the window to see what the weather was like. Clouds with leaden underbellies promised more rain. She couldn't help listening to Brianna explaining to Doyle about Renata's being a stripper. They talked a few minutes, then Brianna hung up without asking Doyle where he'd been.

"Why didn't you ask him about last night?"

Brianna shrugged. "He'd just lie. That's the way men are."

Taylor cradled the telephone receiver in the palm of her hand, but couldn't bring herself to dial her mother's number. Brianna had left fifteen minutes ago, and Taylor knew her mother was expecting the call. She could almost see her mother lying on her bed, propped up by an armada of Frette pillows, watching the telephone on her nightstand.

Taylor forced herself to punch in the number. Her mother answered on the first ring.

"Hello. It's me. How are you feeling?"

"Did you meet Renata? What did you think?"

The breathless quality in her mother's voice caused Taylor's throat to tighten. Her mother had so much emotional investment in finding her missing daughter. It alarmed Taylor more and more.

"Mother, we . . . Brianna and I and Shane Donovan have grave doubts about Renata Rollins. There's not a shred of evidence she's your child. She certainly doesn't look anything like you—not at all."

"She must take after her father."

Taylor hesitated a moment, considering how to break the news about Renata's occupation. "Renata is working in a club here . . . as a stripper."

Two beats of silence. "She takes off her clothes in front of men?"

"Yes, she does," Taylor replied, although this didn't quite cover the risqué performance. "It's a vulgar, disgusting act."

"Oh, my." An audible sigh came over the line, and Taylor could just imagine the disapproving grimace on her mother's face. "She must have had a terrible life to take up stripping."

"I'm not sure why Renata works as a stripper. She seems bright enough to hold down a good job."

Taylor didn't add what Shane had told her. Many strippers doubled as prostitutes, and that accounted for the bulk of their income.

"I spoke personally with Caleb Bassett before you went there," her mother said. "He seemed to think—"

"Mother, I've met the man. He's . . . charming but a little strange." As much as she hated to, Taylor mentioned the private detective. "Shane thinks he's a hustler. There just isn't any proof this stripper is your child. The woman is a con artist, that's all."

A muffled silence followed and Taylor heard the soft rustle of the silk comforter her mother kept over her. Even in the Miami heat, she was now cold all the time. Taylor sucked in a stabilizing breath, realizing, yet again, she would soon lose her mother.

"I want to meet Renata."

Oh, no. Have mercy, Taylor thought. Nothing good could come of this.

Quite possibly, Renata would cause her mother's condition to become worse. Taylor too clearly recalled the spite in Renata's voice when they'd been discussing her mother.

The rich bitch.

"Mother, don't put yourself through this. Take my word for it. This woman is *not* your daughter."

"I still want to meet her."

"What good would meeting Renata do?" Taylor asked, her voice sharper than she'd intended.

"I'm sure if I saw her, spoke with her . . . I'd know."

Taylor put her hand over her eyes, imagining her vulnerable mother meeting Renata. Before this illness her mother would have been disgusted by a stripper. Such a person would have been an embarrassment, and Vanessa Maxwell wouldn't have wanted her friends to find out.

The woman on the telephone was different. With death so close, her personality had changed in ways Taylor didn't quite understand.

Still, Taylor loved her so much that just the thought

of losing her caused a dull ache deep in her chest. Her father had died, then Paul had disappeared. Somehow she'd come through without breaking down.

Could she survive another loss?

"You've got to bring Renata here." Her mother's voice had slipped to a mere whisper. "Promise me . . . you'll do it."

Shane was wiping a dab of shaving cream off his earlobe when he heard the knock at the hotel room door. He cinched the towel around his waist and answered the door.

Taylor. Shit.

She had a way of finding him half dressed. Okay, so he was practically naked.

"Mother insists on meeting Renata in person," Taylor said the second he opened the door.

Then she noticed his nearly nude body. A flush inched up her cheeks, but to give her credit, she kept talking without missing a beat.

"I don't know what to do. I'm afraid she'll accept Renata on faith because she has some deep-seated psychological need to be reunited with the child she gave up."

Shane backed up and let Taylor step into his room. Her face was totally pink now, but he didn't move toward the bathroom, where a fluffy terry-cloth robe hung on the back of the door.

He let the tension in the air build before saying, "You're probably right. Vanessa wants to believe this is her daughter. Unless we can prove Renata is a fraud then your mother will accept her."

Taylor walked over to the window where the drapes were open, revealing a sullen gray sky. The wind squalled through the trees, a harbinger of yet another storm. He couldn't tell if she did it to avoid looking at him or if she was thinking.

He ducked into the bathroom, dropped the towel, and shrugged into the robe. When he stepped into the room again, Taylor was still gazing out the window.

He walked closer, and she said, "I promised Mother that I would bring Renata to Miami."

"Sounds like a one-way road to hell. Renata's social skills are . . . questionable. Are you sure your mother is ready for her?"

She turned to him, her eyes troubled. The blush had disappeared, leaving her skin pale. "It won't be pleasant. That's for sure, but I have no choice. Do you think we can convince Renata to come to Miami for the weekend?"

Man, oh, man. Get real. He was positive Renata was playing hard to get.

"Let me talk to her."

There was no answer at Renata's when Shane called. He had no choice but to phone Caleb. The man answered on the second ring, his voice a redneck's ludicrous attempt at an English accent.

Some women might find Bassett captivating, but Shane's bullshit tolerance was down to zip, so he came right to the point.

"What's it going to take to get Renata to come to Miami for the weekend? Vanessa Maxwell wants to see her."

"Really? I'm surprised."

"Cut the crap. Let's get this settled."

Shane knew whatever Caleb had said to Vanessa when they'd originally spoken had convinced the woman that Renata was her daughter. This request wasn't a shock.

"Well, I may be able to convince my daughter. She's sitting right here. We're about to have breakfast."

What a strange relationship. For a second, Shane wondered if they really were father and daughter. He'd have a better idea when he saw them together. There was a certain chemistry between couples who were involved.

"Talk to Renata then call me here."

Shane gave Caleb his room number at the Windsor Court, then hung up. He walked over to the window where Taylor had stood less than an hour earlier. She'd gone back to her room to pack.

Are we having fun yet?

Getting close to Taylor was one thing, this was another. He had the crazy-ass feeling that he was in the middle of something more complicated than he'd bargained for. He tried to ignore his suspicions, but he couldn't.

He'd brought this on himself by seeking out Taylor. Now he had no choice but to help her.

The phone rang, interrupting his thoughts. It was Caleb Bassett with Renata on the extension.

"I had a hard time convincing her," Caleb began.

Yeah, and I'm the pope.

"I have to give up three nights of shows," Renata said. "Weekend shows when I make the most money."

Here comes the pitch for money.

"We think five thousand dollars should cover it," Caleb said, all traces of his attempt at a British accent gone.

"I don't know," Shane said, although this was less than he'd expected them to ask.

"I have to have the money or I'm staying here."

He could almost see the belligerent thrust of Renata's jaw as she made her demand.

"Caleb has to come, too. I'm not going there alone."

Shane silently congratulated himself. These two must be lovers. Okay, so, did that mean Renata wasn't Vanessa's missing daughter?

Not necessarily.

Doyle Maxwell smiled inwardly as Raoul and Trent emerged from the jail. He'd put up the money for their bonds, but they'd have to return for trial—if it came to that. Alan Friedman, the pricey lawyer, had advised Doyle that they should accept a plea bargain for a lesser charge.

"Thanks," Raoul said. "I owe you one."

"Ditto," Trent added, giving Doyle a quick hug. "I can't thank you enough."

"Don't thank me yet. We haven't seen the end of this."

Raoul shrugged, but he didn't look as cocky as he usually did. A night in a cell with Miami's scum had taken him down a notch, Doyle hoped. He led them to the lot where his Mercedes was parked.

"Mother doesn't know anything about this, does she?" Trent asked.

"No. I haven't told anyone."

"Not even Brianna?" asked Raoul.

Doyle thought he detected a hint of disdain in Raoul's voice. It was no secret that he and Brianna were extremely close. He planned to tell her, consult with her on the best way to play this drug arrest to his advantage, but the arrogant Cuban didn't have to know about it.

Brianna didn't have to know everything, either.

He'd managed to keep his financial problems from her. She'd married him for his money; she'd leave him if he lost it. This drug arrest could very well be key to reviving his finances.

"No, I haven't mentioned anything to Brianna." He unlocked the sleek black Mercedes by pressing on his key. He opened the door, saying to Trent, "I think your mother is going to be too preoccupied for the next week to find out about your arrest. She's invited Renata Rollins to come stay with her."

Trent dropped into the front seat, his shoulders sagging. "That woman proved she's related to us?"

"No. The investigator hasn't been able to prove or disprove the woman's story, but your mother still wants to meet her."

"Why?" Raoul asked from the backseat as Doyle took his place behind the wheel.

It's none of your damn business, Doyle wanted to say, but he kept his cool. In time the uppity Cuban would get his.

"Vanessa thinks she'll be able to tell if this is her daughter."

"I don't think she's in any condition to—"

"Mother is obsessed by this," Trent cut off Raoul. "Her illness has made things worse."

Doyle drove the car out of the dark structure into the blinding Miami sunlight. "*Obsessed* is a good word. Vanessa wants Renata and her father to come here even though there's no proof the woman is her daughter and—get this—Renata works as a stripper."

"You're kidding. My mother wouldn't—"

"Jesus H. Christ!" Raoul said. "I think we need a plan."

For once Doyle agreed with the cocky Cuban.

Chapter 8

The defining moment.

For every person there is a moment—often just an instant—when a decision must be made, a choice that will alter the course of their life. It's always fun to watch . . . and wait to see which choice a person will make.

"People seal their fate with the decisions they make."

Right now, he was watching the Maxwells cement their fate. Of course, Vanessa's fate had been sealed by her decision.

The bitch was getting what she deserved—a slow agonizing death.

"That doesn't mean Vanessa doesn't deserve some more torture. If finding the daughter she gave up—her defining moment—is her heart's desire, then she should meet her child."

A crack of laugher reverberated off the walls. It took a few moments for the sound to die away, leaving a hollow, tomblike echo.

"Be careful what you ask for. You just might get it."

The appearance of Renata Rollins in Vanessa's life should prove interesting. How would the family react?

There's more than one way to torment a person. Cancer alone isn't enough. Vanessa needs to suffer a whole lot more.

The way he'd suffered.

"I wonder if Vanessa needs to know the one daughter that she's *positive* is her own has been marked for death?"

He checked another laugh. This just kept getting better and better.

"Let Taylor's death come as a surprise."

Has Taylor experienced a defining moment when she must make a life-altering choice?

"No, but she will when she faces her killer."

Shane stroked Auggie's head as he brought Vince Walker up to speed on the situation with Renata Rollins. He hated boarding Auggie. The dog needed socializing, not isolation, but he hadn't made any friends who could take his pet.

Maybe he would never have real friends. He was too much of a loner to let anyone get close to him.

"The Rollins woman and her father are flying in tomorrow to spend the weekend with Vanessa. I bought their tickets and promised I'd pay them when they arrive. That should wipe out the advance Vanessa gave us. We'll need more if we're going to continue investigating Renata."

Nodding, Vince's eyes cut away from Shane. The E-mail icon on his computer screen was blinking.

"Let me see what this is."

Shane stroked Auggie's gloss-black fur, thinking about Caleb and Renata. He hadn't seen them together yet, but he would this weekend. Then he'd know if they were lovers.

The situation bothered him, yet no one else had mentioned it. Maybe it was the age difference between Caleb and Renata that had fooled Taylor and Brianna. Caleb was old enough to be Renata's father, but the age difference didn't mean he wasn't her lover.

"Nothing important," Vince said, turning away from his computer. "I was hoping it was info on some of Maxx's competitors. While you were gone, I took a preliminary look at their computer security problems. I'd say someone is trying to ruin their business to head off a deal with one of the big cosmetics firms."

"What makes you think its a competitor? Couldn't the problem be in-house?"

"Possibly, but the major players with the security codes all stand to gain if the business is sold."

"Really? Someone like Taylor might see it as a family venture and not want to sell."

"Nope. Taylor would like to start a firm specializing in online games. You know, the kind where you play on the Net against people all over the world. She's working on a trivia game right now."

Shane nodded, taken by surprise. He thought he knew a lot about Taylor, but this information was brand new.

"Raoul wants Trent to start a company with him. A cosmetics company like To The Maxx. According to my sources, what Raoul wants, Raoul gets."

"That leaves Vanessa and Doyle. I don't suppose Vanessa cares all that much, considering her health."

"She favors a sale and has been letting Doyle handle the preliminary discussions with two of the big firms after the company. Doyle needs the money. He lost a bundle in the market. Like a lot of people, he loaded up on tech stocks and got killed.''

"Why am I not surprised?"

"Yeah, Doyle's a bit of a high flyer with a dynamite young wife.''

Vince chuckled, and Shane knew that although Vince was a poster boy for the single life, he had the hots for Brianna.

"Doyle and Vanessa get along now, but they didn't at first. Doyle was really close with his twin brother, and when Vanessa came along . . . well, things changed. For years, he barely spoke to Vanessa.''

"Interesting,'' Shane said, mentally kicking himself.

His usually infallible sixth sense hadn't picked up on any hostility between Doyle and Vanessa. If people didn't speak for years, it usually meant there was latent anger that could be detected.

No doubt his mind had been on Taylor, and it had distracted him.

"What brought Vanessa and Doyle together?"

"You'll love this.'' Vince chuckled. "Vanessa supported Doyle when he wanted to divorce his wife. It seems Sophie Maxwell despised Vanessa. The woman did everything she could to keep Vanessa out of the elite social groups.''

Why wasn't he completely surprised? Vanessa had been mellowed by time and illness, but Shane knew a social climber when he met one.

"You'd be amazed at how many enemies Vanessa Maxwell has,'' Vince added. "Any one of them could want to ruin To The Maxx.''

"Clue me in.''

"Raoul Cathcart is at the top of the list. Although no one knows it, Vanessa tried to pay Raoul big bucks to get out of Trent's life. He refused and he's had it in for Vanessa ever since.''

"How'd you find out, if no one knows?''

Vince rocked back in his chair; his dark eyes reflected his amusement.

"You'd be amazed at what people tell their hairdressers and manicurists. Stuff they wouldn't confide in their best friend. Why? Because it's someone who'll listen and agree with them.''

"Damn straight, they'll agree or lose a customer.''

"Raoul has been going to the same beauty shop for years. For a hundred bucks, his hairdresser told me the story.''

Go to a hairdresser? God forbid.

"Vince, you already said Raoul wants to go into business with Trent. The start-up money has to come from the sale, right? Why would he want to sabotage a deal?''

"It defies logic, but there's something strange about Raoul. He spent six months in a private psychiatric hospital. I'm trying to get his file, but I haven't had any luck yet.''

Raoul was not what he would call a guy's guy, and something about him had disturbed Shane, yet he couldn't quite put his finger on it. He was going to have to keep his mind off Taylor and watch the players this weekend.

"Who else has a grudge against Vanessa?'' he asked Vince.

"Brianna, possibly. Vanessa backed Doyle when he wanted to leave Sophie, but she didn't bargain for a Cuban lap dancer. Except for family functions, when Doyle has to be included, Vanessa never sees Brianna.''

"Do you think Brianna cares?''

"Hard to say, but you know women.''

Don't go there.

To say he knew women—out of the sack—would be like saying he was a rocket scientist. His longest so-called relationship had lasted two months, then he'd received a new assignment and was transferred to the other side of the world.

"Sophie, the ex-wife, has every reason to want Maxx to go under," continued Vince. "She took a huge settlement instead of alimony. If Doyle goes bust, she isn't hurt."

"Okay, suppose Sophie or Brianna or even Raoul were behind this, they wouldn't have the expertise to tamper with the company's computer files."

"True, but it wouldn't be hard to find a hacker who could."

Vince studied the screen saver on his computer for a moment, then added, "There's another possibility. Lisa Abbott, Trent's former wife, was really hurt by the divorce. Her background is finance. She'd have the know-how to access the system."

"Trent might have told her the security code when they were married."

"Right. I'm taking a closer look at her. I wouldn't be surprised to find she's one of those 'hell hath no fury' women."

Shane remembered the striking brunette on the morning he'd introduced himself to Taylor. He stroked Auggie's head, trying to imagine Lisa sabotaging the company. She didn't seem to be the type.

But who knew? When it came to understanding the female mind, he was clueless.

"Here's what we decided to do," Trent told Taylor as they drove to the airport that evening to meet Renata's flight from New Orleans.

"When the Rollins woman arrives let's see if we can pay her off. Raoul thinks we should offer her twenty-five thousand dollars but be prepared to go to fifty. I'm kicking in some, Doyle's paying his share, and we want you to come up with a third."

Taylor listened, thinking how much her brother had changed. Once he would have consulted with her first before agreeing to a plan like this. Now he listened to Raoul, then took action without running it by her.

"I don't know," she replied. "I promised Mother—"

"I know, but this is only going to upset her. You said so yourself."

Trent drove the Beamer onto the expressway. As usual, the cars were bumper to bumper.

"A stripper. Just our luck. Raoul says she probably turns tricks on the side."

Taylor didn't mention that Shane had said the same thing. Why prejudice Trent unnecessarily? They might very well have to deal with this obnoxious woman.

"I don't think Renata will take the money," she said.

"Why not? It has to be a fortune to a woman like her."

"True, but she's strange. It took some convincing to get her to come here. Money might not move her the way it would other people."

"Come on. I'm not buying that bridge. After all, Shane had to pay her to make up for her lost wages."

Trent nudged the car into the fast lane, as if it would do any good.

"If she sees Mother's house in Coral Gables, she's likely to insist on a lot more money," he said. "With luck we can arrange a payoff and put her on the next plane back to the Big Easy."

* * *

"Did we get lucky or what?" Trent asked. "They've changed their minds and decided to stay in New Orleans."

Taylor watched the pilot and copilot walk away from the baggage claim area. The flight attendant had already confirmed that no more passengers were on the plane.

"Maybe they missed the flight. You'd think they would have called, though. I gave them my number and my cell number."

"Do you think they phoned Shane, since he set it up?"

Taylor pulled her cell phone out of her purse, then grabbed her Palm Pilot to find Shane's number. When he answered, she explained the situation, but he hadn't heard a thing from Caleb or Renata. He said he would try to find out what happened.

"Mother's going to be really disappointed. When I spoke to her this morning, she was so excited." Taylor walked beside her brother toward the exit. "She expected them for dinner. I'm sure she's gone over every little detail. You know how she is about entertaining."

They were in the parking lot when Taylor's cell phone beeped. It was Shane.

"You're not going to believe this," he said. "They took an earlier flight. They're already at your mother's house. From what your mother told me, they're all getting along like old friends."

"You're kidding."

She covered the phone with her hand and told Trent what had happened.

"Why didn't they call? They could have saved us a trip to the airport."

"Beats me," Shane said. "Your mother seems convinced Renata is her daughter."

"Great. Well, we're on our way there. Do you want to meet us?"

She didn't know what prompted her to invite Shane, but she had the feeling she could use the help with Renata and Caleb. No telling what she might find when she arrived.

"Sure. I'll get there before you will. I have an idea how we can get a DNA done on Renata, but it'll be expensive."

"I'm sure we can come up with the money. Trent and Doyle are ready to pay Renata a chunk of money to get rid of her."

"I doubt that's going to work. If Caleb and Renata think she might inherit money from your mother, why would they settle for less?"

"You're probably right." They had reached Trent's Beamer and she climbed in, asking, "What about the DNA? I thought you said there was no way around the waiting list."

"Don't mention this to anyone yet. I'm looking into sending the sample overseas to Germany where there's a first-rate lab without the waiting list problem. It's expensive, but if I can arrange it, we could get results in about a week."

Chapter 9

Shane watched Taylor across the dining room table as she talked with Renata. The stripper was on her best behavior and Caleb had dropped the phony British accent, but Shane wasn't fooled. He figured the pair had sized up the mansion and Vanessa's expensive jewelry. It was worth their while to be charming.

Were Caleb and Renata lovers? No, he didn't think so. He'd observed them closely while they'd had cocktails around the pool. He didn't pick up any chemistry between them.

Unless they were incredible actors, which he doubted, they weren't lovers.

Had Caleb Bassett actually raised this woman? He wouldn't bet the ranch on it.

"Renata, I think you should move here," Vanessa said unexpectedly. "Then we could get to know each other better."

Trent broke the astonished silence, saying, "I'm sure Renata has her own life in New Orleans and her work."

Her work? Get real.

They hadn't discussed "her work" since Shane had arrived. Caleb or Renata could have mentioned it earlier, but Vanessa seemed to be conveniently ignoring the subject. He suspected she often overlooked things she found unpleasant.

"I don't think I'd be interested in moving here, but I could stay a while and visit," Renata said with a smile.

"Wonderful!" Vanessa clapped her hands.

Are we having fun yet? Taylor was trying to smile and appear pleased, but Trent didn't bother.

"You'll stay, too, won't you?" Vanessa asked Caleb.

"If my little girl wants to visit, I'll stay with her."

Was he a good father, or what?

Shane waited while the maid served dessert. Mango gelato in a crystal brandy snifter. Proof positive the rich were different.

Before this group got any cozier, it was time to mention the DNA. It would be awkward for Taylor to bring it up. He needed to do it.

"You know," he said to Renata, "we could settle the question of whether or not you are Vanessa's daughter with a DNA sample."

"That's not necessary," cried Vanessa. "I know she's my daughter. I can *feel* it."

Vanessa's attitude took Shane by surprise. He'd expected Caleb or Renata to object because they had a lot to lose if the DNA came back negative, but he'd assumed Vanessa would want independent confirmation.

Go figure.

"Mother, this is a good idea," Taylor said.

"Yes, it would put all our minds to rest," Trent added.

"It would be a waste of time and money." Vanessa's tone was even firmer than before, and Shane could see why she'd made enemies over the years. Vanessa was difficult to deal with when she wanted her way.

"We talked about it this afternoon when we arrived," Caleb told them. "Renata has to be Vanessa's daughter. She's the right age. I adopted her in a town less than ten miles from where Vanessa gave birth."

Vanessa reached over and patted Renata's hand lightly. "I don't have much time left on this earth. I want to spend it getting to know my daughter better."

"We'll have fun," Renata said.

Define *fun*. Shane bet it would involve spending Vanessa's money.

Taylor had to admit she was jealous.

Her mother was obsessed with Renata. It didn't matter that she was a stripper with crude manners and no education. Her mother sincerely believed Renata was her daughter.

She adored her.

What little time she had left to live was going to be spent with Renata, forgetting the daughter who had loved her for a lifetime.

Unbelievable.

She lounged back on her sofa and tried to concentrate on the late night news, but in her mind's eye she saw the way her mother had been earlier in the evening. She'd kept touching Renata's hand or putting her arm around her.

Taylor had longed to run out of the room, but pride and the iron will that had helped her in business kept her at the table. She tried to understand what it would have been like to give up a baby.

Her mother had been worried all these years about her child. Naturally, she needed to make up for lost time. Any mother would react the same way.

"Don't take it personally," Taylor said out loud.

Her words did nothing to banish a deep, yearning ache to turn back the hands of time and have her mother to herself again.

A knock on the door startled her, and she jumped to her feet. Crime wasn't a problem in SoBe, but you never knew. She peered through the peephole and saw Shane standing there with Auggie. He'd left her mother's house before she did, and she hadn't had an opportunity to talk to him.

She swung open the door and warm air surged into her air-conditioned apartment. Lively music drifted on the breeze, coming from one of the nearby clubs. Even though Taylor was about to go to bed, SoBe was just waking up.

"I saw your light. I'm taking Auggie for a walk. Do you want to come with us?"

Taylor bent over and stroked Auggie's sleek, dark head. "Yes. We should talk."

They walked the short block to Ocean Avenue, speculating on why Renata and Caleb arrived so early without letting anyone know their change in plans.

"I think they knew we'd try to get rid of them," Taylor said. "They wanted to make sure they met my mother."

"You may be right," Shane said. "It doesn't matter now. They're here to stay. We have to decide how to deal with them."

"If only Mother would allow us to run a DNA test. I wouldn't feel as bad if Renata really is the missing baby."

"I've been thinking about it. Can you get into your mother's home while they're out somewhere?"

"Sure. I grew up in that house. I have a key. I'll just have to make up a story for Pablo and Maria, the Cuban couple who work for mother."

"Okay, get in and find Renata's hairbrush. Take a few hairs with follicles, if possible. Then get some of your mother's for comparison."

They paused to let Auggie sniff a poodle passing with an elderly woman. Taylor knew how hard Shane was trying to socialize Auggie.

"Why hairs with follicles?" she asked.

"The follicle is easier to test. Hair products, especially dye and bleach, break down the hair. It can be used but it's more difficult."

"I feel strange sneaking around behind my mother's back, but . . ." She looked into Shane's eyes, not certain how to put this. "Something about those two isn't right. That's my gut feeling. I don't believe she's my half sister."

"I can't find any records to prove anything. The DNA will be conclusive."

They stopped and sat on a bench at Lummus Park. Auggie settled himself at Shane's feet. The long, narrow park flanking the shore was filled with sun worshipers by day, most of them wearing little more than their tans. At night, the park was usually deserted, the chic set having migrated to one of the trendy SoBe clubs.

"What's with the lifeguard stations?" Shane asked.

"Fun looking, aren't they? Hurricane Andrew destroyed all the old lifeguard shacks. Some politician decided the new ones should be conversation pieces. Right over there is the spaceship designed by Kenny Scharf. He's a pop artist. Doyle has a couple of his works."

Taylor was a little amazed that she could sit here

so comfortably with Shane and discuss something as mundane as the unusual lifeguard stations. She'd been on edge when she'd been around him before, but since they'd returned from New Orleans, she'd become more comfortable with him.

And less comfortable with her brother.

Trent was like a different person now. She could blame Raoul, but in all fairness, each person was responsible for himself. Maybe Trent had gone so many years pretending to be straight that she'd never really known him.

"I understand you're a trivia buff," Shane said.

"Yes. I don't know why but odd bits of information fascinate me. I keep track of them on my computer. If we sell To The Maxx, I'm going to start a computer game company."

She couldn't help smiling inwardly. "Today I came across an interesting fact. A turtle's sex is determined by the temperature of the sand when the eggs hatch."

"Be still my heart."

"Oh, stop." She punched him lightly on the arm. "I thought it was interesting."

"Some people are easily amused."

"Okay, so what amuses you?"

"You do."

His eyes gazed unwaveringly into hers. Something intangible and frighteningly elusive passed through her. She wasn't attracted to Shane, was she?

No, of course not. Seconds fractured and it seemed as if a full minute passed before she could speak.

"Let's stick to business," she said a little more sharply than she intended. "Has your company had any luck with the computer security breach at To The Maxx?"

"Vince worked on it while we were in New Orleans. I started checking today. I wish I could tell you exactly what the problem is. We changed the security codes, but the problem hasn't gone away."

Taylor shook her head, angry with herself for the oversight. "We should have systematically been changing those codes all along, the way other companies do."

"Don't blame yourself. A cosmetics firm shouldn't expect to have these problems."

"Any idea who it might be?"

Shane hesitated for just a moment before replying. "We're not sure, but Vince thinks your mother may have made some . . . enemies over the years."

As much as Taylor loved her mother, she had to admit the woman could be ruthless at times. "I'm sure Aunt Sophie, Doyle's ex-wife, ranks right at the top of the list. She'd love to hurt Mom and Doyle."

"She's one possibility," Shane agreed. "Raoul is another. Did you realize your mother tried to buy him off to get him out of Trent's life?"

"Oh, tell me she didn't."

Actually, Taylor wasn't all that surprised. Her mother acted as if she didn't mind Trent's homosexuality, but she had concealed it from her friends for as long as possible.

"I don't think Raoul would ruin the business. I'm sure he's counting on money from the sale to start his own company."

"You never know. He spent some time in a psychiatric hospital," Shane told her. "He might not be all that stable. We're checking into it."

"Really? I'm surprised. Raoul seems very self-absorbed but not unbalanced."

"Sometimes it's hard to tell. Often the person you think you know turns out to be someone else entirely."

There was an odd note in Shane's voice. Taylor wondered if he was trying to tell her something. Perhaps it was his oblique way of referring to Trent's sudden lifestyle change.

"Have you looked at the company records for anyone we terminated?" she asked to get away from a personal discussion. "It hasn't happened very often, but I can think of one man who worked in accounts receivable. My father fired him just before he died. His name was Jim Wilson. Several companies called for references, but we couldn't recommend him."

"I'll look into it." Shane stood up and Auggie leaped to his feet. "We better start back. It's getting late for those of us not on the club circuit."

They walked in silence along Ocean Boulevard. Throngs of people spilled out of the clubs and cafés. Music throbbed in the air and along with it came a certain sexiness. SoBe was for the young and hip and scantily dressed.

She couldn't help noticing the way the women they passed gazed at Shane. He wasn't classically good-looking, but she had to concede he was attractive in a masculine way. His angular face was rugged, the dominant feature being blue eyes that bored into you.

She mentally gave herself a hard kick. Why was she thinking about Shane? Why wasn't she thinking about Paul Ashton, the love of her life? A warning voice whispered in her head.

Memories fade.

Like a watercolor image, Paul's blurred face appeared on the screen in her mind. Then faded. As soon as she got home, she was going to look at her pictures of him.

"There's one other person we're investigating," Shane said, breaking into her thoughts. "Lisa Abbot."

"Lisa would never sabotage Maxx," Taylor cried, outrage filling her.

"Are you positive? She has the financial background to know her way around a sophisticated computer system. She could have gotten the code from Trent when they were married."

"She couldn't have done it. She was out of the country until this week."

Shane stopped and gazed down at Taylor. "No. She's been in Miami for over a month."

Taylor stared at the photograph of Paul Ashton. How vividly she recalled the day she'd taken it. It seemed like yesterday but it was nearly three years old.

He'd come into the bedroom she used as a home office, asking, "What are you doing?"

It was Saturday morning and she was supposed to be relaxing, but she'd momentarily forgotten her promise to Paul. She'd been answering her E-mail and had downloaded an article on Perlane sent to her by a colleague in England.

Paul came up behind her, put his hands on her shoulders, and began massaging. "Okay, babe, what's more important than going to the beach?"

"Nothing."

She'd promised not to make her life all about work, but sometimes it was difficult. Her computer game, the cosmetics business seemed to consume all her time.

Paul was right. It wasn't fair. She needed a personal life, downtime when she could enjoy herself.

Enjoy time with Paul, a man who swept her away from work into a world of fun and simple pleasures like a Saturday morning stroll along the beach, people watching and waiting for SoBe to wake up after another late night at the clubs.

"An E-mail about Perlane, right?" Paul asked, staring over her shoulder at the computer screen.

"Yes. It's from Ethan in London where they've used the gel for years. It's a little like collagen," she felt compelled to explain. "It plumps up your cheeks or lips and gives them a glow."

"You're beautiful exactly the way you are." He kissed the curve of her neck.

"Thanks, but with age, women begin to sag and wrinkle. Perlane can be injected without the allergic reactions many women have with collagen."

"Why is that?" he asked but he didn't sound really interested.

"It's a biosynthetic form of hyaluronic acid, which is a natural substance found in the body. That's why there are fewer reactions to it than—"

"Hey! I give up. Are we going out or are you going to spend a beautiful day in front of your computer?"

"You're right. I'm outta here."

She logged off and stood up. Paul swept her into his arms, then kissed her.

"I've been waiting my whole life for a woman like you. I don't want to waste a lot of time hanging with a computer. Right?"

"Right," she agreed, thinking about how she'd spent her life before meeting Paul at Bash, a trendy SoBe club. It had been a rare night out with friends, but Paul had brought new meaning to her life.

Live.

Don't just devote yourself to work. Enjoy the beach, the galleries, the cafés, the clubs, the people. The SoBe life.

He'd led her out of the office, saying, "I have a plan. Let's walk to Brew Ha-Ha, get coffee, then head for the galleries instead of the beach. Let's see what's new. Okay?"

"Great idea," she'd replied, knowing he'd suggested this because she loved art.

Work had consumed her for the past few weeks. The galleries would have changed exhibits and there would be new, exciting artists to view. She blessed Paul for keeping her out of the confining business world she lived in each day.

She hadn't truly felt alive until Paul had come into her life.

Chapter 10

Doyle savored his morning cup of coffee in the sunroom of the Coconut Grove mansion he'd purchased because Brianna had admired it. She was still upstairs getting dressed, but she would be down in a few minutes.

He prayed she wouldn't initiate sex.

Again.

It had been almost a week since Brianna had returned from New Orleans. She wanted sex all the time, which wasn't unusual. She'd always been a sex kitten, but there was something . . . forced about her lovemaking now.

He wondered if she was having an affair and covering it up. He supposed he could hire an investigator and have her followed, but he wasn't really sure he wanted to know.

The last thing he could afford right now was another expensive divorce.

"What do you think?"

Brianna swanned into the room in an electric blue sundress and matching high-heeled sandals. Like most Cuban women in Miami, Brianna favored bright colors and flashy jewelry. After years with Sophie dressing in drab clothes, it was a refreshing change.

"You look gorgeous, darling."

The maid appeared with *café con leche* for Brianna. Doyle preferred American-style coffee, but Brianna had grown up with Cuban food and liked espresso diluted with a splash of steamed milk.

"I've been thinking," Brianna said, sitting down.

Doyle released a pent-up sigh of relief. He could tell from her expression this wasn't about sex.

"Thinking about what?"

"Renata and Caleb."

Last night Vanessa had thrown another one of her command performances. They'd gone over to dinner to meet the newly found daughter and her father. Like Taylor and Trent, who'd suffered the same fate the previous evening, Doyle was convinced Renata was a fraud.

Too bad they'd missed the opportunity to pay off the stripper and get rid of her before Vanessa had been taken in by the broad. Now that Renata knew how wealthy Vanessa was, they'd pay hell getting rid of her.

The way Vanessa fawned over the woman amazed Doyle. He'd watched her operate through the years, manipulating his brother, social-climbing with a vengeance, and mercilessly dropping people when they were no longer useful.

His former wife had a pedigree dating back to Flagler and the earliest of the wealthy families who'd come to Miami. He didn't give Sophie credit for much, but she had seen through Vanessa and had refused to introduce her to any of her society friends.

Vanessa was a beautiful woman with a cunning streak. Under normal circumstances, she would have cut any ties to a stripper. But as the saying went, these were *not* normal circumstances.

"What about Renata and Caleb?" Doyle asked.

"I know what's bothering me about them. It came to me while I was putting on my lipstick. They have some hidden agenda."

"Sure, parting Vanessa from her money while trying to act as if they aren't interested in material things."

"No, it's something else. The way Caleb watches Vanessa tells me something else is going on."

"Well, she's a beautiful woman, even if her health is failing. He wouldn't be the first man to fall for her."

"Maybe, but I *feel* it's something else."

Doyle finished his coffee and waved off the maid when she appeared to refill his cup. He hadn't told Brianna about Trent's arrest because just as he'd begin she would initiate sex; but now seemed like a good time.

"While you were in New Orleans, Trent and Raoul were arrested for possession of crystal meth."

"Dios mio," cried Brianna. "How terrible."

"Don't tell anyone. Vanessa must not find out. Her health is too fragile."

"What about Taylor? Does she know?"

"I haven't told her."

"You should. She might be able to help her brother."

"I'll see if I can catch her at the office and have a private conversation."

Brianna sighed. "It'll be the end of Trent. I know. I saw enough ice in Calle Ocho."

"Ice?"

"Crack, speed, meth, crystal. The drug has a lot of names. In Calle Ocho it's called *hielo*—ice."

Doyle would rather forget Brianna's past life in Calle Ocho, the heart of Little Havana, but at times it was helpful. She knew things, had seen things he hadn't.

"Did you ever try it?"

She waved the hand with the rock he'd given her. The bauble splintered the morning light into a rainbow of colors.

"No. Growing up, I saw what drugs do to people. It wasn't going to happen to me."

"Apparently it's the drug of choice among Miami's gay men."

"I'm not surprised. It intensifies your sexual drive. You go on a hunt for sex like some wild animal, and you have sex much more frequently than normal."

Doyle couldn't stop the frown tightening his face. Brianna was describing herself—especially lately.

"I'm not on ice," Brianna said, reading his mind the way she often did. "I'm too fat to be hooked. Those addicts never eat, never sleep. You know what that makes you look like."

"I see," he replied, relief obvious in his voice.

"I love you. That's why I like to have sex so much. I want to keep you happy."

"I am happy. You know I love you, darling." He meant every word. He'd never loved anyone the way he loved Brianna. "I don't want so much sex. I just need to spend time with you.

The words slipped out before he could stop them. He didn't want her to think he was an old man who couldn't get it up as often as she liked.

Tears glistened in Brianna's eyes. "I'm glad you love me. I love you so much it hurts."

"You're a treasure and a huge help to me," Doyle

said, congratulating himself for defusing the sex thing in a loving way even though it had been accidental. "That's why I want you to tell me how to use this drug thing to our benefit."

It took a minute to explain how he'd bailed out Trent and Raoul and kept the whole incident from Vanessa.

"What I'd like to do is use this to stop Trent from imposing Raoul's ideas on To The Maxx. I have two potential buyers in the wings. I don't need any new products or for the company to go in another direction."

"What about the computer tampering?"

"That's enough of a problem in itself. I'm stalling the buyers until we have it resolved. If they knew about it, hell, the deal would go up in smoke."

Brianna thought for a moment, gazing across the room. "We could have a worse problem than the computers or Raoul."

"What's that?"

"Renata. You heard her last night. She's so-o-o interested in the company. What if Vanessa dies and leaves her share to Renata? She might not want to sell."

"Of course, she'd want to sell—" Doyle stopped himself. Brianna was too perceptive and right too often to ignore her warning.

"She's a stripper with no education, but she wears enough makeup to stock a counter at a SoBe spa. What could suit her more than owning such a company?"

Taylor was sitting in her office, checking some of the latest ads for To The Maxx products. Since their line was sold only in beauty supply outlets, spas, and beauty salons, the advertisements didn't have to be as expensive or as slick as those of department store cosmetics.

To The Maxx advertised in beauty supply catalogs and professional publications. Still, she needed to make sure each ad showed their products to their best advantage.

Her mind kept drifting back to what Shane had told her. Lisa had been in Miami for over a month.

She'd never called.

Why not?

They'd been best friends since Yale. How could Lisa have come home and not told Taylor she'd returned? There had to be an explanation, but Taylor couldn't quite bring herself to call and ask.

No matter what the reason, Taylor was convinced Lisa could not be the one tampering with the computers. Lisa had been devastated when Trent left her, but she was not the vindictive type.

Lisa had a lot of integrity and self-respect. When Trent divorced her, she'd refused to take any money, saying she could support herself.

"Good morning. Am I interrupting?" asked Trent as he walked into her office.

"No. I'm just going over the new ads."

Trent dropped into the chair beside her desk. "Have you heard the latest about our so-called sister? Mother bought her a red Mercedes convertible."

"I'm not surprised," she replied, although she was shocked and a little hurt. This had happened so soon. "Mother must want to make up to Renata for lost time."

"I think we can expect her to change her will."

Taylor checked the anger she felt rising from deep inside her, saying calmly, "You're probably right."

"I see it coming."

"There might be something we can do about it."

She rose, walked across the room, and shut her office door. It took a minute to explain her plan to sneak into Renata's room to get hair for the DNA test.

"Good idea," Trent said, suddenly more upbeat. "If we can prove she isn't the missing child, Mother won't leave her a dime."

"It's not the money," Taylor said, being totally honest. "If this woman was her child, I wouldn't mind, but I don't believe for one second she is."

"We're protecting Mother from con artists."

Trent smiled at her, and for a moment, it seemed like old times when he would drop into her office just to chat.

"I have an idea for a new product," Trent said with another smile.

"Uncle Doyle doesn't think we should develop any new products while we're considering selling the company, and I agree. Remember, I gave up on developing a collagen-type product like Perlane, which is so popular in Europe."

"I want you to try this." Trent pulled a small bottle out of his pocket. "It's shampoo. Use it and tell me we shouldn't develop a similar product."

"To The Maxx already has an excellent line of shampoos, and we have a very loyal following according to our sales. Our shampoos are just about our bestselling product."

"This is from France. Leonor Greyl's Moelle de Bambou is the best shampoo in the world. Raoul tells me the hottest beauty salons in New York are pushing it."

Raoul.

She might have known.

Once, she'd had misgivings about selling the company that had meant so much to her father. Now she thought it would be a good idea. Let Trent go into the cosmetics business with Raoul. There would be a lot less family friction then.

Her heart was in designing computer games. So far she hadn't had the time to do much more than work on Trivial Moments. This job took too much of her time.

"If you look at the ingredients in Moelle de Bambou, you'll see there's no sodium lauryl sulfate or sodium laureth sulfate. None. Nada. Zippo."

"Wow!" She checked the bottle and saw he was correct. "Without the sulfates this shampoo won't have *any* lather."

"So it won't damage the hair's cuticle. Right?"

She nodded. It was an industry practice to add sodium lauryl sulfate or the milder sodium laureth sulfate to shampoo to produce lather. Professionals knew it damaged the cuticle of the hair, a big problem for women with longer hair. Not cutting it as often as men meant women didn't have new, healthy hair.

"You know the public expects lather when they shampoo. They won't buy a product that doesn't lather. They won't think it's working."

"Raoul says they'll get used to it, if we start at the top with the best salons. Then word will spread downward."

"I don't know. It's hard to change expectations. Vintners know screw tops protect the wine better than corks, but they've shied away from them because the public associates screw tops with cheap wine."

Trent stood up. "Try the shampoo, then we'll talk again."

He was out the door before she could utter another word. She had no intention of encouraging him. Now was not the time to spend the huge amount of money it would take to develop and test a new product.

She credited her business acumen for telling her to

side with Uncle Doyle and refuse to allow Trent to bring Raoul into the business. It had strained her relationship with her brother, but she could only imagine how disruptive Raoul would be if he actually worked here.

Unable to concentrate, Taylor left her office and walked down the hall to the finance division. To The Maxx had a sleek, minimalist environment, with wide halls to showcase contemporary art and give the company a gallerylike ambience.

Behind doors of frosted-milk glass were different departments. A band of high, narrow windows at the ceiling allowed natural light to come in all around the building. She thought it was the most beautiful and unusual office building she'd ever seen.

In the finance section, Shane and Vince were working on the computer security problem. The men had their heads together, studying something on one of the monitors. She stood there a moment, thinking about last night.

Taylor had to admit something about Shane was beginning to appeal to her. Last night she'd gone back to her apartment and taken out the pictures of Paul. They'd evoked memories of happier times, yet when she put them away and went to bed, she kept thinking of things Shane had told her.

Despite her best efforts, Taylor's heart rate kicked up a notch as she watched Shane. The macho type had never interested her, but once she'd begun to know Shane, she realized he exhibited a power and depth of character that was very compelling.

She sensed he wanted her. She knew it in the primal way a woman always senses a man is sexually attracted to her. She had to concede she found his interest exciting.

"Taylor, do you have a minute?"

While she'd been daydreaming, Uncle Doyle had
come up behind her.

"Sure, I was just going to remind Shane to check
on Jim Wilson. He might have a reason to sabotage
us, but it looks as if they're really busy. I don't want
to interrupt."

"Let's go into my office," he said, without comment-
ing on the employee her father had fired.

He turned and headed down the hall toward the
office that had once been her father's, and Taylor
followed.

Inside, he closed the door, which was unusual. Taylor looked around at the office. Uncle Doyle had done
nothing to change it except put Brianna's picture on
the desk.

The same industry awards lined the walls along with
pictures of Duncan Maxwell with famous celebrities
who used his products. A blow-up of his one-hundred-
and-twenty-foot Swan sailboat dominated the back
wall. Stately potted palms with ferns around their bases
softened the room.

There were two chairs facing the glass and chrome
desk. Instead of sitting behind the desk as he usually
did, her uncle sat in one of the chairs and gestured
for her to sit beside him in the other.

"There's something I need to tell you," he said.

Once again, she was reminded of her father. They
had been identical twins who shared the same manner-
isms. His habit of shrugging one shoulder never failed
to bring a pang of sadness.

"I'm listening," Taylor said when he seemed to
hesitate.

"Your mother's not to know anything about this.
Understand?"

"Yes," she replied, expecting a new plan to get rid
of Renata.

"While you were in New Orleans, Trent and Raoul were arrested for possession of crystal meth."

Shock caused words to wedge in her throat. All she could do was listen to the rest of the story. Shane was right, she decided when her head began to clear.

You never really knew anyone but yourself.

She could never have imagined her brother taking drugs. He didn't smoke and never had. He rarely drank.

Taylor kept silent, a cramp in her chest, until she was certain she could speak. "What are we going to do?"

"For starters, I'm making it clear to Trent that I don't want him ramming Raoul's ideas about this business down our throats."

She thought about the shampoo back on her desk but didn't mention it. Uncle Doyle already hated Raoul. He'd be furious to learn Trent was pushing another of Raoul's ideas. A very risky one at that.

"Trent needs help. There must be a doctor or—"

"We don't know he's addicted. This might be the only time he took meth. I didn't think to ask, but it doesn't physically appear as if he's hooked."

He was explaining the physical changes to watch for when his secretary knocked on the door.

"Taylor, your mother's here with her daughter. She'd like you to give Renata a tour of To The Maxx."

Chapter 11

Fuming, Taylor watched Renata fill her large straw handbag with samples of To The Maxx products in the promotions department storeroom. Without so much as asking if Taylor had appointments or something important to do, her mother had left Renata with Taylor while Caleb took her to the hospital for her weekly blood test.

"I never had enough money to buy fancy cosmetics like these," Renata said, helping herself to handfuls of To The Maxx lipsticks.

"Let's go into the laboratory where they're blending our perfume."

Taylor led the way down the hall connecting the main office to the adjacent building where the products were manufactured, before Renata could wipe out all the samples intended for a trade show next week.

"This is some operation," Renata said when they entered the perfume facility.

It was difficult for Taylor to tell if there was genuine awe in Renata's voice or if she was merely acting the part. When you looked at her, Renata still had the hard edge of the stripper—overmade-up. Even though her newly discovered "mother" had bought her a boatload of new clothes, Renata chose things that made her look like a hooker.

Her personality had softened since that night in New Orleans. Taylor was certain it was an act, but she was grateful the woman wasn't being mean to her mother. The way the stripper had sounded in New Orleans made Taylor expect the worst.

But the two of them got along just fine. She tamped down a surge of jealousy, knowing her dying mother desperately wanted to believe she'd found her long-lost daughter.

Her mother was dying. Let her be happy.

"What does that machine do?" Renata was pointing to an expensive stainless steel machine the company had recently purchased.

"It presses the fragrant extract out of magnolias and lilac petals. What comes out is called an essential oil, the basis of all perfume."

Taylor waved to an older man with a full head of curly white hair.

"I'll have Marcel, who heads this department, explain the details."

Marcel ambled over, his bum knee obviously bothering him again. Taylor had tried so often to get him to go in for a knee replacement that it had become a sore subject between them. Marcel seemed to think the entire operation would shut down if he wasn't here every day.

Taylor introduced him to Renata without saying they

were related. If Renata noticed the omission, she didn't show it. In fact, Renata never said she was Vanessa Maxwell's daughter. It was always Taylor's mother who brought up the subject.

"The first thing to know about fragrance," Taylor said, "is it changes on the skin. Each of us has a unique body chemistry, so the scent develops differently on each of us."

"The top note," Marcel said as he sprayed a bit of To The Maxx on the pulse point on Renata's wrist, "is our first impression of the fragrance."

Renata sniffed her wrist. "Yummy."

Taylor couldn't help thinking their perfume was a marked contrast to the heavy, cloying scent Renata wore.

She told her, "Give it a few minutes, then smell it again."

"What you'll have then," Marcel added, "is the middle notes, or the heart of the perfume."

"Later, when the perfume has dried and been on your skin for a while, the base note is what lingers," she added.

Taylor led them over to the counter where they were testing the latest batch of their perfume.

"Did I get a sample of this?" Renata asked. "I wear Unforgettable but I might give this a try."

"Yes, you have a couple." Actually, she'd taken at least a dozen.

"Explain to me exactly how you make perfume," Renata said with what appeared to be genuine enthusiasm.

Clearly charmed, Marcel launched into a step-by-step explanation. Taylor supplied a few details, but mainly she observed the dark-haired woman who was posing as a member of the family. Renata asked questions, many of them very intelligent, and seemed so interested that Taylor was suspicious.

Then Taylor got it.

Renata was going to dazzle her mother with her knowledge. Taylor knew her mother would be impressed.

No doubt about it.

Taylor's father had been the driving force behind the company, but her mother flitted in and out of To The Maxx regularly. She was a smart woman who knew each product thoroughly.

"You must love working here," Renata commented when they'd finished and were walking back to the main building.

"It's very interesting," Taylor replied, noticing something almost wistful in Renata's expression.

She supposed To The Maxx seemed glamorous to a stripper in a seedy club. She didn't have the heart to say it was a lot of number crunching and dealing with vendors and distributors. It was hard work, and it took a strong person with sharp business skills to do her job.

"Do you think there's something here I could do?" Renata asked.

Taylor nearly tripped over her own feet. Renata around full time? God forbid.

"Since you're going back to New Orleans, you must want to spend your time seeing the sights."

Like the Miami sun, hate burned in Renata's dark eyes for a second, then it vanished so quickly Taylor thought she'd imagined it.

"Didn't your mother tell you? Caleb and I are staying. Vanessa says there's plenty of room at the house."

"Really?" Taylor smiled—or tried to. "She hasn't mentioned it, but I'm sure you'll enjoy living there."

"A job here would be just perfect. It'll give me something to do besides shop."

Over my dead body, Taylor thought. "My mother needs to spend time with you. She hasn't long to live, you understand."

Renata smiled and tossed her long hair over her shoulder in a gesture of defiance. "Vanessa doesn't need me around all day. She's got Caleb. They play mah-jong by the hour and hardly pay attention to me."

This was news to Taylor, but she didn't comment.

"For sure Caleb won't be getting a job. He has a bad back."

The bitterness Taylor had noticed in New Orleans had returned with a vengeance. It almost sounded as if Renata hated her father. Again, Taylor wondered what kind of man sat at home while his daughter worked in a strip joint.

There was something going on—more than they knew about yet. She needed to have Shane continue checking into Renata's background.

"So what about a job?" There was a challenging, almost threatening glint to Renata's eyes even though her tone was casual.

"Look, my mother wants to believe you're her missing daughter, but I don't buy it. Not for one second."

"Who's to say I'm not her daughter? You can't prove I'm not."

Taylor was damn well going to try. An idea had already formed in her mind while they had been discussing perfume.

"It doesn't matter," Taylor snapped. "I'm not letting you hang around here."

"I wouldn't hang around. I would work."

"You don't get it, do you?" Taylor kept her voice low, but anger punctuated every syllable. "I don't want you here. Stay with Mother. Make her last days happy ones."

"Taylor, I'm here!"

She turned to see Brianna sailing down the hall. She often came to have a late lunch with Doyle. Taylor held in a sigh of relief, grateful to Brianna for diverting the conversation.

"You've met Renata," she said the instant Brianna was close enough to talk.

"Of course." Brianna's smile was easy, charming. Her trademark. "It's great to see you. Isn't this, like, a totally amazing place?"

"Totally," Renata agreed. "I was just asking if there was a job here for me."

If Brianna was shocked by the statement, it didn't show in her face. "Why would you want to work here?"

"I love cosmetics. I always have. Since I was young enough to swipe my grandmother's lipstick, I've adored makeup." She looked directly at Taylor. "I'm just the person to work here."

"I don't know," Brianna said when Taylor couldn't utter a word for fear of losing her temper. "It's a lot of hard work, and it isn't very glamorous."

"I'm used to hard work," Renata said, a sharp edge to her voice.

"I'm sure you are," replied Brianna. "I used to be a lap dancer before I married Doyle. I'm used to hard work. I wouldn't want a job here unless I desperately needed the money."

"I want to work here."

There was a feral undertone to Renata's voice now. It triggered a warning bell in Taylor's brain. This woman was determined to cause trouble.

There was only one way to get rid of her—the DNA test. Now was the perfect time to collect samples. Caleb was at the hospital with her mother.

If Renata could be kept here, Taylor would have enough time to run to her mother's house and get hair samples. It was the perfect opportunity.

"Brianna, I have to call one of our vendors in California. Could you show Renata the anti-aging lotions our product development department is testing?"

"Sure. Tell Doyle I'm here. We have lunch reservations at Café Baci."

Taylor liked the trendy dining spot with its unique menu and metallic domed ceiling, but she knew reservations there were hard to get. She couldn't count on having Brianna stall Renata for as long as it would take her to drive to her mother's home and collect the hair samples.

Taylor rushed away. "I'll be back in a minute."

She found Shane Donovan still hovering over the computer with Vince. "Shane, could you help me?"

He spun around, obviously glad to see her, and he smiled, a surprisingly endearing grin that gave her a flash of what Shane must have been like as a young boy.

A devil.

Adorable.

She'd become extremely conscious of his virile appeal and the way her feelings for him were changing.

"What's up?" he asked.

She motioned for him to come with her, out of Vince's hearing range. "Renata's down in product development with Brianna, but she has to go to lunch with Doyle," she said in a breathless rush. "Could you show Renata the accounting department and then take her upstairs to the executive dining room for lunch? That'll give me time to get to my mother's house and collect those DNA samples."

"Not a problem," Shane replied. "I'll stall Renata for as long as I can."

Taylor flashed him a grateful smile, but she couldn't help thinking a man like Shane Donovan wouldn't have a bit of trouble "stalling" a woman, even a hard-as-nails person like Renata.

"Shane, are you still checking into Caleb and Renata's background? They've decided to stay here with Mother, and I'm dead certain something about those two is really wrong."

Shane moved closer and put his hand on her shoulder in a gesture that was almost intimate. "Your mother pulled the plug. She paid us for what we've done, but she said it was no longer necessary to look into their past. She just told us this morning. I didn't have the chance to tell you."

"I'll pay you whatever it takes," she said, her words barely above a whisper.

Those two con artists weren't going to take advantage of her dying mother.

Doyle came back from lunch with Brianna, in the best mood in a long time. It didn't last five minutes. On his desk was a stack of messages. One of them was from the family attorney, Ridley Pudge, an old friend and classmate at Duke. The message was marked "urgent" and said to call immediately.

Doyle sank into his chair and dialed Ridley's office. "What's happening?" he asked as if he weren't worried when his friend came on the line.

"I just want to give you a heads-up. Off the record, right? You never heard this from me."

"Of course. You know you can count on me."

Sweat peppered Doyle's upper lip and he swiped at it with the back of his hand. What now?

"This morning Vanessa called for an appointment. I'm booked until next week, but she insisted on getting in tomorrow, so my secretary consulted me. Vanessa wants to change her will.''

"Thanks for letting me know."

"That's all I'm going to be able to tell you. I shouldn't have mentioned it at all but . . .''

Doyle knew the "but" referred to the loan he'd once made Ridley when he was between wives and strapped for cash.

"Thanks, Ridley. I'll see you at the club."

Vanessa's changing the will wouldn't affect him financially, but it could very well affect Taylor and Trent. And To The Maxx.

At lunch, Brianna had told him about showing Renata around the company. His wife was convinced the stripper truly wanted a position at the company.

Jesus Willie Christ!

If Vanessa died and left Renata part of Maxx, the woman might be able to block the sale of the company. Doyle pressed his hand over his closed eyes, wondering how much longer he could sustain his lifestyle without an infusion of cash.

Not long. Six months maybe.

The only hope he had of making any money was a monumental rebound in the stock market—a pipe dream—or the sale of Maxx. He couldn't do anything about the market, but he could engineer the sale of the company.

This computer snafu had slowed things down but hadn't stopped it entirely. Vanessa's death and the subsequent inheritance problem could.

If only there were a way to get rid of the Rollins woman. He picked up the phone to call Brianna on her cell phone. She might have an idea.

* * *

Shane lingered over coffee in the executive dining room with Renata, discussing—hell—embellishing—what little he knew about To The Maxx. He was an expert in computer security. He didn't know mascara from lip gloss.

"Just what is your position in the company?" Renata asked.

She was a whole lot smarter than she let on, he'd decided just after he'd relieved Brianna, saying Taylor had an important appointment and he would finish Renata's tour of the company.

"I'm a consultant," he hedged. "Computers are my specialty." He didn't add anything about how a Special Forces guy got into computers.

"Why does To The Maxx need an independent consultant? They have a whole accounting department."

Good question.

"I just check to make sure the computer security hasn't been breached. You know how important it is to protect the formulas for the various products."

He leaned closer to the sultry brunette. "Trade secrets are stolen every day. Where better to infiltrate the system than the accounting department?"

She bought it, nodding, eyes wide. "Of course."

A few minutes passed as they sipped their coffee in the minimalist executive dining room on the top floor of the building. Out of the sweep of glass, Shane could see the lush greenery of Coral Gables. The office building was a short distance from Vanessa Maxwell's home. Taylor should be back any minute. She'd told him that she would find him when she returned.

"I intend to learn this business from the ground up," Renata said. "Where should I start?"

* * *

Renata gazed at her reflection in her makeup mirror in the guest suite Vanessa had given her. Wow! Pricey cosmetics did make a *huge* difference.

A red Mercedes convertible. Getting written into the will. Life was good.

A far cry from tricking and stripping.

Her luck had changed. She didn't want anything to jinx her *mojo* now. She wished she could visit Marie Laveau's grave. Lighting a candle, running both hands over the Xs would ensure her lucky streak kept going.

"You look great, baby."

Caleb had come into her room without knocking. If the old bag didn't like him so much, she'd dump him. When she got her mitts on the dough, she would.

She'd had enough of him.

A lifetime, it seemed, even though she was young, and it really hadn't been that long.

"I told you to knock."

The old fart's reflection smirked at her from the mirror.

"You've made quite an impression on Vanessa. It's smart to ask to work at her company and act like you're interested."

"I *am* interested. I don't know what she plans to leave me, but I want to know enough to start my own cosmetics business."

Renata was pleased with herself. It hadn't taken much to convince Vanessa to get her a job at To The Maxx. Taylor—the bitch—was going to have to learn to deal with her.

"I say we take the money and head for Mexico, where it'll last forever. Neither of us will ever have to work again."

She spun around to face him. "I don't rightly recall you working."

"My back's bad, honey. You know that."

She turned around again and found the glistening tube of Maxx lipstick. "It was easier to let me support you than work."

"There's no point in fighting. I got you here. We'll be rich in no time. Vanessa won't live much longer."

"What will it take to get you out of my life?" she asked.

Caleb's reflection disappeared from the mirror. He stalked out of the room and slammed the door behind him.

This was the end, and he had to know it.

She'd give him some money to get him out of her life. Let him go to Mexico. A man with his charm and looks could use the money while he found another woman to support him.

She was staying right here.

Chapter 12

"Fate sends people into our lives to test us."

Interesting concept, he decided, mulling over the words. Had Shane Donovan been sent by fate, or was some other force at work?

"What in **hell** *is* Shane Donovan doing in Miami?"

He was dangerous to have around. No, more than dangerous.

Shane was trouble, pure and simple. If he nosed around enough, he could screw up everything. He couldn't allow that to happen. What was needed was a preemptive strike, something to throw off everyone.

Especially Shane Donovan.

That's the ticket. Send everyone into a tailspin.

Divert attention.

What would work the best?

Thinking and planning were essential. Patience was a virtue, but time was short now.

A preemptive strike had to be made immediately.

"Yes!" he cried. "Brilliant idea."

He knew exactly what his next move would be.

Was he a genius, or what?

Shane answered the knock on his door without looking through the peephole to see who it was. Auggie's wagging tail told him that Taylor was here. A first, he thought, turning the doorknob.

She'd come to him.

"I know it's late," Taylor said as she stepped inside and patted Auggie.

"It's barely ten," he said, closing the door.

"I have the samples." She handed him a small bag with two small plastic baggies inside.

"Did you have any trouble getting them?" he asked. They hadn't been able to talk privately when Taylor had returned to finish showing Renata around the offices.

"No. It was easy. I just gave Maria an excuse for being there. She didn't pay any attention to me. She was too busy mopping the entry so it would dry before my mother returned."

She hesitated a moment. "I even had time to look through Renata's things."

"Go on. You can't mean it. You did that?" He was joking, but Taylor took him seriously.

"I felt like a creep, but I couldn't resist. I didn't find anything worth mentioning. A lot of cheap makeup and phony jewelry. A closet full of new clothes. That's it."

"What did you expect to find? She's smart enough not to leave anything incriminating around. Did you get a chance to go through Caleb's things?"

"Yes, but there wasn't anything interesting except . . ."

"Except?"

"I can understand my mother buying Renata clothes, but why would she buy clothes for Caleb?"

Shane walked to the dining room table, where he had a FedEx mailer addressed and ready to go. He put the samples inside, saying, "She probably feels guilty because he raised her child. He doesn't have much—"

"What about his place in New Orleans? Those looked like genuine antiques to me."

"They leased it furnished." He led her over to the sofa, and they sat down. "I have a contact on the New Orleans police force. He says neither of them have a criminal record in Louisiana—a least not under the names they are currently using."

"If Bassett is Caleb's last name and Renata is truly his daughter, then her last name must be Bassett."

"Right, Sherlock."

She giggled and gazed at him with what he hoped was real interest. For once, Paul Ashton wasn't hovering between them. Now was the time to tell her the whole truth.

She'd be pissed, he decided, but she needed his help too much to dump him.

"Did you have your friend check under the last name of Bassett?"

"Yes, but there wasn't anything. The Louisiana DMV issued a driver's license to Renata Rollins."

Unfuckingbelievable! He'd chickened out and hadn't told her a damn thing.

"I don't suppose the strip club has her Social Security number."

He chuckled, deciding now really was not the time to bare his so-called soul. Why tell Taylor something that was damn sure to hurt her? Wait until their relationship was on a more solid footing. He was making progress with her.

"No. The club pays the girls in cash. My contact did have one interesting comment. Girls come and go at the club. They're all hookers."

Taylor put her hand over her eyes, then whispered, "Maybe she's an exception."

"I hate to be the bearer of bad news, but the cops who work the area know Renata by name. They never arrested her for prostitution, but word has it she's into rough sex. She gets big bucks for it."

"No wonder she wants to live here. She had the nerve to ask me for a job at Maxx."

"Just what you need."

"I told her to forget it."

Shane leaned down to pat Auggie who was sitting at his feet. Something was going on inside the company, and it wasn't as simple as someone sabotaging them. He decided not to worry Taylor until he knew exactly what was happening.

"Can you keep a secret?"

If she only knew how damn good at keeping secrets he was.

"Sure. I won't tell anyone."

He made an X over is heart.

Just in case.

He had the smarts not to hope to die.

"We had a meeting tonight at the SoBe loft my brother shares with Raoul. Uncle Doyle and Brianna were there along with Trent. Of course, Raoul was there. He's gay, you know, like my brother."

No kidding.

"So, we're all a family. We needed to discuss what to do about Renata. Uncle Doyle discovered my mother intends to change her will."

Why was he not surprised?

"We're all afraid that if Renata is left part of the company, she might block the sale or hold it up for a while. We want to outmaneuver her."

"The DNA is your best bet."

"Yes. Everyone is counting on it." She shook her head slowly. "There were a lot of other ideas tossed out. Raoul even wanted to hire a Cuban hit man he knows to kill her."

"What? That's crazy."

"You're right. I told them I wouldn't listen to talk like that, but the men thought it wasn't a bad idea."

"I know Renata is excited about To The Maxx, but when the time comes, I think money will be more appealing to her than actually working. I'd give her a hard, grunt work job right now, so she won't think it's glamorous."

"I don't want her around—period."

"What if your mother insists?"

Taylor stared at the wall for a moment, thinking. "I guess I wouldn't have any choice. My mother is dying. I don't want to upset her."

"If it comes to it, give her a grunt job."

"She can have my job. It's not glamorous."

"I think she'd take it in a heartbeat. Then you could work on your computer game."

Taylor thought a moment. "I'm trying to find a way to make longer trivia work in a game format. Like the saying, 'It's raining cats and dogs.' It comes from the Middle Ages when floors in houses were dirt and the roofs were thatched straw. It was where animals went to get warm."

"Wait a minute," he said, edging closer to her. "How would they get up on the roof?"

"There was always a woodpile on one side of the house. It went up to the roof or close enough for the pets as well as rats and mice to jump up to where the heat was rising and the straw was warm. But when it rained, the straw became slippery and the animals fell off the roof.''

"So, it was raining cats and dogs, right?"

"Right. I need to get it down to a few lines for it to work in this game's format." She gazed off across the room for a moment. "I could save the longer trivia for another game. That might be a better idea than trying to force interesting trivia into one-liners."

She was so cute thinking about the game. He was tempted to kiss her, but hell, he'd ruin everything. He'd waited this long, come this far to find her. He could bide his time.

Taylor walked into the Coral Gables home where she'd grown up, calling, "Mother, it's me."

"Terrace," Pablo informed her with a Cuban accent, "breakfast."

Taylor braced herself, thinking how much she dreaded this, but after leaving Shane last night, she'd been unable to stop thinking about her mother changing her will. Her uncle and brother were upset enough to talk about taking drastic measures like hiring someone to kill Renata.

The fine hairs across the back of her neck prickled just recalling the way Raoul had suggested it, as if it were a viable option.

She should have walked out right then, but she hadn't. Expecting her brother and uncle to pounce on Raoul, she'd stayed only to listen to the men seriously discuss it for a moment until she cut them off. Brianna, of course, had sided with her.

Getting her mother alone to have a talk might help, she thought. Taylor had hardly seen her mother—and never alone—since Renata had arrived. She wanted to gauge her mother's frame of mind and give her a chance to explain why she was changing the will.

Taylor needed to stall her until the DNA test was completed.

"Good morning, darling," her mother called.

Taylor walked into the terrace room overlooking the pool and garden. The room was the most casual in the house with its sunny exposure and West Indies decor.

Taylor mustered a smile for Caleb, who was sitting at the table with her mother. She'd taken an instant dislike to the man when she'd met him in New Orleans. Part of it was instinctual, but the way he allowed his daughter to work in a strip club while he did nothing increased her feelings.

There was something else about him that disturbed her, but she couldn't quite put her finger on it. In his own way, he was charming especially when he was around her mother.

"Hey, Taylor," Caleb said while she kissed her mother's cheek. "Have some breakfast."

Why was he offering her breakfast in her mother's house? He grinned at her, trying to be nice, but she couldn't muster a smile.

"I've eaten. I just stopped by to see how Mother is doing."

"I'm fine," her mother replied, her voice upbeat. "The blood work shows no change from the last test."

"That's great!"

No wonder she seemed so happy. Her previous tests had shown she was steadily becoming more anemic and her immune system had gone haywire. The doctors monitored it with a weekly blood test and adjusted her medications accordingly.

"You came by yesterday afternoon while we were at

the hospital," Caleb said, his dark eyes assessing her under drawn brows.

Taylor sat in the rattan chair next to her mother, grateful she had a cover story ready. Beneath a thin veneer of charm that had her mother fooled, Caleb Bassett was a cunning man with a ruthless streak.

"I had a meeting with a new vendor, and I wanted to pick up the notebook my father kept in the library on using botanicals in cosmetics. Much better than chemicals."

"I see," he said, still staring at her.

An unwelcome lurch of fear struck Taylor, and she realized Caleb knew she'd been in his room.

How?

She'd been so very careful. Refusing to be cowed, she brazened it out and kept looking at him.

"Is Renata still asleep?" she asked.

"Oh, heavens, no," her mother replied, obviously missing the undercurrent between Taylor and Caleb. "She so excited about To The Maxx. She wanted to be there when it opened."

It was all Taylor could do not to groan out loud. Of all the nerve. The stripper knew how Taylor felt about her, yet she'd gone over her head to Vanessa.

"You told her that she could have a job?"

"Of course. Just like me, Renata has a knack for cosmetics," her mother gushed. "When she came home yesterday, she knew almost as much about the business as I do. She just *loves* it."

Caleb's smug smile told Taylor all she needed to know. The family was in real trouble. She didn't know exactly what Caleb and Renata were up to, but she wasn't letting them get away with it.

She stood up, saying, "Mother, may I speak to you alone for a few minutes? You'll excuse us, won't you, Caleb?"

"Sure," he said, picking up the paper on the chair beside him, "take your time. I'll be right here reading the news."

Her mother swayed as she rose to her feet, and Taylor was reminded of how frail the once vivacious woman had become. The blood test may have shown no deterioration, but anyone who knew her mother could see she was slipping fast.

She took her mother's arm and led her out of the terrace room, down the hall, and to the library where her father had reigned for so many years. The formal room could have been part of a library in an Ivy League college. Dark wood, leather-bound books, maroon suede wing-back chairs.

No one had touched this room since her father's death. Just being here made Taylor feel the power of his presence.

Some people will be with us always, in the way we live, the way we love. This saying often came to mind, she realized, because it was so true.

Her parents had shaped her life. They weren't perfect, but what family was? Still, the power of their love had made her secure.

Their love had given her inner strength. And now she was going to need it.

"Is something the matter?" her mother asked.

Taylor didn't really know what to say. She'd been warned not to mention the will and get the attorney in trouble.

"I just haven't had a chance to talk to you privately in so long. How are things going? I understand you invited Caleb and Renata to live with you."

Her mother gingerly lowered herself into a chair, and Taylor sat on the ottoman in front of her.

"Yes, I want to get to know my daughter. What better

way is there? It took a lot of doing, but Caleb convinced Renata to move here."

Taylor summoned a half smile and managed to nod.

Caleb. Who else?

The mother she'd known all her life would have been too savvy to allow a man like Caleb to manipulate her. And she wouldn't have accepted Renata as her daughter without better proof.

"I'm surprised you're not spending more time with Renata," Taylor said, trying to edge into a conversation about the stripper.

Her mother's smile was straight from the heart. "I have Caleb to keep me company. I want Renata to start a new career. She's never had the benefit of a first-class education the way you have."

A surge of bitter jealousy threatened to force her to say something she might regret. Taylor bit down on the inside of her cheek and reminded herself that her mother had a terminal illness.

Don't upset her.

The DNA test couldn't come back soon enough. Taylor realized there would be no reasoning with her mother until she had proof Renata Rollins was not her daughter.

"I understand how you feel about Renata," Taylor said, remembering Shane's advice about finding some difficult job for the stripper to do. "I'll see Renata learns the business, but if we sell it, the new owners may not keep any of us."

"We'll cross that bridge when we get to it."

"So, what are you doing today?" Taylor asked, although she already knew her mother had an appointment with the attorney about her will.

"Caleb's taking me to lunch at the Shore Club," she said.

It was one of SoBe's newest and hottest hotels.

Another pastel-colored beachfront spot where the hip, young crowd liked to be seen. It wasn't her mother's style at all.

"Caleb can't believe I haven't eaten there yet."

No doubt her mother was paying for this luncheon. Taylor waited for her mother to add something about the attorney, but she didn't. There was a hint of the old sparkle in her blue eyes as she smiled at Taylor.

"Renata tells me you and Shane have something going on, true?"

Holding raw emotion in check, Taylor managed to say, "That's ridiculous. Where would she get that idea?"

Her mother gazed at her for a long moment. "You know, I never liked Paul Ashton. He wasn't your type. Renata's right. Shane Donovan would be good for you."

Chapter 13

"You need to see me?" Taylor asked Shane.

She'd driven from her mother's home to work, where her secretary handed her an "urgent" message from Shane. Thinking hard, she'd walked to the finance department to find Shane. Why would Renata say something was going on between them?

Was the stripper determined to cause trouble?

Of course, was her immediate response. Then she reconsidered. To be totally honest, Taylor had to admit she was attracted to Shane.

But how would Renata know it? Had she picked up on something Taylor hoped wasn't obvious to most people?

"Yep, I wanted to talk to you." Shane swung around from the computer terminal to face her and smiled.

Her heart beat a little faster and she did her best

to disguise her body's reaction by keeping a straight face as he looked at her.

"What do you need to talk about?" she asked, determined not to sound excited to see him.

There was a disturbing nuance to his smile.

What was it about him that made her forget she was in love with another man? There was a mysterious side to him that she didn't quite trust, yet she couldn't help being drawn to Shane in a way that defied her previous experiences with men—even Paul Ashton.

Shane was all business. "Renata arrived really early this morning. I was the only one here except for the security guards. She claimed your mother had a job for her."

"Right," she replied, trying not to notice how broad his shoulders were or the masculine dusting of a beard along his jawline even though it was barely noon. "As you predicted, my mother gave Renata a job."

Without consulting me.

"I told Renata you'd found her a place in the shipping department."

"Shipping?" It was the lowest rung on the company ladder.

Shane frowned, saying, "Didn't we agree to give Renata a position that would demonstrate this is not a glamorous company, if you were forced to give her a job? Didn't we want to make her work her buns off?"

"Absolutely. I don't want Renata to see Maxx as an easy job with lots of perks and no downside."

Shipping meant broken nails, packing material that made you sneeze, and a killer deadline to make the UPS pickups.

Shane nodded thoughtfully. "That's why I told her that you wanted her in shipping—to learn the business from the bottom up."

Taylor tried not to chuckle, remembering when she'd been thirteen and her father had sent her into shipping for the summer 'to learn the business.' It had been hell on earth. Hot and cramped and seething with workers who hated her because she was the owner's daughter.

Have fun, Renata.

"Good thinking," Taylor said. "How did she take it?"

"Renata was thrilled—or pretended to be. She claims to want to learn all about the business—everything."

Taylor almost shuddered. Exactly what her father had wanted to hear years ago when she'd started in shipping. That's what she'd told him despite keeping the white lie to herself. Even then she'd wanted to run her own game company.

"How are you progressing on the computer security problem?" she asked.

"It's coming along."

"There's one other person I told you about. Jim Wilson. My father let him go. Jim knew a lot about computers."

"I'll check into it."

"Do you think it'll take much longer to fix the problem?"

"I should have a report for you in a few days." His words although, spoken in an even tone had an ominous quality to them.

"Is something wrong?"

He hesitated for an instant. "I think what's happening may be worse than sabotage."

"Worse?" The word vaporized on her lips. Oh, God, she didn't need any more trouble right now.

He led her to the computer terminal he was using. "See this picture?"

On the screen was a full-color photograph of a bottle of Maxxed Out. "It's our product for treating damaged hair."

"Right, and it's just one of many pictures on your Web site featuring all your cosmetics." He studied her intently for a moment. "Have you ever heard of steganography?"

She shook her head, becoming more troubled as he spoke.

"It's a Greek word for *covered writing*. It's a way of hiding messages in plain sight. To read the concealed message the user has to have a special program on his computer and know the code to get inside your site."

"Are you saying there's a hidden message in that picture of Maxxed Out?"

"Yes. See what happens when I run it through the program I have on my laptop?"

He pointed the arrow at the 'o' in Out and double-clicked. The entire picture vanished from the screen and was replaced by script and numbers.

"What's this?"

"That's what I'm trying to figure out." He double-clicked again and the original picture reappeared. "Don't mention a word about this to anyone—your uncle, your brother, even your mother."

"All right, I won't, but you must have some idea about what's going on. Why would anyone want to hide messages on a cosmetics Web site?"

"Because it's the last place the police would think to look."

She dropped into the chair next to him. "Something illegal?"

He put his hand on her shoulder and nodded. "Why else would anyone take the trouble to hide messages? It's one of the ways child pornography is distributed over the Internet."

"Oh, God, no," she cried.

He squeezed her shoulder gently, saying, "Don't worry. It's not kiddie porn. There aren't any pictures. It's a lot of script and numbers. I'm trying to figure out just what they mean."

She looked around at the other cubicles in the finance department. "Someone here must have done this."

"Not necessarily. Talented hackers can get into any computer anywhere. The question is, who and why?"

Doyle Maxwell hung up the telephone, wondering how much longer he could hold off the prospective buyers. He was running out of excuses why they couldn't visit To The Maxx and inspect the books.

Jesus Willie Christ. He needed this deal in the worst way. What was taking Shane and Vince so long to figure out the computer security problems?

He buzzed Taylor's office but her secretary told him that she was down in the shipping department. Shipping? What was she doing down there? Trent oversaw shipping, not Taylor.

He tried Trent's office, but his secretary told him that his nephew wouldn't be in until after lunch. Then Doyle remembered Trent and Raoul had an appointment with the attorney concerning their drug charges.

The courts had become much stricter. His nephew and his 'buddy' would have a tougher time dodging this one than they might have several years ago.

And it would become even more difficult to hide the truth from Vanessa. That's when he would have Trent and his meddling lover, Raoul on the ropes.

Doyle hustled down to the shipping department and found Taylor talking to Renata Rollins. What in hell was the stripper doing? It looked as if she was packing boxes for shipment.

He held back in the entrance to the area where the open loading dock accommodated shipping trucks and allowed the outside air to swamp the huge room with suffocating heat laden with humidity. Who would work under these conditions?

"What's going on?" he asked as he walked up.

Renata stared at him with defiant brown eyes. "I'm learning the business from the bottom up. Taylor thought I should start working here first."

Taylor flashed him a look that said she'd explain later.

"It's fascinating," the stripper told him.

Fascinating, my ass, he thought. The other workers were Cubans who spoke Spanish all the time. The job was tedious and boring, but he supposed if you wanted to really learn the business, shipping was the place to start.

It suddenly struck him that Brianna was right—again—Renata wanted to become part of the company. When they had offers for the business, money alone might not satisfy Renata.

If she inherited a chunk of Maxx from Vanessa, the stripper might not be willing to sell. That would be disaster. He needed to sell—now.

Once again, Doyle considered Raoul's suggestion. Doyle had liked the idea as had Trent, but Taylor had taken the high road, insisting no one discuss the "ultimate option." The swishy Cuban knew the Miami underworld like no one else Doyle had encountered.

Now, seeing Renata here, listening to her discussing Maxx as if she expected to inherit it, made Doyle reconsider. What right did this bitch have to call the shots? Where had she been during the past twenty years when his brother had nurtured the company into a first-rate cosmetics business?

"Taylor, I need to go over some advertisements with you," Doyle said, knowing his niece would realize he wanted to speak to her alone. He rarely had anything to say about their ads, which were Taylor's responsibility.

"I'll see you later," Taylor told Renata as she walked away.

"What's she doing here?" Doyle asked.

Just as Brianna had predicted, Taylor told him Vanessa had insisted on giving Renata a job. His tie was suddenly too tight. He touched his bare skin and discovered he'd worn an open-neck shirt.

"I'm really worried about Mother," Taylor confided. "She's so wrapped up in Caleb and Renata. Why? Could one of her medications be distorting her perspective?"

"Possibly," Doyle replied, although he personally thought guilt was the primary factor.

Vanessa had been a hard-core society wife, but she did flit in and out of Maxx with suggestions. She'd stepped on—and over—countless people until she'd got what she'd wanted through her husband, Duncan.

Her ability to maneuver his brother had been a wall between them until Doyle realized fighting Vanessa was useless. This sudden insight had occurred just as he was preparing to divorce Sophie to marry Brianna.

Vanessa's support had deflected flack from his family and had paved the way for Brianna—at least to a certain extent. Although welcoming Brianna to the family, Vanessa had never admitted his new wife into her circle of society friends.

"Did you talk to your mother about seeing Ridley this afternoon?" Doyle asked, thinking about what his attorney friend had told him about Vanessa wanting to change her will.

Taylor hesitated a second too long. "Mother never mentioned her appointment with the attorney. All she wanted to talk about was Renata working here. She's determined to have Renata learn the business."

"Maybe it's because you aren't interested."

"Possibly," Taylor replied. "Mother may want to propel my father's legacy into the new millennium. She says she feels the need to make up to Renata for all she's missed."

Doyle didn't argue. Who knew what was going on in Vanessa's mind? He'd spent the better part of his adult life fighting her—and losing.

He led Taylor through the double doors into the hallway leading back to the main building, where the air conditioning cooled the building to a reasonable temperature. Let the stripper spend her time with a pack of sweaty Cubans.

"Have you talked to Vince or Shane?" he asked. "What's happening with the computer security investigation? I have two buyers champing at the bit. I have to keep putting them off because I don't want them to find out about the security problems."

"They're working on it," Taylor replied.

"It's taking a hell of a long time. I think we should get another team in here to expedite things."

"No. Don't do that. Shane is almost through."

Something in her voice alarmed Doyle. Taylor was not a good liar. What was going on?

"Does Shane have any idea what the problem is?"

"Not exactly," answered Taylor, "but he says he'll have an answer in a few days."

A few days.

Everything seemed to be boiling down to 'a few

days.' An answer about the computer security. The
DNA results.

Time was everything, he decided. And it was running
out. He needed the money from the sale of his brother's company. Computer glitches and strippers posing
as long-lost daughters were nothing but trouble.

What could he do?

Renata pinned the tiny gold bar with a single bead
of jet dangling from it on her dress. She'd driven her
hot new Mercedes convertible to Little Havana right
after work to buy the *arichanet*.

Not that she believed in their Santería crap, but
she'd always been a little superstitious. She'd gotten
it from her grandmother, who'd raised her with a
healthy fear of haints—ghosts—and other creatures
who roamed the hallows in the dead of night.

Her life had taken a new turn.

Renata needed her *mojo*—her good luck charm—
now more than ever.

She had to work a bit longer with Cubans who gave
her the willies. The way they looked at her and jab-
bered in Spanish would make anyone superstitious.

She'd told the Cuban bitches to fuck off and die.
But for good measure, she'd bought the *arichanet*.

Santería stuff, but it might protect her. Okay, it was
Macumba, the black magic some Santería followers
worshipped like those who believed in Marie Laveau's
black arts.

Candles. Xs on tombs.

Followers of Santería sacrificed chickens. Animal
rights activists had taken them to the Supreme Court.
The judges upheld their right to practice their religion
the way they always had.

Native Americans smoked peyote in their services.

Santería believers could have animal blood sacrifices of chickens.

Renata had never been to a blood sacrifice, but the concept intrigued her. "Ashes to ashes. Dust to dust. If God won't have you, the devil must."

Then the innocent animal's jugular was slit open. Its life blood spilled onto the dusty earth, saving the true believers.

A loud rap on her door then Caleb barged in, saying, "I thought we'd hit the clubs after Vanessa goes to bed."

"No way. I can't. I'm bushed. I spent all day bustin' my ass in the shipping department."

"What's that pin you're wearing? Some fancy piece Vanessa gave you."

"Don't I wish. The *arichanet* cost me five bucks. Cubans use them to ward off the evil eye. You know, bad luck or worse."

"Don't tell me you still believe that shit. Who'd give you the evil eye?"

"Cuban workers."

"Come on. Get real."

"I've always been superstitious, but I'm feeling lucky these days. It doesn't hurt to take precautions."

Chapter 14

It was late afternoon and Shane was studying the computer screen's sophisticated steganography. It still had him stumped. The scrambled letters and the numbers beside them had to be some sort of code.

What did it mean?

His mind drifted to Taylor, and he remembered looking at the photograph of a beautiful blonde and listening to Paul Ashton. They'd been sitting in a bar in Bogota's Soluna district.

Soluna, a melding of the Spanish word for sun—sol—and the Spanish word for moon—luna. That's what Colombia's drug lords wanted—the sun and the moon. So far, it looked as if they were going to get it.

"Taylor's my babe in Miami," Paul told him as he placed three pictures on the small table. "Of course, when I'm here, I have Miranda. She's one hot number. When I'm in Rio, there's Alia."

Shane had kicked back the dregs of his Tequila, unable to take his eyes off the picture of Taylor Maxwell. She reminded him of Heidi, a girl he'd gone to school with years ago.

Heidi had been intelligent and pretty in that refreshing girl-next-door way. Nothing had ever come of their relationship, but Shane often wondered what had happened to her.

Now there was Taylor gazing up at him from the photo, reminding him of the past and what it was like to care about someone. He had suddenly missed the real world. His work seemed oppressive and futile.

Could anyone ever get the best of these criminals?

"Got a woman here?" Paul asked.

"No. My trips are too quick. I fly in, broker a shipment of coffee beans, then I'm gone."

Posing as a coffee broker trying to secure steady supplies of coffee beans for the American market was Shane's DIA cover. He was actually working to cut off the stream of illegal drugs from Colombia that funded various terrorist organizations.

And flooded America with drugs.

Paul had picked up Taylor's picture and tucked it in his wallet along with photos of the other women he'd already bragged about. They'd all been pretty, but none of them had been as appealing as Taylor.

"For the right price, I can help you bring a load of coffee beans through rebel territory," Paul said.

"Not just any beans. Beans from the Obergon region. They have the acidity level we need."

Paul nodded, and Shane knew he'd passed the test. If he'd been faking being a coffee broker, he wouldn't have known Americans, unlike South Americans and Europeans, preferred coffee that was highly acidic.

"I'll get you what you need," Paul told him. "I'll ship them for you."

Shane haggled over the price—just for show—Paul had taken the bait. He intended to conceal cocaine in with the shipment of coffee beans.

After that day, Shane hadn't been able to get Taylor out of his mind. When he'd completed his mission, he'd flown straight to Miami and took Vince up on his job offer. Then he went to find Taylor. He'd expected the real woman to shatter the image he had in his head.

Just the opposite.

Taylor Maxwell was even more interesting in person than she'd been in a photograph. She had a complex personality that Ashton—the crazy son of a bitch—hadn't appreciated.

Shane had intended to satisfy his curiosity then leave, but seeing Taylor in person had taken his infatuation to a whole new level. Meeting her and getting to know her had made leaving impossible.

The phone on his desk rang, jolting him back to reality. "Shane?" the sultry voice asked. "It's Renata. I think something funny is going on down here in shipping. Could you come check?"

Apprehension waltzed up his spine in a way it hadn't done since he'd been assigned to the Colombian task force. Renata Rollins was cunning and deceitful, he thought. She might have discovered something or she might be playing a game.

Who knew?

Taylor nuzzled into her pillow, the noise threatening to awaken her, being kept at bay by the comforting down. It had been well after midnight when she'd fallen asleep. Disturbing images of her mother and Renata had kept her awake for hours.

"POLICE! OPEN UP!"

Taylor lifted her head from the pillow. Groggy. Surely she was dreaming. Cocking one ear to the side, she listened more closely.

"POLICE! OPEN UP!"

Oh, my God! She sat bolt upright, wondering if this was real. Or was this just another nightmare?

The clock on her nightstand said it was almost eight. She'd forgotten to set the alarm. She'd overslept and now she'd be late to the office.

She jumped out of bed, grabbed her robe, and trudged down the hallway toward the living room door. Peering through the peephole, she saw a police officer and a detective in a suit. The detective was holding his badge up for her to see.

Something must have happened to Trent, she decided, recalling what Doyle had told her about his arrest for possession. She swung open the door, asking, "What's going on?"

"I'm Detective Morse and this is Officer Jennings," the man said as he snapped his wallet shut and put it in his pocket. "Are you Taylor Maxwell?"

She managed to nod, a suffocating sensation tightening her throat.

"Where were you between nine o'clock last night and three this morning?" the detective asked.

"Right here? Why? What's this all about?"

"Was anyone with you?"

"No. I live alone."

Shane appeared, bringing Auggie back from his morning walk. "Taylor, is something wrong?"

Blood pounded in her temples and her knees quivered. Something was *terribly* wrong.

"I don't know. They haven't said what this is about."

Shane walked over to her side, and she had to admit she was enormously relieved to have him with her.

"What's the problem?" Shane asked.

"Renata Rollins was murdered last night."

"No!" Taylor gasped. How could she be dead? Renata had been so alive—so ambitious. So in your face. Could she possibly be dead?

"How? Where?" Shane wanted to know.

"She was shot in her sleep some time between nine last night when she went to bed and three in the morning. We're questioning people, checking alibis."

"I had no reason to kill her," protested Taylor. "I barely knew her."

"That isn't what Mr. Bassett says."

Shane put his arm around Taylor as they sat on her couch. The police had left, saying they were questioning everyone involved.

"Who would want to kill Renata?" Taylor asked.

"It could have been any number of people, even someone from New Orleans. Who knows?"

"You're right. Even Raoul talked about having her killed. Of course, it was just talk."

Shane wasn't nearly as positive as Taylor sounded. Who knew what a desperate person might do.

Anger glittered in her eyes as she gazed at him, asking, "Why would Caleb implicate me?"

"Good question. Did something happen yesterday morning when you visited your mother?"

"No . . . not exactly. Caleb did ask me why I'd come by the house the previous day. I had my excuse ready, but I don't think he believed me. I had the feeling he knew I'd been snooping in his room."

"Taylor, listen to me carefully." He pulled her a little closer, and she gazed up at him, concern etching her face. "You could be in serious trouble if they don't find the killer immediately. Your fingerprints are going to be all over that room."

"Oh, my God." She muffled a gasp with a clenched fist. "You're right. When I snatched the hair sample, I went through Renata's things."

Shane checked his watch. "Let's get to the office and see what Trent and Doyle say. It might be smart to contact an attorney now."

Shane stood in the back of Doyle Maxwell's office and watched as Doyle talked with Taylor and Trent. Off to one side stood Raoul and Brianna.

"We could all be in trouble," Doyle was saying. "None of us have alibis. Even Brianna spent last night at her mother's."

"Her heart's been acting up, and I'm the only one who can convince her to go to the hospital if necessary," explained Brianna. "You see, in Cuba, you went to the hospital to die."

"Then your mother is your alibi," Trent said.

"She was in the bedroom, and I slept on the living room sofa. I could have slipped out and she wouldn't have known, but why would I?"

Shane decided Brianna could have pulled the trigger if she realized how financially strapped her husband was. Getting rid of Renata before she could squelch a deal to sell the company could be the motive, but Shane believed this was a long shot.

"Honey," Doyle said to Brianna, "don't worry about it. Everyone knows you wouldn't kill a fly."

"Then why did the police question me?"

"They questioned all of us," Raoul said. "They're just gathering facts."

Shane studied Raoul and saw his pale blue eyes were glazed and his fingers were trembling slightly. Unless he missed his guess, the Cuban was sprung on meth.

"You two weren't together last night?" Shane asked Trent, watching Raoul out of the corner of his eye.

"No," Trent said, his voice so low he was almost whispering. "I was home by myself."

"We had a fight," Raoul said with a shrug. "I was out walking along Ocean Avenue."

Shane would bet the fight was over crystal meth. Raoul was getting hooked, and Trent wanted him to stop.

"What are the odds of this happening? None of us has an alibi," Brianna said.

"Shit happens," Shane said under his breath.

Doyle picked up the telephone. "I'm calling Alan Friedman. He's a first-rate criminal attorney. He'll know what to do."

It didn't take a rocket scientist to guess what the lawyer would tell them. Don't talk to the police without a lawyer being present.

"I called Mother," Trent said while Doyle contacted the attorney. "The doctor gave her a sedative and she was sleeping."

"I think we should go over there," Taylor said. "When she wakes up, she'll need us."

Shane drove Taylor to her mother's Coral Gables home. Yellow and black crime scene tape was strung across the driveway and yard. Uniformed officers were stationed at the front door. They let them inside, but told them most of the house was off-limits until the investigation was complete.

Caleb Bassett was standing in the hall just outside the door to Vanessa's bedroom. "What are you doing here?"

"I came to see my mother."

"She doesn't want to see you. Not after what you did."

Shane grabbed the front of Caleb's shirt and shoved

him up against the wall. "Don't you dare accuse Taylor. She—"

"Was jealous of Renata. Vanessa changed her will, leaving everything to Renata." Caleb glared at Taylor with sadistic intensity. "That's right. Everything. She loved my little girl, and now my baby's dead."

"I'm sorry about Renata," Taylor said, struggling to control her anger at his accusation. "I didn't kill her."

Taylor tiptoed into her mother's bedroom while Shane kept Caleb outside. The blackout drapes were drawn, the only light coming from the luminous dial on the bedside clock. She waited a moment until her eyes adjusted to the lack of light.

Taylor admitted she hadn't liked Renata, but she never wished the woman dead. Renata hadn't had a good life, and now she would never have a chance at making her life better.

Her mother's small frail shape was huddled into a fetal position beneath the covers. Oh, God, she thought. Renata's death would destroy her mother. She'd been so convinced the woman was her daughter.

"Caleb, is that you?" her mother called, her voice hoarse from crying.

"No, Mother. It's me." Taylor walked over to the bed and switched on the lamp on the nightstand.

Taylor bit back a gasp. Not only were her mother's beautiful blue eyes bloodshot and red from crying, all the color had leached out of her face. Her lips trembled as she attempted to speak.

"Should I call the doctor?" Taylor asked.

"N-n-no, there's nothing anyone can do. Renata's dead."

Taylor sat on the edge of the bed and took her

mother's hand. "I'm so sorry. It's such a tragedy. Renata had everything to live for, especially now."

"She was your sister, you know."

Half sister, Taylor mentally corrected her mother.

"We were just getting to know each other," Taylor fibbed. She hadn't wanted anything to do with the stripper who was trying to pass herself off as her half sister.

"I miss her so much." Tears seeped from her mother's eyes and trickled down her pale cheeks.

Taylor reached for a tissue on the nightstand, then gently dabbed away the tears. "Do the police have any idea about what happened?"

Her mother scooted into an upright position and Taylor helped adjust the pillows behind her head. "All they've said was that someone shot Renata at point-blank range."

"Did anyone hear the shot?"

"No. I didn't hear a thing. Neither did Caleb."

"Was there any sign of forced entry?"

"I don't know, but the burglar alarm wasn't on, and the gate to the pool area was unlocked. Anyone could have gotten in very easily."

"You're usually more careful," Taylor said before she could stop herself. "You always set the alarm."

"Not since Renata and Caleb came. Renata liked to go out to the clubs at night. She'd come home very late, and she didn't want to fool with the alarm. I got out of the habit of setting it."

"Did she go out last night?" Taylor asked, wondering if some nut had followed her home.

"No, she was exhausted from working in shipping, and she wanted to get to work early again. She kissed me good night around nine—"

Her mother's voice cracked and she gulped hard, tears again slipping down her cheeks.

"That was the last time I saw her. I'll never see her again. I'll never have the chance to make up for giving her away."

Taylor didn't know how to deal with her mother. She couldn't help wondering if her mother would be this upset had she been the one to die.

"Oh, Mom, don't be so hard on yourself. You did the best you could."

"No, by changing my will I may have put her life in danger." Tears still shimmered in her eyes, but her voice had the steely edge Taylor remember from her youth. "That's what Caleb says."

Caleb again. The man had far too much influence on her mother. Could she possibly be thinking someone in the family was responsible for Renata's death?

"You all knew I was going to change my will, didn't you?"

Taylor saw no point in denying it. "Yes, we did."

"Caleb warned me not to use Ridley Pudge. He was a family friend, and he would tell, but I wouldn't listen."

Caleb was right, she silently conceded.

Her mother's stare was so accusing, it sent a tremor through Taylor.

"Mother, surely, you don't think one of the family killed Renata."

"I don't know what's going on . . . I'm so heartsick. So confused."

"Mother, please don't think . . ." Taylor let the words trail off, not knowing what else to say and realizing Caleb had planted the seed of suspicion in her mother's mind.

"Caleb spoke to Renata last night just as she was going to bed. She told him she'd been threatened with death, and"—her brittle voice faltered—"Renata believed one of you was behind it."

"Who threatened her?"

"One of the Cubans in the shipping department, but she was just a messenger."

Taylor squeezed her mother's hand, puzzled by what she'd just heard. "I can't imagine why any of those Cuban women would threaten Renata. It doesn't make sense."

Her mother nodded very slowly, and Taylor could see just what a toll this had taken on her.

"Why would those women be mean to my girl?" her mother asked. "And what was Renata doing in the shipping department? It's miserable down there. Just miserable."

"She wanted to learn the business from the ground up," Taylor managed to say with a straight face. Undoubtedly Renata would have preferred to start in sales where she could sample all the products.

Her mother's pale blue eyes assessed her the way they had when she'd been a teenager and trying to get away with something.

"Renata never had a chance," her mother said, "to be all that she could be. All that she should have been."

Chapter 15

"Life isn't about the chances you're given. It's about the chances you take."

No-see'ums buzzed through the sultry night air, riding a beam of moonlight. In the distance, strains of salsa music blared from a radio tuned to WQBA, Miami's Spanish-language station.

"The preemptive strike was chancy given the short time I had to plan. But life isn't about waiting to be given a chance. It's about seizing the moment—making your own chances."

The wail of a police siren cut through the night. It wasn't coming this way. Why would it?

No one knew the truth, and no one ever would.

Who would be clever enough to figure it out?

Shane Donovan thought he was hot shit, but he didn't have a clue.

"With Renata dead, everyone is in a tailspin. Just the way I wanted it."

The radio clicked off and the sudden silence seemed oppressive to him. The dead air almost had a physical weight to it. The silence became louder and louder until it pounded in his brain like a drumbeat.

What was there about noise that comforted? In the distance, two alley cats geared up for a fight, yowling to the heavens in long, high-pitched screeches that were death threats.

Ah, that's better.

"Vanessa is really in agony. Just what I wanted. By the time I'm done, Vanessa will suspect everyone in the family of killing Renata—even Taylor, her own daughter. Little does she know I'm going to kill Taylor as well."

The cats were fighting now, clawing and screeching. The sounds ripped through the hot, thick night air like fingernails on a chalkboard.

Perfect music.

"Taylor doesn't have long to live and getting cozy with Shane Donovan isn't going to save her."

"My mother's so upset, so confused," Taylor said to Shane. "I think Caleb has convinced her one of us killed Renata."

"That man is nothing but trouble."

"Mother has known me my whole life. How could she think I could possibly harm anyone?"

"Did she come right out and accuse you of it?"

"No, but I could tell she was suspicious."

"She's not herself right now," Shane told her. "Caleb Bassett isn't helping."

It was after ten and they were sitting on Shane's sofa with Auggie at their feet. Shane's arm was around her, the way it had been almost constantly since they left her mother's home around noon.

He was so close she could smell the elusive citrus-like scent of his aftershave. Taylor was drawn to his strength. Suddenly, the intimacy she'd been working so hard to avoid seemed comforting.

Trent had taken off with Raoul, and she couldn't reach him. Her best friend, Lisa, was still missing in action even though the murder had made the head-lines of the *Miami Sun.* Brianna and Doyle were at the hospital with her mother, who'd taken a turn for the worse.

Shane Donovan was the only person she had right now. A steady, reliable man, she decided. She hadn't liked him at first, but she'd changed her mind.

The phone rang and Shane jumped up, saying, "I'll bet that's Vince."

He'd called Vince earlier in the day to get him to use his contacts on the police force to see what evi-dence they had. Taylor listened, watching Shane and noticing two deep lines of worry appear between his brows. Evidently it was Vince and what he was saying was upsetting.

"What's wrong?" she asked the second he hung up.

"Nothing really. It's a good new bad news deal."

He lowered himself into the place beside her and put his arm around her again. He kissed her forehead lightly.

"The bad news is the police found your fingerprints in Renata's room, which is no surprise."

It was impossible to steady her erratic pulse. "Are they going to arrest me?"

"No. The good news is they also found several sets of prints they haven't yet identified. Your brother's prints, as well as Raoul's, are also in the room."

"What? That's weird. I can't imagine why they would have been there."

His eyes darkened as he held her gaze. "You need to consider the possibility your brother might have killed her."

"No, not Trent. He couldn't."

Her protest didn't have as much conviction as she would have liked. More and more lately she'd discovered she didn't truly know her brother as well as she thought she did.

"That's all the police have—fingerprints. They're in the process of getting search warrants for the three of you as well as Doyle and Brianna. They'll be looking for the murder weapon."

"They won't find it at my place. I don't own a gun."

He frowned, his eyes level beneath drawn brows. "Do you know anything about Santería?"

"Not really. It's Cuban. A mix of voodoo and religion. I don't know much about it, but Brianna probably does. Why?"

"Vince said Renata was wearing an *arichanet* pin when she was murdered. It's a bead of jet that dangles from a gold bar."

"A pin on her nightgown? How odd."

"Apparently, it's supposed to help ward off a hex. What bothers me about it is Renata called me down to the shipping department just about closing time yesterday. She complained one of the Cuban women had put a hex on her. She wanted me to move her to another department."

"What did you tell her?"

"I told her to talk to you."

"She didn't contact me. Maybe she was waiting until the next day." Baffled, Taylor rested her head against Shane's sturdy shoulder. "The women in the shipping department are Cubans and they may believe in Santería, but I can't imagine them putting a curse on Renata. Why would they?"

"Good question, but I spoke with Renata and she was upset. She is—was—a very superstitious woman."

"Did she say who put the hex on her?"

"No." Shane shook his head. "I should have asked, but I didn't, and now it's too late."

"You know, a hex is one thing. Cubans can be very superstitious, but Caleb claims Renata told him her life had been threatened."

"Really? She told me the hex was supposed to bring bad luck. She didn't mention any death threat. Something must have happened after I left."

"I find it difficult to imagine Renata being frightened by a hex. She seemed too tough to me."

"She was superstitious enough to take the trouble to drive over to Calle Ocho. Vince says that's where those—*arichanet*—jet pins are found."

"If she'd been frightened, you'd think she would have bought a gun."

"Maybe she had. Who's to say she wasn't shot with her own gun, although that doesn't seem likely. How would the killer have known where she kept the gun?"

"You don't suppose Raoul Cathcart hired someone to kill Renata?" Taylor wondered out loud. "He claims to know the best hit man in Miami."

"A pro didn't shoot Renata. According to Vince's contact, a pillow was used to muffle the sound. A professional hit man would have had a silencer on the gun."

"I suppose you're right." She heaved herself to her feet. "It's been a long day. I'd better go."

"I'll walk you home."

Shane stood up and led her to the door. Auggie trotted behind them, wagging his tail, obviously hoping for a walk.

"I'm a light sleeper. If the police show up in the middle of the night with a search warrant, I'll be right over."

Clouds gloved the moon, and the light in the courtyard was out. Something moved in the shadows and Auggie lunged toward it. A tomcat streaked across the flagstones and disappeared into the bushes.

Shane chuckled. "Once Auggie wouldn't have dared chase a cat. He's becoming a regular dog now."

She paused to unlock her door, then turned to thank him for helping her today. She honestly didn't know what she would have done without him. Shane's gaze was as soft as a caress and just as seductive.

His lips dangerously close to hers, he traced the high arch of her cheekbones, then slowly eased the tips of his fingers into her hair. Suddenly, her blood thickened like warm honey. She knew he was going to kiss her, but she couldn't bring herself to pull away.

Gently covering her mouth, his lips pressed against hers. Strong arms drew her into the heat of his body, forcing her to acknowledge the hard length of his legs and powerful chest. His tongue brushed her lips, and with an inward sigh, she opened her mouth. Her arms slid upward, a scant inch at a time. Finally, one arm circled his neck while the other clung to his shoulders.

Shane's arms tightened around her as his tongue mated with hers. Desire, dark and urgent, swept through her, chasing away her attempt to think rationally. The longer he kissed her, the more she needed him to keep kissing her.

Too soon, he pulled back, and she heard her own serrated sigh with a surge of embarrassment. Lordy, what he could do to her without half trying.

"I'll be here tonight if you need me," he said, his voice slightly husky.

* * *

Taylor was in her nightgown and ready to climb into bed. Had she no willpower? Why couldn't she resist Shane?

She still loved Paul, didn't she? Becoming involved with another man felt as if she were betraying him.

"Get a grip," she mumbled to herself. "It's been almost three years. Life goes on. Just be careful. Take your time."

She heard a knock at the front door. Expecting the police with a search warrant, she threw on a robe and answered the door. Lisa stood there, smiling, a hot-pink shopping bag in her hand.

"Look what I've brought you," she said, walking into the apartment as she handed Taylor a paisley canister. "Here's my first product, Love Dust. It's dried ground honey and guarana. That's a root product from the rain forest. It looks like amber talcum powder, but it's totally edible."

Taylor couldn't believe her friend was rattling on about what was obviously some *Kama Sutra* product when Taylor's life was in such turmoil.

"You use the miniature feather duster inside to whisk the love dust all over his body. If he hasn't ravished you by then, you lick it off."

"Off who? What's this all about?"

She swallowed hard, trying to control her anger. She'd put off calling Lisa and asking her why she'd returned to Miami without contacting her. Now, here she was, practically accusing her of having an affair.

Lisa tossed her dark hair over her shoulder, a familiar gesture, but one that Taylor now found irritating.

"Come on. I was here half an hour ago. I saw you kissing that hunk. What was his name? Shane something. I left and went back to my shop to bring you the Love Dust."

"Oh, for God's sake. It was just a kiss." She put down the canister. "It didn't mean anything. I have too many problems to be thinking about men."

"Something's wrong. I can tell."

"What planet have you been on?"

Lisa's dark eyes darted back and forth. "I've been working day and night to get my shop up and running. I've been sleeping there on a futon. I know I haven't been around much . . ." She tried for a smile. "I'm sorry. What did I miss?"

"Everything."

Taylor flopped onto the sofa and patted the seat beside her for Lisa to sit down. She couldn't stay angry with Lisa for long. They'd been friends for too many years, been through too much. Lisa was hurting and using this *Kama Sutra* business to take her mind off her troubles.

It took Taylor a few minutes to tell Lisa all that had happened since they'd last seen each other. Taylor hadn't quite realized how monumentally her life had changed in such a short time. Lisa hadn't even met Renata and now she was dead.

"You're telling me the police suspect someone in your family killed Renata?" Lisa asked. "Unbelievable."

Taylor nodded slowly. She hadn't told Lisa about the fingerprints in the room or the Santería business. Undoubtedly Shane wouldn't want his sources compromised.

"Shane's a security expert," Taylor felt compelled to say. "He's working for the company. We've been having some problems with our computer security."

"Really?" Lisa's dark eyes were fixed on hers, and

Taylor tried to gauge her sincerity. "What kind of problems?"

"Sabotage. Messed-up invoices and stuff like that," she replied, skirting the whole truth. "Did Trent ever give you the computer codes?"

"No, and I wouldn't do anything like that."

The outrage in her friend's voice chilled Taylor. What was happening to her? She was beginning to suspect her brother of . . . well, not murder, but he could possibly be somehow involved. And now she was sounding as if she thought Lisa was behind the security breach.

"I was just wondering," she said, making this up as she went, "if Trent had them written down somewhere at home where they might have been stolen. I have the codes over there in my desk in case I need them."

"No, but he might have told Raoul. God only knows what he might do. He's, like, one of the biggest skanks around."

Taylor nodded, trying to appear as if she were considering this. Actually, she hadn't realized Lisa knew anything about Raoul Cathcart. Of course, any number of people might have told her.

"I wasn't totally honest about when I returned," Lisa said, her voice troubled. "I came back to Miami and had a private detective look into Trent's new life. I wanted to know where I'd gone wrong before I could truly let go of the past."

"Oh, Lisa, there's nothing you could have done. My brother is gay. He tried to fight it, and I'm sure he loved you as best he could. I think my father's death freed him, allowing Trent to finally live his life the way he wanted."

"I know," Lisa replied in a broken whisper. "I'm okay with it now."

Taylor wonder if she really was okay with losing

Trent. Thinking of Paul, she knew how hard it was to get on with your life when someone you loved was taken away.

"The Buddhists call it *bodhichitta*, which is a Sanskrit word for the openness of heart and mind. I opened my heart and mind to the truth. I hadn't failed at love nor had love failed me. You have to accept your fate, your destiny. Some things are not meant to be.

"That doesn't mean I don't care about Trent. He's a wonderful person. I don't understand what he sees in Raoul—other than he's drop-dead gorgeous."

"Trent and Raoul were picked up by the police last week for possession of crystal meth," Taylor said. "It was my brother's first arrest and hopefully his last, but if Raoul has a previous record, it could be a problem."

"Can't you talk to him?"

"I'll try. Believe me, I'll try."

"That's all you can do."

They sat in silence for a few minutes. They'd missed so much of each other's lives in the year Lisa had been away. Taylor felt their friendship ebbing away. They needed to reconnect, spend time together.

"Tell me about your business," Taylor asked. "You have a shop. Where?"

"Right here in SoBe on Fifth Street just off Ocean."

"Great location."

Taylor thought about the wonderfully restored art deco buildings in the area. After decades of neglect the pastel colored buildings had been restored. Versace had started the trend, and after his tragic murder, the renovation of SoBe's architectural treasures became his legacy.

"I have several products being produced for me like the Love Dust."

"How'd you know what to do and where to go?" Taylor was slightly insulted Lisa hadn't come to her.

Producing a product and getting it packaged wasn't easy, but after her years at Maxx, she knew exactly what to do.

"I hired a consultant. I didn't want to bother you," Lisa said. "You need to spend your spare time working on your computer game. I contacted Jim Wilson."

"Why would you call him? My father fired him when he worked for us." She didn't add that he was one of the people she suspected of tampering with their computers.

"Do you know why your father fired Jim?" Lisa asked, her voice pitched low.

"Not exactly. My father rarely fired anyone. He must have had a good reason."

Lisa started to say something, then stopped, looking away.

"What aren't you telling me?" Taylor asked.

Her friend looked at her again. "I thought you knew. Jim was fired because he was having an affair with your mother."

A wild flash of disbelief ripped through her, but the concerned expression on Lisa's face made her think. When Jim had been fired, Taylor had been so wrapped up in Paul Ashton that she hadn't been paying attention to much else.

"I didn't realize. I—"

A loud knock on the door interrupted her. This time it was the police.

Chapter 16

"Have you fixed the computer problem yet?" Doyle asked Shane.

"I'm working on it," Shane told him. "It's much more complicated than we originally thought."

"Maybe we should get someone else to help you."

Shane cursed under his breath. The fewer people who knew about the coded writing hidden on To The Maxx's Web site, the better. Now he had no choice but to tell Doyle what he'd found or risk having him hire another person. Vince had been helping him, but when Renata was murdered, the family wanted Vince to work on the case.

"Pull up a chair," Shane said. "I need to show you something."

It took a few minutes to explain the situation to Doyle. As they talked and watched the screen, Shane decided Doyle knew nothing about this. He seemed genuinely shocked and upset.

"This just keeps getting better and better, doesn't it?" Doyle stood up. "I guess I'll have to come up with another excuse not to meet with the prospective buyers."

"Tell them there's been a death in the family."

"Right. They've probably read about it in the papers by now," Doyle said as he walked away.

MURDER IN PARADISE had been the banner headline in the *Miami Sun*. Shane had scanned the article. It threw suspicion directly on family members—especially Taylor.

The paper made a big deal of Taylor's home being searched, as well as the loft Raoul and Trent shared. They speculated the police were looking for the murder weapon, which was correct. But the authorities had been able to keep secret the reason these homes had been searched was linked to the fingerprints at the crime scene.

He didn't know about Trent's loft, but Taylor's apartment looked like an explosion in a Chinese laundry when the police had finished. He'd stayed up most of the night helping Taylor put things away.

The police hadn't found the gun yet, but they still considered Taylor and Trent to be prime suspects. Shane wouldn't be surprised to learn Trent and Raoul had killed Renata, but he knew Taylor had nothing to do with it.

They were getting closer each day, and he liked the way their relationship was developing. This was exactly what he had in mind when he'd moved here to find Taylor.

What he needed to do now was to discover who killed Renata. Until the murder was solved, Taylor would be under constant pressure. She wouldn't be able to lead a normal life.

Hell, who could?

Reporters swarmed around the office and their apartment building. The police could drop by at any moment. He'd lived under pressure like this—worse, actually—but Taylor hadn't.

She was a strong woman, but being in the center of a murder investigation and having her own mother suspect her, coupled with problems at the office was enough to emotionally cripple anyone.

Vince walked up unexpectedly, saying, "The police questioned the Cuban women in the shipping department. One of them admitted she'd hexed Renata."

"Why?"

"It seems someone who spoke Spanish called her and offered her a thousand dollars to scare Renata. Half the money was delivered to her home by a messenger service. The other half came after she spent the day hassling Renata."

Shane rocked back in his chair and gazed at Vince. "She doesn't know who it was. Right?"

"You got it. The messenger service reports a woman dropped off the money, paid in cash, and they don't have any idea who she was."

"What could the woman in shipping say that would frighten someone like Renata? I was around her quite a bit. She wouldn't scare easily."

"Apparently, Renata had always been superstitious. Maybe she wasn't really frightened, just wary and superstitious." Vince grinned, slowly shaking his head. "Hey, I've lived here all my life. A lot of Cubans take Santería seriously."

Shane had spent enough time in small villages in South America to know how superstitious people could be.

"Santería is white magic. You know, good magic, not black magic. That's Macumba, an evil form of Santería."

"Was it what the Cuban woman used on Renata?"

"Apparently. The pin Renata was wearing is most often used on babies to ward off the evil eye. Even YUCAs—young urban Cuban Americans—who are educated and affluent put those orichanets on their babies. When you're very young you're vulnerable, is the theory."

"Go figure." Shane stared at the computer screen for a moment. "This code thing has me stumped. I want to make a copy and send it to a buddy of mine in the DIA."

Vince nodded. They both had been trained by the Defense Intelligence Agency but had worked in different fields. Shane knew someone who specialized in computers and used a sophisticated DIA computer to crack codes.

"While we wait for the results, I want to help you with this investigation." He didn't add his real reason was clearing Taylor.

"Okay, start with Trent and Raoul. See if they can explain why their prints were in Renata's room. I've found a contact who copied the files at the psychiatric hospital where Raoul Cathcart was treated. I'm going to meet her this afternoon."

"You're not going to believe what just happened."

Doyle looked up from his desk and saw Taylor at his office door. Her stricken expression twisted his guts. What now?

"Come in and shut the door."

Taylor did as she'd been told, her motions jerky like a robot. He knew she'd been up all night and had told her to take the day off, but she wouldn't listen. A major vendor had flown in from the West Coast. She had to meet with him.

"I just ran over to see how Mother is doing. Caleb says she doesn't want to see me—or any of us until the killer is caught."

"Did she tell you this herself?" Doyle didn't like Caleb, hadn't from the moment they'd met.

"No, he claimed she was asleep, and I believe him. He said she was angry with me for sneaking into the house to get the hair samples for the DNA test. He called me a conniving brat who was interested only in my mother's money. If I'd really cared about her, I would have been nicer to Renata."

"I guess the police told them your explanation for why your prints were at the scene."

"Probably. Does it matter how they found out? With Caleb living there, spewing venom, she's not likely to be open-minded. He has altogether too much influence over my mother."

Something clicked in the back of Doyle's mind. Brianna had mentioned the relationship between Vanessa and Caleb seemed odd to her, but she didn't know what about it was bothering her. He trusted his wife's instincts.

Something was wrong.

"You're right. Caleb does have too much influence over your mother. He used Renata to get close to her. Even in death, he's going to use your mother. They'll have to plan the funeral and grieve together."

"You're assuming Caleb is really Renata's father, and he's actually mourning her."

"They didn't seem to have a father-daughter type relationship. That doesn't mean Caleb can't fake grief. With all of us on the suspect list, Caleb is the only person your mother can lean on."

Taylor remained silent for a moment. "Could Caleb have killed Renata?"

"Why would he? She was the one who was going to inherit from your mother, not Caleb. With her gone, what does he get?"

"You're right. I'm betting they were fakers. They were planning to split the money. Being the mooch he is, Caleb will hang on and live off Mother for as long as possible. Remember, he wasn't working in New Orleans. Renata supported them by stripping."

Doyle hated to see Vanessa go to her grave alienated from the daughter who loved her. Trent was a different story. He hardly knew what went on in his nephew's head these days.

Barefoot, hair tousled, Trent answered the door to his loft in the trendy section of SoBe near where Shane lived. Trent hadn't come in to work today, and his machine was picking up his calls. Shane figured Trent was avoiding the media and drove over to his home.

"Something wrong?" Trent asked.

"Nothing new. I wanted to talk to you for a minute."

Trent stood aside and Shane walked in, instantly noticing the open drawers and emptied bookcases. Visible from the entry, the kitchen appeared to have every cabinet open, the contents tossed on the counter. Odd, Trent seemed like the kind of guy who would have cleaned up immediately after the police searched.

"I'm helping Vince investigate Renata's murder. The sooner we find out who really killed her, the better off you and Taylor will be."

"Don't the police have any new leads? They didn't find the gun here or at Taylor's. When are they going to look into that woman's background and see who might have wanted her dead?''

Shane didn't blame Trent for being bitter. All of Miami was talking about the case and pointing the finger at Trent or Taylor. It would dog them the rest of their lives if the killer wasn't found.

"According to our sources, the police don't have any new leads. They're relying on the fingerprints in the bedroom as the first and most important clues. There are a few sets they haven't identified yet. We may get a break there.''

Trent cleared a space on the sofa and flopped down. His eyes—so much like Taylor's—were bloodshot and puffy. Shane doubted he'd gotten much sleep last night, either.

"I need to ask you why your fingerprints and Raoul's were in Renata's room.''

"I'll tell you what I told the police.''

Shane couldn't help wondering if what he was going to hear would be the truth. He also wondered why Vince's contact at police headquarters hadn't told him about Trent's excuse.

"We were over for dinner last week. To be friendly, Raoul asked to see the dresses Renata had bought at Miami Spice. She took us to the guest suite and showed us a dozen new outfits. Dresses, shoes, bags—the works.''

"Your mother and Caleb must have explained this to the police. If there was a reasonable explanation for your prints being at the crime scene, your place would never have been searched.''

Trent heaved a sigh. "Just my luck. Mother and Caleb were in the den playing mah-jong when we told them good night. We were going dancing at Amnesia with Renata. Before leaving, we stopped to check out her new clothes. They didn't see us go into the room.''

Okey dokey, this was going to get ugly. Shane thought Trent was telling the truth.

But who knew?

No alibis. Fingerprints at the scene. A motive to kill. Taylor and Trent and good old Raoul had run out of luck. Or put it another way. How could the killer be so lucky?

"I have a few questions for Raoul," he said. "Know where I can find him?"

Trent closed his eyes for a moment, then stared up at the loft's exposed steel beams. "Unless it's the police, no one is allowed to see him for a week. I checked him into a rehab clinic in Key Largo this morning."

Shane nodded, recalling Taylor's confiding in him about the drug arrest. The last time he'd seen Raoul, the guy had appeared to be sprung on meth, as they said in SoBe.

"That's what you two were fighting about the night Renata was killed."

"Yes. I told Raoul we were through unless he got help. He finally agreed."

Shane left Trent in the loft staring up at the ceiling. He suspected Trent knew how difficult it was to get a person off meth once they were hooked.

His cell phone vibrated; it was Vince.

"I have the report from the clinic. It seems Raoul tried to commit suicide several times. That's why he was hospitalized."

Shane wondered if Trent knew this. If so, he had more reason to worry. Meth screwed up the best of minds. Troubled ones were history.

"Get this," Vince continued as Shane walked along the crowded street, his phone pressed against his ear. "His wealthy girlfriend checked him in and paid for the clinic."

To start your membership, simply complete and return the Free Book Certificate. You'll receive your Introductory Shipment of FREE Zebra Contemporary Romances. Then, each month as long as your account is in good standing, you will receive the 3 newest Zebra Contemporary Romances. Each shipment will be yours to examine for 10 days. If you decide to keep the books, you'll pay the preferred book club member price of $15.95 – a savings of up to 20% off the cover price! (plus $1.99 to offset the cost of shipping and handling.) If you want us to stop sending books, just say the word… it's that simple.

BOOK CERTIFICATE

Yes! Please send me FREE Zebra Contemporary romance novels. I only pay for shipping and handling. I understand I am under no obligation to purchase any books, as explained on this card.

Name _____

Address _____ Apt. _____

City _____ State _____ Zip _____

Telephone (____) _____

Signature _____

(If under 18, parent or guardian must sign)

Offer limited to one per household and not valid to current subscribers.
All orders subject to approval. Terms, offer, and price subject to change. Offer valid only in the U.S.

Thank You!

CN112A

PLACE
STAMP
HERE

Ill..l..l..lll....lll.l..l.ll.l..l..ll.l..l..lll..l.l

Zebra Contemporary Romance Book Club
Zebra Home Subscription Service, Inc.
P.O. Box 5214
Clifton , NJ 07015-5214

"Girlfriend? He's gay."

"Not back then apparently. The psychiatrist's notes were full of how much he loved this girl and wanted to marry her. She'd dumped him. That's why he tried to kill himself."

"How long ago was this?"

"Almost three years."

"No mention of any homosexual tendencies?"

"None. He could have discovered his true feelings when he moved from Palm Beach down here."

"Possibly. Or maybe he's bisexual. I'm told that's very in these days." Shane dodged a group of Japanese tourists with garlands of cameras around their necks.

"He could be stringing Trent along to get the money to set himself up in business."

Shane returned to the office and copied the material off the computer to send to the DIA. He called his friend or mentor, really—the man who'd trained him to use the sophisticated new field computers developed by the Defense Department to track terrorists.

Hank Olfeld had agreed to put the information into the agency's computer, but it would have to be done in off-time, when the DIA didn't need to use the computer. Best guess was, it would take several days, maybe as long as a week, to decode the expertly hidden material.

Shane didn't mind. The way this murder case was progressing, he could use his time to clear Taylor.

"Dios mio!"

Shane turned and saw Brianna sailing down the hall. He jumped up. "What's the matter?"

Brianna saw him and stopped. "I was listening to Cristina being interviewed about her television show tonight."

Shane hadn't been in Miami long, but even he knew "Cristina" was Cristina Saralegui, the Latina talk show host who was wildly popular in Miami.

"Experts are going to roast the police for not immediately arresting Taylor and Trent and taking them in for paraffin tests."

"Test for gunpowder residue just because their fingerprints were at the murder scene, when both of them had been in the house and might have entered the room. No way." Shane raked his fingers through his hair. "I'll bet the cops had a hard time convincing a judge to issue a warrant based solely on the prints."

"This is just going to make more trouble for them."

"Got that right," he said as she rushed off to Doyle's office.

Shane turned to finish getting the material for Hank. The front office receptionist rushed up to him, a FedEx envelope in her hand.

"This just came for you."

"Great." He took it, thankful he'd insisted on written DNA results. He'd figured Vanessa would need to see it in writing to believe it.

Chapter 17

"Graveyard shift. Saved by the bell. Dead ringer. Which is best?" Taylor asked Auggie.

She was in her apartment, working late on her computer game to take her mind off the murder. Shane hadn't come home, but he'd given her a key and asked her to take out Auggie. The dog was great company, making her realize how much she wanted a dog of her own.

She reread the information and tried to condense it down to a single line for her computer game. In medieval times so many people had been buried alive—by mistake—that people were interred with a string around their wrist. It led up through the coffin and dirt to the ground above, where it was attached to a bell.

Someone assigned to the "graveyard shift" would listen and know when a person was "saved by the bell" or was a "dead ringer." Fascinating, she thought, but she couldn't see how to put the information into a single line for her Trivial Moments game. She set it aside for the longer answer trivia game forming in her mind.

She went on to the next bit of trivia on her list, still reading out loud to Auggie. "People in the Middle Ages married in June because they took their yearly bath in May. They were still smelling pretty good by June, but to make sure brides carried bouquets to hide any body odor."

Taylor couldn't help giggling and thinking how traditions like this had evolved through time. These days a bridal bouquet was a work of art, and brides spent hours at a spa pampering every inch of their bodies before the wedding.

The knock on her door caused her to flinch. The media had hounded her all day long. They'd left several hours ago, but she expected them to return tomorrow.

Until another suspect surfaced, she was in the spotlight.

A cautious glimpse through the peephole revealed Shane. She swung open the door with Auggie at her side. The dog's tail swished through the air, and he danced on his hind legs as Shane walked into the apartment.

"I took Auggie for a walk, then brought him over here. I didn't want him to be lonesome," she said, but in reality she'd been the one who'd been lonely.

"Hey, boy." Shane bent down and ruffled Auggie's ears with both hands. "Miss me?"

"Of course he misses you. Bring him to the office. No one will care."

Shane rose to his feet and gazed into her eyes. Something in Taylor's brain clicked.

Bad news.

"Shane, what's wrong?"

He led her to the sofa, saying, "Nothing's wrong . . . exactly." They sat down, and he put his arm around her. "The DNA report came back."

"What were the results?"

"Renata is—was—your mother's daughter. No question about it. The DNA matches."

A suffocating sensation tightened her throat. Oh, my God. The woman she'd despised had been her sister. Half sister. Still, they'd been related, and Taylor had never given herself a chance to get to know Renata.

"I treated her so badly," Taylor whispered.

Shane pulled her close. "Don't be too hard on yourself. Just because she was the missing baby doesn't mean she was a good person. I think it was pretty obvious she intended to take what she could get."

Blurred shapes throbbed and swirled, swarming through Taylor's brain. Renata stripping. Renata sitting next to Caleb. Renata with her mother.

Taylor's mother.

Their mother.

"I wonder what kind of life she had. It couldn't have been good. She ended up working as a stripper."

A surge of guilt expanded in her chest, crushing the air out of her lungs. It took a minute for her breath to return.

"I had every advantage, every opportunity. She had nothing."

His large hand cradled her face. "Don't beat yourself up. What could you have done? Your mother gave her away."

The heartrending tenderness in his gaze startled her. She'd known he was attracted to her, but now the look in his eyes said so much more. It was as if he cared about her and had been concerned how this news would affect her. Touched, she looked down at Auggie, not knowing what to say.

"Your mother was *so* sure Renata was her daughter," Shane said. "Caleb had to have told her something over the telephone to convince her."

"Do you think Caleb adopted Renata the way he claims?"

"The records show he had a daughter, but was she Renata?" Shane shook his head. "I doubt it. They don't have a father-daughter relationship. More likely, they hooked up somewhere and Renata told him the story."

"I think you're right. A father wouldn't laze around while his daughter worked as a stripper."

"True, but there are men around who are real users. They'll say anything to a woman, do anything to get what they want."

Something in his eyes, his voice, alerted her. Was he trying to tell her something? She thought about it for a moment and decided he was warning her about Caleb.

"Just because Renata's dead doesn't mean Caleb's leaving, does it?"

"I'd be blown away if he did," Shane said. "He's gotten tight with your mother. Now he'll make himself indispensable."

Taylor rested her head against Shane's shoulder and tried to think. She kept seeing Renata, a hard, bitter woman, and wishing she had done something to make up for Renata's past. Despite Shane's reassuring words guilt gnawed at her.

Why hadn't she given Renata a chance? Taylor had been too quick to condemn her as an impostor. She closed her eyes, her heart aching.

She could have helped Renata so much. Maybe she

had been interested in the business. Taylor could have taught her all about Maxx.

Instead, she'd condemned her to "shipping hell" as the workers called it. There she'd sweated out the last day she was alive and had her life threatened.

Why? Why? Why?

"I've sent the codes on your company's Web site to a guy I know in the Defense Intelligence Agency," Shane said, breaking into her thoughts.

Taylor opened her eyes and lifted her head off his shoulder. She recalled seeing the screen saver on his laptop when they'd been in New Orleans. The initials DIA were on the screen.

"Did you once work for the DIA?"

This close, Taylor saw the minute stitches of black in Shane's blue eyes. She also detected a flicker of something in those eyes. It lasted only a split second, but Taylor had the distinct impression Shane was weighing whether or not to tell her the truth.

"Yes, I was with the Cobra Force. It's an antiterrorist unit formed way, way back before we knew just how big a terrorist problem we were going to have. The Cobra Force members are trained by the military, then operate out of the Defense Intelligence Agency."

"What did you do with them?"

Again something flashed in his eyes.

"Most of the time we concentrated on the drug cartels. A stunning amount of drug profits goes to terrorists groups."

"Really?"

"You bet. Terrorists often control the land where coca trees or poppies are grown. Drug cartels pay them a lot to produce the stuff."

"I remember reading the only good thing the Taliban did in Afghanistan was to stop the poppy growing."

"They're the exception that proves the rule. Most terrorist groups support drug cartels. It's an important source of income."

From the very beginning, she'd sensed an air of mystery about Shane. He was a good man to have on her side, she decided.

A dangerous man if crossed.

A man with secrets.

"Part of what I did required extensive knowledge of military field computers. That's why I'm working with Vince now, but I'm not an expert with codes. While my friend works on the codes, I'm going to help Vince with the murder investigation."

"Do the police have any new leads?"

"No, and I think they're spending too much time trying to pin it on you or Trent because of the fingerprints. They aren't developing new leads. Trouble could have followed Renata from New Orleans or wherever she was before that."

"Caleb might be very helpful, if he's willing to cooperate." Taylor thought a moment, concerned about her lack of an alibi. "Won't these DNA results convince the police I went into Renata's room to get hair samples?"

"Possibly, but I believe they're looking at motive. Except for crimes of passion, money is the number one reason people kill each other."

Something inside Taylor fractured into a thousand jagged pieces. Renata, who never had anything, probably died because their mother had changed her will.

"Renata died because she stood to inherit a large sum of money."

"Not necessarily," Shane said, his arm still circling her shoulders.

He tapped on her forearm, thinking. "We obtained a copy of the new will. Your mother didn't leave Renata

money. She left her fifty percent of To The Maxx.
That's your mother's share of the company. Right?''

"Yes. My father willed half to her, and the rest is
evenly split between uncle Doyle, Trent, and me.''

"If Renata had inherited those shares, she could
have prevented the sale of the company. That may be
the reason she was killed.''

"True . . .'' Taylor stopped herself from saying: Why
would she?

"Renata may have been genuinely interested in
learning the business. I was so quick to judge her. So
determined not to like her. If only I'd given her a
chance.''

"Stop it.''

Shane gathered her against his warm body and
pressed his lips to hers, caressing her mouth more
than kissing it. She inhaled the sweetness of his kiss
and admitted to herself that she'd been longing to
have him kiss her again. She'd tried not to be attracted
to him, she honestly had, but it didn't work.

A series of slow, shivery kisses made her pulse skitter,
a fluid warmth seeping through her. The quivery heat
spread, and desire, pure and elemental, invaded every
inch of her body.

"Aw, hell. I can't get enough of this,'' Shane whispered.

"Don't stop,'' she heard herself say.

His tongue melding with hers, Shane cupped her
breast with one hand, and the nipples instantly peaked.
A tiny moan escaped her throat. She couldn't resist
spearing her fingers through his thick hair. It sifted
between her fingers, wavy and surprisingly soft.

This time he groaned, a low rumble deep in his
chest. She couldn't help smiling inwardly, proud of
her feminine power over a man who outmatched her
physically.

He was teasing a nipple through her lacy bra before she even realized he'd unbuttoned her blouse. She clutched a fistful of his hair with one hand. She let the other coast down his torso.

His impressive chest felt as hard to the touch as it looked. Beneath her fingertips, his heart beat with rapid, pounding thuds. Her hand came to rest on his muscular thigh.

"Go for it." He lifted her hand from his thigh to the iron heat of his sex.

"What's this? A mouse in your pocket?" She tried for a joke, but her voice sounded raw, thick.

"Oh, hush."

She gripped him hard, not quite able to feel him the way she wanted through his slacks. He groaned, a moan so deep it almost sounded as if he were in pain.

She nudged her hand inside his pants and stroked his turgid penis through his cotton underwear. She slid her thumb inside the soft fabric and caressed the velvet tip of his penis.

For a second, he froze.

Then he bent down to kiss her breast. Sucking a nipple through the sheer lace of her bra, he slid his hand under her skirt.

She was already moist, aching for his touch when his fingers found the wet heat between her thighs. With expert precision, he stroked her.

"You're awfully good at this," she whispered.

"I'm inspired."

Waves of sensation built, lifting her as if she were weightless. The next instant, release hit her with a mind-numbing geyser of golden light, a glorious jolt of pure pleasure. It sapped every ounce of tension from her body, and she slumped bonelessly against the sofa.

"No way. We're just getting started."

Shane ripped off his clothes and had hers in a pile beside the sofa in an instant. Suddenly, she was flat on her back, the powerful length of his body pressed against hers.

He thrust deep inside her, then burrowed farther. A second ago, she'd been sated, ready to fall asleep. Now her heart lurched, then pounded so furiously she could feel it throb in her temples.

In a heartbeat, desire hit a flash point, almost out of control.

She clutched his shoulders, digging her nails into his bare skin, and arched upward as his hips hammered away, driving her toward yet another pinnacle.

"Don't stop," she cried out, although she had no indication he could be stopped.

Her body contracted, a flood tide of pleasure washing over her, cresting. She cried out, "Oh, yes!"

Slowly the sensation retreated, leaving her languid. A moment later, Shane threw his head back with a guttural moan and squeezed his eyes shut. He went rigid, every muscle tensed, his face a grimace. His breath rasped, a serrated sound that filled the room.

After a minute, he opened his eyes and gazed down at her. "All I can say is—wow!"

"Wow doesn't quite cover it."

"Are you complaining? We can try to improve on it. We'd have more room in your bed."

He stood up and gave the mesmerized Auggie a quick pat. His penis hung heavily between his powerful thighs. He was so masculine, so heart-stoppingly male, that her throat constricted.

When had she last felt this glad to be in a man's arms? It had been so long.

Too long.

Chapter 18

Shane stood beside Taylor the following morning as they waited for someone to answer the door at her mother's house. He'd spent the night with her. Most of the time they'd gone at it like minks in heat—not that he'd ever witnessed minks screwing, but word was out on those little critters.

When they'd taken breaks and talked, Taylor had continued to express guilt about Renata. Nothing he said could make her feel any better.

He didn't think she should blame herself. Who would have guessed?

Renata didn't look like her mother, and no one could prove she was the missing baby. But Taylor, for all her success in the business world, had a sensitive side.

He liked her all the more for it. Aw, hell. Who was he kidding? He'd fallen in love with her.

He should be grateful Taylor's guilt was focused on Renata. He'd half expected her to regret making love to him, because of Paul Ashford.

The worthless son of a bitch.

"Missy, so happy you come," Maria said with a Spanish accent as she opened the door.

Shane noticed the glimmer of tears in the maid's eyes. Uh-oh. Now what? He put his hand on the small of Taylor's back.

"What's the matter, Maria?" Taylor asked.

"Your mother . . . *mala.*"

Mala. Bad.

Shane listened as Maria told Taylor in broken English. There had been a mix-up at the lab. The test results Taylor's mother had received belonged to someone else. Her blood work showed she had taken a turn for the worse.

Shit.

The doctor had called yesterday with the bad news. Beneath his hand, Taylor's body went rigid. Shane knew she was upset because her mother hadn't contacted her.

"Where is she?" Taylor asked, concern etching her beautiful face.

"Bed."

"Is she asleep?"

Maria shook her head. Shane followed Taylor through the quiet house to the master bedroom suite.

"Mother, it's me," Taylor called softly from the sitting room adjacent to the master bedroom. "Shane's with me. May we come in?"

It was a long moment before a faint "yes" came from the bedroom. Taylor led the way into the nearly dark room. The shades were drawn, blocking out the scorching Miami sun. The only light came from a small lamp on the nightstand next to the bed.

Vanessa Maxwell's head was propped up by a bank of lavender pillows. All the color had vanished from her face, leaving it the color of wax. Her blue eyes were glazed. Shane figured she was on heavy-duty pain medication.

"Mother, why didn't you call me?"

"I didn't want to bother you or Trent. You have enough problems right now. You don't need mine." Vanessa's tone was chillier than usual by several degrees.

Taylor sat on the bed beside her mother and took her hand. "I love you. Nothing in my life is more important than you."

Shane waited for Vanessa to say she loved Taylor, but the woman merely gave a wan excuse for a smile.

"Tell me what Dr. Field said."

"They gave me the wrong blood test results. I'm actually severely anemic."

"Is it bad enough to warrant a blood transfusion?" Vanessa nodded.

Christ! Shane swore under his breath. He knew during the advanced stages of myeloma patients became severely anemic and required blood transfusions. Their immune systems went wacko, and they had to have chemotherapy or they would die.

Even with chemo, it was a terminal illness.

Taylor was in for a rough go. He planned to be at her side the whole way.

"Have the police found out who killed my baby?" Vanessa asked.

"No. Apparently, they don't have any new leads. Vince and Shane are working on it. We *all* want to find Renata's killer."

Vanessa didn't answer, but she was looking at her daughter with reproachful eyes. How could she possibly think—for one second—Taylor had anything to do with Renata's murder?

He knew every plane, every line, every nuance of Taylor's face. If her feelings were hurt, she didn't show it. She continued to gaze at her mother with a loving expression.

"My fingerprints were in Renata's room because I went in there to get hair for a DNA test."

"I know. The police told me how you explained the prints. I guess they're still suspicious because your prints were in so many places."

Taylor glanced at him, and he tried to reassure her with a slight nod. Evidently, Caleb was slowly poisoning Vanessa's mind. How long would it be until she openly accused Taylor of murder?

"I know it was wrong, but I looked through her things. That's why my fingerprints were all over the place."

"What did you expect to find?"

"Proof she wasn't your daughter." Shane heard Taylor's quick intake of breath. "I was wrong. The DNA results came back late yesterday. Renata was your daughter."

Suddenly, tears brimmed in Vanessa's eyes. "I never doubted it for one moment."

"How could you be so sure?" Shane asked, speaking for the first time.

Vanessa hesitated for a second, then said, "Instinct. Mothers know things, feel things."

"I'm truly sorry I didn't get the chance to know her," Taylor said.

"You would have liked Renata. She was a wonderful, intelligent person," Vanessa told Taylor, a hint of censure in her tone.

"You're right. I'm sure I would have liked her."

Shane had a real problem with this, but he kept his

mouth shut. Just because Renata was her daughter did not elevate the woman to sainthood.

Caleb Bassett sauntered into the room. "What are you doing here?"

Just the sight of the jerk made Shane want to piss in his gas tank or punch his lights out. Something.

"I'm visiting my mother," Taylor answered.

"You should be at the station, helping the police."

A curse clawed its way up Shane's throat, but he managed to bank it. Taylor was a pro. She could handle this man. If not, Shane was here for backup.

"They've searched my apartment. I've answered every question."

"She's done everything she could," Shane added.

Caleb shot him a look that was close to a death threat. Shane damn near grabbed the bastard by his throat, but he knew a fight would only drive a bigger wedge between Taylor and her mother.

Caleb's dark eyes cut to Vanessa, and he beamed her a smile. "How are you feeling?"

"Weak. Too weak to do anything but lay here."

"When are you going for the transfusion?" Taylor asked. "It'll give you strength."

"She's due there at one," Caleb answered.

"I'll take you," Taylor said.

"No. Caleb is taking me."

They were standing outside Vanessa's house talking twenty minutes later. Shane knew Taylor would have stayed longer, but after Caleb had come into the room Vanessa became colder by the moment.

"She thinks I killed Renata," Taylor said yet again. "I can't believe it."

Shane pulled her into his arms and hugged her.

She leaned into him, needing to be comforted. Holding her felt so damn right.

"She never actually accused you, but I agree. Caleb has your mother seriously considering the possibility. We're going to find the killer. Then she'll know the truth."

"We've got to hurry. I've worked with the local myeloma chapter, and I've seen myeloma patients go down fast once they reach this point."

"Okay, I'll get right on it."

He reluctantly let her go, and they walked to their cars, promising to keep in touch by cell phone if anything came up. As he drove off to interview Jim Wilson, the man who'd been fired from the company over his affair with Vanessa, Shane thought about Taylor's mother.

She could be a bitch.

Vanessa had seemed charming when he'd first met her, and Shane admitted he hadn't paid much attention to her. He'd been too focused on Taylor. Now that he'd been around her more, he understood why some people didn't like her.

Get over it.

Vanessa was Taylor's mother, and Taylor loved her. He'd do whatever he could to make Taylor happy. Their relationship was progressing just the way he had hoped.

She didn't need to know how he'd found his way into her life. Man, oh, man. He'd have to tell her eventually. But now wasn't the time.

Taylor had all the bad news she could handle.

Doyle prided himself for holding his temper in check while Trent pitched some half-baked shampoo that didn't lather. Another one of Raoul's ideas.

"We're selling the company soon. We don't have the time or the money to develop another product." He steepled his fingers and gazed across the desk at his nephew, and decided now was the time to lower the boom. "If you bother me with one more of Raoul's ideas, I'm telling your mother about your arrest."

"You wouldn't."

"Wrong. Don't try me. Save Raoul's ideas for when you two go into business together."

Personally, Doyle thought Raoul was using Trent. Raoul would probably dump him if someone richer came along.

Brianna sailed into the office, her smile breaking the tension. Usually, he looked forward to having lunch with her. But not today.

With the sale of the company on hold, he was being forced to have a talk with her about money. He had to put the brakes on their spending immediately.

"How's it going, Trent?" Brianna asked.

Before Trent could answer, Taylor walked into the office.

"Bad news," she said in a choked voice. "Mother is so anemic she has to have a transfusion."

Trent said, "I thought her test results were okay."

Doyle listened while Taylor explained about the mix-up at the laboratory where the blood sample was processed. Vanessa didn't have long to live, he thought.

"Mother is beginning to believe one of us murdered Renata," Taylor told them.

"Is Caleb still hanging around?" Trent asked.

"Yes, and it seems they're pretty close. I wanted to take her for the transfusion, but she wouldn't let me. Caleb is going with her."

Trent shook his head. "This sucks."

Doyle's stomach pitched as a terrible thought occurred to him. What if Vanessa didn't will her shares to Trent and Taylor? He'd thought with Renata dead, Vanessa would put the will back the way it had been. But if she blamed her children for the stripper's death, no telling what she might do.

Jesus Willie Christ. The way things were going they were never going to sell To The Maxx.

What in hell was he going to do for money?

"I need to talk to you about something," Doyle told Brianna.

They were sitting in the upstairs gallery overlooking the main floor of Norman's restaurant, having just ordered lunch. Doyle thought Norman Van Aken was the best chef in Coral Gables—in all of Miami, for that matter.

He liked eating at great restaurants and ordering fine wine at night. He enjoyed showing off Brianna. He had no intention of giving up his lifestyle, but they were going to temporarily cut back.

"You want to talk to me about money," Brianna said, taking him by surprise.

"Yes. How did you know?"

She lifted her eyebrows. "Last week I went to use my American Express card and it was refused. Then I went home and checked in your office. We were overdue on most of our bills."

"Were?"

"I paid them with money from my account."

When they'd married, Brianna had kept her own bank account. He had no idea how much was in there, but it couldn't be a lot.

"I'm sorry you had to spend all your money. I'll repay—"

"No, you won't. For better or for worse, remember?"

She leaned over and kissed his cheek.

"Besides, it didn't empty my account. I'd saved a lot by the time you married me. I wasn't going to be a lap dancer forever. I planned on opening my own boutique."

"Thank you. I'm sorry. I—"

"Stop saying you're sorry. Tell me how bad it is and what we have to do."

He explained the economic measures he planned on taking. Brianna surprised him with a few ideas of her own.

"Lunches at expensive places like this will be out," she told him. "I'll bring in food from home or we'll go have a picnic somewhere."

"This isn't going to last forever," he assured her.

"I wouldn't count on the company selling anytime soon. After what Taylor told us about her mother, I wouldn't be surprised if Vanessa left her share to charity or something."

Doyle nodded. "We'll have to live on my salary then."

"I could get a job. I—"

"You don't have to work."

"I want to work. I want to help. I'm not one of those—what do you call them?—trophy wives. I love you. We're in this together."

Doyle honestly didn't know what to say. Brianna had always said she loved him. Until this moment, he hadn't believed her.

She really did love him.

Pretty amazing.

It made anything he had to do worthwhile.

Anything.

Chapter 19

"Most people go to their graves their song still in them."

The quote from the legendary jazz singer Billy Holi-day fit Renata Rollins perfectly. Of course, there'd never been a doubt.

"She went to her grave when her life was just begin-ning."

She deserved to die.

"Her song wasn't worth hearing anyway."

The sun dipped below the palm trees, throwing long, skinny shadows with tufted tops across the lawn. Miami was nothing more than New Jersey with palm trees.

And sticky heat.

And palmetto bugs.

And condos.

The pool was the center of life in those cookie-cutter condos, he'd observed. Not much swimming. Just a lot of bald-heads and blue-hairs cooling off in the shallow end, gossiping.

Life in Miami.

Renata Rollins would never know the condo life. Or any other life. She'd served her purpose.

A preemptive strike had been made.

He had to develop new plans immediately.

Vanessa's condition was deteriorating, accelerated, no doubt, by grief over Renata's death. Suspecting someone in her family was responsible only added to her worries.

What a shame. Poor, poor Vanessa.

It would be too soon to kill Taylor right now. Vanessa was already suffering. She could linger for weeks, months. Who knew?

Murdering Taylor might be premature. Even though she deserved to die much, much more than Renata had. Taylor, the bitch who'd fallen into Shane Donovan's arms.

He had an ironclad rule: Never play your ace until you're positive you didn't need it any longer.

"Taylor is the ace. I'm not taking Taylor out—just yet. Let her screw Shane all she wants. Let her *think* she's safe with him."

A little scare might be . . . interesting as well as amusing.

It would throw off Shane Donovan, if nothing else. The prick was nosing around way, way too much.

"Sex in a basket. Kink in a basket. S and M in a basket."

Lisa Abbott smiled up at Shane, her dark eyes full of mischief.

"Jim's good at marketing, don't you think? For our

clients who are in a hurry or don't know how to plan their sex lives, these baskets are perfect."

Shane had tracked Jim Wilson to Midnight Lace, Lisa's trendy love boutique in SoBe. Jim was out, but Lisa expected him in a few minutes. Meanwhile, she obviously adored a captive audience.

"Sex in a basket is for those into traditional sex. It has aromatherapy body oils and scented candles. Condoms in exotic flavors like piña colada and mango. It also has Love Dust, my own invention. I gave some to Taylor for her to try."

"Mmmm. Love Dust."

He looked at the small canister of amber powder with the miniature feather duster. He imagined dusting every inch of Taylor's body with it.

"You lick it off," Lisa informed him as if he couldn't figure it out on his own.

"What's in 'Kink in a Basket'?"

"Heads Up Cream in four flavors: cinnamon, chili, menthol, and spice. You know, the cool/hot thing."

He didn't know squat. Obviously, he'd been out of the country too long.

"Two dildos. The French model is the favorite. Glow-in-the-dark condoms—flavored, of course. Superglide, the wonder lubricant for when you want . . . things really slick."

"Beats Mazola."

"The SoBe update of the *Karma Sutra* is included. It has illustrations of interesting positions people may not think of on their own. Oh, yes. There's edible panties in a variety of yummy flavors."

"I guess S and M in a basket is pretty much self-explanatory."

Lisa giggled. "Yes, but I've added a few innovations of my own. Furry handcuffs, for example. The metal ones are too uncomfortable, especially if you wear them for hours."

Hours in handcuffs. No friggin' way.

"There's a serious leather whip that can be converted into a tickler-style whip made of French rabbit fur."

"I guess American rabbits are too scratchy."

"No, but Jim says people pay a premium for French imports. They have cachet."

Lisa picked a small black leather book out of the wicker basket.

"I've written an S and M manual, featuring various bondage techniques for those couples with a limited imagination where—"

"Lisa, could you give me a hand with this? I'm double-parked."

A man in his early forties left a stack of boxes at the door and went to move his car. SoBe being SoBe, horns were impatiently blasting.

"Jim's back." Lisa dashed to the door. "More Love Dust. We can't keep it in stock."

Jim Wilson was much younger than Shane had expected, considering the affair. Vanessa had to be at least twenty years older. So what? She was beautiful and rich.

While Shane was waiting, he helped Lisa carry in the cartons of Love Dust. It was another five minutes before Jim Wilson returned, parking being a real challenge in SoBe.

Tall and toned with sun-bleached blond hair, Jim Wilson was so tanned he might have just hopped off his surfboard. He eyed Shane, who was helping Lisa unpack the boxes, with male possessiveness.

So that was the deal. He had a thing for Lisa. Shane wondered if it was mutual. Lisa had barely glanced at Jim.

"Shane Donovan." He extended his hand, and Jim shook it, his grip firm. "Mind if I ask you a few questions?"

"About what?"

"He's a friend of Taylor's," Lisa told him. "A good guy."

Jim appeared to have his doubts, but he didn't verbalize them.

"There have been some computer problems at To The Maxx."

"Ask me if I care."

"I know they terminated you, but—"

"They fired me. It had nothing to do with the way I did my job."

Shane waited for him to say more, but Jim stood there, his clenched fists rammed into the pockets of his khakis.

"I understand you had an affair with Vanessa Max—"

"Affair? Hell, no."

He slanted a glance at Lisa.

"Look, I had a little too much to drink at one of the company parties. Vanessa had been coming on to me all night."

"It's true," Lisa said. "I was still married to Trent then. I remember the party. Vanessa liked to flirt with the younger guys. I think she deliberately tried to make Duncan jealous."

"We ended up doing it in the cabana. It was a quickie. That's all. Somehow Duncan Maxwell found out. He fired me the next day.

"Then he tried to ruin my career. I put To The Maxx on my resume, and when potential employers called, Duncan made it sound as if I were a criminal."

Shane sympathized with the guy. He hadn't known

Duncan Maxwell, but from what he'd seen of Vanessa, she was a woman he wouldn't care to cross.

"I couldn't get a job without saying where I'd been for the previous five years. I was working as a bartender until Lisa came along."

Shane had checked into Jim's background and knew this was true. Okay, he'd had his back against the wall, but you'd think he could have found *something* in the accounting field.

"Where were you tending bar?" Shane asked, as if he didn't already know.

"El Tambor in Calle Ocho," Jim replied in a belligerent tone.

"Why Little Havana? Why not one of the trendy bars in SoBe or one of the posh resorts?"

"Tips are better in Little Havana. Cubans are much more generous than Americans."

Live and learn.

Shane wasn't positive he was buying this, but Cubans seemed to flash more cash than their American counterparts.

"Someone's been tampering with To The Maxx's Web site. Your name came up."

"I'll bet it did. Disgruntled former employees always come under suspicion."

Jim shot another glance at Lisa, who was watching them.

"I had nothing to do with it. Why would I risk a criminal charge?"

Shane nodded, as if he agreed, but he knew there were ways of using public computers like those at libraries to hack into a company's Web site. All it took was a little knowledge of computers and a copy of the *Hacker's Journal.*

Or Jim could have come across the codes to the Web site when he'd been working at To The Maxx.

People were notoriously sloppy about keeping secret passwords hidden. He'd heard about one case at the DIA where an employee had written the password on a Post-it and put it on the bottom of his keyboard.

"I'm sure you wouldn't want any more trouble."

"Got that right." Jim spit out the words. "I have a good job now. I'm not going to blow it."

Shane knew Lisa was paying him well to help her market Midnight Lace's products online as well as at the love boutique. Since adult sex Web sites fueled as much as eighty percent of the Internet's business, it was a safe bet Midnight Lace's offerings would be a hit.

"I needed to ask," Shane told Jim. "The family's been having a lot of trouble lately."

"Jim had nothing to do with any of their problems," insisted Lisa.

So that's how it is, Shane thought. He detected an utterly female note of protectiveness and something he couldn't quite describe. But his gut instinct told him Lisa cared—okay, more than cared—about this man.

"I don't suppose either of you ever met Renata Rollins." Shane knew this was a long shot—out of left field, really. What possible motive could either of them have for killing Renata?

Lisa studied the sex basket display for a moment before saying, "We met her briefly one night at the Living Room. She was there with Trent and his lover to go dancing. Trent introduced us, we said a few words, then we left."

"That's right," Jim added just a little too quickly.

Shane knocked on the condo door. Doyle Maxwell's first wife, Sophie now lived on Fisher Island. The exclusive island floated like a preening swan in the waters off South Beach.

No bridges connected the island to the mainland, so Shane had taken the ferry over. Fawning attendants had washed the salt spray off the Rolls and Jags as they drove off the ferry. Noses in the air, it had been a quick spritz for the Jeep he'd bought used.

Sophie herself answered the door. Shane had expected a maid, considering these condos were in the two-million-and-up range. Most were occupied seasonally by wealthy Northerners who wanted to escape the cold.

"As I told you on the telephone, I know nothing about what goes on at To The Maxx."

She led him to a prissy white sofa, and they sat down.

"When I was married to Doyle, he had his own investment firm. He didn't start to help run his brother's company until Duncan died."

Shane studied the pudgy woman with hair more gray than brown. She was a stark contrast to the sexy Brianna. Unlike many women in Miami who indulged themselves with the latest fashions and kept cosmetic surgeons up to their eyeballs performing liposuctions and face-lifts, Sophie didn't appear to care how she looked.

Not that she could be mistaken for the homeless. Her clothes were expensive but frumpy, and her hair had been styled recently. She just didn't have the air about her that said she could be bothered trying to look any better.

A gold cross on a filigree chain hung from her neck. The information Shane had gathered indicated Sophie was a devout Catholic and always had been.

"Were you very friendly with Duncan?" Shane asked.

Sophie studied his face with solemn brown eyes.

Here was a woman who thought fun was a four-letter word, he decided.

"When Doyle and I were first married, we spent all our free time with Duncan until he married Vanessa."

Shane detected more than just a trace of bitterness. "What happened then?"

"Vanessa did her best to split up the brothers. She was nothing but a redneck hick without an ounce of breeding. A jealous, possessive woman who didn't want her husband to spend any time with his brother."

"How did you two get along?"

"She *tried* to ingratiate herself. My family has money, connections. I saw right through her."

Shane nodded. One of the first things he'd noticed about Vanessa was how impressed she was with a person's social connections. She'd asked him about his family.

"I'm related to Margaret Tuttle on my mother's side. My father was a Vanderbilt cousin. I belong to all the best women's clubs."

"I see," Shane replied, thinking how radically Vanessa had changed since her illness. She was openly acknowledging a stripper was her daughter.

"Vanessa wasn't interested in me. She wanted my friends. She's one of those hicks obsessed with wealthy people. We see quite a few of them down here."

Sophie's eyes drifted across the elegant condo that seemed to belong to another person. "There were lots of other things, too."

Shane waited, then prompted her. "Like?"

"She never went to church. Duncan took Taylor and Trent to church, not Vanessa."

Shane listened, beginning to suspect something.

"Several people have told me Vanessa could be an outrageous flirt. Did she ever come on to Doyle?"

"Not exactly. Vanessa ignored my husband, made

him feel like an intruder in his brother's home. But I could tell she was more attracted to Doyle than she was Duncan.''

"Really?"

"Absolutely. The woman is a hussy."

Hussy? He didn't think that word had been in use since the fifties.

"Was there ever . . . anything between them?"

Sophie gave a little huff of disgust.

"At the time, I didn't think so, but then my husband threw me over for a lap dancer in Little Havana. Who knows what else he did?''

Shane was on the ferry returning from Fisher Island when Vince called him on his cell phone.

"Guess what? Raoul walked out of the rehab facility.''

Shane wasn't one bit surprised. Crystal meth was one of the world's most addictive substances, worse than heroin. At least heroin addicts could be given methadone.

The cravings for crystal meth were often too great. No matter what you had to lose, you'd take that gamble for the next fix. Evidently, the cravings had become too strong for Raoul to resist.

"Where did he go?" Shane asked.

"Disappeared into thin air. But he might turn up anytime.''

Shane told him about his conversation with Sophie and with Jim Wilson. "Gut instinct here, Jim is holding back something. Why would such a qualified accountant with a degree from Wharton work as a bartender in Calle Ocho?''

"Some illegal operation."

"Possibly," Shane conceded, although he hated to

think Lisa had fallen in love with the wrong man again. "They admit meeting Renata once at a club called the Living Room. Jim worked in Calle Ocho. On the afternoon of her death Renata went to a botanica in Calle Ocho for a pin to ward off a hex."

"Santería is popular in Little Havana, but you don't see it associated with bars. It may be a coincidence—not a connection."

"I don't believe in coincidences."

Chapter 20

"How are you feeling?" Taylor asked her mother.

"Better . . . I guess."

Taylor had swung by her mother's house after working late, to see how the transfusion had gone. Her mother was propped up by half a dozen pillows in the family room, watching television. Seated nearby, Caleb munched on handfuls of cashews and eyed Taylor as if he expected her to pull a gun and shoot him.

"What did the doctor say?"

"She'll be all right for now," Caleb answered for her mother.

Taylor tried not to be frustrated, hurt. Her mother seemed more interested in the television program than talking to her. She ignored Caleb and directed her question to her mother.

"What does it mean that you're all right for now?"

"She's all right until her next blood test."

Taylor resisted the urge to make a sarcastic remark. Caleb Bassett might have a veneer of charm—to some people—but he was truly a loathsome man. She certainly hoped he hadn't raised Renata. The woman's last years had been hard enough.

Taylor could only imagine what a childhood with Caleb would have been like. Shane was scheduled to investigate the man, but with the murder, he hadn't had the time.

"Mother, when is your next blood workup?"

Her mother turned her head toward Taylor. Her blue eyes were a glazed dull gray. No doubt the pain medication caused the listlessness.

"Next Thursday."

A little over a week, Taylor thought as her mother turned back to the television. Taylor hated to ask the next question, but she had to know.

"Does the doctor think he'll have to put you on chemotherapy?"

"You'd like that, wouldn't you?" Caleb said.

A rush of red-hot fury blurred Taylor's vision for an instant. She clamped her mouth shut to keep from lashing out. She refused to give him the satisfaction.

"You'd get a kick out of seeing your mother suffer, wouldn't you?"

Taylor jumped to her feet. "What a horrible thing to say! Just who do you think you are?"

Caleb's smug grin kicked her anger up another notch.

"I don't know. Vanessa, who am I?"

Her mother turned to them, a puzzled expression on her face, as if their words were just registering and she was trying to sort them out. Taylor wondered if this creep was overmedicating her.

"Caleb is . . . is . . . my friend."

"I'm your daughter and I love you."

Taylor sank onto the sofa beside her mother. So far, she hadn't mentioned Renata's death or blamed her for it. Caleb must have been lying when he'd told her that her mother didn't want to see her.

"I'm worried about your health, Mother."

Her mother looked at Taylor blankly for a second. "I'm worried about you, too."

"Me? Why?"

"That worthless photographer isn't the man for you."

Paul really had tried to please her mother, but Vanessa had been positively glacial to him. It had embarrassed and angered Taylor. She had tried to talk to her mother about her attitude. Stubborn to a fault, Vanessa had insisted Taylor could do better than Paul.

Those arguments seemed like ancient history in light of all that had happened. Why would her mother bring up Paul? He had been gone two years, and she was with another man.

She didn't want to analyze how she felt about Shane. With Caleb present, now wasn't the time to tell her mother she was seeing Shane.

The man in her life wasn't the issue. Her mother *almost* sounded as if she thought Paul was still living in Miami.

"Mother," Taylor began, testing, "Paul isn't around anymore, remember?"

"Of course I remember," she snapped, but Taylor wondered if the drugs were playing tricks with her mind.

Caleb downed another handful of cashews, then smiled, obviously enjoying this.

Her mother patted her hand. "He wasn't the man for you. Shane Donovan is your soul mate. Renata said so."

Renata again.

When was the last time her mother had told her how much she loved her? Not since Renata had appeared.

"Renata knew things. Saw things." Caleb tapped on his temple with his index finger. "That's why the Santería scared her. She musta' known something terrible was going to happen to her."

Taylor did not want to discuss Renata. It only upset her mother and drove them further apart.

Exactly what Caleb Bassett wanted.

"The doctor won't tell me how much medication my mother is supposed to be taking—or anything about her condition. I'm her daughter. I need to know if that creep is overmedicating her or something else is wrong."

"Telling you violates a patient's right to privacy and could have legal ramifications."

Curled up on Shane's sofa, Taylor listened to Shane and stroked Auggie's silky head. It was comforting to have someone to talk with. She'd come home from her mother's angry and upset, not knowing what to do.

When she'd arrived to an empty apartment, Taylor's first thought had been to call Lisa, but her friend wasn't home. If she was still at Midnight Lace, she wasn't answering the telephone.

Taylor had reached for her laptop to work on her computer game the way she often did when she found herself home alone and edgy. It wasn't beside her purse.

She remembered packing it up and putting it on top of her desk. She'd been so preoccupied with her mother that she'd left the office without taking it.

Gazing out the window, she wondered if she could

get to sleep. Like a beacon, Shane's lights had been shining across the courtyard.

She'd rushed over and had been astounded at how glad she was to see him, to be able to talk with him. She hadn't realized how close they'd become in such a short time.

"The doctor explained about patients' rights," she told Shane. "Still, I think he should have been more concerned when I told him I suspected she was over-medicated, but he didn't seem to care."

"Why don't you ask Maria to check on the amount of medication your mother is taking?"

"I don't speak Spanish well enough. My mother insisted I take French—a refined language."

Taylor shook her head, remembering the arguments she'd had with her mother over this.

"In Miami you need Spanish, not French."

"I'll ask her for you."

Taylor stared at Shane for a second, surprised. "You speak Spanish?"

"Fluently."

"You're kidding!" she cried, and Auggie looked up at her, startled.

"This is your lucky day. How can we get in touch with her without your mother or Caleb knowing?"

"Easy. There's a separate telephone line to the servants' quarters."

"Let's call her right now."

She found the number in the Palm Pilot she kept in her purse, dialed it, and handed the telephone to Shane. Taylor smiled as she listened to him speaking Spanish. There was something so reassuring about being with Shane.

Paul hadn't made her feel so . . . safe. In many ways, she'd nurtured him, encouraging his career, enduring his criticism of her family.

She'd tried not to compare the two men, but at times like this, when she was so stressed with worry, it was difficult not to wonder what Paul would have done. Of course he would have tried to help, but Shane had the skills to get things done.

She still loved Paul and would give anything she had or hoped to have to bring him back home. But Lisa was right. The chances of Paul being alive were slim to nonexistent.

Life goes on.

Sad but true, she thought as Auggie rested his head on her knee, looking up at her with soulful eyes. She and Paul had been together a little less than a year. Now he'd been gone almost two years.

He wasn't coming back.

Shane was here, helping her up when she needed it the most. They'd had great sex, and she'd tried to tell herself that's all it was.

Sex. Nothing more.

She could handle sex. There had been men in her life before she fell in love with Paul. She was a young woman with a normal sex drive, for God's sake.

Taylor had assumed all Shane had wanted was sex. Wrong. He'd insisted on doing as much as he could for her by trying to solve the murder.

And helping with her mother.

Losing Paul was heartrending, but if her mother died believing she was a killer, Taylor knew she'd never get over it.

Her mother wasn't always the easiest person in the world to get along with. She could be overbearing, difficult. Pretentious.

But she was her mother, and Taylor loved her.

Shane hung up the telephone and broke into her thoughts, saying, "Okay, here's the deal. When she gets a chance, Maria is going to write down the names of the medications your mother is taking, then call me here. She'll leave a message if I'm not home.

"Apparently, your mother has a number of prescriptions. We just want Maria to watch the painkillers. Those are the ones Caleb may be using to up the dosage."

"If he is, what can I do?"

"You and your brother need to talk to your mother. I'll take care of Caleb while you do it."

"Why would Caleb overmedicate my mother?"

He grazed a fingertip upward from her knee and under her skirt.

"Come on, Taylor. You're smarter than that."

"He's trying to get her money."

"Bingo."

He framed her face with his hands and kissed the tip of her nose. "We've done all we can do for tonight—for your mother. It's time we took care of each other."

"I can't." Her voice trembled.

"Why not?"

His lips hovered over hers, and it was all she could do not to close the gap. "Too much is going on in my life. Things are happening too fast."

"Okay, I can understand how you feel, but I think you're afraid."

She raised her eyebrows and shrugged. *I'm not afraid of sex. I'm afraid of love.*

"I'm going home."

"No, you're not." He pulled her close. "You're spending the night here in my bed. Right, Auggie?"

At the sound of his name, the dog's tail whipped through the air. Taylor had to smile, her heart beating faster than Auggie's tail. Being here in Shane's arms felt so . . . special.

Why should she deprive herself?

He swept her off the sofa into his arms and carried her to his bedroom. She didn't protest when he lowered her to the bed and gave her a quick kiss.

"Just a minute."

She waited in the dark, one hand over the side of the bed petting Auggie. A scratching sound was followed by the flare of a candle. A second later, Shane lit another candle.

Strange, she thought. Shane didn't seem like a guy who would have candles in his bedroom. She sniffed, then inhaled more deeply.

Jasmine and vanilla.

"Lisa gave you aromatherapy candles."

"Gave? Hell, no." He lit another candle. "She made me buy them. Sold me Love Dust, too."

Taylor moaned softly to herself. Anticipating. She started to unbutton her blouse.

"No, you don't. I want to undress you."

He straddled her, his knees beside her hips. He took his sweet time unbuttoning her blouse. When he finished, he shoved the panels aside and gazed down at the lacy bra covering her breasts.

The candlelight shimmered over her exposed skin, and the fragrant scent of vanilla mingled with jasmine filled her lungs. Taylor smiled up at Shane, a fluid heat unfurling from deep within her body.

"We're just right for each other," Shane told her as he eased her skirt down over her hips.

She shimmied a little to help get it off. "Just right."

The words kindled something she thought she'd lost when Paul had vanished. A second chance. Not at love, she told herself, but at a relationship.

She was fine alone. The last two years had proved how self-sufficient she could be, but she didn't want her life to be so solitary.

All work—the company and her game—nothing more. Life was meant to be lived, shared.

Standing beside the bed, he removed his clothes, stripping down to black briefs. Black silk.

"Mmmmmm," she purred. "Lisa's just too naughty."

"What are you talking about?" he asked, lowering himself down beside her. "Don't you think I picked these up on my own?"

She reached out and cupped his sex through the satiny fabric. Hard and hot.

"No. You're the practical type. Lisa put you up to this."

He removed her hand, then unhooked her bra. A rush of cool air peaked her nipples, and Shane bent down to tease one with the tip of his tongue. Just as she was settling in, enjoying each stroke, he stopped.

"Time for the Love Dust."

He had a canister of Lisa's ground honey concoction. Using the small feather duster, he brushed the amber talc across her breasts. Alternating short and long, then swirly movements, he whisked the power across her body.

He stopped and set the canister on the nightstand. "Now for the real fun."

"Define *fun.*"

"This is my idea of fun. Let me know when you're having a good time."

He licked the Love Dust off her nipples, suckling each taut bud gently as he did. With every stroke, pleasure radiated downward, a melting sweetness pooling in the moist heat between her thighs.

Shane lifted his head and pressed his lips against hers. His mouth tasted like warm honey. The scent of it was light, sweet. The kiss sang through her veins, sending her pulse rate even higher.

A taste of honey, she thought.

The scent of jasmine and vanilla.

Now this was aromatherapy, the treatment her tired soul needed.

"Shane," she murmured, arching upward against the masculine length of his body. "I—"

KA-BOOM! The concussion rocked the bed. The sound of shattering glass was followed by a woman's piercing scream.

In a heartbeat, Shane was on his feet. "Stay there!"

He yanked on his trousers, then grabbed a gun from the nightstand. He sprinted out of the room, and Taylor followed, the sheet wrapped around her.

The living room glowed brilliant orange. For a second, she thought his apartment was on fire. Then she realized the light was coming from a pillar of flame shooting into the night sky.

From her apartment.

Chapter 21

Shane hugged Taylor to his side. She'd stopped trembling half an hour ago when the firemen had arrived to put out the blaze in her living room, but he knew she was still upset.

"I don't think they meant to kill you." Shane tried to assure her. "My guess is someone tossed a small pipe bomb into your apartment. Did you leave the front door unlocked?"

"Yes. I'd planned to be at your place for just a few minutes."

They were standing in the courtyard, gazing into the living room through what had once been a lovely art deco window. It was raining, a hot, tropical drizzle that made the air thick, hard to breathe.

The bomb squad was raking through the charred remains. Beside them Auggie sniffed the smoky air. He barked twice and pointed like a bird dog.

"Why's Auggie doing that?"

Shane hated to tell her that Auggie had just confirmed what he'd suspected.

"He's detected the scent of an explosive substance. That's what he did for the military."

"Why didn't he smell it earlier?"

"The fire was releasing too many odors at once, and the rain made tracking the smell confusing. All that's left is a very faint trace scent." Shane leaned down and petted Auggie. "At ease, boy. At ease."

"Why would someone bomb my place?"

It wasn't the first time she'd asked. Hell, it was at least the hundredth time he'd asked himself the same question.

"I wish I could explain why someone would do this." He thought a moment. "It's almost like a warning. If you'd been home, the noise would have awakened you, and you would have run out the back door."

"Warn me about what?"

"Good question. If not a warning, then why?"

Two of the policemen on the bomb squad walked over to them. "It was a small pipe bomb. We have enough of it intact for the lab to check."

Taylor asked, "Do you think you'll be able to find out who did it?"

The older man with the ruddy complexion and receding hairline shook his head. "I doubt the lab analysis will help ID the perp. It's a simple device. A kid could have made it."

The second man added, "With what's out on the Internet making something like this is a piece of cake. It would be more helpful if someone had seen the person."

"At two in the morning?" Taylor shook her head. "I—"

"Taylor, thank God, you're all right."

Trent rushed into the courtyard, his brows drawn downward in a concerned frown.

"How did you—"

"Mrs. Bryant called me. She didn't think you should be alone." Trent threw his arms around his sister and bear-hugged her. "All the way over, I kept praying not to lose you. I don't know what I'd do if I lost someone else I love."

The two men from the bomb squad stepped away, saying they'd be back when it was daylight. Shane watched them leave, wondering how he could help Taylor.

Next time, she might be killed.

"Have you heard from Raoul?" he asked Trent.

"No. Not a word." Trent's arm was draped across his sister's shoulders. "I pray he's all right."

Shane mustered what he hoped was a sympathetic expression. But a thought hit him like a sucker punch to the gut.

With Renata and Taylor dead, only Trent would be left to inherit his mother's fortune.

Calle Ocho, the heart of Little Havana, meant strings of small shops and cafés crammed together like cigars in a box. Signs in Spanish and throngs of people who, forty years later, still called Cuba home.

Shane walked along the sidewalk, looking for El Tambor, the bar where Jim Wilson had been working. The scent of sweet Cuban coffee and the heavier odor of cigars wafted through the midmorning air. Salsa music thumped from the shops, pulsing with life, the beat of Calle Ocho.

Vendors maneuvered pushcarts loaded with *coquito*, coconut candy, around elderly men in guayaberas puffing on cigars while they hovered over non-stop games of dominos. Shane was fluent in Spanish, and he picked up snatches of conversation as he passed.

He found El Tambor on a corner next to a bakery. Sheets of plywood had been nailed across the front door. The place appeared to be permanently closed.

He strolled into the bakery, ordered a *medianoche*, a "midnight" sandwich of ham, cheese, and pickles, invented for people who'd partied all night, but served early in the morning. After he and Taylor had finally gone to bed, he hadn't been able to sleep.

A warning voice kept whispering in his head.

Taylor is in danger.

His sixth sense had served him well in countless missions.

How could he help Taylor when he didn't know what—or who—he was up against?

The nagging sense of frustration gnawed at him. The problems at To The Maxx, Renata's murder, the fire-bombing all seemed to be random events. But he suspected they were somehow linked.

If he could solve the puzzle, he could save Taylor.

Before it was too late.

He hadn't mentioned his suspicions to her yet, not wanting to worry her unnecessarily, but the more he thought about it, the surer he became.

"Why is El Tambor closed?" he asked the woman behind the counter in Spanish as he paid for the *medianoche*.

"The police raided it."

"When?"

"Two nights ago."

"Why?"

"No one knows."

Shane walked out, wondering when Jim Wilson had left El Tambor and come to work for Lisa. A couple of weeks, maybe longer. He'd need to check.

* * *

Taylor supposed she should thank her lucky stars. There was a lot of smoke damage to her apartment, and the contents of the living room were a total loss, but her clothes had survived, as well as the things in the kitchen. Her laptop with her Trivial Moments game on it, almost finished, had been safe here at the office.

She tried to concentrate on the sales reports her assistant had put on her desk earlier. Skimming through them, she saw sales of their newest products were brisk in Southern California, Texas, and Greater Miami. Women in these areas were quick to try new beauty supplies.

It meant Maxx would have to plan special promotions to spur interest in their newer products in other parts of the country. Taylor thought small samples to be given away in beauty supply stores worked the best. But it was expensive.

Uncle Doyle knocked on her door, just as she was wondering if he would approve the expenditure.

"What happened at your place last night?" he asked, frowning.

"Someone threw a firebomb into the living room. Luckily, I was across the courtyard at Shane's."

"Why would anyone . . ."

"You've got me. I didn't think I had an enemy who would resort to this." Her scalp prickled as she recalled the orange flames leaping from her front window.

"Could it have been a mistake?"

"I'd like to think so. It was the dead of night, and the courtyard isn't very well lit. The rain made it harder to see. Perhaps the person didn't read the street number correctly."

Uncle Doyle sat in the chair beside her desk. "Maybe they got the wrong apartment."

"Shane and I are the only ones on the ground level. The other two units are upstairs."

He shot her a penetrating look.

"You think the firebomb was intended for Shane?"

Her uncle shrugged, lifting just one shoulder the way her father had. "He's a man who's likely to have more enemies than you. Just how much do you know about him?"

Not enough, she silently conceded.

"Shane's a good man. He worked for the Defense Intelligence Agency."

"Doing what?"

"I'm not sure. Something to do with antiterrorism." She thought about it for a moment. "Even if Shane were the target, why a firebomb? It made a lot of noise. He could have run out the back door."

Still frowning, her uncle studied her. "Be very careful."

"I will. I guess I should tell my mother before—"

"I phoned Vanessa and told her you were at work."

Normally, her mother would have called her to make certain Taylor was okay. But these weren't normal times. Vanessa Maxwell wasn't herself.

"How long is it going to take to repair your apartment?"

"You know Mrs. Bryant. She'll get a zillion quotes before she does anything."

"Doesn't she have insurance?"

"Yes, but this morning she told me it doesn't cover fires that are the result of a 'criminal act.' She'll have to pay for the repairs."

"Do you need a place to stay? Brianna would be thrilled to have you move in with us."

"No, I'm fine, but thanks for the offer."

She didn't add that she was staying with Shane, although her uncle was savvy enough to figure it out.

Taylor changed the subject. "I was going over the latest sales reports. Our newest products aren't taking off the way I'd like. I think we should make up samples to give away in beauty supply stores. I know it's going to cost—"

"We've got to do it. Target San Francisco and Seattle and Boston. Skip flyover land."

The marketing people called the middle section of the country "flyover land" because the major markets were on the coasts. The part of the country you flew over to get to each coast was often ignored in marketing campaigns. Taylor believed this was a mistake, but she had to admit immediate results could be seen when large metropolitan areas on the coasts were targeted.

"We need to keep this company growing," her uncle continued. "We may not be selling it anytime soon."

"Why do you say that? Shane's friend should have the computer mess figured out any day now."

"I spoke with Ridley Pudge last night. He called Vanessa to see if she wanted to change the will back to the way it was now that Renata is dead. She told him she was thinking it over, and she'd let him know."

Taylor didn't care about the money, but it cut deep to know her mother was having second thoughts about leaving her anything.

"It's my mother's money. She can do whatever she likes."

"They released Renata's body. The funeral is on Friday. We'd all better go."

"Yes," she agreed, although she dreaded it.

She could just imagine how grief-stricken her mother would be. Considering her failing health, this was an ordeal she didn't need.

"There's something else," her uncle said quietly. Too quietly.

"What's wrong?"

"I got a call last evening from Raoul. He wanted a hundred thousand dollars to leave Miami."

Taylor closed her eyes for a moment, remembering how upset Trent had been last night. He hadn't heard a thing from Raoul. While Trent had been worrying, the man he loved was trying to squeeze money out of the family.

"What did you tell him?"

"I told Raoul to forget it. Not only don't I have that much cash, I wouldn't interfere in Trent's life by getting rid of his . . . friend."

"Mother once offered him money. He might—"

"He called her first. She refused to give him a dime."

Taylor slumped back in her chair. "I'd like to think my mother wised up and chose not to meddle in Trent's affairs, but I'm afraid she's changed. It's either the medication or Renata's death. Maybe both. But she's not the same person anymore."

"I'm sorry, Taylor. I know how hard this is on you. I wish we'd never found Renata."

"She was my mother's daughter. The DNA proved it."

"I know, but she was trouble with a capital T."

Hot rain pelted the grass, a blessing after the grilling Miami heat, he decided. The palms bent sideways in the wind, moaning their loneliness.

Standing a death watch.

There wasn't a damn thing to do except watch the lightening flash in jagged blue streaks, zigzagging across the pitch-black sky.

And wait for the thunder to boom an ominous warning.

"The bomb hasn't frightened Taylor enough," he

said out loud. "She doesn't even *suspect* she's next to die."

It was too soon to kill her, of course.

"Never play your ace prematurely."

The rain pecked against the window, a distraction. The wind had clocked around and was now blowing from a different direction, flinging rain sideways.

That's it!

Come at this from a different direction. Really challenge Shane Donovan. The prick deserved it.

Put the fear of God into Taylor.

How should I begin?

Every waking moment your killer is watching you.

He chuckled to himself. The bitch deserved to die. The sooner she knew the end was near—and worried about it—the happier he would be.

Chapter 22

Shane waited at his apartment with Auggie for Taylor to come home. He knew she'd dropped by her mother's home after work. It was raining again tonight. A real storm this time, complete with thunder and lightning.

The telephone rang and he grabbed it, hoping it was Taylor, but it was Vince.

"I got the information you wanted."

Shane had called Vince after he'd left Calle Ocho. He'd asked Vince to use his connections in the police department to find out why El Tambor had been raided.

"The two brothers who own El Tambor were laundering bingo skim money."

"Bingo skim? You mean from the Seminoles' casinos?" Shane asked.

"That's right. It's supposed to go directly to the

tribe, but a few Seminoles got greedy and took some off the top. They funneled it through El Tambor into a private bank account.''

"El Tambor's owners must have taken a cut.''

"Absofuckinglutely.''

"Was Jim Wilson in on it?''

"It's hard to say. He was there at the time, but he got out before the raid.''

"Sounds a little too convenient for me. He's an accountant, a smart guy. He must have known what they were doing.''

"Maybe one of the brothers will cop a plea and roll over on everyone involved," Vince said. "Even if Wilson was in on it, does that mean he tampered with the Web site?''

"Possibly. The coded material could refer to off-shore bank accounts or it could be a way of letting the Seminoles involved see where the money is going.''

"It would work. Post the info on the Web site, but keep it cleverly hidden. People could be anywhere and never have to meet face-to-face. The police would have a hell of a time linking all of those in on the scam.''

Shane discussed the firebomb with Vince and learned the police had no leads. He hung up, thinking about Taylor. They were close now.

Was it time to tell her the whole truth?

Putting it off would only make it harder. He didn't know how she'd take it. She had a lot going on right now, and the firebomb had added to her problems.

He wondered how she felt about their relationship. He loved her, no question about it.

Deep in her heart did she still feel a flicker of love for Paul Ashton?

Did she still pray at night for him to return?

Taylor walked in a few seconds later. Just one look at her face, and he knew things had not gone well with her mother. Now was not the time to bring up Paul Ashton.

"What's the matter?" He put his arm around Taylor and pulled her close.

"My mother insists on giving an elaborate funeral for Renata. She wants me to call her friends and let them know about the services. It's going to be so hard on her. I don't know if she has the strength to live through it."

Shane kissed her forehead. "Man, oh, man. I don't know what to tell you."

"A smaller graveside ceremony would be better, but she won't hear of it. If Trent had been there to help me, I might have talked her into it, but he's off looking for Raoul."

Shane led her into the kitchen, saying, "I fixed us a seafood salad. Why don't we eat?"

"You made dinner?" A hitching little smile tugged at her lips. "A guy after my own heart."

He patted her cute butt. "I'm after more than just your heart."

She sat down, and he poured her a glass of pinot grigio, then served the simple salad he'd prepared earlier. While he worked, he explained what he'd learned about Jim Wilson and the bingo skim.

"You think our Web site is being used by criminals who are stealing money from Native Americans?"

"It's a possibility. Whatever is going on can't be legal or someone wouldn't have taken the time to hide it on your Web site in code."

"Lisa has hired Jim. He might do something to ruin her business."

"Or get her into trouble with the law if he hides anything on her Web site."

Taylor took a forkful of salad and chewed thoughtfully for a moment. "I should warn her. After all she's been through, it wouldn't be fair to not let her know she's hired a criminal.''

"We can't prove a thing—yet. If you tell her about the problem with the Web site, she might mention it to Jim. He could delete it before we can prove anything.''

"I already told her. I asked her if she knew the codes, if Trent had left them around when they were married. I had the codes on a piece of paper in my desk at home, so I wondered if Trent had, too. Of course, they were destroyed by the fire.''

Shane checked his watch. "Let's see if we can meet her for a drink after we finish. If she hasn't already mentioned the problem with the Web site to Wilson, we can warn her to keep quiet.''

Two hours later, Taylor was sitting in the VIP section of Bash, one of SoBe's trendy clubs. Her head had been throbbing since the meeting with her mother, and the music here wasn't helping.

"It's not like Lisa to be late," she told Shane.

"She's probably hung up in traffic.''

They ordered *mojitos,* the Cuban cocktail made from lime juice and rum. Taylor recalled what her uncle had said earlier that day.

"Shane, do you think someone might have intended to firebomb your place, but got mine by mistake?''

"What?'' Shane's dark brows shot up.

"Well, your work before you came here put you in contact with dangerous people, didn't it?''

Shane gazed at her in the intent way she'd come to expect.

"If any of them had a grudge against me, they'd try to kill me. That firebomb was meant to scare—not kill.''

"I guess you're right, but the courtyard is a little dark, and it was raining. It could easily have been a mistake."

"I'd like to think it was a mistake, but I'm worried." Shane put down his *mojito*. "I think you might be in danger."

For a second, Taylor didn't take him seriously, but then she realized his expression, his eyes were steeped in genuine concern.

"What kind of danger?"

"I don't know, but one woman is already dead. I want you to be very careful. Don't go anywhere alone. I'll follow you to work. People are around you all day. If you need to go to your mother's or someplace, I'll take you."

"Who would want to harm me?" She'd asked herself this question dozens of times and still couldn't come up with an answer.

"It's probably linked to your mother's money or the sale of the company. I'm not sure. My gut instinct says you're in danger."

Shane wasn't the kind of man to cry wolf, she decided. He was truly worried about her. A strange, alien sensation unfurled deep in her chest.

Gratitude and perhaps something more.

When times were bad, the way they were now, having someone care about you was priceless.

"I'm wondering if Raoul might be involved in this somehow," she said, then took a sip of her drink. "He asked Uncle Doyle for a hundred thousand dollars to get out of Miami, out of Trent's life."

"He did? Interesting. The man has a strange past. At one point he was suicidal and had to be hospitalized after a breakup with a woman. Then he moves to SoBe and decides he's gay."

"Men are often conflicted about their sexuality.

Look at my brother. He was happily married—or so we thought.''

"Raoul could be bisexual. It's very 'in' these days. It really isn't any of our business. What matters is whether or not he's involved in this mess. Money would be a good reason to kill. With you and Renata out of the way, Trent would inherit your mother's money.''

She shook her head. "My mother hasn't decided what to do about a new will. She may not leave either of us anything.''

"Does Trent know this?''

"No. Uncle Doyle is going to talk to him tonight. He's going to tell him about the will and about the money Raoul wants.''

An old memory tiptoed out of one of the dark corridors of her mind. Those first days after Paul had disappeared, she'd been frantic. Trent must be feeling the same way.

"I think it's selfish and cruel of Raoul not to call my brother and let him know he's okay.''

"Got that right. We're dealing with more than one selfish guy. Caleb is the wrong person to be with your mother. She's too vulnerable.''

Taylor tried not to think of how much her mother had changed, how their relationship had changed. "I expected her to ask me to move home while my apartment is being repaired, but she didn't. She barely asked about the firebomb. It was almost as if . . .''

"As if what?''

"As if she thought I'd done it to get attention or something.''

Shane put his hand on hers. "I'm sorry, babe.''

"It's just that I know I'm going to lose her, yet in a way, I've already lost her. We used to be close. She could be difficult at times, but we got along. I—''

She nudged Shane. "Here comes Lisa with Jim. Oh, my God. He's got his arm around her."

"See if you can get her to go to the rest room with you. Tell her what's going on and emphasize how important it is to keep quiet."

"Hi!" Taylor greeted her friend, her voice a little *too* bright, but Lisa didn't seem to notice.

"You remember Jim, don't you, Taylor?"

"Of course."

"I heard something on the news about a firebomb at your place," Jim said.

Taylor wondered if he was telling the truth. She'd watched the evening news with her mother. She hadn't seen anything about it. A little firebomb was nothing compared to other crimes in Miami.

"What happened?" Lisa asked.

"We don't know," Shane said. "It might have been a mistake. A drug deal gone bad or something. Luckily, Taylor was with me."

"Oh, my Lord! How scary," Lisa said. "I wish you'd called me. I didn't know a thing about it until Jim saw it on the news just after you called me this evening."

"It was a crazy day," Taylor replied. "I didn't have a moment to myself."

"I know what you mean," Jim said with a smile directed to Lisa.

"You're working for Lisa, I hear."

"No, we're working *together*," Lisa said with a smile Taylor hadn't seen since Trent had left her. "Midnight Lace's Web site is doing gangbuster business."

"Really?" Taylor heard herself say.

"The Web site is doing better than the shop. You have no idea how many women out there in Middle America have no place to go for things like aromatherapy oils and candles and—"

"Furry handcuffs," Jim said with a grin.

"How about piña colada flavored condoms?" Shane added. "I'll bet they're not available in Sioux City."

Taylor wanted to laugh, but she couldn't. This was her best friend, and she was obviously involved with this man who might very well be a criminal. He would break her heart—again—and ruin her business. Lisa might even go to jail.

The waitress sashayed up to them and took Jim's order for a white chocolate martini, and Lisa decided on a *mojito*. Taylor couldn't help noticing the attractive blonde kept eyeing Shane.

"I'm glad you called the shop," Lisa told her. "Jim and I have been working way too hard. We needed a break. Sorry we were late, but the rain made the traffic worse than usual."

Taylor nodded. "Friday is Renata's funeral. My mother is so, so stressed. Do you think you can come?"

"Of course, I'll be there." Lisa touched Jim's arm. "We'll be there."

"Sure," Jim replied, but he didn't sound thrilled.

"I need to run to the ladies' room." Taylor stood up. "Lisa, come with me."

"I don't need—"

Taylor shot her the old "trust me" look from their Yale days, and Lisa excused herself. The music was too loud to talk until they were inside the black marble and stainless-steel rest room.

"Lisa, are you and Jim . . ."

"We're living together in the loft over my shop."

Lisa hugged Taylor with a little squeal of delight.

"I never thought I'd be happy again, but I am. Jim's the perfect partner. We work together, then test the love toys after dark."

"Lisa, the security firm investigating problems we've been having think Jim could be involved in tinkering with our Web site."

"Jim? No way!"

Taylor recognized the hostility simmering in her friend's dark eyes. "Just listen to me, please."

Lisa's nostrils flared as she breathed hard. Taylor waited for a moment while a young woman in a crotch-high dress washed her hands and left them alone in the VIP rest room.

"The police shut down the bar where Jim worked for laundering bingo skim money. There's a good chance he was involved. Don't tell me a man with Jim's looks and talent couldn't find a better job than tending bar.

"He's the prime suspect in the tampering with Maxx's Web site. Now he's working on yours. I'm concerned he'll ruin your business or get you unknowingly involved in some criminal activity."

Lisa crossed her arms in front of her chest. "He's been a tremendous help. His ideas, the speed at which he got us online, amazes me. There's no funny stuff on my Web site."

"You might not realize it. I don't understand exactly how it works myself, but there are passwords and concealed icons people can click on to access hidden material. If there hadn't been some glitches with our orders, we might never have found the secret text."

"Jim's a good man. He's had a run of bad luck—thanks to your mother—but we've become close. He wouldn't do anything to hurt me."

Taylor could have pointed out Lisa had been deceived before, but she didn't. Their friendship was frayed at the edges. She didn't want to make things worse especially since she didn't have any proof yet. She'd learned her lesson with Renata.

"Please, just do me one favor. Don't tell Jim about the hidden text on our Web site."

It took Lisa a moment to agree. "All right. I won't mention it."

"Thanks," Taylor responded, relieved, yet knowing this man was bound to drive them further apart.

"You need to realize your mother is a very manipulative person. I'm giving him another chance. We're going to make a fortune at Midnight Lace. Watch and see."

Chapter 23

Doyle left Brianna visiting her mother in the hospital and went to see his nephew. Trent hadn't come into the office all day, which was very unusual. Doyle knew he'd been prowling the streets of Miami trying to find Raoul.

The conniving little swish had been out hustling the family for money, but he hadn't bothered to call Trent. Doyle didn't want to break the bad news to Trent, yet what choice did he have? Sooner or later, Trent would learn the truth, and he might blame Doyle for withholding information.

Doyle hiked up the steps to the trendy SoBe loft Trent had purchased after his divorce. He rang the bell and waited, hearing the sound of classical music coming from the stereo.

The door swung open. "Oh, hi. I was expecting SoBe Pizza," Trent said.

Doyle expected to be invited inside, but his nephew stood there waiting for him to say something.

"I dropped by to talk to you about Raoul."

"What about me?" Raoul poked his head around the corner.

Doyle said a silent curse for getting himself involved in this mess. He didn't understand the gay life, and he never would. Still, Trent was family.

When his brother had died, Doyle had been at the hospital, holding his hand. "You're the stand-up guy now. Take care of the family."

What a family. Dysfunctional from the word "go." Taylor was the nearest to normal, and even she had fallen for a worthless wanna-be photographer more interested in the family's money than his own career. As far as he was concerned Paul Ashton's disappearance was a blessing in disguise.

"Glad to see you, Raoul," Doyle said. "I came by to ask if Trent had heard from you. I know how worried he's been."

Raoul turned on the smile that had charmed countless women and just as many men.

"That rehab was not working. Lectures all day long. Then meditation. That's not what I need."

Doyle begged to differ but knew it would do no good. Brianna had clued him in on the tricks crystal meth plays on the mind.

"I'm having a Sober Living By the Sea companion come here to help Raoul," Trent said.

Doyle didn't bother to ask what this was costing. He had money problems of his own. This was Trent's life and money, not his.

"Renata's funeral is on Friday. Your mother has invited everyone she knows. I think you two should be there."

"Of course," Trent said. "Who's handling the arrangements?"

"Taylor."

"Good old Taylor," Raoul said with a smirk.

Doyle struggled to control himself. He'd lost it far too often lately.

"I think you should visit your mother. Make your peace with her. Don't go to the funeral and she'll wonder if you're the killer."

"Has Her Majesty rewritten the will?" Raoul asked.

"I don't know," Doyle replied, although he knew she had not.

"She's balking, torturing the family. Right?"

Doyle hated to admit this was dead-on, but it was. Vintage Vanessa Maxwell. Manipulate everyone. Keep them guessing.

"We could drop by your mother's in the morning before work," Doyle said, "and see if there's anything we can do for the funeral."

Trent's eyes shifted to the side, and Doyle knew he was less excited than Doyle had been when Brianna suggested the visit.

"Great idea," Raoul said with a megawatt smile. "Patch it up with your mother."

Taylor looked up from her desk and saw Brianna sail into her office. "Okay, I'm here to help. Where's the list?"

"What list?"

"Doyle said your mother gave you a list of people to call about the funeral tomorrow."

"Right," Taylor said. She'd been putting off calling everyone, uncertain of what to say. "I appreciate the help."

Brianna smiled, and for a moment Taylor's world lit up.

"You said we were friends. I want to help you any way I can."

Those heartfelt words spoken in a New Orleans hotel seemed to belong to another person in another lifetime. But Taylor had meant everything she'd said. Brianna was special. Even if she left Doyle, Taylor would think of her as family.

Taylor handed Brianna the printout from her mother's address book. "I don't know how many of these socialites are in town, or how many can make it on such short notice, but let's try. You take half the list. I'll take the other."

An hour passed more quickly than Taylor realized. She'd reached many of the people on her part of the list and left messages for those she hadn't been able to contact. She inhaled deeply, immensely relieved to have done what her mother had asked, and grateful to Brianna for halving the load.

The interoffice light on her telephone monitor blinked. It was Trent. Brianna had told her about Raoul's sudden reappearance at the loft. Taylor also knew Doyle had not told her brother about the way Raoul had tried to get money from the family.

"Got a minute for me?" Trent asked when she answered the interoffice telephone.

"Sure. Your office or mine?" she said, using their old joke.

"Mine." Trent sounded very serious.

Taylor marked her place on the list of those to call and rushed down the hall to Trent's office. "What's up?" she asked as she came through the door.

"I went to see Mother this morning with Uncle Doyle."

"I saw her last night. She was . . ."

"Not herself."

"True. I'd called the doctor before about her medication. I know she's in pain. The myeloma is getting worse, but—"

"That Caleb person is giving her more painkillers than is good for her."

A small weight lifted off Taylor's heart. This was her brother, the person she knew so well that they could communicate almost without words.

"Exactly what I thought. Shane and I are having Maria monitor the number of pain pills she's taking. We should know soon if anything is off."

Trent nodded, his brows furrowed. "She seemed happy to see me."

Taylor didn't say her mother's reaction to her had been disturbingly cool.

"Mother says she's putting the will back to the way it was—more or less."

Interesting, Taylor thought. Her mother had told Ridley Pudge she hadn't decided how she intended to rewrite her will.

"What do you think she means?"

Trent barked a short laugh. "Who knows? I just think it's a good sign she isn't blaming us so much for Renata's death that she's written us out of the will."

Taylor wasn't positive this meant her mother didn't blame them—especially her—for Renata's murder. Every time she was around her mother, Taylor felt guilty even though she'd never done a thing to harm Renata.

"Raoul and I have plans for our share of the inheritance."

Raoul.

His name alone curdled her blood. Brianna had

told her about Uncle Doyle finding Raoul at Trent's loft.

Now they had plans for Trent's share of an inheritance that might not happen for months or—with luck—a year, maybe even longer.

It seemed morbid and greedy to Taylor.

"I don't like discussing Mother's money so callously. We need to get through the funeral and make sure she has a happy life until . . . the time comes."

"You don't have to bite my head off," snapped Trent. "We know she's going to die. What's wrong with discussing our plans?"

Taylor walked out of his office without saying another word. For a few minutes there, she thought the old Trent had reemerged. She'd been wrong.

Her brother had changed so much, he might as well be a stranger.

"Let's get a bite of lunch," she said to Brianna when she walked back into the office. She couldn't face making another call about the funeral right now, especially when the next person on her list was Aunt Sophie, Doyle's ex-wife.

As they walked upstairs to the company's dining room, Brianna gave her a rundown on the people she'd contacted. They sat at a small table near the window with a view of Coral Gables and, in the distance, Biscayne Bay.

"I'm dreading the funeral," Taylor confessed after they both ordered salads. "I'm not my mother's child when it comes to caring what people think, but after all the publicity about Renata's murder and the police searches, people are going to be looking at me and wondering.

"You know how people are. Some will think I killed Renata to keep her from inheriting the money. Others will think . . . oh, I don't know."

Brianna reached for her hand and curled her fingers into Taylor's

"You can't let it bother you. The gossip mill will churn, and there's nothing you can do to stop it. True friends will never believe you killed Renata."

"I know you're right. I just wish the case was solved. Not to shut up the gossips, but so my mother can have peace of mind."

The waitress delivered their Cobb salads, and they ate in silence for a few minutes.

"Is Shane taking you to the service?" Brianna asked.

"Yes, he is."

Taylor could have added Shane wasn't letting her out of his sight except at the office where other people were around. She'd discovered the man was as stubborn as an Arkansas mule. He was convinced she was in danger and nothing she said could change his mind.

"I'm happy you found him."

Taylor almost said she was happy, too, but somehow it seemed disloyal to Paul. After sleeping with Shane, she didn't allow herself to think about Paul often, but once in a while guilt would prick at her.

"I wonder how Paul would have handled all this."

"Well, he wouldn't have liked Renata. He—"

"I meant you getting tried in the press for Renata's murder."

"I have no idea. The worst we went through was Mother's attitude. Paul wasn't good enough for me. What she really meant was her socialite friends expected me to marry a rich man, not a struggling photographer."

"First Trent, then Renata. Your mother has had to accept a lot that once would have upset her."

"I admit I'm surprised that she's come such a long way. She even approves of my relationship with Shane. Of course, Renata gave her the idea."

Brianna put down her fork and pushed her plate aside. "How do you feel about him?"

There was no point in trying to deceive Brianna. "I like him . . . a lot. It's nice to have someone who's there for you when you need him. He's kind, intelligent."

"Sexy."

Taylor couldn't bank her smile. Indeed he was sexy. They told each other they shouldn't have dessert, then decided to split the chef's specialty, key lime pie.

"Brianna, be honest with me. No one in the family liked Paul except Trent. What did you think of Paul?"

"I found him funny, charming, but I also thought he was more interested in himself, his career, than anything or anyone, even you."

Their key lime pie came, and they attacked it. "Yummy," they murmured in unison.

"Shane's a different story," Brianna said. "From the first night I met him at your mother's, I've thought he was totally taken with you. He was polite to everyone, but he made zero attempt to be charming to anyone but you. It was almost as if he was obsessed with you."

So much had happened, Taylor hadn't thought about her first impressions of Shane. She'd caught him staring at her apartment. He'd watched her even though she hadn't been aware of it.

"What are you thinking?" Brianna asked.

"About the first few times I saw Shane. My intuition told me something was wrong."

"Before anything had gone wrong." Brianna scooped up the last of the pie. "A woman's intuition is a powerful weapon, sometimes our only weapon."

Taylor nodded, saying, "Maybe what I was picking up was an aura of danger. He worked for the Defense

Intelligence Agency on a counterterrorism unit. There are things he can't talk about."

"Can't, or won't?"

"Have you heard anything from your friend who's trying to crack that code?" Doyle asked Shane.

"The DIA sent Hank to Germany for a week to train some men there. He left several days ago. He'll be back soon and get right on it."

"It can't happen fast enough. I don't want the prospective buyers to get cold feet."

It couldn't happen fast enough for Shane, either. He was betting Jim Wilson was involved. The more he thought about it, the less certain he was that the company problems, the murder, and the firebomb were all linked.

He had the nagging feeling he was missing something. And it royally pissed him off.

He wanted to help Taylor more than he could remember wanting anything. Something or someone had put her at risk. The sooner he could fit pieces of the puzzle together, the more likely he could help her.

What a crock! The police were at a stalemate on Renata's murder and the firebombing. He and Vince weren't having any luck either.

"Raoul's back with Trent," Doyle told him, then filled him in on the details. "Trent's hiring this 'companion' to help with Raoul's drug problem. Have you ever heard of it?"

"Sure. I read about companions in *People*, I think. Movie stars and rock stars often have addiction problems. Companions go everywhere with them and make sure they don't take drugs."

"Then Raoul's companion is going to have his hands full."

"Companions get rock stars through their tours or movie stars through filming, but it doesn't deal with the underlying problem."

"Of course not. Trent ought to realize that."

"The addiction doesn't just disappear. The cravings remain. You need money to feed your habit. In the end, you deal or you steal."

Doyle went back to his office, and Shane tinkered on the computer, easily hacking into Sun World Bank's database. It took him nearly an hour to check the Maxwell family's financial records.

Not that he knew what he was looking for, exactly.

But the old "deal or steal" phrase triggered something in his brain. This had to be about money. Who in the family was spending beyond their means? Who might be desperate for money?

Doyle Maxwell was tapped out, his overdraft privileges had been revoked, and he was several payments behind in his mortgage.

Very interesting.

He checked Taylor and Trent, but couldn't come up with anything unusual. With Raoul hanging on Trent's coattails, he could easily need money soon.

Vanessa Maxwell was another story. She had transferred large sums of money from her brokerage account a few weeks ago—about the time she had learned about Renata.

Most of the money was gone now. Lots had been spent in stores, beauty salons, and spas when Renata had been alive. There were several hefty checks made out to Caleb and Renata herself.

Why would she give money to Caleb? The check was written before she was taking so much medication, so she must have been thinking clearly at the time.

What happened to Renata's money? None had been found in her room.

He scrolled through Vanessa's account and came upon another entry.

"I'll be a son of a bitch," he muttered out loud.

Chapter 24

Taylor stared at the dark hole in the ground, imagining Renata Rollins—so lively, so full of life, spending eternity six feet under.

Why hadn't she taken the time to get to know her?

How could she have judged someone so quickly, so harshly?

Walk a mile in my shoes.

She should have remembered that saying earlier. It was so true. What Renata became was the result of the life she'd led. She hadn't had all the privileges Taylor had taken for granted.

Suddenly, she saw Renata as a young girl. She was playing hopscotch on the sidewalk.

Smiling.

Happy.

What had happened to that little girl?

"Are you okay?" Shane whispered.

She nodded and leaned into his body, savoring the comfort of his arm around her. Getting through the service inside the chapel had been more difficult than she'd anticipated. Sobs had racked her mother's frail body, and Taylor had longed to move across the pew to hold her.

But an aisle separated them, an aisle and Caleb Bassett. He sat beside her mother, his arm around her, offering her his handkerchief, whispering to her.

Mercifully, the service had been short, delivered by a minister who knew nothing about Renata. He described her as "an innocent lamb called to heaven" and "a woman whose compassion for others and charitable works would be remembered through eternity."

Trite phrases, she'd thought, but she didn't blame the minister. He'd never met Renata, and no telling what Caleb and her mother had said about her.

Still, she couldn't help wishing someone who'd known Renata well had been on hand to deliver the eulogy. Taylor couldn't imagine going to her grave, surrounded by strangers.

At least a hundred people had come, more than Taylor had expected, but only a handful had ever met Renata. Taylor supposed she should be thankful her mother's friends were in attendance. Even though they hadn't known Renata, their presence might comfort her mother.

If anything could.

Shane guided Taylor to the white folding chairs placed alongside the open grave. They took seats next to Brianna and Uncle Doyle. Across from them on the other side of the grave were Raoul and Trent, beside her mother and Caleb.

Mourners were still filing out of the chapel and down the short walkway to the grave site. For a change, the temperature was mild, the humidity lower than normal. Overhead, a gull coasted on a thermal, searching for a meal along the nearby shore.

It was a beautiful setting, Taylor thought. A good resting place for the sister she'd never got to know.

Vines flush with bright pink geraniums spilled over a coral wall. An ancient banyan tree arched gracefully over this part of the graveyard. It would be shady and cooler here even in the heat of summer. The scent of gardenias floated through the air from the trellised arbor a few feet away.

"It's a beautiful casket," Brianna whispered.

"Lovely."

Taylor realized her mother had orchestrated this funeral the way she had all of her parties. While Taylor had taken care of the messy details like calling everyone, her mother made certain everything was beautiful and done with taste.

Perfect.

Banks of white flowers, from exotic orchids to huge jungle roses, had cascaded from elaborate arrangements inside the chapel. The casket, a glossy mahogany with polished brass hinges, was covered in a blanket of white orchids. Along the top, sprays of white rosebuds, twined through curly willow branches, reached heavenward.

The grave site had been carpeted with hundreds of thousands of white rose petals until not a speck of brown dirt could be seen. Somehow the florist had managed to apply the petals to the earth on the sides of the freshly dug pit.

But it still looked like a grave, Taylor thought.

Dark and deep.

She glanced up at Shane as the minister cleared his throat to deliver the final prayer. Shane was gazing down at her, his eyes concerned. She laced her fingers through his.

When she glanced up, Caleb caught her eye. The look he gave her literally did make her skin crawl. She had to get her mother away from this man.

Taylor's temples throbbed, a headache brought on by tension. After the funeral, everyone had come back to her mother's house. They were barely twenty minutes into what she expected to be an ordeal lasting several hours.

"I could use a Tylenol," she whispered to Shane.

"This is a good time to talk to Maria. She'll know where to get an aspirin, and I can ask her about your mother's medication."

"Let's hope we can find her."

An army of caterers swarmed through the house, carrying trays of appetizers, setting up elaborate food stations and a buffet table the size of a tennis court. A bar had been set up outside by the pool in addition to the bar in the house.

A troop of florists must have been here earlier. Taylor doubted a single white rose or white orchid was left in Miami.

They found Maria and Pablo back in the servants' quarters, the kitchen having been taken over by the caterer.

"*Maria, tenga aspirin?*" Taylor tapped on her forehead, feeling silly for her butchered Spanish and wishing yet again she'd taken it instead of French.

Maria had worked long enough here to understand the stabbing attempts at her language, Taylor decided as the woman led her to the small bathroom nearby. No doubt Maria understood English better than she could speak it, having worked for the family for almost twenty years.

Taylor popped three pills and washed them down

with the glass of water Maria offered. Back in the sitting area, Shane began to question Maria in Spanish.

The maid produced a list of medications she'd copied off bottles in the master bathroom. The writing was large and childlike. Beside each entry was a numeral for the number of pills in the bottle.

"Look at this." Shane pointed to the Vicodin count. "I'd say she's mainlining the stuff."

"I'm not sure what Vicodin is, exactly. I know it's a painkiller, but she's been on Percocet. Is Vicodin stronger?"

"You bet, and more addictive. It's a manufactured opiate. In the ghetto they call it 'rich man's heroin.' Its effects are similar, but instead of injecting it, you swallow a pill."

"If she's taking so much, she'll run out. Then the doctor will know there's a problem."

Shane put his hand on her shoulder. "Honey, don't count on it. Our health system is on the verge of collapse. Doctors are so overworked and hassled with insurance claims, they don't always have the time to check. Her doctor may not remember when he last wrote a prescription, or for how many pills."

"You're right. I need to call him. This time he *has* to listen to me." Taylor thought a moment. "No. I'll go see him. Maybe if I handle this in person, we can help Mother."

"Good idea," Shane replied. "Let me ask Maria what she thinks about the situation. She's a smart woman, and she's known your mother for a long time."

Taylor listened while Shane spoke in rapid Spanish to Maria. The maid answered, gesturing with her hands. Pablo added something in a quieter voice. Without understanding more than a few words here and there, Taylor knew the couple was upset.

"What's wrong?"

Shane turned to her. "They don't like Caleb. They say he takes advantage of your mother. He snoops through her things. Slips out at night after she's asleep and doesn't come back until nearly dawn. He gives her pills even when she doesn't ask for them."

A surge of something too bitter and painful to be mere anger swept through Taylor. The man had managed to hook up with Renata and take advantage of her. Now he was after her mother, who was in a weakened, helpless state.

"Maria, Pablo, *gracias,*" she said in a strained voice. "*Muchas gracias.*"

She walked toward the door, planning how she'd confront Caleb, while Shane spoke to the couple in Spanish. When Shane joined her, she explained what she wanted to say to Caleb.

Shane guided her out the side door into the pool area, where a few guests were milling around, munching on appetizers and sipping drinks.

"I'm not sure confronting Caleb will get you anywhere."

"What am I supposed to do? Sit back and let him OD my mother or bilk her out of God-only-knows-what?"

Shane cupped her chin with his large hand and looked down at her. "Do you want to drive a bigger wedge between yourself and your mother?"

"Of course not."

"I suspect Caleb is just dying for you to pounce on him. That way he can go to your mother for sympathy."

"You're probably right," she conceded. "What are we going to do?"

"I suggested it before, and I still think it's best if you and Trent talk to your mother. You're her children. Tell her your concerns. I'll keep Caleb out of the way.''

"All right," Taylor agreed, although she had serious reservations about this working. Not only was her mother cool to her, but the last time she'd been with Trent, they'd disagreed. How much could she count on her brother?

"Taylor, Shane, there you are." Lisa walked toward them, her arm through Jim Wilson's.

"Thanks for coming," Taylor said with as much sincerity as she could muster. As with her brother, her last words with Lisa hadn't been pleasant.

"That was some funeral, even for Miami," Jim said.

The pressure of Shane's hand on the back of her waist kept Taylor from making a sarcastic remark. This accountant, who looked more like a surfer, had no right to criticize her mother.

"You know Vanessa," Lisa said. "She knows how to do things to perfection."

Personally, Taylor had thought this was over the top, even by her mother's standards. But she wouldn't admit it to anyone except Shane.

"Taylor, why aren't you inside?" It was Aunt Sophie.

"Hello, Aunt Sophie. You remember Lisa? And Shane Donovan?" Taylor turned to Jim. "This is Jim Wilson."

Aunt Sophie acknowledged each of them with a short jerk of her chin. "You should be inside with your mother. That odious man is with her. It's your place to be at her side, not his."

Before Taylor could respond, Aunt Sophie grabbed her arm and propelled her in the direction of the living room.

"I saw that slut with my husband. You'd think he'd leave her home when it's a family occasion like this."

"Aunt Sophie, they're married. It would be *strange* if he didn't bring her."

Aunt Sophie's eyes blazed with a malevolent light. "That whore is trouble. She got my husband away from me with Santería."

"Magic? Oh, Aunt Sophie, you don't believe that."

"She gave him one of their love potions and put a hex on me."

Taylor exhaled deeply, realizing the Tylenol hadn't kicked in yet. "Why haven't you ever mentioned this?"

"I just found out."

"Who told you?"

"Never mind," she snapped. "I have my ways."

Taylor had never seen her aunt so unbalanced. True, she led a life steeped in religion and society-style charity work, but now she seemed more distraught than she'd been right after the divorce.

Betrayal was a terrible thing. As was loss, Taylor decided. She'd finally moved on with her life. Why couldn't Aunt Sophie?

Inside, it appeared that everyone had arrived. A crowd surrounded her mother who was—miraculously—still standing. She should be sitting down, conserving her strength.

"Trent's with her," Taylor told her aunt. "She doesn't need me right now."

"So is the slut."

Taylor had noticed Brianna standing with the group but hadn't mentioned it, knowing what Sophie's reaction would be.

"You like her, don't you?" Aunt Sophie's voice had an accusatory edge.

"Yes." Taylor told herself not to feel guilty. Brianna was her friend and deserved her loyalty.

"She used Santería on you, too."

"I don't believe in it," Taylor responded with as much patience as she could muster.

"I've seen evidence of it."

Taylor glanced over her shoulder, hoping to find Shane coming to rescue her. Instead, Raoul Cathcart was bearing down on her, a knockout blonde at his side.

"Hello, Mrs. Maxwell," Raoul said to Sophie with a charming smile. "You look beautiful in that navy suit."

Taylor hadn't realized Raoul knew Sophie. Evidently, Trent must have been to Fisher Island to visit his aunt.

"This is my companion, Fallon James." He beamed another smile, and Taylor wondered what her brother saw in this man. "She's at my side every moment to be sure I don't touch any drugs, not even alcohol."

"He's been a good boy so far," Fallon said.

Taylor managed a weak smile. She thought a rehab program would have been better because it dealt with the causes of addiction. What would happen when the companion left?

"We're discussing Santería," Sophie told Raoul. "Do you believe in it?"

"Of course. I'm part Cuban. My mother swears by it." Raoul chuckled. "Beware of the evil eye."

"Excuse me," Taylor said. "I need to find my brother."

"He's in the library with Doyle," Raoul told her as she walked away.

It took her a few minutes to walk through the crowd, accepting condolences from people who hadn't met Renata, and get to the library. She knocked on the door. Uncle Doyle called out for her to come in.

"Am I interrupting?"

"No," Trent said, "we were just discussing what to do about Caleb Bassett."

"That's what I wanted to talk about."

She explained what Maria had told them about the Vicodin and the way Caleb behaved.

"I think Trent and I should take Mother aside and tell her how concerned we are. Shane said he'd keep Caleb out of the way while we did it. Perhaps, Uncle Doyle, you could help him."

"Good idea," Doyle replied. "I'll get Brianna, too. Caleb can't keep his eyes off her."

"I guess we should wait another hour or so until the crowd thins out," Trent said without a hint of enthusiasm.

"What's the matter?" she asked.

"Money," he said. "I was asking Uncle Doyle for a loan, but he's short of cash, too."

"I can loan you a little," she said, even though she would have to take it from the account she'd set up to start her own business.

"A little won't help. We need to sell the business."

"I'm hoping your mother will agree to a sale just as soon as this computer mess is cleared up."

No one had to tell her that Trent needed the money to help Raoul. A companion like Fallon had to cost a bundle.

Oh, Trent, she thought. Don't do this to yourself.

Chapter 25

Shane stood beside Brianna, who was talking to Caleb. Doyle was at the bar set up near the pool, getting Caleb another Johnnie Walker.

What a crock!

The jerk-off did not need another drink. He was in the bag already.

Taylor and Trent told Caleb they were putting their mother to bed. The man was too busy drooling over Brianna and kicking back expensive Johnnie Walker Blue Label to pay much attention to what Vanessa was doing.

"Where did you live before New Orleans?" Brianna asked Caleb.

Shane had coached Brianna and Doyle about information the three of them should try to get out of Bassett. It wasn't going to be easy. Bassett's eyes had shifted to the side at the question.

The man was drunk but not stupid.

"Lived here and there, darlin', here and there. Why?"

"Your accent is so interesting. When we met you in New Orleans, you sounded British. Now you seem Southern. Mississippi or Arkansas."

Caleb's sly smile revealed little.

He shrugged, lifting the shoulders of the lizard-green-and-purple print Versace sport coat he'd put on after the funeral. No doubt the guy didn't think black was his color. The trendy Versace jacket could have got him arrested in Des Moines, but no one looked twice in Miami.

"Here's your Johnnie Walker," Doyle said as he walked up and handed Caleb another drink.

"Thanks." He looked around at the nearly empty pool area. "It was a helluva' party. A nice send-off for my baby."

"Do you think the police are going to solve the crime?" Brianna asked.

"Nah, they aren't even trying."

Caleb swigged his whiskey, then leered at Brianna's low-cut neckline. For a grief-stricken father, the man was having a damn good time.

"Do you think Renata had made enemies where she lived before?" Doyle asked. "That person could have—"

"Nah. Everyone in New Orleans adored her."

Gimme a break.

"It's a shame. She was so young," Brianna said. "She had her whole life ahead of her. I started out as a lap dancer not much different than what Renata was doing, and look at me now."

Caleb didn't need any encouragement. He couldn't keep his eyes off Brianna's impressive cleavage.

"I'm starting a new life here in Miami," Caleb

announced, after kicking back the rest of his drink. "No more selling insurance for me. No, siree."

"What are your plans?" Doyle asked.

"I've always been innerested in real estate. I've got a hankering to sell condos. There are a lot of retirees down here looking for them."

Shane could see Caleb as a successful real estate salesman. Stranger things had happened. The man could be persuasive and charming. When he wanted, he could beam a smile bright enough to light up Miami.

"May I get you another drink?" he asked Caleb. "I'm getting myself one."

"Sure. Johnnie Walker Blue Label. Make sure they don't give me the rotgut Johnnie Walker."

"Gotcha'."

Shane would have bet his life Caleb hadn't had Blue Label until he came to Miami. He held out his hand palm up, took the glass, and turned before Caleb could notice he wasn't letting his fingers touch the glass.

Not that Caleb was paying attention to anything but Brianna.

While they'd been talking, Shane had an idea. Lift Caleb's fingerprints off the glass, make copies of the print, and run it through police databases in nearby states.

See what turned up.

Swans do not wax poetic about their lives as ugly ducklings, but Caleb's reluctance to discuss his past indicated the man had something to hide. Shane had noted the comment about selling insurance. Caleb hadn't been doing squat in New Orleans.

So why had he mentioned selling insurance? Granted, he had been selling insurance long ago when his house had burned down. Had he continued to sell it for years?

There weren't many insurance companies. As with most other businesses, the sharks had gobbled up the little fish. Assuming he'd been using the name Caleb Bassett, it shouldn't be hard to check.

"The guy over there in the green jacket needs a Johnnie Walker Blue Label on the rocks," Shane told the bartender. "Make sure it's Blue Label."

"We're out of Blue. He drank it all. We've got Johnnie Walker Gold Label. Will that do?"

Shane nodded, thinking Caleb had consumed a fifth of whiskey. Okay, it had been over a five hour period, but still . . .

He slipped into the kitchen, where the caterers were cleaning up, and wrapped the glass in a paper towel to preserve the fingerprints. He caught a glimpse of Raoul down the hall. He was kissing the blonde who was supposed to be keeping him off drugs.

Go figure.

He dumped the ice in the sink and ducked into the pantry to use his cell phone. Vince answered on the first ring. Shane explained what he wanted to do, and Vince agreed it was a good idea.

"I wish I had the time to go to Arkansas and do some checking on Bassett. But I don't want to leave Taylor right now. I can be more help here with the murder investigation."

"If my company was bigger and had more men, I could send one of them."

Vince was just starting out and specializing in computer security. He'd given Shane a job because they'd known each other from the DIA. In a year, if they worked well together, Shane was going to buy half the business. Then they could expand.

"I doubt a hundred men could turn up much on Bassett. I'm betting he covered his tracks."

* * *

While Trent pulled the drapes and turned down the bed, Taylor took her mother into the dressing room and helped her change out of the black Chanel suit she'd worn to the funeral. Her mother was unsteady on her feet and her hands shook. Taylor couldn't tell if it was from exhaustion or drugs.

"It was lovely," Taylor said because she felt she should. "Everything was perfect."

"Yes. I thought it went well. So many of my friends came."

"We have Brianna to thank for that. She did the lion's share of the calling."

Her mother didn't comment. She tottered off into the bathroom. Taylor didn't follow. Instead, she returned to the bedroom area.

"Mother is in the bathroom."

Trent was standing in front of a table where there was an arrangement of family photographs in sterling-silver frames. In the center was the last publicity picture taken of Duncan Maxwell for the To The Maxx catalogue.

"I miss him. Don't you?" Taylor asked.

"Totally. He'd know what to do."

"He wouldn't want us to sell the company."

"I'd like to keep it and run it with Raoul, but I don't have the money for the buyout."

"Trent, why are you so pressed for money? If it's none of my business, just tell me, but if there's any way I can help, I will."

Trent turned to her, a glimmer of the brother she once knew reflected in his eyes.

"Thanks. I appreciate the support. I don't need the money right this minute, but I will. It's going to take a lot to get Raoul back on track."

That's exactly what she thought the money was for. Maybe she'd misjudged Raoul. She'd like to believe her brother's time, money, and most of all, love wasn't wasted on a vain man who'd dump him in a heartbeat if something better came along.

"What are you doing?" Their mother's soft voice came from behind them.

Taylor turned, saying, "Looking at the picture of Dad. Missing him."

"I miss him, too." Tears glistened in her eyes.

Taylor rushed to her side. "Let me help you to bed." She guided her mother to the bed and steadied her as she slipped between the sheets.

Without makeup, her mother's skin was a worrisome ash color. Her eyes seemed clearer than they had the other day, but they held a world-weary expression.

The day had taken its toll, the way Taylor had known it would. It didn't seem fair to have this discussion now, but who knew when they'd have another chance?

Trent sat down on the foot of the bed. "Mother, we're concerned about you."

She looked up at them from beneath half-closed lids. "It was an exhausting day, that's all."

Taylor eased herself down onto the bed, not knowing how to begin even though she'd mentally rehearsed this at least a dozen times. "We're worried because your blood work isn't good."

"We knew this day would come. Didn't we?"

Taylor nodded with a quick glance at Trent. This sounded like the woman who'd raised her. She faced the world head-on.

"Yes, we've all been aware of the progression of the disease," Trent said.

"It's only a matter of time until I die."

Taylor wanted to deny it, wanted to shout it to the

heavens, but what would be the use. They all knew the truth.

"With luck and proper treatment, you'll have quite some time," Trent said.

"We're concerned about the amount of painkillers you're taking," Taylor said.

"How do you know how much I'm taking?" Her mother's voice was soft, as if she didn't have the strength to raise it, but there was a distinct bite in her tone.

Rather than get Maria in trouble, Taylor said, "We see it in the way you look, the way you talk. Your eyes don't look . . . right."

"I haven't had a pain pill all day. Caleb wanted to give me one several times, but I didn't want to miss a thing. I just took one now. I'm waiting for it to work."

"Is Caleb giving you those pills more often than you're supposed to take them?" Taylor asked.

"I-I'm not sure. I'm in a lot of pain, you know. I-I need . . ."

Taylor reached for her mother's hand. "We know you're in pain, and we don't want you to suffer. But . . . if you're doped up and groggy how can you enjoy yourself?"

"We'd like to have a nurse come in to help you. She can administer the proper amount of medication and take care of you," Trent added.

"I don't want a nurse. I've got Caleb."

"Mother, he doesn't dress you or put you to bed," Taylor pointed out.

"Maria is here if I need her."

"That means Caleb gives you all your medication," Trent said. "What happens when he leaves? I'm sure he'll be going soon, now the funeral is over."

Her mother's head slowly swung from one side of the pillow to the other in an attempt to shake her head. "He's staying here with me while he gets a real estate license."

Oh, great, Taylor thought. Just great.

She squeezed her mother's hand. "Do you think Caleb's staying here is a good idea? What will your friends think?" Taylor asked because she thought her mother might still care about impressions the way she once did.

"You saw them today. They like Caleb."

Being totally honest, Taylor said, "With him around, this place doesn't seem like home. It's not the family home it once was when Dad was alive."

"You can't blame Caleb for being a little hostile. You two are prime suspects. That's why they searched your homes."

"And didn't find a thing," Taylor reminded her.

"Mother," Trent spoke up. "Uncle Doyle and I were in the library this afternoon. Someone has been going through the files. We think it's Caleb."

"Is your jewelry safe, Mother?" Taylor asked.

"And To The Maxx's formulas," Trent added.

"Of course, it's all in the safe except for a few pieces of jewelry I wear every day."

She studied them a moment, then closed her eyes. It was a few seconds before she opened them again.

"I know what you two are thinking, but you're wrong. Caleb is a good man. He's Renata's father. He'd never do anything to hurt me."

"I wish I could agree. You know he's out at the clubs every night."

Taylor didn't know this for a fact, but judging from what Maria had told her, where else would he go at night?

"Of course he goes out at night. Caleb needs to have a little fun. He's with me all day. It must be dreadfully depressing."

"Why don't you give him the money for his own apartment, where he can study for his real estate license?" suggested Trent.

"I need him. I need him here with me."

Those words confirmed the full extent of the hold Caleb Bassett had on their mother. Taylor had suspected this, but held out hope that the woman who'd raised her would be savvy enough to see this man was a con artist.

"I love you both very much," her mother told them. "I'm so proud of each of you."

"And we love you." Trent stood up and walked to the head of the bed and kissed his mother's cheek.

Taylor leaned forward and kissed her other cheek. "Love you. Love you so much."

"Hey, what's all this lovey-dovey stuff?" Caleb sauntered into the room and the air filled with the scent of Johnnie Walker.

"We're family," Taylor said, forcing a pleasant tone. After all, it was clear they would have to deal with this man. "We love each other."

"Sweet. Right sweet." Caleb took her mother's hand and kissed it. "Do you need your medication?"

"No. I've taken it."

Caleb looked at Taylor and Trent. "Then we'll get outta here and let you go to sleep."

"Love you." Taylor kissed her mother again. "I'll drop by tomorrow on my way home from work."

"Good night, Mother," Trent said.

"I love you both," their mother said, her voice faint but charged with emotion.

Caleb followed them out of the master suite. Taylor waited until they were in the foyer adjacent to the dining room before saying to Caleb, "Don't overmedicate my mother. Don't give her pain pills more often than the directions indicate."

"She's in a lot of pain."

"I know, but being so doped up that she's out of it isn't good for her. I want her to enjoy what time she has left."

Caleb shrugged. "Think of me as family. I'm Renata's father. We're as good as related."

He left them and strode out toward the pool. As soon as Caleb was out of sight, Trent whispered in her ear, "Christ! You don't suppose he's convinced Mother that he's family, and she's going to include him in the will?"

"We got nowhere," Taylor told Shane as they left the house and headed to her car. "My mother isn't going to tell Caleb to leave."

"We didn't have much luck with him, either. He's a wily old coot. But Caleb did give me a few ideas."

She listened to him explain about the glass and the insurance angle as they walked through the sultry night. She could hardly concentrate. She was bone-weary and more worried than ever about her mother.

Thank you, God, for sending me Shane.

Her brother's comment about the will disturbed her. At times he appeared to be himself. Yet at other times, he seemed obsessed with money.

And Raoul.

They'd parked her Beamer under a streetlight. It shone down on an envelope tucked between the windshield wiper and the glass.

"It can't be a parking ticket," she said as they approached.

"Don't touch it."

They stared down at the envelope. In big, bold computer generated block letters, TAYLOR MAXWELL was written across the front.

Taylor pulled it out, and Shane grabbed her hand. "It's probably just a condolence note."

"Maybe, but let me open it. If it's a letter bomb, I don't want it to explode in your pretty face."

He walked about ten feet away, turned his back to her, and she heard him rip open the envelope.

Silence.

He turned around and strode back to her, a grim expression on his face.

"I was right." He handed her the single sheet of paper. "You are in danger."

She scanned the words.

EVERY WAKING MOMENT YOUR KILLER IS WATCHING YOU.

   PREPARE TO DIE, TAYLOR. PREPARE TO JOIN RENATA.

Chapter 26

Outside Shane's bedroom window an alley cat yowled, a harrowing sound. Taylor jerked upright. He knew she hadn't been asleep, and neither had he.

After finding the threatening note, they'd gone to the police station. The detectives working the case took the note seriously, especially after the pipe bomb. They didn't come out and say they no longer considered her a suspect in Renata's death, but Shane noticed a change in their attitude.

"It's just a cat," he told her as he sat up and pulled her into his arms.

"I know. I'm a bit jumpy. I can't imagine why anyone would want to kill me."

They'd been over it and hadn't come up with an answer. He hated to ask this question. The police should have inquired, but they hadn't yet.

They probably would soon. He needed to know now.

"Do you have a will? If you died, who would inherit your money?"

"I have very little money. My father left me a small trust fund. Trent received exactly the same amount. My father was a big believer in children making their own way. He left everything to my mother, thinking she'd live a long time, and we would have proven ourselves before she died, and we inherited his money."

"Who would inherit what you do have?"

Two beats of silence. "My brother."

Shane didn't have to verbalize his thoughts. With Taylor dead and her mother's death imminent, Trent stood to inherit everything.

"Trent wouldn't do this. He may have changed, but he's still my brother." Taylor pulled out of his arms and scooted backward to rest against the headboard. "Why warn me? Why not just try to kill me?"

They'd been over this before, but Taylor still needed to talk about it.

"Whoever it is wants you to be frightened." He moved back until he was beside her. "He's getting a kick out of this."

"I'm not giving him the satisfaction of letting him know I'm frightened. I'm going about my business just as I normally would. Don't tell anyone about this. I don't want my family worried, especially Mother."

Shane leaned over and clicked on the small lamp beside the bed. Auggie was curled up on the floor. He lifted his head and cocked it to one side. Shane gave him a quick pat.

"Now wait a minute. How can I protect you if the people who can help watch over you don't have a clue?"

"Then whoever is trying to scare me will know I'm frightened."

"Not necessarily. I want you to let me tell the people

who can keep an eye on you at work. Doyle can be the most help."

"And Trent. He's there every day."

Shane didn't want to say what he was thinking.

"He's not behind this," Taylor repeated what she'd told him a few minutes ago, more emphatically this time. "I know my brother and he would never kill anyone."

He leaned sideways and kissed her cheek.

"Money is usually the reason people kill unless it's a crime of passion, which tend to be spur-of-the-moment killings. This killer has an agenda. If we knew what it was, we'd know who was behind this."

Shane didn't rule out the money angle, but it seemed less likely given the threatening note, and the pipe bomb, which had been the initial warning. The killer was getting off tormenting them.

"I'm glad I have you," Taylor said, her voice a shade shy of a whisper. "Together we can beat this."

"Count on it."

"I've been thinking. Anyone who came to the house after the funeral could have put the note on my car."

"Someone could have driven by and put it there."

"True, but it seems more likely it was someone at the funeral. Right?"

"Probably. This person isn't striking at random. He has a gripe or some vendetta." Shane thought a moment. "People are usually killed by someone they know."

"Someone I know wants me dead," she replied, a quaver in her voice. Biting her lip, she looked away. "Is it possible Caleb Bassett is the one?"

"Possible but unlikely, I think. Why would he kill Renata? She was the goose that laid the golden egg. His entree to your mother and her world."

"Maybe it's Jim Wilson. He has a grudge against the family."

"We're checking him out. He may have tinkered with the Web site. But why would he kill Renata? Or want to kill you?"

"There's something we don't know, don't understand."

Shane slipped his arm around Taylor and pulled her close. "Don't worry about this anymore tonight. With luck, the police will be able to lift fingerprints off the note or the envelope."

He pressed his lips against hers, caressing her mouth more than kissing it. How in hell had he fallen so hard, so fast, for this woman? Being intrigued by a photograph was one thing.

Falling in love was another.

"Shane, I've been wondering . . . about you."

Uh-oh. Here it comes.

"I know so little about you, about your past."

"What would you like to know?" he forced himself to ask.

"Where did you grow up and what was your family like?"

"I lived in Germany until I was seventeen. My mother's German. She's a wonderful person. You'll like her. She married an American serviceman who was killed in an accident on the autobahn.

"Her family lived nearby and she moved in with them, but she made certain I attended the base school. So I grew up speaking English and German. In high school I learned French."

"Oh, my God. You speak Spanish, too. I took years of French, and I can barely make myself understood when I go there."

"Europeans usually speak more than one language.

I learned Spanish later, when I was in college at Georgetown."

For a moment she studied him intently. "Georgetown. Interesting choice."

"Want a laugh? I was accepted at Yale, but chose Georgetown because I took one look at New Haven and hated it. Georgetown was more like Europe."

"Wow! We could have been at Yale at the same time."

"See? It was fate we finally met."

Fate and the dirtbag—Paul Ashton.

"After college I went into the service and joined Cobra Force. I told you the rest. I worked on classified projects involving drugs and their link to terrorist groups.

"I used a sophisticated military computer in the field for the last two years. That's how I got into computer security. I can't tell you any more about it than I already have."

Actually, this wasn't *exactly* a lie. His last assignment had been classified, but he could tell her about meeting Paul. Not all the details, of course. Those were top secret.

He should let her know the man she'd loved—maybe still loved—was very much alive.

He couldn't risk her leaving him. Not after tonight. When she was out of danger, he'd tell her about meeting that prick and seeing her picture.

"What's your mother's name?"

"Gisela. I have her blue eyes and my dad's dark hair. Everyone else in my family is blond. My grandmother, Rue, is still alive, but my grandfather, Klaus, passed away almost five years ago. He was like a father to me."

Shane corrected himself. "No. He was my father. He raised me and did all the 'dad' stuff."

"Your mother never remarried?"

"Nope. I asked her about it once, and she said she couldn't stand to lose a man she loved again."

"I can understand." Taylor gazed wistfully across the room.

Aw, hell. Why had he said that? What was he thinking?

After a moment's silence, she asked, "Do you talk to your family very often?"

"I usually call on Sunday after they've been to church. I know Grandmother will be fixing a huge lunch. My mother and cousins will be there."

He'd been away a long, long time, but a Sunday never came that he didn't think about his family.

And miss them, especially his grandfather.

The life he'd led with the Cobra Force had turned him into a loner who didn't—couldn't afford to— trust anyone, get close to anyone. He'd sacrificed years to the fight against terrorism, a fight that had become front page news.

Part of him itched to go back. His wiser side told him that he was burned out, more likely to make a mistake than to help.

"Amazing. Our family did the same thing. Sunday dinners were special. Even after Trent and I had our own places, our own lives, we gathered at the house every Sunday evening."

She smiled, then asked, "What about your father's family?"

"They came to visit several times. They're both dead now, and since my father was an only child, I just have distant cousins. I don't know them."

Shane leaned over and clicked off the light. He drew her into his arms, saying, "I'm crazy about you. I'm not going to let anything happen to you. I promise."

This was as close as he'd come to telling her he loved her. Hell, he wanted to say it, but he knew Ashton was still on her mind. It was too soon to use those words, especially since he hadn't yet been completely honest with her.

Taylor snuggled against him. She smelled of his soap, having showered after they'd returned from the police station. He nuzzled her neck, then kissed his favorite spot just below her earlobe.

Well, one of his favorite spots.

As usual, she sighed. That's why it was a favorite spot. A kiss there always meant a sigh.

"Shane . . . I . . .

He told himself it was okay. She wasn't ready to say more yet, but he could see her feelings were changing. He remembered how hard it had been on his mother when she'd faced life without his father. He understood what Taylor was going through.

It would take time.

He covered her mouth with his. Her lips were warm and moist beneath his. With a quick darting motion her tongue sought his.

Like a swift-rising tide, desire built in him, and he could feel it mounting in her as she pressed against him, unconsciously offering herself. This was an honest reaction to him, not the cerebral loyalty to another man who didn't deserve it.

Shane couldn't change the past, but this he could control.

He gazed down at Taylor, her face barely visible in the moonlight filtering through the window. "I should have gone to Yale. I would have met you sooner."

"No. I believe in fate. We were meant to meet now, this way."

He slowly pulled the T-shirt over her head. It would have been easy to reach up under it, but he didn't want anything between them when he made love to her.

His hands slid over her bare skin, so soft, so smooth. She raked his back with her long nails.

Gently.

Erotically.

He lowered his lips to her breast, not intending to kiss the breast itself. He was kissing her heart, and he could feel the steady thud-thud against his mouth.

"Suck on me," she whispered.

He did as he was told and laved one nipple with his tongue, slowly drawing it into his mouth. He was so damn hot and hard, he thought he'd lose it like some horny teenager. He squeezed his eyes shut.

And told himself this was another mission.

Not mission impossible. He'd already accomplished half of what he wanted to do. He and Taylor had a relationship going.

So what if she didn't love him the way he loved her? It would happen with time and luck.

So far luck had been on his side.

Her hand slid between his legs and clutched his erection. "I need you—now."

He let her guide him into her moist heat. Then he told her with his body what he couldn't yet say out loud.

"I don't know what to think," Shane told Vince the following morning in the accounting department cubicle at Maxx, where he hung out when he was there. He'd brought Vince up to speed, telling about the threatening note.

"I made Taylor let me tell her uncle and brother about it. I wanted to gauge their reactions to see if one of them might be involved."

"How did they take the news?"

"They seemed to be shocked. I'd say Trent might

have . . . I don't know. He could have been a little *too* surprised.''

"Go with your gut instinct. The odds say money is the number one motivator for murder. With Renata gone and Taylor dead, Trent stands to inherit everything.''

"Right, but I'm beginning to wonder if money is what's behind this.''

"If not money, then what?''

"I don't know. What I do know is, Taylor needs more protection, but we don't want to tip off the killer. I want to put a tracker on her.''

"Good idea but how do you expect to get one and a tracker monitor to boot?''

They'd both used tracking chips when they'd worked for the DIA. A tiny chip a little bigger than the head of a straight pin had contact glue on one side. It could be attached—unnoticeable—to an article of clothing or jewelry. Wristwatches were a favorite place to conceal a chip, because people took them off only to sleep.

"I have contacts and money. I can get a monitor and several tracking chips.''

He didn't add that he had lots of money. Not only had his grandfather left him a chunk, he'd spent little of what he'd earned. Being conservative by nature, he'd invested in bonds, not stocks, and his money had grown.

He was prepared to use it all to help Taylor.

"I want to chip several people besides Taylor. In her case, I want to know where she is should anything happen. With the others, I want to know where they're going.''

"Others?''

"Trent, Raoul, Jim Wilson.'' Shane paused, then added without thinking, "Doyle Maxwell.''

"No women?"

"Odds say it's a man."

"Women are becoming more aggressive all the time. Once you could bet your life the killer was male. Not anymore."

Shane rocked back in the office chair and studied the ceiling. "Sophie Maxwell struck me as weird. Taylor told me she seemed unbalanced at the funeral. She went on and on about Santería."

"What about Doyle's wife?"

Shane knew Vince had his eye on Brianna. "A long shot. Not worth wasting a chip on her."

"Okay, so who is going to sit around and watch the tracking monitor?"

Shane knew this question was coming. The chips required a tracking device with a screen similar to a radar screen. Someone had to watch and record the movements of the people electronically being reported by the tracking chips.

"I'll pay for two employees whose job it'll be to watch the screen and record where everyone goes around the clock."

Vince nodded. "It'll be great when we're making enough money to hire more people."

The fledgling company had a small office with a secretary in a rundown area of Coconut Grove. The computer security field was very lucrative, and they stood to make a good deal of money once they were established.

Thinking of the cost-cutting they'd done made Shane question Vince. "Did you sweep this place?"

"No. Why would I? We don't have the equipment. I didn't think it was necessary. The problem is with the computers."

"I'm wondering if someone bugged these offices. That's how he'd know Taylor didn't take the pipe bomb seriously. She thought it might have been a mistake.''

"So he sent the note." Vince arched one eyebrow. "I think it's someone right here who doesn't need a bug to know what's up. Either that or someone here tells everything that's going on."

"You mean Raoul Cathcart?"

"Exactly, although I wouldn't rule out the brother."

Shane wouldn't either. "You know, the computer problem might not be related to the murders at all."

"You may be right. Hank Olfeld should be back any day. When he cracks the code, we'll know."

"Let's sweep the place anyway. I'll buy the sweeper. We may need it later for another job."

Vince agreed, and Shane gave him a credit card to purchase the sweeper. He didn't want to leave Taylor—even if Doyle and Trent were here—unless he had no other choice.

Shane hadn't told Vince what he'd found when he'd hacked into the family's bank records. It was illegal, but Shane wasn't above doing something illegal to save Taylor.

He hadn't told Vince about Paul Ashton, either. Vince was as close to being a friend as he'd had since college, but there wasn't any reason to tell him about Ashton.

Chapter 27

Taylor looked up as Shane knocked on the open door of her office and said, "Got a minute?"

"Sure. Come in."

"Let's go up to the dining room. I need to grab a bite."

She started to protest because she was swamped with Maxx sales reports to review, but decided against it. Shane wouldn't interrupt her unless it was important.

Out in the hall, he whispered, "I just heard from the police. The only prints on the note and envelope are mine."

"I expected as much."

To her dismay, Taylor's voice broke slightly. She hadn't thought she'd be this disappointed, but she was.

Shane put his hand on her shoulder. "Don't let it upset you. This guy's clever, but he'll make a mistake."

They walked in silence up to the third floor, where the executive dining room was located. Shane selected a seat at a table next to a wall-mounted stereo speaker.

"I wanted to talk to you away from your office in case someone is recording our conversation," he said, after they'd sat down. "I've sent Vince to buy an electronic device that detects bugs."

"Bugs? You mean someone's listening to us?"

She couldn't imagine it, but then she never expected a killer would stalk her.

"Possibly. I got to thinking. The pipe bomb didn't frighten you. It pissed off—sorry—upset the killer, forcing him to write the note. How did he know you weren't frightened? Either he's someone close to you, or he's listening."

What he said made sense. She hadn't believed the pipe bomb had been meant for her, and she'd said so.

To just a few people.

"The note said 'Every waking moment your killer is watching you.' That might mean he's planted some devices. Otherwise, it's impossible to keep track of what I'm doing all the time."

"We'll know soon," Shane said with what was supposed to be a reassuring smile. "Vince should be back within the hour."

"If the place is bugged, can't we find the recorder? Doesn't it have to be nearby?"

"Only if we're dealing with a rank amateur, which I doubt. The newer devices send a signal that can be picked up a mile away. Our chances of finding the laser disk recording the conversation are zilch."

She gazed across the empty dining room, her mind drifting from their conversation to last night. It was hard to believe this masculine, totally in control man was the same guy who'd been so tender last night.

He'd told her he was crazy about her. She'd been so surprised she hadn't known what to say.

This morning she'd tried to concentrate on the sales reports. She'd even attempted—yet again—to unravel the mystery of who wanted her dead.

But she couldn't help pondering her relationship with Shane.

When she was with Shane, her heart swelled with a feeling she thought had died forever. She'd missed caring about someone and having a man care about her.

Not just any man, but a man like Shane.

Someone you could trust.

Trust with your life.

"Shane . . ." she began, then didn't know quite what to say.

"Yes?"

"About last night . . ."

"What about it?"

Just say it, she told herself. "I didn't know what to say."

She took a deep breath. "After Paul disappeared, I never thought I'd care about another man. I was wrong. I care about you very much."

He gazed at her with a look as soft as a caress. Skimming his fingers across her cheek, he said, "I meant what I said last night. I'm crazy about you."

He lowered his mouth to hers. She kissed him, her eyes wide open. There was more she needed to say.

"Shane, I was in love and when Paul vanished, my life seemed . . . empty. It hurt so much I could hardly function. I don't want it to happen to me again."

She hesitated, then added, "I like you. I care about you, but I'm not going to fall in love with you."

"Okay, I—"

"There you are," called Vince. "I've been looking everywhere."

He handed her a note. She held it so Shane could read it, too.

Your office is bugged.

A chill of apprehension waltzed up her spine.

Vince went over the room with a device that appeared to be a small hand-held microphone like singers used.

"Nothing here," he announced when he finished.

"Did you check any of the other offices?" Shane asked Vince as he sat down at the table with them.

"No, I thought we should discuss it first. Taylor's office was empty. I closed the door so no one would see me."

"Where's the bug?"

"In the telephone."

Shane turned to Taylor. "It's the number one hiding place."

"I left it there."

"Good. Let's sweep the other offices tonight after people leave. I don't want anyone else to know about this except us."

"Why are you leaving the bug there?" Taylor asked.

"We can feed the killer the info we want him to have."

Taylor had an idea. "I could act as if I'm going to be alone somewhere. He'll take the bait and come after me."

"Not so fast," Shane said. "I hate putting you at risk."

"Sounds like a plan to me," Vince said. "You and I could cover her."

"Let's take it one step at a time. First we sweep the other offices."

"What about my apartment and yours?" Taylor asked.

"We'll sweep everything, including our cars."

Shane stood with Vince in the hall outside Taylor's office, where the hidden listening device couldn't record what they were saying. It was early evening and everyone had left Maxx except for the three of them.

"I've checked your apartment and what's left of Taylor's," Vince told him. "Nothing's there. The office building is clean except for Taylor's office."

"Interesting. The killer definitely targeted her and no one else in the family unless her mother's place is bugged."

"We'd need a really good excuse to get in there to check."

"Maybe Taylor could find out when her next doctor's appointment is."

"Do you really think it's necessary to sweep her mother's house?"

"Damned if I know. This whole thing has me strung out. I don't want to miss anything."

"Did you get anywhere checking on Caleb Bassett?" Vince asked.

"Yes. He worked for American Mutual Insurance until five years ago when he filed a disability claim, saying he'd hurt his back. It's just about the oldest scam in the world."

"Where was he working then?"

"Elmira, Louisiana. It's upstate near the Arkansas border. I called the agency where he worked and found a very helpful woman who sounded as if she was eighty years old. She said he was a bachelor who lived alone. The local ladies considered him quite a catch."

"Interesting. Renata wasn't around then."

"Apparently not. I described her to the woman at the agency. She didn't know her, but it's hard to say for sure without going there and interviewing people."

"When did he leave Elmira?"

"About six months after he filed the first disability claim with the state. He picked up his next payment in New Orleans."

"You're thinking he met Renata there, and she told him the story about being adopted?"

"Seems likely. New Orleans is a magnet for weirdos, grifters, and deadbeats as well as artists and musicians. We know Bassett had a daughter at one point, but we don't know where she is."

"Do you think she could have been Renata?"

"Possibly, but I doubt it. I think that woman is married with six kids and living near where she grew up."

Shane was very familiar with the statistics. Rural Southerners rarely moved more than fifty miles from where they attended high school.

"I agree. Most fathers wouldn't sit around doing nothing while their daughters worked as strippers."

"And did tricks on the side."

"You're throwing a lot of money at this," Vince said. "Is it worth it to pay someone to go there and investigate?"

Shane had considered this earlier. "No. I don't see how it matters. Renata is dead. Does it make any difference if Bassett adopted her the way he claims, or if she was merely some woman he met in New Orleans?"

"It might. Taylor seems to think her mother may leave Bassett some money. If we could prove he wasn't the man who raised Renata, she wouldn't leave him anything."

"There's a reputable firm in Montgomery. I—"

"Hire them. I'll pay for it."

"I promised my mother I'd stop by to visit her," Taylor told Shane. She was tired and wanted to go home, but she needed to see her mother.

"No problem. We'll swing by there." Shane smiled at her, and she perked up. "Find out when Caleb is taking your mother to the doctor again. We'll sweep the house when she's gone."

Caleb Bassett answered the door when they arrived at her mother's house and rang the bell.

"Howdy."

Caleb waved them in with a hand clutched around an old-fashioned glass. Amber liquid and ice clinked against the crystal. Johnnie Walker Blue Label, no doubt.

"How's my mother?" Taylor asked.

"Doin' good. She's out by the pool. We're barbecuing ribs."

Ribs? Her mother *never* ate ribs. They were greasy and unladylike to eat.

"There's plenty for the two of you."

If Caleb still blamed her for Renata's death, he didn't sound like it now, she thought. He almost seemed . . . friendly. Scary.

"We have plans," Taylor fibbed. They'd discussed going to Wok on the Wild Side for sushi but hadn't actually decided. "I just want to see my mother for a minute."

"Sure thing."

They followed Caleb out to the pool area, where the barbecue was located. Her mother was lounging on a chaise, a mint julep in one hand.

"How are you feeling?" Taylor asked.

"Pretty good. A bit tired. That's all."

Taylor tried for a smile, thinking her mother looked bleary-eyed. If she was just tired and not in pain, why was she taking so much medication? The answer, of course, was Caleb Bassett.

"When do you see the doctor again?" Shane asked.

"Tomorrow," Caleb answered.

"Do you want me to go with you?" she asked.

"Nah. I'm taking her," Caleb said from the nearby barbecue grill where he was turning over a rack of baby back ribs.

"I want to take you," Taylor told her mother.

"No, honey. Don't leave work. They'll just draw some blood and run the usual tests," her mother said. "Afterward we're going to see Ridley Pudge. I need to straighten out my will."

Out of the corner of her eye, Taylor saw Caleb smiling as he slathered barbecue sauce on the ribs. She had the sinking feeling Trent was correct. Caleb Bassett, by claiming to be Renata's adopted father, was going to inherit some of her mother's money.

"Never try to be a hero, Shane. It won't work."

He stared into the darkness, thinking, planning.

"Shane Donovan *thinks* he's going to be Taylor's hero. But he's a sorry excuse for a hero."

The air was swirling with no-se'ums. Again. Did they ever go away? he wondered. Cicadas and grasshoppers chirped in the sawgrass nearby. Time to step inside where the air conditioning made life in Miami bearable.

Of course, there was no place like Miami. The Sunshine State's best known city. A city with lots to do, hot night clubs, sexy women.

Anyone could disappear in Miami.

Anyone.

"The note got to Taylor. Scared the piss out of her. Now she knows she's going to die."

It was important she realize what she was dealing with—even if he couldn't allow her to know who planned to kill her.

Yet.

Let the cold, macabre reality of her peril sink into her pretty head.

"Taylor will die. She just doesn't know where or when. And her hero can't save her."

This will be her defining moment, he thought. Death defines a person in a way that life never can.

Chapter 28

Doyle knew it was futile to argue with Brianna when she'd made up her mind about something. They were selling the house. Who needed a big, expensive home when it was just the two of them?

"I'm going to work at Miami Spice," she told him over coffee at breakfast. "I'll earn a lot on commissions."

"You don't have to work. We're not that hard up."

She leaned over and kissed his cheek. "I want to work. I need to contribute to this marriage. I've played around too long as it is."

God, he loved her. He'd do anything for her.

"Sophie called yesterday," she said.

His ex never called, and hearing she had made the sweat rise up on the back of his neck.

"Why didn't you tell me last night?"

"I didn't want to spoil our evening."

They'd driven down to Key Largo and had a picnic on the beach. Watching the crabbers and mullet fishermen in the nearby mangroves had been more fun than he would have thought. The sunset had been spectacular.

Best of all, Brianna didn't insist on making love. She'd understood when he'd told her that he didn't need sex all the time. All he needed was her.

"What did Sophie want?"

"She accused me of using Santería to get you away from her. She says she's put a hex on me, on the whole family."

"Oh, Christ! Why now? Why after all this time?"

Brianna's blond hair swung from side to side as she shook her head. "Who knows?"

"You don't take that black magic stuff seriously, do you?"

Brianna gazed at him and didn't say anything for a moment. "Santería is more like white magic. They wear white robes when the *santeros*—priests—perform the rituals. "Castro has a *babalauo*—high priest—that he consults daily."

Doyle chuckled. "Nancy Reagan used an astrologer."

"It's not the same thing," she replied, totally serious. "Now, Macumba is an evil form of Santería. It's black magic."

"Black magic, white magic. Do you believe in that stuff?"

"My mother pinned an azabache on me the day she brought me home from the hospital to ward off the evil eye."

"A pin like the one Renata was wearing?"

"Exactly. I guess I'm a little superstitious."

He couldn't believe a woman who was so intelligent

actually believed in Santería. "Honey, don't worry about Sophie. If she calls again, hang up."

"I will. But for good measure, I'm going to have my mother counter this with a *limpieza*. That's a ritual cleansing to ward off any hexes. She knows how to do it."

"She hasn't been home from the hospital very long. Are you sure you want to bother her?"

"Mmmm, maybe not." Brianna toyed with her empty cup. "Renata was threatened with Santería, too. Do you suppose it was Sophie?"

"I doubt it. Why would Sophie care one way or another about Renata?"

"Revenge. All of this is about revenge."

Doyle didn't argue with her. His wife had a sixth sense about things.

"I have this terrible feeling . . . Taylor's in danger."

"Shane's with her all the time. He'll protect her."

"Sorry this took so long," Hank Olfeld told Shane on the telephone late in the afternoon. "The brass sent me over to Germany. I just got back."

"Did you crack the code?"

"The computer did. It's drugs. Cocaìne mostly. Some heroin."

Shane was so surprised that there was a moment of dead air on his end of the line. He'd been certain Jim Wilson was using the site to launder bingo skim.

"Would you create an attachment and E-mail the data to me?" Shane asked.

"Will do."

"I owe you one."

Shane hung up and walked down to Taylor's office. He motioned for her to come with him so the bug wouldn't pick up his voice.

"My friend at the DIA cracked the code," he told her when they were down the hall. "Drugs."

"Oh, my God! Why our Web site?"

"Good question. I suspect they thought the police wouldn't look there."

"What do we do now? Call the police?"

"We'll have to, but let's wait until Hank e-mails me the decoded info. I want to look at it first."

"Will you be able to tell who they are? Where they are?"

"Maybe. That's what I spent the last two years doing in South America. I tracked drug money being funneled to terrorist groups. But don't get your hopes up. These people are slick.

"That's why they use Web sites like To The Maxx. They can be anywhere in the world and access the information. Or send info to their buddies."

"Our Web server said our site was secure."

"Somebody had the code or hacked in."

Taylor sighed. "We better tell Doyle and Trent."

"Let's keep this to ourselves until I go over the decoded material."

"You think it might be Raoul, don't you?"

"When you've got a habit, you deal or you steal to support it. Just in case it's him, let's not tip him off by telling Trent."

He kissed her cheek and patted her cute fanny.

"Go back to work. Hank's E-mail has probably come through. I'll see what's on it."

On his way back to the computer, Shane's cell phone rang. It was Vince.

"The tracking chips are here and the monitor. That was fast."

"I paid extra for overnight delivery. Will you run the chips by my apartment later? I want to get one on Taylor right away."

"No problem. I've hired two people who can start here tomorrow. I'll train them how to use the monitor."

"The problem's going to be getting the chips on the others without them knowing it."

"You'll think of something. You always do."

He was wondering about how to get the chips on them when he opened the E-mail from Hank. It was drugs, all right. A sizable operation with the shipments coming out of Colombia to cities all across the United States.

He studied the screen and saw a familiar pattern.

Aw, hell.

How stupid could he be? Why hadn't he figured it out?

Taylor curled up on Shane's sofa and watched the Discovery channel, Auggie at her feet. The program featured Florida's endangered manatees.

Vince had dropped by with the chips. Shane had put one on the side of Taylor's gold Ebell watch. The face was mother-of-pearl with tiny diamonds around it. The watch had been a college graduation present from her parents.

The chip wasn't noticeable at all. It should have made Taylor feel more secure, but it didn't. Until Renata's killer was caught, Taylor knew she was going to be nervous.

Even Shane seemed on edge.

He'd been very quiet all evening, which wasn't like him. They usually spent their time talking, when they weren't making love.

He was sitting on the sofa near her. He seemed to be watching the program, but intuition told her something was wrong.

"Shane, is something on your mind?" she asked him.

"I need to talk to you."

His reflective gaze and serious tone set off an alarm bell.

"Let's turn off the television." She clicked on the remote control.

His gazed was so penetrating that it unnerved her even more.

"I didn't just *happen* to meet you. I'd seen your picture, and I *wanted* to meet you."

"My picture. Where did you see it?"

A long moment of dead silence. He reached over to touch her shoulder the way he often did, but stopped and rested his hand on the back of the sofa.

"Where did you see my picture?" she repeated.

"Paul Ashton showed it to me."

He knew Paul and hadn't told her. Why? she wondered, her mind awhirl, considering the possibilities.

"When did you meet Paul?"

"I met him in Colombia."

"Before he disappeared."

Shane hesitated. "Taylor, he didn't disappear. Paul Ashton is alive and living in Costa Rica."

"No." The word came out a garbled, choking sound.

"It's true."

A white-hot prickling sensation shot from the base of her neck downward. No! This could *not* be true.

"What? I don't believe you. I hired detectives. They couldn't find a trace of him."

"By then he was already in Costa Rica."

"No," she cried out, a tortured sound like an animal caught in a trap.

She jumped up, nearly tripping over Auggie, and rushed over to the window. Unseeing, she gazed out

at the shadowy courtyard. A swirling, nauseating kalei-
doscope of pain, relief, shock, and anger besieged her.
She dragged in a breath and held it, trying to regain
her self-control.

It took a few minutes before the gut-wrenching
shock subsided into something calmer but no less pro-
found. Auggie stood beside her, licking her hand.

She sat down again, pulled her legs up, wrapped
her arms around them, and rested her chin on her
knees. "Why didn't he let me know he was alive? I was
so worried."

Shane remained silent.

"He didn't love me, did he?" she heard herself ask.

He put his arm around her. "Baby, I know this is
hard on you."

She shoved him away. "Don't 'baby' me. I want to
know everything."

"All right. I was working undercover in Bogotá. I
met Paul through one of the cartel leaders. He was
posing as a photographer, but he was actually a member of one of the drug cartels."

His words detonated on impact just as if he'd physically hit her. She wanted to scream No! but his words
had the ring of truth to them.

"I can't tell you all the details of the operation, but
we busted it. Paul had valuable information. So instead
of bringing him back here and prosecuting him, they
let him off if he promised to stay out of the country.
The government often makes deals like that to break
up a cartel."

"He could have called me . . . or something." A
remnant of pride resurfaced and morphed into anger.
"He should have. I would have."

"Do you know where he is?"

"Not exactly. Someone else escorted him to Costa
Rica."

"But you could find out where he is, right?"

"I guess. Why?"

"I want to talk to him to tell him what a jerk he is."

"He's worse than a jerk. I don't think you want to talk to him. He's the one using your Web site to traffic drugs. He's back in business again."

"Oh, God." She clutched her stomach and rocked back and forth, silently cursing herself. "I did it. The codes were in my desk in our apartment. I told him what they were for, and he must have copied them."

"I suspect he's been using your Web site for years," Shane said. "I should have guessed it was him, but someone is supposed to be monitoring him."

"It looks like he fooled his handlers." The way he fooled me, she silently added.

"We need to be careful not to tip him off. He'll slip out of Costa Rica and into some other South American country where it will be hard to find him. He should stand trial here."

"I want to talk to him."

"Okay, but you'll need to wait until this operation is busted. I don't think the DIA will handle it, because the money isn't going to terrorists, but I'm going to call them anyway. They can refer it to whomever they want."

"Will there be agents crawling all over the office?"

"Nope. One may come by to interview you, but they can access the Web site from where they are. They'll have Ashton arrested in Costa Rica, then extradited. You can speak to him in person."

What do you say to someone you loved—honestly loved—who turned out to be a heartless jerk and a criminal to boot?

Why hadn't she seen it? She was smart and successful, not the kind of woman who was easily taken in by a man.

"Why didn't you tell me you knew Paul? Why did you wait so long? Couldn't you have told me sooner? Why hide it?" She fired the salvo of questions at him like bullets.

"I don't blame you for being angry. I should have told you, but I was afraid you'd rush off to Costa Rica to find him."

She raised her chin a notch, silently daring him to make her anger go away.

"I had no idea he was using your Web site until I saw the decoded material. He's using a few of his old contacts. That's what tipped me. I remembered what you'd said about keeping the codes in your desk at home. Then it all made sense."

"Were you *ever* going to tell me you knew him?"

"I'm so sorry I didn't. I started to tell you a dozen times. I didn't want to lose you."

Shane lay awake, staring at the pattern the moonlight made on the ceiling of his bedroom. Taylor was on the far side of his bed. Between them it was no-man's-land. She hadn't wanted him to touch her.

He couldn't blame her. She might never fully trust a man again.

Never trust him.

The hell of it was, he'd cushioned the blow as best he could. The bastard hadn't loved her. He'd deliberately used her and bragged about it.

Not only was Ashton a scumbag and a crook, he was a nutcase. Yeah, he could be charming, especially around women, but there was something 'off' about the son of a bitch.

Shane had argued with the brass not to let Ashton go, but they wouldn't listen. Now they'd be forced to deal with another of Ashton's drug networks.

When Ashton had told Shane about Taylor, it had been with a laugh. He collected women and had a stunningly beautiful girlfriend in Bogotá. No doubt he'd found another babe in Costa Rica.

Shane hadn't laughed. In the photograph there had been something in Taylor's eyes that had tugged at his heart. He'd found himself thinking about her all the time.

He hadn't expected to fall in love with her, but he had.

"Are you asleep?" he whispered.

"No."

"I just want you to understand one thing. I love you. I'll never do anything to hurt you."

She didn't say a word.

Chapter 29

After letting Auggie out to relieve himself, Taylor gave the dog a quick pat. "I'll be right back to feed you."

She left Shane sleeping and slipped out of his apartment. She'd hardly slept at all. She wasn't the type to be angry for long, but she was furious with herself, with Shane.

And most of all with Paul Ashton.

She unlocked the back door to her apartment. The place smelled like the inside of an ashtray. She hoped the outfit she'd come to get didn't reek of smoke.

In her bedroom, she meant to go straight to the closet, but stopped and opened the drawer where she'd kept her pictures of Paul. She didn't bother looking at them. Instead, she ripped them into a dozen pieces and flushed them down the toilet.

It was a childish thing to do, she silently conceded,

but it made her feel better. The jerk had vanished, and she'd searched for him, so frightened and heart-sick she'd barely been able to function. The malaise had lasted nearly two years, threatening her health, her career.

All the while, he was living it up on drug money—made by using her Web site—in Costa Rica.

"Don't dwell on the past," she said out loud. "Get even."

The clothes in the closet did smell of smoke. Some fabrics absorbed the odor more than others. The moss green Dana Buchman suit she planned to wear wasn't too bad.

Not too good either. A spritz of Febreze and a dash of perfume should fix the problem.

While she was in the closet, she made a pile of clothes to be taken to the dry cleaner to get rid of the smoky smell. She'd made one run after the fire-bombing. It was time for another trip. At this rate, her cleaning bill would rival the national debt.

She was leaving the bedroom when the telephone on the dresser rang. Staring at it, she wondered who would be calling this early.

Unless something had happened to her mother.

She rushed over and grabbed the receiver. "Hello."

"Mornin', darling."

She dropped the clothes on the floor and sank down on the bed. It had been two years since she'd heard his voice.

Paul Ashton.

The jerk. The drug dealer.

Calm down, cautioned her inner voice. Don't tell him off. Let the authorities catch him. Seeing him in prison will be the best revenge.

Don't let on you know he has been tampering with the Web site.

"Did you miss me, Taylor? I sure missed you."

"Oh, my God! P-paul, is it really you?"

The quaver in her voice was real. She was so furious with this man that she could barely grind out the words, but she hoped he would mistake it for heartfelt emotion.

"I thought you were dead."

"No, sweetheart. They tried, but it takes a lot to kill me."

"You were being held captive?" she asked, all innocence.

"Something like that."

"Where are you?" The connection was too clear to be Costa Rica.

"Right here in Miami."

Uh-oh. What was he up to?

"What's going on? I've been worried sick."

"I know, darling. I'm really sorry, but I've been through hell, believe me. This is the first chance I've had to contact you."

"Why? What's happening?"

"It's very complicated. I need to explain it to you in person."

He sounded so sincere she was almost fooled. "All right. When?"

"Meet me at Brew Ha-Ha in, say, fifteen minutes."

"Okay."

Paul hadn't changed. Not one bit.

He still expected her to drop everything for him. She remembered how she used to worry about him and his phony career. She'd even downplayed her own success so he would feel better about himself.

Well, she'd been dumber than dirt. He was handsome, charismatic but without substance. Her mind flashed to Caleb. Another charmer without depth.

The opposite of Shane Donovan.

"Let's see Paul try to talk his way out of this," she said out loud.

She was wearing shorts and a Marlins T-shirt. Later she would come back and get ready for work. Combing her hair, she decided against makeup—not even mascara.

Who cared what Paul thought?

She wasn't wasting any time trying to look pretty for him. She grabbed a pair of sunglasses from the drawer. Even this early the Miami sun would be brutal.

It was a short walk to Brew Ha-Ha. She didn't go back to Shane's apartment for her purse. If he was awake, he would want to know where she was going, and he would insist on coming with her.

This was private and personal. She needed to hear what Paul had to say.

Alone.

As she was leaving the courtyard, she ran headlong into Trent. One look at her brother, and she knew he'd been crying.

Raoul.

What had the creep done now?

"I need to talk to you," he said, his voice brittle with emotion.

"What's wrong?"

He stared at her for a moment, then said, "Raoul's marrying Fallon."

"The companion you hired for him to keep him off drugs?"

"Turns out her father is Rupert James."

"The media tycoon who lives in Boca Raton?"

"You got it. Fallon's loaded and in love with Raoul. He left with her last night."

"That's awfully fast, isn't it?"

Trent shrugged. "I asked Raoul to move in with me the first week I met him."

Taylor knew she should feel sorry for Trent and say something sympathetic. The words wouldn't come. It might hurt now, but Trent would eventually find the right person.

Raoul was not the one.

"I guess Raoul's bisexual, isn't he?"

"Yes. I knew it from the very beginning, but I thought he cared enough about me to become my partner. I wanted someone I could spend my life with, someone who'd let me be myself. I thought I'd found that person."

So had I, but we both were wrong. Paul Ashton was an even bigger skank than Raoul.

It was amazing that someone as smart as her brother could be fooled by a man like Raoul, but then, she'd been deceived as well. They were siblings and more alike than she'd thought lately.

"Before Raoul left, he confessed to being the one who tried to scare Renata off by having the Cuban woman in the shipping department hex her. He also went to see Aunt Sophie and convinced her Brianna put a hex on her marriage."

"Why would he do such a thing?"

"He wanted to make trouble for Uncle Doyle because he refused to let him work in our business."

"That's really immature. What did he have against Renata?"

"Raoul would be the first to admit money means a lot to him. He thought Renata was going to inherit 'my fair share' and it bothered him."

"Enough to kill her?"

Trent took a deep breath, then expelled it, blowing upward and ruffling the dark hair across his forehead. "I don't think so, but I can't be one hundred percent sure. I never thought he would leave me for a woman."

Taylor glanced at her watch. Fifteen minutes had passed since she'd spoken with Paul.

"Trent, I want to talk to you, but I have to meet Paul for a few minutes at Brew Ha-Ha."

"Paul? You're kidding!"

"No. I'm afraid not."

"He's back? Where's he been?"

"I don't know. He's going to explain everything to me."

"How can a man just disappear, then pop up again? Something's fishy."

"I'll find out when I talk to him." She didn't want to take the time to explain what a fool she'd been about Paul Ashton.

"Paul better have a damn good excuse. He put you through hell."

She handed him the key to her apartment. "Wait for me, please. I want to tell you all about it."

Rushing off, a spasm of guilt hit her. She should stay and let Trent talk out his problems the way they once had. Another part of her wanted to nail this creep in the worst way.

She hesitated, slowing her pace. Nothing she could say to her brother would ease his pain. Nothing.

Time would heal his battered soul, give him perspective. Eventually he would understand Raoul had done him a favor.

Paul was waiting for her outside Brew Ha-Ha. Honey blond hair shagged back into a ponytail the length of a cigar.

Tanned.

Toned.

Megawatt smile.

Exactly the way she remembered him.

He was wearing a tank top underneath a loose fitting blue cotton dress shirt rolled back at the cuffs to reveal a black widow tattooed on his forearm. That was new—and disgusting.

Taylor mustered a smile and made a determined effort to conceal the anger roiling inside her like a detonated grenade.

She touched his face with the tips of her fingers. "I never thought I'd see you again."

A strange smile—one she didn't remember—curled his lips upward. "I'm back."

Something hard jabbed her in the ribs. She looked down and saw the shiny chrome barrel of a gun. In a flash she weighed her options.

A few people were having coffee behind them under the shady banyan tree at Brew Ha-Ha. Paul's back was to them, and his loose fitting shirt concealed the gun. One scream would bring help.

One scream and a bullet would pierce her heart.

"My car's parked down the street," he said as if they were discussing the weather. "Move."

Auggie's cold nose on Shane's arm awakened him. He rolled over and looked across no-man's-land and saw Taylor wasn't on her side of the bed.

"Did she let you out, boy?" he asked Auggie.

Of course she had. Taylor adored dogs and was obsessive about Auggie. She was in the bathroom or making coffee.

Would she be in a better mood today?

Probably not.

Betrayal cut to the quick. She wasn't easily going to forgive him for not telling her about knowing Paul.

He took a leak, then wandered down the hall to the second bathroom, which was outside the bedroom he'd converted into an office. She wasn't there.

She wasn't in the kitchen.

Okay, she was pissed and had gone to her apartment. Something clicked in the back of his brain.

He recalled seeing her watch with the newly attached chip on the nightstand at her side of the bed.

"Aw, hell!"

Not bothering with underwear, he pulled on a pair of jeans and grabbed a T-shirt. Spearing his fingers through his wild hair, he raced out of his apartment, Auggie at his heels.

Across the courtyard, he banged on her back door with his clenched fist. A few seconds later, Trent answered the door. His red, puffy eyes barely registered.

"Where's Taylor?"

"She'll be right back. She went to meet Paul Ashton."

Like a sucker punch to the gut, the air whooshed out of Shane's lungs. It was a second before he could say, "Oh, shit!"

Doyle walked down to Taylor's office. She still hadn't arrived. Strange, he thought. Taylor was usually among the first here, especially on a day when they had scheduled a meeting with an important vendor.

Trent hadn't come in either. The whole damn place was falling apart. The family wasn't very interested in running the business. The sooner it was sold, the better.

His secretary raced down the hall toward him, calling, "Mrs. Maxwell is on the telephone. She says it's an emergency."

Doyle rushed back to his office and picked up the telephone. "Vanessa, what's wrong?"

"Taylor just called me," Vanessa said, tears in her voice. "She's been kidnapped."

"Kidnapped?"

Doyle dropped into his chair, suddenly feeling wrung out. Old. He'd never had children. Taylor was like the daughter he'd never had. How could this have happened to her?

"A-are y-you there?" Vanessa was crying now.

"Yes. I'm here."

He stared at his brother's photographs on the wall. One of them was Taylor's picture on the day she graduated from Yale. He'd been as proud of her as had her parents.

Maybe prouder.

"Who took Taylor? What do they want?"

"S-she she didn't—or couldn't—say. She's going to call back."

"Okay. Stay calm. Obviously this is about money. We should prepare to raise—"

"Should I call the police? Taylor warned me not to but—"

"I'm going to get ahold of Shane Donovan. We'll come to your house. Don't do a thing until we talk. Understand?"

"Yes, but Caleb thinks we should have the police—"

"I don't care what he thinks. You listen to me. We need to discuss this and come up with a plan—if you want to see your daughter alive again."

He slammed down the receiver, perspiring so much a trickle of sweat ran down his temple into his eyebrow. He swiped his forehead with his cuff and yelled at his secretary to get him Shane's cell phone number.

While he waited he called Brianna. "Bad news, honey. Someone has kidnapped Taylor."

"I knew it," cried Brianna. "I knew she was in danger."

His secretary handed him Shane's number, and he

told Brianna, "Meet me at Vanessa's as soon as you can."

He punched in Donovan's number, and he answered on the second ring.

"Why did you leave Taylor alone?" he demanded.

"How do you know Taylor's alone?" Shane shot back.

"Because someone has kidnapped her. She called her mother to tell her."

"Paul Ashton has her. I'm here with Trent at Brew Ha-Ha. People saw her get into a car with him."

"Ashton? I thought he was dead."

"No. It's a long story. I—"

"Meet me at Vanessa's as soon as you can. Bring Trent with you."

"I'll get Vince, too."

"Good idea."

"What does Ashton want?" Shane asked.

"Who knows? According to Vanessa, Taylor didn't say who kidnapped her. She's going to call back with more information."

"Trust me. Ashton has her."

Chapter 30

"Everybody calm down," Shane ordered. His tone was so sharp that Auggie, seated at his side, flinched. "Crying and arguing isn't going to do Taylor any good."

"I say we call the police," said Caleb.

"That's sure to get her killed," Trent retorted.

Shane had already explained to the family gathered in the library about Paul's using their Web site and about his drug escapades in Colombia. They'd been shocked except for Vanessa, who was already crying so it was hard to tell what she thought.

"The question is, what does Ashton want?" Doyle said. "Money? Why didn't he just ask for it?"

"I don't think this is about money," Brianna said. "It's about revenge."

Shane raked his fingers through his hair, silently

cursing himself, yet again, for letting Taylor out of his sight.

"He hasn't asked for money," Shane said, "because he wants us to sweat."

"Why make Taylor call?" Vince asked. "Why didn't Ashton call himself?"

"He doesn't want us to know he's involved," Shane told them. "Trent just happened to run into Taylor, and she told him who she was meeting."

"He doesn't realize we know," Caleb said, "unless Taylor told him."

"Give her some credit," Shane ground out the words. "She wouldn't tell him."

"Lower your voices," Vince ordered from the doorway. He'd been using the electronic device to check the house for bugs.

"Find something?" Shane asked.

"There's a bug in the den and in the terrace dining area."

"The places the family gathers," commented Doyle. "Paul would know this."

"No bugs in here?" Vanessa asked with a faraway look. She'd seen Vince check the room and had listened to Shane explain, but it obviously hadn't registered.

"Nothing in here, honey," Caleb said.

"This was my brother's lair. We rarely used this room until lately," said Doyle.

"We can talk freely in here," Vince told them, "but keep your voices low, so the other bugs don't pick up anything."

"Why not remove them?" asked Caleb.

"I don't want Ashton to know we suspect anything," Shane replied. "Plus we may want to feed him false information."

Trent asked, "Why is he doing this?"

"Good question," Shane said. "I think Brianna may be correct. He sees this as payback time. Right, Vanessa?"

Taylor's mother gazed at him a moment, then nodded. "I suppose . . . it's possible."

"What are you trying to say?" Caleb asked.

Shane waited to hear Vanessa's reply. From checking her bank account, he was fairly sure what she was going to tell them.

"It's no secret," Vanessa said. "I never liked the man. None of you did either."

"True," Trent agreed while Brianna and Doyle nodded.

"I was afraid Taylor would marry him," she continued. "I wanted to get some dirt on Paul, so I hired a private detective."

"Who did you use?" asked Vince.

"Rick Masters. He tailed Paul for three months." Vanessa waved her hand toward the desk. "He gave me a complete written report."

"What did it say?" Shane asked.

"Paul was dealing drugs. I thought it was just a simple, small-time operation. Mr. Masters gave me no reason to believe he was a major player, or that he was using our Web site."

"What Masters observed were probably petty-cash operations," Shane said. "The serious money goes into offshore accounts. And remember, Ashton was pretending to be a struggling photographer. He didn't want to—"

The doorbell rang, and Trent said, "That'll be Lisa."

"You called Lisa?" asked Brianna.

"Yes. She and Taylor were very close when Paul was around. She may know something that will help us."

A moment later, Maria brought Lisa into the library.

Trent had already told her about the kidnapping, and he spent a minute explaining about Vanessa having a private detective shadow Paul.

Shane tried to keep his cool by petting Auggie. He hated wasting time, but Trent was right. Lisa might have valuable information.

"Taylor's like a sister to me," Lisa told them. "I'll do anything to help her. So will Jim."

"I don't know what he can do," Vanessa said sharply.

"He's available if we need him." Lisa took a deep breath. "What I'm going to say has to be kept secret. I know you all suspected Jim of tampering with the Web site and maybe even murder."

"We know Jim didn't touch the Web site," Trent said.

"He had nothing to do with Renata's death," Lisa said. "He was working at El Tambor on an undercover assignment with the police department. His brother is a detective, you know, and he got Jim the job because of his special accounting skills. Jim cracked the case, but he could get killed if anyone finds out what his role was before it comes to trial."

Interesting, Shane thought. He wouldn't have guessed that one.

"Maybe we should call his brother and see if the detective can help us," Caleb said.

"Paul might kill Taylor immediately if we go to the police," Brianna said.

"I agree," Doyle added. "When she calls again, act as if you haven't a clue who took her."

"Right," said Shane. "Ask her who kidnapped her and see what she says."

"I will," Vanessa responded. "I'm not taking any medication. I need to be as clear-headed as possible."

"Do you want to tell us how you got rid of Paul?" Shane asked.

"I thought about calling in the police, but I decided it would take too long and he might plea-bargain or something."

"Quite likely," Vince said.

"You don't know Paul," Vanessa continued. "He had a mesmerizing personality, and somehow he got his hooks into Taylor. I was afraid he'd persuade her that he was framed or reformed or something."

"I know what you mean," Brianna said. "Paul has a way about him. He fascinates most women."

Vanessa nodded. "So I went to see Paul and told him if he didn't leave Miami, I would go to the police."

"That's when he hit you up for one hundred and fifty thousand dollars."

"To relocate," Vanessa told Shane. "I thought it was worth every penny to get rid of him. I never imagined this would happen."

Shane hadn't seen it coming, either. It took balls to come back to the States after cutting a deal with the government. Either that or Ashton was stone crazy.

"I offered Raoul money, too, at one point. Then Caleb made me see how wrong it was to interfere."

"People have to make their own mistakes," Caleb said. "How else are they going to learn?"

"While I'm owning up to what I've done, I need to tell all of you something important." Vanessa sat up straighter and glanced sideways at Caleb. "I knew Renata was my daughter without a DNA test. You see, I met Caleb at the foster home. He was my first love. He was Renata's father."

It took a minute for her words to really register with Shane. Everyone else was just as surprised, judging by their slack-jawed expressions.

"Why didn't you tell us?" Trent asked, his voice tight with emotion. "Then we wouldn't have given Renata such a hard time."

Good point.

Vanessa heaved a sigh. "I should have. I wish with all my heart I had, but I didn't think you and Taylor would understand about Caleb."

"Oh, Mother, of course we would have understood."

"I didn't want her to tell," Caleb said. "It's best to keep the past in the past. I've done things I'm not proud of, and I didn't want to embarrass Vanessa, but I'm a new man now."

Yeah, right.

"How did you get Renata?" Brianna wanted to know.

"The foster mother took the baby from Vanessa. She came to me to get me to sign the consent form. I refused to give up my daughter. I took her and raised her. She was the light of my life."

Sure, so you let her support you by stripping, Shane thought. He leaned down to pat Auggie and hide what had to be a disgusted expression on his face.

As if reading his thoughts, Caleb added, "I never wanted Renata to be an exotic dancer, but she was stubborn beyond belief. She was like that from the time she could walk."

"She took after me," Vanessa said wistfully. "I'm too stubborn sometimes."

"You had to be to survive," Caleb said.

"This is a crisis," Vanessa said, "and I need everyone to understand Caleb is like family. He's going to stay with me until my time comes. He'll be at my side through all of this."

"So will we," Brianna told Vanessa. "So will we."

"I don't know what I'll do if my actions get both my daughters killed."

"You think Paul killed Renata?" asked Lisa. "Why? He didn't know her, did he?"

"No, but it was a sure way to get back at Vanessa," Shane said, "and throw the company into chaos."

"He made a mess of things at To The Maxx. That's for certain," Doyle said.

"Ashton bought himself some time while he continued to make money using the Web site," Shane added.

"Paul was here often enough," Trent added. "He would know how to get into the house even if the alarm had been activated. He could easily have slipped in and killed Renata."

"Right now we should be concentrating on finding where Ashton's holding Taylor." Shane knew he sounded impatient, but they couldn't afford to waste time. "I've thought about this and decided he must have her in a private home or some secluded spot."

"Most likely," Vince agreed. "It's hard to get a woman out of the car, up the stairs or elevator to an apartment at gunpoint without risking someone seeing you and calling the cops."

"It's possible but not likely," Shane added.

"I contacted the DIA on my way over here," Vince told them. "Ashton disappeared from Costa Rica about two months ago. His handler didn't know how he got out of the country, but obviously he came to America again with a phony passport."

"He'll have a new name," Shane explained. "Otherwise, the second his real name went into the computer at Customs, he'd be arrested."

"What he's done so far fits the profile of most fugitives," Vince told everyone. "He's returned to an area he knows."

"Do any of you have any idea where he might go?" Shane asked. "You all knew him. Think about places he might have mentioned."

"He loved SoBe. I mean *loved* it," Lisa said. "Loved

the clubs, the beach. While Taylor worked, he hung out on Lummus Beach, where all the babes are.''

"Was he known at the clubs?" Shane asked.

"Oh, absolutely. It's hard to get in unless you grease the bouncer.''

"Who wants to check the clubs?" asked Vince.

Lisa volunteered. "Jim will help me. We'll cover as many as we can tonight."

Shane asked, "Does anyone happen to have a picture of Paul?"

"I'm sure I must have a photo taken at a family dinner those first few months Taylor was dating him. After then, he rarely came," Vanessa said.

"Trent, do you still have our pictures?" Lisa asked. "We had snapshots of the four of us, remember?"

Trent nodded. "I know just where they are."

"Paul looks about the same," Shane said. "The people at Brew Ha-Ha told us he had blond hair worn in a short ponytail."

"Do you think he'd risk showing up at one of the clubs looking the same?" asked Lisa. "What if someone recognized him?"

"Who would know to report him to the police as long as he kept a low profile and didn't get into trouble?" Shane asked. "Besides, he's arrogant and sure of himself. I doubt if he see this as a risk."

"He must live fairly close," Trent said. "Taylor had just talked to him, and they were meeting a short time later."

"Good thinking." Shane wondered how he'd missed getting this information from Trent earlier. He'd been so thrown by Taylor's disappearance, he hadn't thought to ask.

"What area is like SoBe and nearby?" Shane asked. He hadn't been in Miami long enough to know the city the way he needed to if he was going to save Taylor.

"Mid-Miami Beach," Doyle said, "just north of here."

"There are a lot of exclusive hotels like the Fontaine-bleau Resort, and high-rise condos in the area," Trent said. "There are some private homes."

"This is when the pictures will be important."

Shane stood up and strode across the room, talking to everyone. Auggie dogged every step.

"Go through the photos and meet back here in two hours. We'll blow up the best shots of Paul and show them around the mid-Miami area and the clubs."

"If only Taylor had put on her watch," Vince said when the others had left and Caleb was helping Vanessa go through her pictures. "We could find her in no time with that chip."

"It's too bad, but there's nothing we can do about it now. We need a plan and luck."

"We need more manpower," Vince said.

"I've got the money. Hire people and put them to work." Shane thought a moment. "Maybe we should hire this Rick Masters. He tailed Paul once—"

"Fuhgettaboutit," Vince said in his best Sopranos impression. "The guy's a has-been who does nothing but spouse-peeping. It took three months for him to nail Ashton. Come on."

"You're right, but I'm going to ask Vanessa for Master's report. I want to read it. There may be something in there to help us."

"We need to put a recorder on Vanessa's phone for the next call."

"Right. I figure it'll be a day or more. Ashton wants us to sweat out every second."

"That's a good thing," Vince replied, obviously try-ing to give him some hope. "He has to keep her alive to make the call."

"I'm guessing there will be several calls. It has to do with the drug info on the Web site."

"What makes you think so?"

"I've had experience with the guy. Ashton might kill for revenge but money is his god. I think he knows—somehow—we've decoded the Web site. He needs to set up another site and transfer the information. He must get the new info to his suppliers and dealers."

"That'll take time, especially if they aren't using E-mail, which they won't if they're smart. Otherwise, it leaves a trail prosecutors can use. Everyone will have to check in at the Web site and get the new information, using the code."

"Know what this means?" Shane asked, then answered his own question. "There's a leak at the DIA. Someone tipped Ashton. That's why he grabbed Taylor—to buy time. The moment his contacts have been notified, he'll kill her."

Chapter 31

Handcuffed to the bed, Taylor stared up at the ceiling of the fishing shanty where Paul had taken her. Cobwebs streeled from the ceiling, and mildew covered every surface, especially the musty-smelling old mattress under her.

Paul had forced her to drive south to Big Pine Key, which was almost to Key West. It was one of the larger islands, a wilderness of scrub, mahogany, and gumbo-limbo trees. Mangroves lined the shore where crocodiles preyed on the raccoons, otters, and miniature Key deer that were a tourist attraction in the area.

Who would think to look for her here?

No one. Not even Shane.

Trent would have told him that she'd gone to meet Paul. Surely, her mother had said she'd been kidnapped. Paul wouldn't let her mention his name, but they would know.

The sun set, and in the gloaming she saw a red-tailed hawk fly across the sky, riding an updraft. The shack consisted of one room with a single window, a bed, and a chair. A fishing porch was cantilevered out over the inlet.

Paul had handcuffed her to the bed and left, saying he needed to use a telephone. He had a satchel full of stolen cell phones. He'd made her use one of them to call her mother just outside Miami, then he'd tossed it in the ocean.

No doubt he wanted to call someone and use a land line in case the police were monitoring cell calls. Would her mother have notified the police even though she'd been warned not to? Taylor couldn't guess. Her mother wasn't herself these days.

Suddenly, she had a disturbing thought.

What if Paul didn't come back?

From the look of it, no one had been here for several years. If she died shackled to this rusty wrought-iron bed, no telling when someone would find her.

Paul must be coming back.

For some reason, he didn't want her dead yet. She was supposed to make another telephone call home. There had to be a way to tip off Shane.

A key word or phrase.

Like what?

"Think, think hard," she whispered.

She fell asleep trying to come up with something. The sound of a car engine on the single lane dirt road and the flash of headlights through the grimy window awakened her.

Paul banged his way through the door, his arms full, a flashlight in one hand. It arced around the small room, catching the cobwebs and turning them silver.

She smelled alcohol on him and knew he'd been

in a bar somewhere, using the telephone . . . and waiting. For what? Who?

He dropped an orange plastic bucket on the bed. "If you need to go to the bathroom, use it."

She didn't say a word as he set some things on the floor. One of them was the bag she'd seen in the trunk earlier. He was packing enough heat to wipe out a banana republic.

Why so many guns?

He returned to the car and brought in a Styrofoam ice chest and several bags of groceries. Judging by the supplies, he planned to be here several days. Enough time for Shane to find her if only she could slip him a clue.

Paul lit a kerosene lantern, and the shanty suddenly filled with amber light. He rummaged through one bag.

"Hungry?" He tossed her a protein bar and a bottle of water.

She didn't touch them.

"Sweetheart, don't pout. You've got to eat, right?"

"I'm not pouting. You won't answer my questions. What's the point in talking?"

He filled a plastic cup with ice from the cooler, unscrewed a bottle of Grey Goose, and poured it over the ice. A crackling sound filled the hot room.

"Want some?"

She shook her head.

"Might as well enjoy yourself."

"When are you going to let me go?"

Without responding, he knocked back a bit of vodka.

"Why are you doing this? I never did a thing to hurt you."

She'd questioned him before, but a sullen stare had been his only response.

"I have a right to know why you kidnapped me."

He studied her a moment, and in the amber light his green eyes had a feral glow. What had she ever seen in him?

"You were always so . . . so perfect." He smiled, more to himself than her. "You tried so hard to nurture my career, when I was already a star. You didn't know it. You felt sorry for me."

"No, I didn't I—" She stopped herself from saying she had loved him.

"You thought you were better than I was."

"That's ridiculous. I . . ." She let the sentence die, admitting on some level she had felt superior, and he'd picked up on it.

"You and your mother both."

"That's no reason to—"

"If you want to know, let me finish."

He capped the vodka and stowed it in the ice chest. He swung the shanty's single chair around backward and sat, the drink in his hand.

"Your mother paid me to get out of your life, you know."

Taylor wasn't surprised, given her mother's attempt to buy off Raoul.

"She knew I was dealing drugs long before you all discovered the codes on the Web site."

"She never mentioned it."

"Not to you, but she tipped the cops. They busted me in Colombia."

Taylor knew this was dead wrong. Shane and the DIA had caught Paul. She didn't correct him for fear he might do something to Shane.

"Do you have any idea what it's like to be exiled to Costa Rica? You might as well be in jail. Can't go anywhere, can't do anything without notifying and getting permission from your handler." He swigged a bit more of the vodka. "Thanks to your mother and her big mouth."

Taylor kept quiet, comprehending the source of his anger for the first time. Granted, Paul and her mother were like oil and water, but she never suspected his hatred ran so deep.

An extremely abnormal reaction. There had to be more to it than this.

"It took me almost two years to rebuild my network under my handler's nose. What the feds didn't find was the Web site. They're not half as smart as they like to think.

"I've got a world-class hacker in Japan. He's in the DIA computers, and they don't even know it. I knew the second they cracked the code and told Donovan."

"Is the Japanese man the one who tinkered with our Web site?" she asked just to keep him talking. The more she learned, the better chance she'd have at saving herself.

"You bet. I gave him the codes you kept in the desk. Pretty dumb on your part. Even dumber not to change the codes regularily."

She nodded slightly, as if she agreed, just to keep him going.

"Now, Donovan's going to tell the police all about it unless your mother convinces him to hold off a few days."

"Why a few days?"

"I need to let my contacts know where the new Web site is. Until everyone of them checks in, I want to keep your site operational."

Taylor heard herself sigh. "Why didn't you have me tell my mother to keep Shane from calling the authorities?"

He laughed, a brittle, grating sound.

"You're kidding, right? Donovan's not calling the police as long as I have you."

"All of this is to get back at my mother?"

He thought about it a moment, swirling the nearly melted ice in the glass. "I wanted to teach you a lesson, too. Never look down on a man, never think you're better just because you have more money and a fancy education."

"I didn't look down—"

"I'm enjoying your mother's suffering," he cut her off, obviously not caring what she was going to say. "I went through hell. Why shouldn't she?"

"Mother has myeloma, you know. It's a terminal illness. Don't you think she's in enough pain?"

"Pain?"

He shot out of the chair, spun around, and went into the cooler again. This time he grabbed an apple.

"I'll tell you what pain is. It's sitting on your ass in Costa Rica. No air conditioning. No decent nightclubs. Total boredom."

"Poor baby."

The sarcastic remark slipped out before she could stop herself. For a second, she thought he was going to backhand her. But he merely smiled.

The smile from hell.

"You'll think 'poor baby' before we're through."

He chomped into the apple and deliberately chewed noisily.

"I promised myself if I ever got out of that hellhole she put me in, I'd make your mother miserable. Then I found out she was dying, and she was searching for the daughter she gave up.

"Know what? That pissed me off even more. My mother dumped me like your mother dumped Renata."

In his eyes the cold truth dawned. That's it, Taylor

thought. He hates Mother because he blames her for the way his own mother rejected him. He was a complicated man, and she had sensed a dark undertow to his personality. She'd attributed it to his artistic nature, but now she knew the truth.

He despised her mother for several things. Her mother hadn't been responsible for the bust-up of the drug ring. She certainly hadn't given him up for adoption. The only thing her mother was guilty of was thinking Paul wasn't good enough for her.

"I was adopted by the sorriest couple to ever walk the planet. As soon as I was eighteen I ditched them."

"You told me they were dead."

"I told you a lot of things you were stupid enough to believe."

He was right, and hearing him, of all people, say it made her even angrier with herself.

"Did you ever try to find your mother?"

"No. Why would I? She unloaded me."

"Maybe she regretted it the way my mother did."

Paul snorted and took another bite of apple.

"I doubt it. She and your mother are exactly alike—selfish bitches."

Despite being in the hot, stuffy shack, goose bumps sprang across her shoulders and ran down her arms as a disturbing thought hit her.

"You killed Renata, didn't you?"

"You just figure that out?"

"Why? You didn't even know her."

"Donovan was nosing around. I needed to distract him."

He chuckled, obviously pleased with himself. He's crazy, she decided. Truly demented.

How could she have lived with this man and not known?

The crazier a person is, the more sane he can appear.

She seemed to remember that from a psych class she'd taken at Yale.

Still, you'd think she would have noticed . . . something. This was a man who'd killed in cold blood because he needed a distraction. A man who hated his own mother so much that he blamed another woman for what his mother had done.

"I could have used one of these babies on Renata." He reached into a bag and pulled out a pistol with a silencer on it. "But I wanted it to look amateurish, like one of you did it."

Again he laughed.

"Best of all, your mother went for it. Torture can be subtle, you know. She's grieving for the daughter she just found, and she's blaming you or Trent for her death. Now she knows she's going to lose another daughter."

Taylor had realized he planned to kill her, but this was the first time he'd admitted it. She should have been shocked, but all she could do was stare at him, transfixed.

"The beauty of this whole deal is no one knows I'm here," Paul said. "When it's over, I'm moving to LA. I already have a new name. I'm starting a new life."

The sun was rising over Biscayne Bay when Shane rendezvoused with Vince, Jim and Lisa. They'd been showing a picture of Paul around the clubs.

Auggie at his side, Shane had checked as many houses as he could in the mid-Miami area until it was too late to ring a doorbell. Then he and Auggie had walked the streets for hours.

He'd given Auggie the T-shirt Taylor had slept in the last night they were together. Auggie hadn't been trained to track people, but he had a hell of a nose, and he thought Taylor hung the moon. With luck, Auggie might catch her scent.

His luck had run out.

They didn't find a trace of Taylor.

"He's been spotted at several of the clubs," Lisa told them.

"But none of the bouncers knew where he lives," Jim added.

"I had another thought," Lisa told them. "Paul's pretty buff. He used to work out every day at Fit For Life."

"In the morning could you check the health clubs?" Shane asked.

"Sure. We'll do it, but there's a lot of them."

"I'm sure Trent and Brianna would be glad to help," Vince said. "Start here in SoBe and move north."

"I'd start in mid-Miami," Shane said. "Ashton's arrogant enough to hit the clubs because he knows Taylor isn't into that scene. I doubt he'd risk running around SoBe in daylight."

"Yeah, he's too smart for that," Vince agreed.

Shane told them to go home and get some sleep. He drove back to Coral Gables, where Doyle was waiting by the telephone with Caleb and Vanessa. Doyle answered the door and they walked down the hall to the library, Auggie at their heels.

"Brianna's in bed," Doyle said.

Caleb was dozing in a chair, but Vanessa was awake.

"Taylor hasn't called?" Shane knew the answer to the question before he asked.

"No," Vanessa said.

"He wants us to sweat, but if this is about the Web site, he'll have her call soon."

"Do you think he might let her go if we do as he says?" asked Vanessa.

"I seriously doubt it. He doesn't realize we know he's involved. He can't afford to let her live."

"I agree," Doyle said. "We have to find her before it's too late."

"Why don't we all get some sleep," Shane suggested. "We want to be fresh in the morning."

"Good idea," Doyle said.

"Tomorrow at nine when the offices open, I'm going to check rental agencies," Shane told them. "I doubt if he purchased a house, but I'm having the group check the real estate agencies, after they cover the health clubs, just in case."

"I had Maria make up a guest room," Vanessa said. "You and Auggie may sleep there."

Shane thanked her and left for the bedroom with the report the private detective had given Vanessa after he investigated Ashton. He doubted he could sleep, but he was determined to try.

He needed to stay as sharp as possible. He was so upset he had to force himself to concentrate.

He read the report. Vince was right. Masters didn't seem to be too hot a detective. He was pretty vague about many details, making Shane think he'd deliberately padded the bill.

Masters had managed to follow Ashton all over the place. He'd seen him sell a minor amount of cocaine. There were even a few snapshots of the transactions.

Chapter 32

By morning, Taylor had a plan. It was a long shot at best, but it was something.

On the bed next to her, Paul stirred. He hadn't touched her. Thank you, God. She'd been forced to pee in the bucket, which was humiliating enough without having Paul try to have sex with her.

"My arm hurts," she said more loudly than necessary.

She wanted to wake him up. She needed to get Paul to put the handcuffs on her left hand. She was much better with her right hand.

His eyelids at half-mast, he gazed at her, grunted, then rolled over. She nudged him with her knee.

"For Christ's sake, let me get some sleep."

"It's nearly eleven o'clock."

This was a lie, but it got his attention.

He vaulted out of bed, then looked at his watch.

"What? It's barely eight."

"It seems later. I am not wearing my wristwatch." A major mistake. If she had it on, Shane would have found her by now.

He pulled a banana out of a grocery bag and wagged it at her. "Want something to eat?"

"No, but please switch the handcuffs to the other side. My arm is killing me."

"Quit nagging. I'll do it in a minute."

He went outside and she could hear him going to the bathroom in the bushes. She said a quick prayer that her plan would work.

Paul returned and pulled the key to the handcuffs out of his pocket. "I'm going to leave them off for a minute while you call your mother."

He unlocked the handcuffs and put them on the other side of the bed. Next time her left hand would be tethered to the bedpost. She wiggled her fingers, trying to get back as much circulation as possible.

Handing her a cell phone he'd taken out of the duffel bag, he said, "Call your mother. Tell her no one is to touch the Web site even to take orders. Tell her if she does it, the kidnappers will release you. Get it? Kidnappers. Plural."

"Why don't you let me go after I make the call?"

"I might." He ran his index finger across her lips. "If you're good."

He was lying. She'd be dead if her plan didn't work. She studied the keypad on the cell phone.

"Go on. Call Vanessa. Tell her exactly what I said, but don't mention my name."

"What if she asks who has me?"

"Say you don't know their names."

Taylor dialed the number, and her mother answered on the second ring with a feeble hello.

"It's me."

"Thank God. I've been so worried. Are you all right?"

Taylor detected a hallow sound, indicating her mother had put the call on the speaker phone, which meant there were others in the room. Taylor prayed Shane was there. Someone else might not understand what she planned to do.

"Yes. I'm okay."

"Hurry up. Get on with it," Paul whispered.

"I'm going to be released if you do exactly what I tell you."

As she spoke, Taylor pressed the 2 and the 7 on the small cell phone pad.

Paul didn't seem to notice. He turned to rummage in the cooler.

She pressed the 5, 3, and 9.

"There's some interference on the line," her mother said.

Taylor kept talking. "Mother, go to To The Maxx and make sure no one touches the Web site, not even to check for orders. Understand?"

Paul had gotten a bottle of water. He threw back his head and drank it. Taylor again pressed the same sequence of numbers.

"There's a beeping noise on the line," her mother said.

"I don't know who the kidnappers are, but they mean business."

Paul smiled, obviously pleased. He turned and searched through one of the grocery bags.

Taylor punched in the numbers again.

This time her mother didn't mention it. Taylor bet someone in the room—probably Shane—had told her not to say anything.

Paul turned to her. "Warn her not to call the police."

"Mother, if you call the police, I'll be killed."

"I love you." Her mother's voice wasn't much more than a whisper.

"I love you, too," she said. "Tell Shane I love him."

Paul yanked the phone out of her hand and hit "End."

Tell Shane I love him.

The way she'd said those words, almost a plea, brought a treacherous lump to Shane's throat. He'd never heard that kind of emotion in her voice. It sent a shiver of sheer longing tripping up his spine.

God, how he loved her.

He hadn't realized he was capable of such love. It came from a deep, secret place he hadn't known existed.

Doyle cut into his thoughts. "What was with the beeping? Why did you tell Vanessa not to mention it again?"

"Taylor was trying to signal us with the phone pad, I think."

"It sounded like cell phone interference to me," Caleb said.

"No. It happened three times, and she ignored Vanessa's comments about it. She didn't want Ashton to know."

"She said kidnappers. Do you suppose there's more than one?" asked Vanessa.

"I doubt it. He just wants to throw us off."

Shane was thinking about the beeping, and Auggie was gazing up at him as if he'd recognized Taylor's voice on the speaker phone. "I'll run right over to the company and make sure no one uses the Web site." Doyle walked toward the door. "I'll make up some story about a virus."

As Doyle left, something occurred to Shane. "There are letters on the keypad. Maybe she was spelling out something."

"It was just beeps," Vanessa said. "How do we know what numbers she was hitting?"

Then it hit him. The Discovery channel program.

"Each number on a telephone keypad has a slightly different tone. An electronic enhancer will tell us. Taylor and I saw it on a TV program. She was smart enough to remember it."

He grabbed the small tape recorder they'd used to record the conversation.

"Recording studios have enhancers."

He rushed to his car and drove off toward Miami with Auggie. He used his cell phone to locate a recording studio. For a hefty fee, they would let him use their enhancer.

Tell Shane I love him.

"I love you, too, babe. Don't worry. I'm going to find you."

Shane looked at the numbers he'd gotten using the electronic enhancer. Taylor had pressed 2, 7, 5, 3, 9. She'd done it three times, selecting exactly the same numbers in the same sequence.

The numbers probably weren't a street address. It was too long for most of Miami, but he'd get Vince to check—just in case.

The phone keypad letter clusters for those numbers were: *abc, pqrs, jkl, def,* and *wxyz.*

It had to be a place, he decided. A word jumped out at him. The last three letters spelled key.

Taylor was somewhere in the Keys, not in Miami at all.

Which Key?

There were only two letters left. They didn't spell a complete word.

Initials.

It had to be initials.

If only he were more familiar with the area. Remembering the private detective's report, he rushed out to his car. Ashton had gone to the Keys several times to do drug deals, but the investigator hadn't said which Keys.

Shane took the map out of the glove compartment. There were so damn many Keys. Thirty-four major ones and countless blips without names.

Big Pine Key jumped out at him.

She had pressed the *b* and *p*. Had to be it.

Why was the damn thing so big? It was one of the largest keys.

He would search every inch if he had to. Auggie might be able to help. Another idea occurred to him.

He used his cell phone to call Rick Masters. The PI had been down there. He might know where Ashton would go on that Key.

Shane was surprised to find Masters in his office. The way his luck had been going, the guy might have been in Tibet on an assignment. He explained what he wanted.

"You know, I'm not in this business for my health. I—"

"I'll give you my credit card number."

Shane yanked it from his wallet and rattled off the numbers. He didn't bother to ask how much. If Taylor died, no amount of money could bring her back.

"Yeah, I did tail him down to Big Pine Key a coupla' times."

The detective's voice alone conjured up the image of a Florida cracker who hated Cubans and had a beer belly slopping over his belt.

"Fishin's real big in Big Pine. So's diving. There's lots of canals—"

"Where did Ashton go?"

"I'm gettin' to that part."

Shane heard him take a drag on a cigarette.

"There's this here shack fishermen used in the thirties. Since then better ones have been built. With air and fridges for beer."

"I'm familiar with them."

"I figure Mr. Ashton liked this one because it's hidden. I had a helluva' time tailin' him out there 'cause nobody goes to that part of the Key."

Taylor watched Paul leave, her jaw still smarting from when he'd slapped her. She had known saying it was a risk, but one worth taking.

If she died, she wanted Shane to know how much she loved him.

She wasn't surprised Paul had been jealous enough to hit her. "He thinks he is God's gift to women."

Once she'd thought so, too. Now, she knew better.

Shane was the kind of man a woman could count on. Masculine yet surprisingly sensitive.

Why hadn't she told him how much he meant to her?

Because she hadn't realized the depth of her emotion until it was too late. Facing death makes you take stock of your life.

Maybe that's why her mother had changed so much. The elitist woman was able to take in a redneck like Caleb Bassett and accept a daughter who was a stripper. When death was imminent, it wasn't what you had or who you knew that counted.

Life was about loving and being loved.

Taylor tried to imagine never seeing Shane again. Never being able to share anything with him.

She'd thought she had loved Paul, but looking back, she realized they'd had a shallow, meaningless relationship based on sex and good times.

Shane had come into her life when she was facing crisis after crisis. He'd been wonderful.

Supportive.

Helpful.

"A man of action, not just words," she muttered under her breath.

Her thoughts turned to her mother and Trent. Uncle Doyle and Brianna. She might never see *any* of them again. She might not have the chance to tell them how much they meant to her.

The pain of what she stood to lose reverberated through her, a keening cry of despair that took sheer willpower to suppress. Her chest ached with tears she refused to shed.

"Purge those negative thoughts," she said out loud.

She prayed Shane remembered the Discovery channel program and had decoded her keypad message. She didn't know what else to do. Paul had taken the duffels with the cell phones and the guns with him.

Even if she somehow managed to get the drop on him, Taylor realized she was still handcuffed to the bed. Maybe she could convince him to switch hands again, and attack him before he could recuff her.

"Wait a day or so," she told herself. "If help doesn't come, you've got to give it a shot."

Paul had gone to someplace that had electricity so he could plug in his laptop and see which of his contacts had checked in at the Web site. When they'd all contacted him, Taylor's time would be up.

He wouldn't hesitate to kill her.

* * *

Shane followed the smarmy detective's directions down the long highway where the ocean came within six feet of his Jeep in places. Sure as hell, he wouldn't want to be on this road during a hurricane.

It was dark now, the sun having set two hours ago. After decoding the message, Shane had immediately driven out of Miami with Auggie. He'd put his gun in the trunk of the car. He'd left a message for Vince on his cell phone, but he hadn't bothered to contact anyone else.

"No one but Vince can help me," he told Auggie.

He'd considered calling the police, but if Ashton even thought the police were around, he would kill Taylor on the spot.

"I have to rely on myself."

And the Glock in the trunk of his car. The light-weight gun had only been fired on a practice range.

Shane had been in some tough spots, but he'd never actually had to kill a man. He'd wounded several during a firefight in Cuidad del Este, the terrorist haven in South America.

"This time might be different. Right, Auggie?"

Auggie gazed at him as if he actually understood. Shane tried to remember when he'd last fed the dog.

"I'll make it up to you, boy. A Big Mac once we have Taylor with us."

Big Pine Key bustled with life as he turned off MM 33. Masters was right. It appeared to be a haven for fishermen and divers.

He drove by Barnacle Bed and Breakfast. The sign read: *barefoot oceanfront living with panache.*

Yeah, right.

Masters had told him the B and B had been built in the shape of a star, but all Shane could see were odd angles. Nearby was another B and B. Hansel and Gretel must have designed it.

He sped by, then began looking for the dirt side road leading out to the fishing shanty.

"What if she isn't there?" he asked Auggie. "What if I misinterpreted the message?"

The dog gazed up at Shane with such soulful eyes that he almost missed the side road. It went on for over a mile, the way Masters had said, fizzling out from anything resembling a road to become little more than weed-choked tracks in the dirt. It led him into a thicket of dense shrubs, too short to be trees, too tall and thick to be ordinary bushes.

It was darker than Hades; the only light visible came from his car. If Master's directions were correct, he was getting close. His headlights would tip off Ashton and ruin Shane's plans.

He parked the car, put his cell phone on the dash, and rolled down the windows. It was night but hot and as humid as a steam room. Auggie's brains would fry if he left him in the car with the windows up.

"Stay," he told Auggie.

He went around to the trunk and pulled the Glock out of its case. Why hadn't he brought a flashlight? The night air sheened him with perspiration as he trudged down the dirt road into the darkness.

Around the bend, he saw a dim light.

Chapter 33

Taylor stared at the cobwebs trailing from the ceiling, while Paul typed something on his laptop. She tried to calculate how long it would take for Shane to realize she'd been sending a message and decipher it.

What if her mother hadn't contacted Shane?

It was possible, she decided, but Uncle Doyle or Brianna would have told Shane what had happened. She needed to stay calm. It was too soon to expect help to arrive.

"Know what the most common crime in America is?"

She asked the question to annoy him. She'd been doing it since he returned and it gave her a perverse thrill.

"Cheating the IRS," he said without looking up.

"WRONG! That's number two. It's jaywalking."

He shot her a warning glance. "Don't interrupt

me with any more of your trivia crap. I'm trying to concentrate."

That's why I'm hassling you.

Through the grimy window, she saw a movement. It could be a nighthawk. Big Pine Key was full of them.

She watched the window out of the corner of her eye. If it was Shane, she didn't want to attract Paul's attention. The window was directly in front of him. He was concentrating on his laptop, but the satchel with the guns was at his feet.

BANG! The door burst open with a shower of splinters and the doorknob smashed a hole in the flimsy plank wall. Shane strode into the room, a gun leveled at Paul.

A rush of relief coursed through Taylor—so intense it brought scalding tears to her eyes. In her heart of hearts, she'd never given up hope. Somehow she'd known Shane would decipher her message.

"What the fuck?" Baffled shock contorted Paul's face. The laptop dropped to the floor.

"Unlock the handcuffs—now."

"Shane, be careful. He has a bag of guns at his feet."

"Hands in the air," Shane yelled.

Paul slowly raised his arms.

"The key to the handcuffs is in his pocket."

"Slowly reach into your pocket and get the key," Shane said.

Paul took his sweet time but finally pulled out the tiny key.

"Unlock the cuffs."

Paul hovered over Taylor, and she saw her reflection in his eyes. She also saw raw fury like a rabid dog.

He inserted the tiny key in the lock. It popped open, and Taylor yanked her wrist free. Her arm was numb from being in one position so long, and her fingers tingled from lack of proper circulation.

"Are you okay?" asked Shane.

"Yes. I'm fine."

"Stick out your wrists," Shane told Paul.

"Can you cuff him?" he asked Taylor. "Or do you want me to do it while you hold the gun on him?"

"I'll do it." Taylor had never handled a gun and didn't trust herself in such a crucial situation.

Paul shoved his hands at her, palms up. Taylor opened the handcuffs and adjusted them for a man's larger wrists. Her right hand tingled, the circulation not quite normal. She fumbled as she attempted to clamp the handcuffs over his wrists.

"Need help?" Shane asked.

"I think I've got it now." She had the cuff on one wrist but couldn't quite clamp it shut.

Shane took a half step forward. Taylor looked up, her mouth open to tell him to stay back. The handcuffs slipped through her numb fingers and hit the floor. She dove after them.

In a lightening flash, Paul yanked a small switchblade out of his shirt pocket. The knife was at her throat in a heartbeat.

"Toss the gun onto the bed or the bitch dies."

Please, God, this couldn't be happening, Taylor thought. Tears blurred her vision. How could she be so clumsy?

Paul would kill Shane, too.

And get a big kick out of it.

"You heard me," Paul yelled. "The gun."

The Glock hit the mattress—*thunk*. With his free hand, Paul grabbed the gun.

"I was going to wait a few days before killing her," Paul told them. "You've forced me to come up with a better plan. A murder-suicide. That way the police—

should they ever find this place—won't look for anyone else."

"The police are on their way." Shane's voice was calm.

"You're bluffing. I remember you from Colombia. You thought you were hot shit. You wanted to take me down yourself so you can be little Miss Perfect's hero."

"He is my hero," Taylor said. If this maniac killed them, she wanted Shane to know how much he meant to her. "He's been there for me in a way no one—"

"I love you, Taylor."

"Oh, pul-leeze." Paul waved the gun, motioning for Shane to come over to the bed.

Shane walked over and stood beside Paul.

"How did you find us?" Paul asked.

"Taylor sent a message when she called."

"Impossible! I listened to every word."

"I did it by pressing the keypad while I talked." Despite the knife pricking her jugular, Taylor couldn't help being proud of herself.

A crackling laugh split the night air.

"Well, hell. Aren't you the smart one," Paul said. "That's what I liked about you. Beauty and brains."

"It won't do you any good to kill us," Shane said, his tone level, calm. "Help is coming. You don't think I drove all the way out here without telling someone, do you?"

"It doesn't matter," Paul replied. "I'm trying to decide which of the two of you to kill first. Who'll suffer the most seeing the other one die?"

"You're one sick bastard," Shane said.

"You're just pissed because I outsmarted you."

"He found me when—"

With a ferocious snarl, a streak of black bounded into the room.

Auggie.

He lunged for Paul, fangs bared like a wolf. He whirled around, aiming the gun at Auggie. Taylor grabbed his arm, and the shot went wide. Shane tackled him just as Auggie pounced and sank his teeth into Paul's arm.

Paul howled in pain as he hit the floor, Shane and Auggie on top of him. They rolled back and forth across the splintery wood floor, a blur of arms and legs and dog.

Shane put a hammerlock on him, and Paul was forced to drop the gun. It clanked onto the floor and Shane grabbed it. He pointed it directly at Paul's temple.

"Get the dog off me."

"Down, Auggie."

The dog backed away but kept snarling at Paul, who had blood gushing from his upper arm where Auggie had bitten him. Auggie had always been so mellow Taylor never realized he had such huge fangs or that he would actually bite someone.

"Just for the record," Taylor told Paul, "my mother had nothing to do with you being busted. Shane did it."

"A DIA sting," Shane added.

"Ask me if I care," Paul said, but Taylor could see he would have gone after Shane had he known the truth.

"I never knew Auggie was trained to attack," Taylor said to Shane.

She was lying in his arms in the bedroom of a cottage at Parmer Place in Big Pine Key. By the time the police had arrived and taken their statements, it had been too late to drive back to SoBe, but they'd called her mother to let everyone know Taylor was safe.

"He isn't trained to attack, but like a lot of dogs, he'll instinctively protect his owner. I had him on a 'stay' command. I'm surprised he jumped out of the car window to come after me."

Auggie must have sensed they were talking about him. He put his head up on the bed and Shane petted him, then Taylor took her turn.

"You arrived at just the right time," she told Auggie.

"Saved me from taking a bullet," Shane said. "I wasn't going to let him kill us without putting up a fight, you know."

She gave him a quick peck on the cheek. "I meant what I said. You are my hero."

"And you're mighty clever. I'm not sure I would have thought to use the keypad to send a message."

"I didn't know what else to do. I'm glad you figured it out."

Their lips met, and he kissed her, lingering, savoring the moment.

"So you finally admit it," he whispered. "You're in love with me."

"Yes, I am, and you love me, too."

"When are we getting married?"

"Right away."

"You're that hot for me, huh?"

"Don't get cocky now." She gently punched him. "I want to do it soon because my mother may not have much longer to live."

"Good idea."

"I want her to help plan the wedding. She's great at parties. It'll take her mind off her illness."

"I'll call my mother and grandmother and send them plane tickets. They've been pestering me for years to settle down. They won't believe I'm finally doing it.''

"I want to be married out by the pool at our house. Is that okay?''

"Anything you want, babe. Planning weddings is not a guy thing.''

"Any chance Caleb Bassett will be gone in two weeks? That seems like enough time to plan a simple family wedding.''

"No chance.''

Shane explained to her about Caleb being her mother's first love and Renata's real father. She was stunned. He didn't appear to be the type of man her mother would love, but she'd been very young then.

She listened while he brought her up to speed on the other developments that had happened while she'd been with Paul. She was thrilled to hear Jim Wilson wasn't a criminal. Lisa deserved a good man.

When they arrived at her mother's the following afternoon, everyone was waiting for them. Her mother had brought in a caterer, who had set up an elaborate buffet table.

Her mother was on a chaise by the pool, with Caleb hovering nearby. Taylor rushed into her arms.

"Heavens! I thought I'd lost you.''

Her mother burst into tears, which was unusual. Taylor had seldom seen her cry.

"Don't cry. I'm safe. I'm here.''

"These are happy tears.''

Unexpectedly, Taylor was crying, too.

Tears of joy. Tears of love.

Shane put his arm around her, and Auggie licked her hand. She dabbed at her tears with a tissue Brianna handed her and listened to Shane tell everyone the details of their harrowing experience with Paul Ashton.

"You're very brave," her mother told Shane.

"That's one smart dog," Uncle Doyle remarked.

"Paul murdered Renata," Taylor told her mother. Caleb nodded. "We figured as much."

Taylor doubted this, but didn't call him on it. This man was Renata's father and part of her mother's life now. Taylor would do anything to make sure her mother's last days were happy ones.

"I'm sorry if I acted suspicious of you two," her mother said to Taylor and Trent, who was seated nearby. "It was wrong of me. I should have known better."

"It's my fault," Caleb said, actually sounding as if he meant it. "I thought one of you did it to keep my baby from inheriting anything."

"Don't blame yourself," Vanessa told Caleb. "Anyone in your position would have thought the same way. I should have known better but the stress of finding Renata and all the medication I was taking played terrible tricks with my mind."

"It doesn't matter now," Trent said.

"He's right," Taylor said. "It doesn't matter at all."

"I'm glad everything is straightened out," Lisa said. She was sitting at the foot of the chaise where Jim Wilson was sprawled. "No more blaming innocent people. Forgive and forget, right?"

"There's one thing I'm not going to forget," Taylor said, glancing at them one at a time. "Shane told me how you all pitched in to try to find me. I want to thank you. It means a lot to me.

"There was a time out there when I didn't think I would ever see you all again. Know what my biggest regret was? I hadn't had the opportunity to tell you all how much I love you."

"We love you, too," said Uncle Doyle and the others echoed his words.

Taylor stepped away from Shane and went around the group. She gave everyone a hug and a kiss. Brianna and Lisa started to cry, which brought tears to Taylor's eyes again.

"They're crying because they're happy. Go figure," Shane said.

"Women," Vince said with a shake of his head.

"That's why they cry at weddings." This from Caleb. "They're *so* happy."

"Speaking of weddings," Shane said to the group, "I've asked Taylor to marry me, and she said yes."

Vanessa clapped her hands. "I've been mentally planning your wedding for years."

"We want to be married right here. A small wedding. Nothing fancy," Taylor told her mother. "Two weeks from now."

"I guess we should consider this an engagement party," Trent said. "Let's break out the champagne."

"We have a lot to celebrate," Brianna said.

"We had a family powwow this morning," Uncle Doyle said. "We've decided not to sell To The Maxx. I'm going to stay on with Trent. Brianna's coming to work, too."

The news surprised Taylor a little, but it made her happy. Without Raoul's interference, things would be great again.

"We know you'd rather develop your own game company. You could start it after the honeymoon," added Uncle Doyle.

"I'd like that," Taylor said.

Even though she preferred starting her own company, she was glad they'd decided to keep the business that had meant so much to her father. She was certain Brianna would be a valuable addition to the team.

* * *

It was early evening and everyone was still hanging around, eating and having a good time. Auggie had been rewarded with a steak for his bravery, and he'd fallen asleep at Shane's feet.

Taylor finally managed to get Caleb alone. There were questions she wanted to ask about Renata, but seeing how happy her mother was discussing the wedding plans, Taylor didn't want to spoil things by bringing up such a sad subject.

"I'm sorry for your loss," she told Caleb. "I wish I had gotten to know Renata better."

"You would have liked her. She could be prickly at times, and we fought more than a father and daughter should, but she was a good girl."

"Did you tell her that she really was Mother's daughter?"

"I didn't tell her until I saw the TV program and realized Vanessa was searching for Renata." Caleb paused a moment, and looked across the pool area to where her mother was sitting. "My baby went ballistic. She couldn't believe I'd withheld the truth from her all those years."

Taylor couldn't blame her, trying to imagine what it would be like. "She knew you were her father, didn't she?"

"Yeah, but she thought Mary Jo was her mother."

"Why didn't you tell her the truth?"

Caleb didn't seem to be offended even though her tone was a little sharp.

"I didn't want her hunting for her mother and making more trouble for me. She was hard enough to handle as it was. I loved her. You may not believe that, but I did."

Something in his voice made Taylor suspect there

was more to it than he said. She waited him out, gazing intently at him to see if she could get him to say more.

Finally, he added, "I lost your mother, and there was so much about Renata that reminded me of Vanessa. I didn't want her to leave me to search for her mother."

But then you found out how much money Mother has and you changed your mind. Taylor kept this thought to herself. In his own way, maybe Caleb had always loved her mother.

"Renata really didn't want to come here, did she?"

Caleb shook his head. "Not at first, but I convinced her. Know what? Once she got here, she loved it."

"Did she forgive Mother for giving her up?"

"No. Not really. Renata liked Vanessa okay, but she was out for what she could get."

Taylor thought about how warped Paul had become. Part of it was caused by his feeling of abandonment because his mother had given him up. Renata hadn't lived with it for years the way Paul had. Still it had made her bitter.

"How did she become a stripper?"

Caleb rolled his eyes. "She was determined to be a dancer in Vegas, but she wasn't good enough. She worked awhile as a waitress, then found out she could make more money stripping."

"Were you with her in Las Vegas?"

"Nah. I was selling insurance. She'd gone off to Vegas on her own. I assumed she was dancing. We lost contact. I didn't hear from her for over three years.

"Then out of the blue I got a call. She needed money. We talked, and I convinced her to move to New Orleans."

"Did you see her? Did you know what she was doing?"

"Yeah, I visited. She'd changed her name from

Peggy Sue Bassett to Renata Rollins. She admitted she was stripping. Nothing I could say would stop her.''

Taylor believed him. She hadn't known Renata well, but she had given Taylor the impression she did as she pleased.

"She was a good girl, though. When I hurt my back, she invited me to live with her. Of course I used my disability check for my share.''

Taylor nodded. People, she thought, often led lives she found hard to understand. They made their own choices, and she refused to condemn anyone for it.

But it was depressing to know a man she'd brought home had killed Renata just when she was on the verge of starting a new, better life.

"You're wondering why I never tried to find your mother,'' Caleb said.

"I assumed you did try. Was I wrong?''

"Yes. I never looked. Vanessa was exactly like Renata. She had stars in her eyes. I knew she'd run off to some big city. She'd never be happy in a small town with a guy like me.''

Taylor sighed inwardly. Caleb did truly care about her mother. She doubted she would ever warm up to him, but it didn't matter. It was how her mother felt that counted.

Shane walked up, Auggie at his heels. "What's going on?''

"We were talking about Renata.''

"I think I'll get a Johnnie Walker,'' Caleb said.

Taylor watched him stroll away. She turned to Shane and told him what she'd learned about Renata.

"I had to know,'' she said. "It's been bothering me.''

He pulled her into his arms. "There's nothing you can do to help her now. Stop beating yourself up about it.''

"I know, but—"

"Come on. Let's go into the house and call my family. They'll be so excited."

Arm in arm, they walked into the house where she'd grown up. Once again it was a happy place full of fond memories.

"Oh, my gosh. In two weeks my name will be Taylor Donovan. Sounds good, doesn't it?"

"I love it." He kissed her, a light, sweet kiss. "I love you."

Please turn the page for
an exciting sneak peek of
Meryl Sawyer's
newest novel of romantic suspense,
LADY KILLER,
coming in November 2003 from Zebra Books!

Prologue

Damn, was he good—or what?

Troy Avery stood in front of the penthouse window, gazing at the skyline glittering in the darkness. A skull of a moon skulked above the Golden Gate Bridge, hidden on and off by wind-whipped clouds.

He was still breathing heavily, panting with exertion and the bone-deep satisfaction of another job well planned.

Executed to perfection.

Troy was good because he was so smart. Brilliant, actually. More intelligent than any of the other scholarship students who had been at Stanford with him. Troy had been smart enough to drop out and devote himself to an invention guaranteed to change the world.

"I'm a whole lot smarter than you are," he said over his shoulder to the dead woman sprawled on the marble floor behind him.

"Final call," he had told Francine Yellen as he'd strangled her with the telephone cord.

Hearing the well-known phrase, Francine's eyes had popped out of her head in sheer terror. For once the renowned psychiatrist, who so glibly gave advice on television was at a loss for words.

She'd been a fighter. He'd grant her that much. She'd bucked and kicked and thrashed for a full minute at least. Then she'd gone limp, the air in her lungs exhausted.

The *San Francisco Herald* had dubbed Troy the Final Call Killer. He preferred his own term.

Lady Killer.

It fit better because these women thought they were ladies. He knew the truth. They were bitches who deserved to die.

"Lady Killer. Lady Killer."

He whispered the words under his breath until they thundered through his head becoming louder and louder and louder. A second later, he realized he was shouting the term repeatedly like a mantra.

LadyKillerLadyKillerLadyKillerLadyKillerLadyKiller LadyKiller. . .

Chapter 1

"Aren't there any normal guys around?"

"Define normal."

Jessica Crawford and her two friends broke out in laughter that floated above the buzz in Peaches, the trendy bar near the *San Francisco Herald* where they worked. Several men turned to watch them, but Jessica didn't make eye contact. She was through with men she'd met in bars.

Been there. Done that. There were better ways to meet men.

"Seriously," Zoe said, arching one dark eyebrow the way she often did. "I need to find a normal guy who wants to settle down and have a family."

"Why?" Jessica heard herself ask. "Has your biological clock become a time bomb?"

"You bet," Stacy replied. "Hey, we're all thirty-something, right? So—"

"None of us has seen the big three-two," Jessica said. "Why rush marriage? Let's enjoy dating."

Her two friends stared at Jessica. She gazed back, checking a grin.

"Okay, Jess, what gives?" Stacy, a green-eyed red-head, always zeroed in on things others missed.

"Tell all," Zoe demanded. "You've been so down on men."

Jessica had to admit her acrimonious divorce from the cheating, lying skank Marshall Wolford had left her distrustful of men.

"We need to be careful, but if we screen properly, we can meet great guys."

"I have a fab guy," Stacy informed them as if they weren't totally aware of her year-long relationship with Scott Reynolds.

"Hip-hip-hooray for you!" Zoe lifted her wineglass. "I guess I'm the only one missing out. It sounds like Jessica has met a guy."

Jessica smiled fondly at her friends. Each Thursday night the trio met for dinner. And true confessions.

The three of them hadn't known each other until they'd been hired by the *Herald*. In the last seven years, they'd become close. A blonde, a brunette, and redhead. All of them were attractive, Jessica had to admit. When they were together, the trio drew stares from men.

"I have met someone," Jessica confessed. "An attorney."

Stacy shook her head, her dark hair shifting across her shoulders. "Did you ever notice the term 'criminal lawyer' is redundant?"

They shared a laugh, which drew more male glances in their direction.

"You both told me to start dating again," Jessica said.

"You must admit that it seems strange for you to take up with an attorney . . . considering."

Jess mentally completed the sentence. Considering Marshall Crawford had left her for an attorney in his firm. She'd been angry, broken-hearted, and she'd sworn off all men—especially attorneys.

Jason Talbott was different.

"How you met this man? I want to find a guy," Zoe said.

Jessica hesitated, thinking these were her closest friends, but still . . . there was something unconventional about the way she'd met Jason Talbott.

"I met him online," Jessica confessed. "On Matchmaker.com."

Her two friends stared at her, slack-jawed.

"Well, what did you expect me to do?" Jessica knew she sounded defensive, but she couldn't help herself. "I've hung out in bars and met losers. My friends have introduced me to the three single men they know. Two of them were heterosexual."

"You're right," Stacy said. "I met Scott at Starbucks when I bumped into him and spilled my latte on his slacks. Fate, I guess."

"Okay, tell all," Zoe said in the businesslike voice she used when interviewing people for her financial column at the *Herald*.

"Well, I subscribed to several online dating services to research an article."

Jessica was an extremely popular columnist who wrote New Millennium Lifestyles, a column examining the evolving American culture in a witty, off-beat way. Many of her articles examined personal relationships.

"What happens when you sign up for an Internet dating service?" Zoe asked.

"Scan your picture, then fill out a form about your likes and dislikes."

"I dislike men who aren't good at oral sex," Stacy said with a giggle.

"Stop it. I need to know about cyberdating," Zoe said.

Jessica smiled then took a sip of her pinot grigio. "Guys contact you or you contact guys through E-mail. Then you decide if you want to respond."

"I'll bet that's how the killer found those two women," Stacy said.

Jessica groaned out loud. Two women had been killed in the past six months. Each had been strangled with a telephone cord.

"Fuhgettaboutit," Jessica told her friends in her best Sopranos' voice. "The second was probably a copycat killing. Internet dating is perfectly safe."

"Do you mean it?" Stacy asked.

"Yes. All that shows on the screen is the special name you select for yourself. No one knows who you are or where you live unless you tell them."

"I think Marci does the Internet dating thing," Stacy said. "I remember her saying she met men for the first time at a public place like Starbucks."

All three of them rolled their eyes heavenward. Marci—with an i—was the society editor and a total airhead.

"As much as I hate to admit it," Jessica said, "Marci is right. You e-mail first, but it doesn't last long. Men are anxious to meet you."

"Of course, they want to check out your boobs," Zoe said.

"No wonder Marci loves the Internet. Her new boobs must be a hit," Stacy said.

"Okay, so you meet," Zoe said. "It must be awkward."

Jessica shook her head, sending a spray of long,

blond hair across her face. "No worse than your usual blind date."

"What did you do with this lawyer?" asked Stacy.

"We shot back and forth a few E-mails, then met for drinks at Carmelo's. We decided to have lunch the next day. That's how it started."

"So how do you know he isn't the Final Call Killer?" Zoe asked.

"Pul-leeze. After we met for lunch, Jason invited me to his office. He's an attorney with a big firm in the Contential Bank tower."

"So why does he need an Internet dating service?" Stacy asked.

Jessica put her drink on the small table and leaned closer to her friends. "Jason has been introduced to all the singles his friends know. We live less than a mile apart, but we don't have mutual friends. We would never have met except online."

"Has he ever been married?" Stacy asked.

"No. He's thirty-four and single. I think he wants to settle down."

"See! There are normal guys around," Stacy said.

"Yikes!" Zoe cried, glancing at her watch. "We're outta here. You know how Grant obsesses when anyone is late."

Grant Bennett was editor-in-chief at the *Herald*. He'd invited his executive staff to dinner at Stars. They paid their bill and rushed out to catch a taxi.

Inside the cab, Jessica gazed out the window at the city where she'd grown up. September was her favorite month. Tourists thought summer was the time to visit. Locals knew better. Summer was cool, foggy. Fall brought warmer days and clear skies.

"Anyone want to bet on why Grant invited us to dinner?" Zoe asked.

They'd discussed this earlier. Grant usually had his 'team' to dinner to celebrate something important.

"Could Marci be getting married?" Stacy speculated. "That would thrill Grant no end."

Grant Bennett had handpicked all his reporters except for Marci Haywood. She was Throckmorton Smith's niece, and the owner of the *Herald* had insisted Marci be the society editor.

"She's made no secret of her manhunt." Jess couldn't bank a smile at the thought of Marci leaving. "She also claims a wedding takes a year to plan."

The trio giggled as the taxi bullied its way up the street toward Stars.

"I'll bet Grant has replaced Warren Jacobs," Zoe said.

"Sheesh! You're probably right," Stacy told them. "If a serial killer really is stalking women, the paper needs a first-rate reporter . . . like Chuck."

Just hearing her father's name caused a lump to blossom in Jessica's throat along with a swell of pride. Until Parkinson's had forced him to retire, Charles Crawford had been the best, earning three Pulitzer prizes in his career.

The cab crawled to a halt and double-parked outside of Stars. They paid the driver and winnowed their way through the crowd at the door. Grant had reserved the private room in the rear. Just inside the room a waiter greeted them with flutes of champagne.

Jessica knew Grant didn't usually go all out like this. Throckmorton—call me Mort—Smith rarely read his own newspaper, but he was notorious for keeping his eye on the bottom line.

All smiles, Marci Haywood bounced up to them. "Isn't this fab? Totally fab?"

Jessica averted her eyes from the blonde's surgically enhanced breasts which were pushed upward like pagan offerings above the neckline of the leopard-print sheath.

"I think Grant's won a prize," Marci said, enthusiasm bubbling over the way it usually did when she spoke.

"Pulitzers are awarded in the spring," Zoe pointed out.

"Well, it could, like, be a new prize or something."

Jessica could almost hear her father saying: Having Marci Haywood at the *Herald* has deprived a village somewhere of its idiot.

A waiter arrived with a tray of seasoned scallops wrapped in a thin band of filo dough.

"Yummy," they all agreed.

"Get the recipe," Marci said to Stacy. "I'll use it at my wedding."

Stacy headed off toward the kitchen. As food editor, she wanted the recipe—not because Marci had asked for it.

"You're engaged?" asked Zoe.

"Not exactly, but I have met someone."

"Really? Who is—"

"Find a seat," Grant called from the front of the room.

Jessica and Zoe turned and motioned to their buddy, Duff Rutherford, the health editor to save places for them. Zoe held up three fingers because Stacy had yet to return from the kitchen.

They went a few steps. Jessica stopped and turned, saying, "Sit with us, Marci."

Marci's thrilled smile touched Jessica in spite of herself. Marci was flighty and boring, but harmless.

As they sat down, Duff asked, "Do any of you know what PID is?"

Jessica sighed inwardly. Duff was a sweetie, but he let his job as health editor consume him.

"PID. It must be a new SUV," Marci said.

"No," Duff responded. "It stands for a pelvic inflammatory disease. It's one of the leading causes of infertility."

Stacy slipped into the seat beside Jessica, whispering, "What's this about infertility?"

"Don't ask. You'll just get Duff going."

Up front, Grant tapped on a glass to get their attention. "I'm sure you're all wondering why I invited you tonight."

Tall with a patrician bearing, Grant Bennett had been blessed with razor-sharp intelligence. His pewter gray hair was wisped with silver at the temples, and he wore it a little too long. It brushed the back of his collar, the way it had years ago when Jessica's father had lead her by the hand into Grant's office.

The morning after her mother had walked out of their lives—forever.

Grant was talking about the value of the independent newspaper—an endangered species—in a world dominated by media conglomerates. It was one of his favorite topics, and Jessica forced herself to listen.

"The *Herald* can't pay the same salaries the chain papers do, but we don't have to sacrifice our views to satisfy the suits who live on the other side of the country."

So true, Jessica thought. The *Herald's* reporters had freedom, but to make ends meet, they often wrote more than one column. New Millennium Lifestyles appeared daily, but Jessica also wrote New Millennium Travel, published each Sunday.

"Once in a while I can help out by getting a column syndicated, but it's becoming harder all the time."

Jessica knew the chains liked to syndicate their own people, not the competition. Occasionally it happened. Rock Newman, the *Herald's* sports columnist had been syndicated for several years.

"I've managed to get another *Herald* columnist syndicated." Grant paused, obviously enjoying the way everyone was collectively holding their breath.

Jessica said a silent prayer for Zoe. She was a better financial analyst than anyone at the *Wall Street Journal,* an unqualified success in a male dominated world. She also murmured a prayer for herself—a long shot.

"The Triad Media Group is eager to syndicate this column."

A buzz rippled across the room. Everyone knew this was the largest, best-paying media chain.

Grant cleared his throat and silence fell over the room. "Starting next month, Triad will be syndicating New Millennium Lifestyles."

It took a moment for his words to register. Suddenly, all the air was siphoned from Jessica's lungs. Her first thought was how proud her father would be.

"They wanted to syndicate Jessica because she has a distinctive voice and unusual articles," Grant added when the applause died down.

Oh, my God, she thought. Her column would be read across the country. A dream, a goal had come true long before she'd expected it.

She was so lost in her own thoughts that it took a moment to realize Grant was still standing before them, his expression now grave.

"Just before I came here, I received a very disturbing E-mail," he told them. "The sender claims to be the Final Call killer. He says he strangled a prominent psychiatrist."

"Who?" someone shouted.

"I can't say until the police check out the information. If this isn't a hoax, we'll have a scoop in the morning edition."

"Why wouldn't the killer e-mail a TV station?" Marci whispered to Jessica.

"He wants to see it in print, so he can save it."

"But everyone has a VCR, don't they?"

"True, but serial killers often keep clippings in scrapbooks."

Marci didn't look convinced, but she didn't argue. She probably realized Jessica had learned a lot during the years her father had worked as an investigative reporter.

"Arinda Castro, a high-profile criminal attorney," Duff said. "Vanessa Filmore, a biochemist with several breakthrough patents in the works. What did they do to attract a serial killer?"

"It's hard to say," Jessica replied, "but we'll know more when we find out who the latest victim is."

ABOUT THE AUTHOR

Meryl Sawyer lives in Newport Beach, California. She is currently working on her next work of romantic suspense, which will be published in November 2003. Meryl loves to hear from readers and may be contacted at her Web site www.merylsawyer.com.

Thrilling Romance from Lisa Jackson